NOH
FOOLING
THIS TEACHER

MARGERY A. NEELY

authorHOUSE®

AuthorHouse™
1663 Liberty Drive
Bloomington, IN 47403
www.authorhouse.com
Phone: 1 (800) 839-8640

Published by AuthorHouse   05/25/2018

ISBN: 978-1-5462-0298-1 (sc)
ISBN: 978-1-5462-0297-4 (e)

Library of Congress Control Number: 2017912175

CONTENTS

Dedicated to my parents
Anna Amelia Schneider Neely
Arthur Dorris Neely

In 1899, Congressman Willard Duncan Vandiver in Philadelphia said, ". . . frothy eloquence neither convinces me nor satisfies me. I'm from Missouri. You have got to show me." *2010 World Book Multimedia Encyclopedia:* Version 14.0.0 (r) World Book, Inc. (www.mackiev.com)

PART ONE

HAI TIMES

CHAPTER ONE

S tanding uncertainly inside after she entered the front door of the schoolhouse, Meg Lowe jumped as a lady appeared from a door down the hall.

"Over here," came a cheery greeting from the short brunette lady, dimples showing in her cheeks. "Hi, I'm Althea Ardmore, science teacher. You must be Margaret Lowe." She walked briskly toward Meg.

Meg nodded.

Althea said, "The teachers' lounge is where I was and the supply closet's in there. The lunchroom's down there by that classroom. Mrs. Fritz, our principal, will be here soon. She's organizing a mah jongg tournament at the O Club. She's always organizing: the school, us, ladies' golf tournament, school parents organization, her husband, soup kitchen––or, to be accurate, rice bowl and fish stew kitchen. She wanted to call it Fritz's Food for Friends, but no one could pronounce the 'r' in Fritz so it's just Food Kitchen. She runs it on Tuesdays. She'll be happy to run your off-duty hours, if you let her. Here she comes. Let's follow her to her office. You're on time. 'We' love that."

Meg was thrown by the rapid delivery of information. Tossing a questioning look at the back of the other teacher, Meg Lowe trailed her. The Ardmore lady certainly had an irreverent way to describe the boss to a newly hired teacher.

Meg felt drained of energy as well as brainpower after her two-week trip from Missouri to Japan. Now a bit of apprehension was working itself into her consciousness.

The hall was white and cold and muggy while the air outside had been warm and sunny. Their feet made clipping sounds on the wood floor. The two teachers were waved into an office at the end of the hall by their supervisor. Mrs. Fritz was older and shorter than they were.

"We welcome you, Miss Lowe, Margaret. We are Mrs. Fritz, temporary principal, English teacher, and wife of the President of the School Board. This, you may know, is Miss Althea Ardmore, science and math teacher. You've been here almost a week, and this is the first day we have met you," Mrs. Fritz scolded with a frown between her eyes.

"My apologies. I am sorry but I've been exhausted," said Meg, putting down her heavy briefcase and large purse with relief, "because I was queasy and seasick most of the eleven days on the Pacific Ocean."

At last she had enough energy to describe what she'd been through. At last she had an audience of educated ladies. "I was in a converted hospital ship cabin with 16 other women, in a sling hammock above another woman's hammock. I warned her in plenty of time to get out of the way when I was sick." She gestured with hands on stomach and mouth open. "Then, there was so much to do when I arrived here in Nagoya. I'm sure you've been through it, too, but I've never experienced anything similar before."

Althea Ardmore laughed and the principal pursed her lips pursuant to speaking but Meg continued to chatter in spite of anything the boss lady had been going to utter. She continued, "On Wednesday, from the Chiyoda Hotel where I landed, I was hauled over to the Provost Marshal's Office in the Okaya Building for registration and fingerprints. Next,

I was photographed at the Public Information Office in the Yamato Building for my official Identification Pass. I applied for my PX Ration Card and exchanged my cash into scrip, and *yen,* and *sen*."

"Fine, now, Miss Lowe," the principal began.

Meg Lowe hadn't finished. "I've been shipped, entrained, motor pooled, and bused until I am anesthetized, although I *was* immunized before I left home. Too, I admit that I was told to call you when I arrived. Quite frankly, that is why exhaustion set in until I telephoned you yesterday."

Mrs. Fritz held up a warning hand. "We did not need to hear that *lengthy* commentary. Our men have had far worse to deal with, you must admit. Now, here is your key to the front door. The native janitor will be in each weekday from noon until 1700 hours and will clean your classroom."

She handed Meg a piece of paper. "This paper has our Code of Conduct that we have composed for you to read and sign. We are being careful of the reputations of unmarried teachers who are models for our young Americans. Miss Ardmore will show you to your room and the supply closet, because we have other duties today."

The straight-masted woman sailed away, clouds of gray hair held high, leather purse anchored in her left hand. Meg, wondering why the principal had been short with her, watched Mrs. Fritz go. First, the principal had acted as though she were remiss in not appearing earlier. Second, the lady then took off almost immediately after Meg did arrive in her presence.

Miss Ardmore waved at the principal's wake and turned to Meg, Miss Lowe, still holding the paper in her hand. "Let's go up to your classroom; after that, I'll show you the supply closet off the teachers' lounge down here. Oh, sign that Code thingie later. I'm in a rush, too." She walked out, waiting in the hall for Meg to follow.

"Do I call you Margaret?" Miss Ardmore started for the stairs.

"I'm usually called Meg. And do you go by Althea?" They climbed up tiled stairs.

"Exactly like I introduced myself early on--Althea, Althea Ardmore. See my ring?" Miss Ardmore wiggled her finger. The gold ring held a diamond centered among rubies.

"Beautiful," Meg said. "I hope the guy I'm promised to back home places a duplicate on my finger when we get engaged. He's still in college. I offer my best wishes, or congratulations or whatever to you. Am I the only unmarried teacher here?"

"So far. We have some other new teachers due before school starts in September. No way to tell if they're married, but I doubt it. If they were, they'd already be here as dependants of some military fellow. We are going to have more dependant students this year because families are arriving by the boatload so maybe a mom will be a new teacher for us. My friend, Sharon Sheldon, taught the handful of elementary kids we had last year but will be leaving soon. Her husband's a TDY civvy sleuth."

"A what?"

"Civilian Sherlock Holmes. Very hush-hush." She lowered her voice with a finger over her lips. "Loose lips sink ships, you know."

Meg zipped her lips and crossed her heart, agreeing to observe devout devotion to silence. They strolled along the second floor hallway. It was painted institutional green and paved with linoleum in a swirly grey pattern, a pattern that reminded her of ocean waves, waving, weaving ocean waves.

"You'll find someone to date, I'm sure. Upstairs here are various rooms. My math class meets over there," she pointed to a grey door with an opaque window. "My lab's over there next to it. I won't let the native maid in the classroom or lab, but you'll be welcome to come visit me."

As they walked down the hall, Meg glanced into an open classroom door; tables and chairs seemed to comprise students' desks and seating.

Althea said, "The gym and such are on the top floor just above us. 'We' are less bothered up here by 'Our' principal than those teachers there on the first floor."

"I'm frankly puzzled by my interview with her. Is she an egomaniac––insecure––middle child in ordinal position in the family?"

Althea gave a slight smile. "You social 'science' majors tickle the daylights out of me. Let me expound on the origin of her species. What she first revealed was that she pulled herself up by her bootstraps after the family trudged out of the Dust Bowl into Chicago. She worked her way through a good university there and even obtained a master's degree.

"If you'd have been here last fall, you could've trapped Captain Fritz before he got snared by our Wicked Witch of the Far East. He's a little old in grade, and sickly, perhaps with malaria from when he was a prisoner of war, but that's the Army's business and hers."

"The Fritzes are newlyweds?" Meg laughed. "But where does she get off with that pompous view, then, that 'we' are both Principal and Co-president of the School Board? Isn't that nepotism?"

"No, they both had the positions before they were married, and there weren't many boots on the ground to meet the needs of dependant families arriving by the shipload. He is a repatriated POW, and she came in with the first groups of dependants to set up the school." Althea waved her into a classroom after she opened the door.

"Thanks for elucidating the background. I'll just have to wait to discover if we work well together."

As Meg began to look around her second floor classroom, her attention was caught by Althea going into mimicry of Mrs. Fritz. She strutted around the room, bending a critical eye on each piece of furniture and equipment. "Whereas, *we* are *president* of the School Board, *we* expect obedience to our Code of Conduct Orders, therefore:

"*We* chairs must sit up straight and tall.

"*We* blackboards must start the day with a clean slate.

"*We* chalks must not leave Her in our dust.

"And, *We* desks certainly must not show our drawers!"

She gave a cancan flip to her mid-calf skirt and kicked off a shoe toward her audience with a bump and grind.

Meg laughed at the teacher's dialogue and gestures at the classroom accouterments.

"There, now you're laughing. That's better. When you came dragging in here, and then gave us that lecture about your personal travails, I wondered if you were *her* kind of woman. She's like a dog I saw once, nipping at the feet of sheep to herd them wherever. She'll probably nip your nose if you defy her. I don't dare, myself. I just say, 'Yes, ma'am.'" Althea stepped into her shoe, taunting, singsong, "But my diamond's bigger than hers is."

"Who're you marrying?" Meg asked, seating herself behind a metal desk at one end of the room. She was still tired after the trip and hustle and bustle.

"You've heard what one piece of corn said to the other: 'Don't get in bed with a kernel?' Well, I'm pure corn."

"A colonel? Isn't he too old for you?"

"Dear lady, I'm older than you think, but thanks. He and I have known each other since elementary school and kept in touch after my folks moved us to another town. He was two years ahead of me, and we corresponded throughout the war. He wrote me about the teaching positions opening here, and I applied."

"How great to get together in an exotic land like Japan," Meg said.

Althea said, "Yes, it is. Even though he's been grounded, because of medical reasons, we'll be able to fly privately when we own a plane. He's so enthralled with aeronautical engineering that we have a lot of common interests because of my background in science. He enrolled in law school but never even finished the first year. He's very inventive . . . in more ways than one. I'm as crazy about him as he is about me. He missed a lot of fun during the war years--during his youth, you might say."

"I understand. At my college, the veterans were into training but also after that fun you mentioned. Veterans on the GI Bill simply inundated my college my last two years. They refused to wear Freshmen Beanies." Meg laughed. "Their lingo used acronyms such as 'snafu' and punch my 'TS' card. We had some fantastic parties."

"I can imagine."

Meg reflected, "At least you won't have to go through the agony of building equal status with your husband. You're both are a couple of scientists--your reputations will surpass that held by *Mr. and Mrs. We* Presidents of the School Board."

"I'm confident that we will succeed together."

Meg asked, "Is the wedding soon? I'll have a shower for you. I love to plan parties. What types of gifts do you want?"

"Whoa, there. We're getting married August 20, on a Saturday so that he can have the weekend off. What would I like for gifts? Maybe some Japanese things for a living room. We'll be living in the Kanko Hotel until he is out."

Meg stood up from the swivel chair. She then asked, "Do you live at the Chiyoda, too? I haven't met anyone else yet, people I could ask to the shower. I'll need a list of names and addresses from you."

"Yes, I'm at the Chiyoda and will introduce you around. Come on downstairs, I'll show you the supply closet and leave you then to your work. You'll be busy up here."

Meg followed Althea to the door. The science teacher turned and waved Meg back to the desk. "First, though, pull out the top drawer of the desk––it unlocks the bottom drawer where you can put your purse. Wherever did you get one that big and that odd color?"

Meg picked up her purse and cradled it in her arms. "It's a satchel from a farm warehouse and implement store. I added the snap on the flap. I figured olive drab would not go with anything, therefore would go with everything. I never have to change purses to match my shoes. Plus I can carry my camera and flash attachment easily."

She followed Althea's directions and fit the satchel inside the desk drawer, shut the drawer, and shut the top drawer before reversing the process to retrieve her handbag. Meg left her briefcase on the top of the desk and followed Althea out of the door.

Althea grinned at that description of stylish behavior as they walked downstairs. She then opened a door on the lower floor. "Here's the little lounge with our supply closet. We've been moving over from temporary quarters. We didn't get started last year until October. That's why you're here a month early––to unpack boxes and boxes of supplies."

Meg glanced at the comforting rose paint on the walls and the cushioned chairs of different styles around a long folding table.

Althea pointed at the boxes and then a door leading into a small kitchen. "This building was renovated for us because it had been slightly damaged by a bombing, and, moreover, had been a business building with small offices that became classroom when walls were removed. The Corps of Engineers did a great job for us, because more students are expected next year. The increase in students is why I'll probably teach all year although my fly-boy gets out in January.

"You can find cabinets of notebook paper, carbon paper, stencils, and pencils in here," Althea said opening a cabinet, "and the clipboard where you note name, rank, and serial number for what you remove. Mimeograph machine, typewriter, and a hot plate over there on the cabinet. Coffee cans and all are shelved below. The sink and glassware are in that kitchen cabinet in the closet with the sink. Hello, what have we here?" Althea walked to the wall to look at three boxes that were larger than the boxes of supplies and books.

Meg peered over Althea's shoulder as she opened one box that contained a globe, the oceans painted a glossy blue and continents broken into various colors. "Mine! For my geography class," Meg exclaimed.

"I have no objections but you might have to fight Mrs. Fritz for it."

Althea extricated the globe while Meg excitedly opened another box that had costumes. Meg poked around in the box and pulled out some cloth.

"Are the kids likely to put on *Madame Butterfly* or *The Mikado*? Look at these embroidered robes. They are so soft and silky." Meg held up an unusually long blue robe decorated with a snowcapped mountain running up from the hem. She set it to one side.

In the long box that had held the robe was another swath of cloth. "What's this?" She examined, with fascination, a long stuffed white embroidered cloth. "Colors don't match well . . . pink, red, orange. Blue and green. But, I supposed it's beautiful in its own way." She pulled it out and folded it into a length half her height.

Althea sounded puzzled. "Does seem odd for those *kimonos* to be here. The white embroidered one is an *obi*, a sash." She stooped, found a small box at the bottom of the container Meg had opened, and pulled it out. "Ah. Here're the pillow and clip that hold the *obi* up in the back." Althea touched the materials carefully as she examined them with a critical eye, adding the accessories in strategic places to illustrate their use.

"I would not have figured out how those worked under the *obi*. It makes it be a bustle in the back," Meg exclaimed.

"Myself, I rather doubt those particular musicals would go over too well with the baby-sans around here." Althea started to put the garments back into the box.

"Why would babies see them?" Meg inquired, studying the way Althea removed the clip and the pillow it held from the inner side from the *obi*. That might be a bit uncomfortable when seated in a chair, one's spine forced away from the chair back.

"Baby-sans, dear, are the local girlfriends the guys fraternize with."

"Ooohh, I call them indigenes. I thought GIs weren't supposed to date them. I heard one lady on the train call them gooks, and I thought that was crude."

"You'll learn, you'll learn," Althea glanced at her watch, apparently finding it later than she had realized. "I'm sorry but I do have to go now to keep an appointment. Nice meeting you, Meg. Have lunch with me tomorrow about noon in the Chiyoda Hotel mess. I'll introduce you around to some ladies. So sorry to run off and leave you with all the work!"

Livened up by the process of settling in, Meg hauled boxes of books up to her classroom. She piled them on the four student desks, the wood or metal chairs, and the one long table. After a while, tired of unloading items of little use for her classes, she took a break to walk around the American Village walks and gravel streets to the concrete building housing the commissary outside the southeast gate.

\#

Black measles on her shoes started it all, she later decided. The mildew spots studded everything except people-- towels, clothes, walls, floors--and her favorite sandals, the huaraches. She had set off to find a remedy for the mildew.

At the commissary, she studiously ran her finger down the label of the third brand of bleach, but not a single treatment for mildew could she find. It was difficult to concentrate on the tiny writing, too, on the soap bottles or on the boxes of detergent. Distracting her was an argument over at the check out counter. A young officer (*two silver bars meant a captain, according to her dictionary*) was obviously upset.

"This-register-was-$40-off-yesterday. I can't reconcile the inventory with this register," he hollered, waving the register tape around his head. Clearly, he expected either the wild gestures or his bellowing to teach the Japanese clerk how the register worked. "You didn't ring up the goods correctly."

"Mees-take, *ne*?" giggled the clerk behind her hand, reaching up to take the tape. "*Hai*, I didn't. I do good one more time, suh Cap'n Ahcheh. I p'omise, suh, I fix."

"Yes! Yes, you forgetee ringee up good oncie moree." The distraught captain gave a little sob and closed his eyes.

At Meg's elbow in the laundry supplies aisle, an enlisted man (*four rockers, no chevrons, meant a staff sergeant*) softly commented in an amused accent, "Some mistake, *ne*? Forty dollars would buy a lotta beans, *ne*?"

"Or bowls of soup!" Meg replied. Looking up at him a few seconds from under her long, burnt-honey lashes, she questioned, "You from the south?"

"Arkansas. Howja know?"

"Y'all soun' lak sumbuddy from sou-outh a Missoura whar Ahm from, one a mah neighbors," she mimicked. "Ever see any Re-ve-noo-ers?"

"Actually, my daddy's got a crossroads store up on 66," he answered. "No revenuers since Prohibition, no how. No more moonshine no more. Lotsa tourists travelin' by. He cain't even sell no beer 'til he gets a license."

She returned to studying the bleach. "I don't suppose you know anything about mildew. I'm trying to get rid of spots on my shoes. However, chanting 'out blank blank spot, get out I say' like Lady MacBeth doesn't work for me. And the smell. Foul."

"I've smelled it plenty of times," he said.

Meg strolled up another aisle with the sergeant trailing behind her. "Nothing is going to help get rid of the mildew," she said with a touch of despair dramatically playing in her words.

He thought a bit and, to her delight, came up with some advice. "Back home, we did two things for mildew. One, leave a light on in the closet, if it's 'lectricified. Two, put lemon juice or watery bleach on the spots and leave 'em in the sun; works on clothes, but it should work with polish and a spit shine afterwards on shoes. And, keep 'em polished, like you'd do your ball-glove."

Strolling up one aisle and down another, she found no lemon juice. "Rats."

Slinging her large olive drab leather purse over her left shoulder, she tugged down a gallon of bleach and moved to checkout. The beaming clerk carefully entered a decimal point before the 26-cent price as Meg paid in scrip.

"You play any ball here?" she asked the sergeant who was now behind her in the line. He was carrying two packs of gum.

With a noncommittal grunt, he turned in a complete circle, stepped back, did a wind-up, and tossed the word "strike!" ("strahk") at her. She reached high and triumphantly showed her empty right palm up at the tall guy; he had a fringe of crew-cut red hair peeping from under his hat. She called, "Three! You're out."

"Good catch, ma'am."

"I was a pretty good outfielder in my teens. My mom had a hissy fit." At his puzzled look, she continued, "She caught me at the city park being tagged out at first. Naturally, the boys had to touch me with their gloves. 'Young *ladies* behave with decorum,' and playing rough games isn't decorous. But, most of the time I didn't get caught. My dad and I loved baseball and tuned in all the time to the Cardinals."

"Lemme help with that," he said, taking the bottle, "and indeedy I do play ball. I'm the pitcher, Sergeant Calhoun Paley, 'Cally' to friends, at your service." He put his overseas cap on his crew cut red hair. "Do you live here with your husband?"

"Oh, no. I'm to teach dependants. My name is Miss Lowe, Margaret Lowe. I'm on my way back to the school to unpack boxes of supplies. I had an orientation meeting earlier with the Principal. Being in the orient, that seems apropos, eh?"

He looked puzzled, "If you say so. I'll walk back with you through the American Village to the school." As they were waved through the gate that was guarded by Japanese sentries, he called a greeting the two APs talking with the Japanese gate sentries.

"They're on my softball team--relief pitcher and second base," he said to Meg.

He stopped and called back to the APs, "See ya Tuesday night," as they were waved through. "Oh, wait, Miss Lowe, a minute while I talk with them."

Meg felt a little uncomfortable, waiting on a stranger-- though, he'd told her his nickname so perhaps they weren't strangers anymore. And he was from Missouri. His friends kept eying her. They'd probably tease him about her later. She hid a smile.

"Marty, Phil, wanna practice at 1630?"

They both signaled "yes."

"Okay, see ya later," he nodded and called back over his shoulder at the airmen.

With the practice time settled, the sergeant--Cally-- started walking with Meg again. "Didja catch the bus to the Village?" he asked her. "Civilians can't use the motor pool."

"No. I found out that I could take a Japanese taxi. A lady told me what number to have the operator call and how to do it. She said when the taxi arrived, I should say 'Takee me-*san* hubba hubba American Village School, *ne*?' and point to myself. I did as she recommended. The taxi driver replied, 'Yes, Madam. Quickly.' I felt like an idiot and was embarrassed," Meg chuckled.

They strolled past some houses. "Bit of home, that," she pointed to two tykes on trikes headed down the sidewalk as their mothers talked on the lawn in front of one ranch house. "I'd really like to see your team play," she said and then blushed, wondering if she'd read his signals wrong.

"I'd sure be mighty pleased if Miss Meg Lowe did," the sergeant said with a grin and a wink.

"When are the games scheduled and where are they located?" Pausing, she said quietly, "Or, are you 'fraternizing' with an indigene?"

"No, ma'am, no ma'am. Never met one: they're over in Oklahoma." His blush clashed with his red hair.

"I didn't mean 'Indian'––I meant a Japanese girl. I didn't mean to upset you, Cally. Sorry, I meant are you dating a local girl?"

"No, ma'am! No, ma'am!" he sounded alarmed. "I send a money order home. Don't go to those *geisha* houses. Besides, ever' time I'd'a changed money to *yen*, the rate changed, and I couldn't hardly figure out how much anythin' was from time to time." He sounded indignant, then sighed. "Miss Lowe, I sure would like you to come to the games. There's one here in that ball field between the ring of houses. That's where we play softball. Baseball is played over thataways some miles at another field. Our next game is on Tuesday night with a Navy team. Around 1730. I have a pretty good knuckle ball." He took her arm as they stepped into the gravel street.

"I have a pretty good knuckle sandwich," Meg warned, kidding somewhat.

"My sister'd like you," he laughed.

A sister. "What's her name? Is she older?" Feeling awkward for some reason, maybe it was being in the American Village plunked down in a strange, strange land while kind of flirting with an attractive guy in English. Didn't mention a wife.

"Glory Anne. She and Tonya are both younger."

He sounded confident and sure of himself, so she asked what might turn out to be an intrusive question. "Were you in the war?"

"Yes, ma'am. Drafted when I graduated high school in '42. Was in the Pacific Theater."

"That's when I graduated. What was the war like? We had bits about it but only in the newspapers, magazines, radio, and newsreels."

"I was a teeny-weeny dot hopin' I wouldn't get shot. If you wasn't there, no one can explain it." He dropped her arm. "Come on, we'll walk by the ball field on the way to the school. It's kinda interestin', because the field had to be dedicated or some such word by Shinto or Buddhist priests––desecrated?––somethin' like that."

"Consecrated?"

"Yes'm. Here, past the houses, you can see the bases we've set out."

Meg looked around the lawn with paths between the bases and then she glanced at the backs of dependant houses and a chapel that encircled the diamond and outfield. The buildings hid the ball field from the circle of streets.

He said, "The lights won't be here until next spring, but the poles for them are ready. What happened was that poles for the diamond lights were bein' installed when some bones started turning up about four feet down. Further down, they ran into somethin' solid, but the holes were already deep enough to support the poles. 'A course, a typhoon could blow down anythin' or an earthquake could destroy the lights. Evidently some princess or goddess lived . . . no, a goddess wouldn't have bones . . . or, maybe it was her spirit and some other people's bones."

Meg noticed he had started speaking quietly.

"Well, the priests prayed to some spirits, the same spirits that earlier had said it was okay to put the lights at such and such a time at such and such a place. Some bigwigs were here for the ceremony, and our team and a few people on the back porches of those ranch houses watched. Then, next spring the lights could be purely turned on. It's rather eerie, when you think 'bout it. Hooo," he called out as he made ghostly waves with his hands.

"Ethereal."

"Yawser, eerie, weird. I've played here pretty often and always feel alert––a feeling in my gut," he said, walking slowly around on the grass by the diamond. "It's something like when I witch a well. You know?"

She thrust fingers under her bangs, pacing beside him. The coolness of her turquoise ring felt good against her forehead. She'd chosen the ring because she thought it matched her eye color. She wondered if Cally would notice. "I vaguely remember hearing of it in folklore."

"I take a forked peach branch, hold it so," he demonstrated, "and when it starts to tremble, I know in my gut that there's water down there. We dig the well. Not that I'm superstitious," he laughed, unconsciously crossing his fingers, "but it works."

"You have goose-bumps on your arm," Meg pointed out.

Cally rubbed his arm and started walking forward again. They walked in silence for a few paces out to the street again and went toward the white school building on the corner across the street. Gesturing quickly at a white flower on a bush by a long building, he changed the subject. "Just smell that. Ain't it grand? All these dependant houses have them by the front doors. That long, white building's part of the chapel."

"I see. Those flowers might be gardenias but I have seen them only in corsages before. They are pretty. Nice scent."

They crossed back over the street.

"Here we are." He laid the jug on the ground before the three story white school building and gave her a salute. "Try to come to the game, do."

She returned a three-finger salute. "Sorry, can't remember the Girl Scout oath," she grinned, picked up the bleach, and walked up through the school door.

CHAPTER TWO

G oing back into the lounge, Meg started hauling the globe, other boxes, and some supplies upstairs. She spent a couple of hours unpacking history and geography books, studying their contents, and placing them on white bookshelves.

The number of textbooks seemed barely adequate for her classes. There were only a few helpful references such as two out-of-date atlases, a biography of *U. S. Presidents 1789-1928*, and Charles Dana's *Two Years Before The Mast* that described early California in some chapters. At least she would have her Will Durant's history of the Orient when the trunk arrived from home.

A geography map was already rolled up on top of the blackboard, and she held a framed copy of the Declaration of Independence against the yellow wall opposite. Glancing out a window, she noticed the one-story building and, beyond it, the ball field. She saw someone, oh, it was Cally Paley––what a name that would be for a nursery rhyme––pitch a ball toward the building. He then caught the ball in his glove as it flew back, but his partner was hidden from her view.

As she watched the men practice, she thought back to Cally's description of the consecration of the ball field. Arching her aching back, a mischievous idea formed in her mind. Back home, she was well known for her pranks. One of the best had been when she and her sorority sisters sent haunted sounds into the frat house and the guys caromed around inside, trying to find the source.

She muttered, "Tee hee" and secured her purse in the desk. With a pen, she drew big blackened eyes and a grinning mouth on white paper, picked up several paper clips, and trotted downstairs.

She found a mop in the janitor's closet. As she pulled the mop up, some threads caught on a hinge on the floor. Botheration. She yanked the handle free and hurried to the teachers' lounge. The *kimono* and the wig were still in boxes in the supply closet.

She went to work, first snuggling the wig over the mop, and next, clipping the paper between the wig and the mop. She could shorten the *kimono* by pulling the material in the long skirt up and draping it over her leather belt. With the mop-wig held high, the *kimono* collar would shield her head.

After rolling the wig and mop inside the robe, Miss Lowe stepped out the front door and walked across the gravel street. She nodded to a woman feeding a cat on the front lawn of a ranch-style house. "Going to hang a flag," Meg incongruously said to her, walking past her puzzled face onto and then across the tennis courts where she assembled and donned her outfit.

The mop smelled musty, but a slight breeze outside took care of that problem. She sidled across the outfield up by first base, unnoticed until she wailed, "OOOOO," she wailed, "EEEOOOOO!"

"My god, what's that?"

"Cripes!"

Two guys near the building whirled around and charged, each one dropping a facemask and glove behind.

Simultaneously, the pitcher hurled a ball at the headdress, hitting it right on target. The mop handle clunked Meg in the forehead as the ball hit. The handle left her hands, and her legs gave way.

The two players picked her up off the ground and did not let go of her arms until Sergeant Calhoun Paley spoke. "Is that you, Miss Lowe?" his voice shook as he ran up behind the men.

"You pitched my head off," she laughed with tears rolling down her cheeks. "I gotcha good, didn't I? Oh, if you could have seen your faces! I haven't done such a prank since we spooked the frat house."

The two who held her arms looked grim and angry. Sergeant Calhoun Paley frowned, too, but gestured to them to release her. He introduced his teammates while she shed the *kimono* and scrunched it up around the wig.

"No need for an arrest, fellas. Sergeant Martin, Sergeant Tyler, can I present Miss Lowe, a new teacher in town." To her, he said, "They're APs. Shift around doin' different tasks on patrol."

"Gentlemen, how do you do?"

They both nodded warily, still looking at her sternly. Sgt. Martin was shorter and younger than his two teammates. He had fair coloring—blond hair and blue eyes, and his skin had a slight sunburn. Sgt. Tyler was big boned with brown eyes and hair, standing straight and tall; he had big shoulders and large fists and a dark suntan.

Sgt. Cally Paley searched for a calming comment. "Have you, ah, you still been workin' at the schoolhouse this afternoon?" He bent to look at Meg, obviously unsure how to approach her stunt. He appeared puzzled by the incident. "Why are you out here?"

"Yes, I've been working since I saw you," she wiped her eyes on the *kimono*. "I have a bump on my forehead." Her thoughts tumbled over each other. She was beginning to regret being impetuous and interrupting their practice. She hesitated over how to make amends because the schoolhouse was not yet a familiar place to her. However, it was the only place where she could serve coffee. And, she was the only one in the building so no one would notice.

"No more than you deserve, lady. What do you teach-- dramatics and comedy?" scoffed Sgt. Tyler.

"Oh, c'mon. Let me apologize with a cup of coffee. I can make it in the lounge." She answered his sarcastic tone evenly. "I teach social studies and geography. And, you've been practicing long enough to deserve a break."

The APs looked at Cally, and he hesitated then nodded.

She led the way back across the field, pausing while the men walked over to the building and pitcher's mound to pick up their equipment. As they left the field she waved at the lady who was still outside her house, who now eyed her wearing a prim expression of disapproval that replaced the puzzled one.

Before they entered the schoolhouse, the men took off their cleats and left them outside on the small porch with their gear. They stepped over the bamboo doormat inside. Next to the door was a tall urn that she backed into as she held the door open for her guests. She glanced down at the urn's wide-mouthed, bluish-gray ceramic body, back up at Cally who was addressing her.

"Wouldja have books by Thorstein Veblen and Adam Smith?" The question was from Sgt. Cally Paley. He certainly was working hard on taking charge of the evening's events, trying to find a common ground between his teammates and his new lady friend, she thought. Typical male. He'd find out that she could handle herself in difficult situations.

"Yes, back home. Why?" Meg looked at him with the mischievous twinkle still in her eyes. Was he going to start some lecture about economic theory? She could out-quote him in any debate, because she'd argued both pro and con sides on many subjects when she was a member of the college debate team. It would be fun to surprise him with her debate skills. She'd missed the thrill of arguing since graduating college.

"I've been takin' a two-hour extension course on the GI Bill. I liked what both authors said. I'm now through the economics course, and it's taken me a he––a lot longer than two hours already."

Meg shifted gears to a professional, advisory stance on the subject of coursework. "Oh, a two-hour college course means two hours a week for a semester. Why are you studying that? It can't have anything to do with your Air Corps job, although I don't know what it is you do."

"My MOS is airplane mechanic. A lot of us'll be demobbed in a coupla weeks, and I need to go back helpin' Daddy with the store and gas station business. We want to put my two sisters through college––heaven help them if they turn out like you," he laughed.

She wrinkled her nose and him and motioned the men in the direction of the lounge, singing, "We live in fame, go down in flame, nothing can stop the Army Air Corps."

"Wrong, Teach! Back in July, 1947, it became 'nothin' can stop the U. S. Air Force.' I'm with the Fifth Air Force here. See my patch? Purty, ain't it?"

Meg put the mop back in the janitor's closet as they passed and led the way down the oak-floored hall to the teachers' lounge. The supply closet had a percolator, coffee can, can-opener, and sugar cubes, just as Althea had mentioned this morning. She filled the pot at the sink, put in the strainer, and, after working the can opener, poured six tablespoons of coffee in, and set the pot on an electric burner. Sgt. Martin and Cally sat at the table but Sgt. Tyler ambled around the room, peering in the remaining boxes and opening doors on the supply cabinet.

"While that coffee perks, would you please give me a hint as to what all these initials mean? First, AP." She shook the *kimono* and wig and replaced them in their containers.

"Do you know what 'MP' stands for?" inquired Sgt. Martin.

"Member of Parliament," she replied promptly. Sgt. Tyler guffawed.

"No, ma'am. Military Police. We are Air Force Security Police: AP."

"Oh, okay. Now TDY."

"Temporary Duty."

"That's what another man is." The three men glanced at her. Continuing, Meg explained, "I heard there's a civilian super snoop in town on TDY."

"Who might that be?" casually asked Tyler.

"Another teacher's husband. She's Sharon Sheldon." A glance passed between the two APs. "Bill Sheldon," Tyler whispered to Martin.

The coffee finished brewing, and she took coffee orders. Cally liked his black, Martin took his with a bit of sugar, and Tyler wanted his with the powdered cream. While she was mixing the cups, the men discussed their last softball game. Meg couldn't contribute much, but she enjoyed listening.

Cally turned to her. "What's your next question?"

"MOS."

"Military Occupational Specialty. I told you mine. I'm the airplane engine wizard." Sgt. Cally Paley was grinning as he spoke. He tipped his cup at the other two men who replied with the same gesture. They drank the liquid rapidly and allowed her to pour another half cup each, and that maneuver emptied the pot.

"I see. That's your occupation in the Occupation. Mine, then, is Civilian Occupation Specialty, teacher. There is a COS-T in everyone's education. Get it?"

"Not funny, McGee," said Sgt. Tyler.

"Anything else you want to know, miss?" asked Sgt. Martin.

"What do you mean by sixteen hundred hours?" she asked.

"Twelve noon is twelve hundred, your one p.m. is thirteen hundred and so on. That way I know you do not confuse one a.m. with one p.m. I mean that *most* people wouldn't confuse the times." Sgt. Tyler explained the reasoning behind the nomenclature in a superior tone of voice.

The three men rose while she took the empty cups and coffeepot into the supply alcove and rinsed them. As she went upstairs to get her purse preparatory to returning to her hotel room, she heard them musing about what the building had been before it was renovated. They were standing politely near the front door when she returned.

Sgt. Cally Paley spoke. "Miss Lowe, now, where you off to? You need help carryin' things home or are you leavin' your stuff here?"

"I'm tired and going back to the hotel. I'm leaving that bleach, because I'm going to freshen up my shoes here. And the janitor's mop could stand a bleach bath, too, I think. I need to call a taxi."

"No need. There's a bus route right outside the west gate on the other side of the schoolhouse. It'll take you there fine. I'll walk you over there. Say, guys, would you pick up my gym bag when you go through the ball-field? I'll meet you there shortly to change my shoes. Maybe we can get in some more practice before dark, too."

After donning their cleats outside the schoolhouse, the two APs started off with a vague salute acknowledging his request.

When they were out of earshot, he gave Meg a friendly grin. "Say, wouldja like to walk around town tomorrow afternoon?"

"Yes, yes! I've been jittery about walking anywhere by myself. I'm domiciled at the Chiyoda."

"I guess that means you live there. Here comes the bus right on time."

As they stepped from the gate, two schoolgirls walked by wearing dark blue skirts and white blouses. "Hi," Meg said. They dropped their eyes and clipped away on wooden shoes.

Cally whooped. "'*Hai*' means 'yes' in Japanese, and, ya say '*ohayo gozaimasu*' in the mornin' and '*konnichi wa*' the rest of the day. I forget what the evenin' sayin' is but, by golly, I've taught ya somethin' else." He helped her up the bus steps and stood back. "Bye, Teach. I'll come by around 1300. Bye."

CHAPTER THREE

L ate the next morning, the cafeteria was noisy, and looking around as she was walking in, Meg realized that she had a few more people to become acquainted with. She was used to a large school being empty in the summertime, and the small cafeteria being mostly full of ladies surprised her. Luckily, she immediately noted that Althea was already seated and was beckoning her over to a table where she and her two friends were seated. Meg went through the cafeteria line, pushing along a tray as she collected a little glass of juice and a bowl of cereal. She balanced the tray partially on top of the purse hanging from her shoulder and walked to the table.

"These gals are Sergeant Laura Duncan and Corporal Donna Aldrich," Althea said. She smiled at the new arrival. "My colleague, Miss Margaret call-her-Meg Lowe. I asked them to drop in to meet you. We play tennis together with Sharon Sheldon. You'll get to meet her tonight."

"Nice to meet you-all." Meg unloaded the bowl, juice, and silverware from her tray. She looked for a place for the tray and leaned over to put it on other trays stacked on a nearby table. Seating herself, she asked, "Are you also teachers? Or do you work somewhere else here in Nagoya?"

Duncan, dressed in full uniform, shrugged. "I spend some time going over records, filing, organizing. I've been a WAC in the Air Corps––now we're WAFs." She shrugged again and added, "I work for Althea's fiancé."

"WAF, too," Aldrich added. She was dressed more casually than Duncan, wearing khaki slacks and a shirt without a jacket. "I'm a clerk at Fifth Air Force Headquarters. Translation: a secretary. In the military, nurses are called *medics*; secretaries are called *clerks*; teachers are called *instructors*. It's a man's world. I'm doing the same thing as Duncan, only in another office. We're going to a movie after lunch. Can you join us?"

"Oh, that sounds lovely, but I already have plans. See, I met a sergeant yesterday, and he's going to––"

"*Oooh*," said Althea hooted. "A man, already? Look out, ladies, this one will be getting married before I do!"

Meg smiled as a blush warmed her cheeks. "Oh, come now. It's nothing like that. Although he is quite handsome, I must say. But, Althea, I'm promised to a boy back home, so quit your teasing."

"Ha! Look at her blush in spite of the disclaimer," Aldrich jibed. "Where's he taking you?"

"Please don't say the gardens at Nagoya Hall," Duncan said. "That's so cliché."

"Oh, hush, it's romantic wandering around the grounds and fountain there, and you know it."

"I'm not sure where we're going," Meg said. "But, I'm going to enjoy lunch first. I'm really sick of the crackers and Slim Jane pretzel sticks that I had to eat on the ship because I was so seasick. Then, I do want to walk around the shops I saw from the bus yesterday. They all look small, dark, and mysterious."

"Wait'll you get a good, dark, mysterious whiff of the street traffic. Coal-burning cars!" Aldrich exclaimed.

Althea chimed in, "Honey-bucket carts--smell of effluvium, fumes, phew."

"The ditches full of human waste, and I don't just mean trash," added Aldrich.

"How romantic!" Meg snickered.

Duncan looked at her heavy watch. "I must get to work. Look forward to seeing you again, Margaret." Sgt. Laura Duncan gave a half-salute and marched off, saying, "They'll describe in graphic detail what you'll be inhaling. Don't forget about the fish-oil . . . and that we smell sour to them."

Althea and Aldrich kept chuckling about the cars and carts as they sipped their coffee. Meg looked from one to the other as she ate, wondering if she were being kidded. *Latrines* fertilizing rice-paddies? *Charcoal* fueling cars?

At a lull in the conversation, she turned to Althea. "Why do we smell sour?"

"Because we drink milk and eat cheese."

"Well, I have smelled sour milk, thus that might be true. But I don't understand why we don't smell it on each other. Oh, well." She stopped and thought. "Earlier you said something about my meeting Mrs. Sheldon tonight. What did you mean?"

"Haven't you received the invitation to the Fritz party?" Althea asked.

"No. Where or how would I? Do we have mailboxes?"

"In the lobby is where they are, of course. You should have written an answer by now. Get it on your way out. You're gonna be in trouble. Tell you what, you go ahead and find your mailbox. I'll give her a call and tell her you're coming. It's for 2000 hours at their house. We'll take you with us. It's dress up."

Meg looked down at her flowered chintz dress. "This won't do, huh?" She pulled up her capacious handbag, set a camera and flash attachment on the table, continued burrowing around, and finally retrieved a compact and lipstick. Because she were going to meet Cally, she wanted to look as spruced up as she could in this heat. She freshened her lipstick, put more pancake make-up on the brow bruise, and replaced the items.

"Thank you for protecting me from her displeasure. I owe you one. Nice visiting with you both. I'll say goodbye and see you in the lobby about 7:30, however that translates . . . umm, nineteen thirty-hours. Ha!"

Sergeant Cally Paley, clad in a crisp uniform that outlined his broad shoulders, stood up as Meg walked into the lobby. She motioned "just a minute" and approached the desk. "Can you tell me where to find my mailbox? I'm Miss Margaret Lowe."

The clerk directed her to a wall across the way. She ripped open one envelope to read the handwritten invitation. Tucking the mail in her big purse, she then went over to follow the sergeant outside.

The sergeant greeted her quite formally, and Meg followed suit, although the sudden stiffness between them seemed awkward. They exchanged pleasantries as they walked to the bus stop, and then waited quietly for their bus to arrive. Meg hoped that their whole afternoon didn't go like this. When the bus rumbled up, she boarded it before the sergeant climbed on. After riding a few blocks, they alighted near the area of the schoolhouse and gate where she had left him last night.

She stepped on his toe as he helped her off. "Oh, sorry about that. I didn't mean to hurt your tootsies. Last night, you said I could ask you about military terms. Just what is a spit-shine? You mentioned it as a cure for my huaraches."

"Just what it sounds like." He rubbed the toe of his shoe on the back of his trousers. "Rub on polish, spit on it, and rub more. You have nice polish over your bruise," he teased.

"Thanks ever so much," she replied sarcastically, then grinned. "I guess a spit-shine wouldn't work with my huaraches. They're made of twists of leather. I wore them on the boat. Dumped them in my suitcase wrapped in a towel and dumped them in the closet. That's when the black spots showed up on everything packed near to them, and they smell bad, too."

"We can try something or the other. I'll help."

"Could you come over to the school late Monday afternoon? I need to work over that smelly mop with the janitor, too."

"I'll have to check if I can get off in time when I report in tomorrow. I'm out at the Komaki Airdrome." He paused and looked up and down the busy street. "There are some restaurants and shops. The cooked food is pretty good--lots of soy, rice, fish, and ginger. See two doors down? That's a bathhouse. There are several around town. It's kinda funny. See, the Japanese take lotsa baths . . . together. The prissy Americans made them put separate doors for men and women on all the bathhouses, but they still end up inside together. Up north, some Americans were in one bathhouse when a guy brought in his horse--the Yanks didn't stay long."

"We have one private *out*house on the far field at my folks' farm, but I cannot imagine taking a bath in a bathhouse in front of everybody."

"That was exactly the reaction the American authorities had, but had to relent a bit and ended up just labeling the doors separately for men and ladies."

She followed his glances as he spoke, pointed, and described the various dwellings that were jammed side by side next to the sidewalk: café, gift shop, grocery store, the same stores any town would have. Except for the addition of a separate bathhouse.

"I need my camera," she said, handing him the purse and snapping the flap up. Looking at the camera's back, she commented, "I have some pictures left. Let me take a couple of the street, like those other Americans are doing. Whoops!"

One bicycle swerved toward them with a side of beef teetering over the wobbly back wheel. She had seen bicycles toting stacks of pots, large cartons, huge paper floral displays, even concrete blocks.

She snapped a couple of quick shots.

"I wish I had a movie camera like that fellow over there. Looks like every American on this street is taking pictures." She continued, "I need to find a shower present. Let's look in some shops."

Before they started to enter, Meg noticed a khaki clad GI coming toward them with a smile on his face, and eyes focused on Cally. She stepped toward a door covered with a blue curtain and pushed it aside. Then she stopped because she saw that Cally had whirled around when a GI tapped on his shoulder.

"Hello, Salchow," he growled at a burly soldier carrying two cartons of Lucky Strike cigarettes.

"Well, well. Here's Cally with a dolly. Sergeant Kurt Salchow at your service," he said and grinned at Meg as he doffed his cap in a grand sweep. "What ever are you two up to, other than no good?"

"Just lookin' around," muttered Cally. "This is Miss Lowe. Margaret."

Meg noticed a sharp tone in Cally's voice, maybe it was resentment, in his reply to the Army sergeant.

"Watch what me, myself, and I do, Miss Margaret. Alchemy, sheer alchemy. Turn tobacco into *yen* and *sen* day after day. Makes 'cents', *ne?*" He entered the shop through the curtain.

Sgt. Paley took Meg's arm and moved quickly down the street. A few moments later, Salchow caught up with them, fanning *yen* in one hand and jingling coins in the other. Cally tightened his hand on Meg's arm. She looked at him in surprise.

Salchow crowed. "See, my magic tricks! You should try it." He sang, "The *sen* shines east, the *sen* shines west, and I know where the *sen* shines best––monooneey, monnnney." Then, he fanned the paper *yen* over the *sen* in his left hand, clinking the coins as he crooned, "There, there, Sweet *Sen*. Gonna go get me some Sentory beer."

Salchow smiled as Meg shook off Cally's arm. She raised her camera, clicked Salchow's picture, watched him put the money in his pockets as he admonished them, "Now, if you go into that shop, stay away from my baby-san, Fumiko, in there. I'm off to the races." He sauntered back the way they had come.

"That was odd. I had to apply for a Ration Pass, items limited on it per week. Did he sell both of those cartons for that Japanese money?"

"In sort of a way. Some shops trade for butts. Let's shop somewhere else. Let's use that one down the street. We don't wanna work with any shopkeepers that he uses." Cally had lost his friendly manner as he stopped and looked into a dark shop window. Shook his head and followed her down the sidewalk.

"Well, I don't see why we can't go back to that first one. I caught a glimpse of a vase that might be what I want for Althea. Plus, I don't understand your attitude toward that Salchow." She had reversed direction on the walk, dodging pedestrians in the crowd of short people.

Cally sighed. "He's too high himself, always acting superior when he's done no more than the rest of us during the war."

"I see. I know a couple of people like that. But why don't you just act superior back?" she protested and then suddenly jerked at his arm in alarm. Meg felt of surge of fright at the Japanese woman who was walking backward to their forward pace, literally staring harshly through her eyes. Meg grasped his arm. "Cally, why is that woman walking backwards staring at me?"

"She prob'ly thinks you're blind––hasn't seen blue eyes before. You'll get used ta it. Might want ta wear sunglasses, though. They think my red-hair's funny. I got used ta that and also to someone now and then spittin' after I went by. I paid it no mind though sometimes I wanna spit back."

"I don't like to feel like I'm a specimen under a microscope. Boy, I hope that doesn't happen often. I'll get sunglasses at the PX next time I go."

They entered the dim room of the store where a man in a grey *kimono* bowed, hands crossed into his sleeves, and greeted them in unaccented English. "Good afternoon. How may I help you?"

A girl squatting next to a brazier in the corner glanced at them.

"Hi," glancing at Cally, Meg corrected her greeting. "That is, *hai, konnichi wa.* I would like to see that dark blue vase with the single rose on it, please." She picked up a tiny, delicate deep red vase, something for a dollhouse.

"It is cloisonné. Made at the cloisonné factory here in Nagoya. Pretty, *ne*?"

"I'll take it." She was used to making quick decisions when choosing gifts for other people. Her time had always been full of work that needed to be accomplished; she disliked having to worry about purchases. It was too easy to talk oneself out of buying a certain gift and then having to spend more time searching for the perfect one. Perfect ones didn't exist, in her opinion. Good enough was fine.

She handed the camera to the sergeant and rummaged in her purse. "I have *yen* and *sen*."

"For you, it is fourteen hundred *yen* twenty *sen*, ma'am. I will secure it for you." He inserted the vase into a brocade bag, cinched the top with two cords, and put the vase carefully inside a wooden box. He wrapped a cord around the four sides finishing with a loop on the top.

"Sounds fine." She handed him the foreign money.

The sergeant took the loop on the box and followed her from the shop. "Where did you get all that money?"

"Well, it isn't *Miss Tatlock's Millions* from that funny movie. My salary was raised last year, and I changed some when I arrived. I made $100 a month and saved most of it, because I lived with my folks," she bragged. "Why do you ask where I got the money? That vase cost me little more than four dollars at the exchange rate."

"I seldom see that much at one time. I mentioned that I send Daddy mosta my pay. I told you we're savin' up to send my sisters to college. They'll make real money just like you do." He walked a few steps on past the streams of short, dark-robed people.

She said, "Scrip or *yen* and *sen* don't feel like money to me, anyway. Not like U. S. Treasury Department minted dollars and cents and mills. Five cents in military scrip and five *yen* are simply paper. I do like these *sen* coins. I would really really like some pennies and half-dollars instead of every piece of American change printed in paper, though."

Cally mused aloud. "I might do that exchange like Kurt Salchow did. Be goin' home in a few days when I muster out. And that shop back there has some things that ought ta be popular with the tourists goin' down 66. Those little red bowls and trays and the vases. I might just do that, but I won't admit it to Salchow. He makes fun of things he shouldn't."

After a few paces, he said, "Still, you shoulda bargained and got a better price."

Meg retorted, "The vase is gorgeous. It's Japanese. It's a perfect present for a bridal shower. I do not have to waste time shopping because I'm finished. 'Abracadabra' and here's the gift."

He sighed. "I guess I've been away too long. I'm not familiar with gifts, and weddings, and parties. I'm ready, willin', and able to get outta here. I don't know what Stateside is like anymore havin' spent so much time away."

Meg could look around in any direction in the area and grasp what he meant. "This whole atmosphere on this street strikes me as surreal. Your talking about home, when we're so far away, while my being is in a stream of small people who hardly look at us, much less look like us. The juxtaposition of home and here is like a dream. The smell of food and things I can't identify. The sounds between shrill instruments in one store and Glenn Miller from the next." Meg shook her head in wonderment.

She went on, musing, as they strolled, avoided people, stepped over broken parts of the sidewalk. "*Kimonos* or Western wear, doorways dripping with pink, purple, fuchsia fake wisteria decorations. Jarring colors like Christmas and Easter, senior prom and Fourth of July, Hallowe'en lanterns.

Wooden shoes clicking everywhere. No honking or sirens. Signs I can't read. People passing us without smiling--yet there's no feeling of menace."

"That's because after Nagasaki, the Emperor said 'uncle', and everyone obeys him. Plus they're not able to be a leisure class engaged in consumption, Thorsten Veblen, sir. They're hungry and survivin', sir." Sergeant Cally Paley frowned slightly as he explained.

Meg rejoined, "Still, it's like a mixed up dream. Then there you are considering something that smacks of selling illegal moonshine, I mean that cigarettes for *yen* bit!"

"It's not the same. You haf ta understand that I know where a decimal point goes." He pointed at a jeep going up the street. "That looked like my AP friend, Phil Tyler, and a Japanese policeman. I wonder why he barely nodded at us. Prob'ly don't want to see us together after last night. After that scare you put to us." Cally shrugs. "As I was sayin', I understand money but you haf ta underst--" He was cut off as shrieks cleaved the air.

"EEEE-YAAMAA! ARRRGGGH!" People suddenly leaped from the low doors of the bathhouse down the street. They seemed to defy gravity, the three naked men and two women leaping out, airborne several seconds more than one could credit. Two women and one man had clothes streaming behind, resembling feathered tails floating back from their shoulders. They streaked off in terror. Screams assailed the ears of pedestrians, some of whom turned back to look.

Four people moved to help. Most of the Japanese fled, scurrying into doorways, pulling children with them.

A small man in dark clothes scurried from the bathhouse. The jeep, the one that Cally had waved at, paused. The Japanese cop hopped out to hold back traffic while the driver turned the jeep around.

A slim, uniformed American soldier came striding stiffly out of the bathhouse, his face shaded by his hat, brass on his epaulets, an air of command about his posture. He was followed quickly by a taller man in nondescript, civilian clothes. The officer held up his hand toward the jeep that now swung toward the men. The men scanned the street briefly to their right, but then their glances lingered toward the left where Meg had first pointed her camera.

Meg looked back over her shoulder in the direction the two men were looking but saw only people returning to the street from doorways and Kurt Salchow walking swiftly. The officer showed something to the AP, and both men climbed into the back seat before the jeep inched away. The street tentatively returned to its everyday affairs.

"What was that about?" She now noticed that he had edged her toward the side of the building, perhaps as a protective measure.

"Dunno. Wonder who that officer and other guy was," Cally reflected. "Strange, really."

"I took a couple of pictures. I was focused on the bathhouse when the action started. Lucky where I was looking in the viewer for a change. When they're developed, I'll show you.

"But, I'm surely quite on guard now. We've seen enough for one afternoon, Cally. I've seen enough for one day. I do appreciate your taking me here. Also, I need to go back and get ready for a party tonight at my principal's house." She moved back toward the bus stop. "That shop smelled like a pile of rotten leaves. I hope this vase's cloth covering doesn't smell like that. I'll have to air it out somehow." She put the camera away in her handbag and took the box.

At the gate by the bus stop, Meg glanced toward the school beyond the fence and exclaimed, "Isn't that your sergeant friend from the shop? He's going through the gate into the American Village."

Cally Paley glanced around toward the direction she was pointing. "If so, he's probably going to visit someone in the Village or over to Nagoya Hall. Makes me no never mind."

"He has a different shoulder patch than your 'purty' one."

"He's Eighth Army."

"What is that song he was singing? You looked embarrassed at the time."

"Oh, uh, it's a takeoff on a song about a baby-san."

"And?"

Sighing, "Suntory beer." Singing, "Suntory Sue, Suntory Sue, your hair is black, your legs are bowed, your teeth are a-a-all capped with gold. Suntory Sue, Suntory Sue, there ain't no gal as sweet as my sweet Suntory Sue." He added, "It's a parody of an old song."

"Oh. I get it. Like 'Darlin' Clementine, and her sho-oes were number nine.'"

"Yep. Like that." Cally waited with her for the bus.

"I guess I may see you tomorrow afternoon at the school. Thank you for escorting me around this afternoon, Sergeant."

He gave an impish grin. "My pleasure. Say, have you heard the song, 'Back in Nagasaki where the men all chew tobaccy, and the women wicki wacki woo'?"

"Not recently or often enough," she replied, grinning back.

He grinned, "Please call me 'Cally.' I'll do my best to be there, Miss Lowe.

"Oh, and please call me 'Meg,'" she replied and boarded the bus.

CHAPTER FOUR

Dressed in summer suits and heels, hose seams straight, Althea and Meg watched the Ford sedan sweep up to the door. An officer eased out of the passenger seat and carefully walked up, grinning at Althea and doing a double take at Meg.

He was a couple of inches taller than Althea in her two-inch heels. Politely removing his cap, he revealed thinning dark hair and a widow's peak.

"Meet Colonel Robbie Jones. My fiancé, soon to be my spouse. Together we will be spice. Get it?" she laughed. "Mouse, mice; louse, lice; spouse, spice. This is my colleague, Miss Margaret--call me Meg--Lowe."

"How do you do?" Robbie and Meg said together and smiled. The ladies climbed in the back of the sedan. Meg settled back in the seat, still a bit drowsy from having snatched a couple of hours of sleep after her shopping trip with Cally, her pally. She shook her head briskly at the grade school rhyme and sat up straight.

Consulting a map, Robbie directed the driver through the city. They ended the drive at a neighborhood of one-story dark wood houses hidden in shrubbery. The driver and the colonel climbed out and held a rear car door open for the ladies.

"Come back in an hour and a half. We'll be watching out here," ordered the colonel to his orderly. The trio moved toward a low verandah where lights and conversation filtered through the greenery.

Inside, Mrs. Fritz, wearing a silky mauve gown, and her husband, wearing full dress Army uniform, comprised a welcoming committee. The hostess' grey hair and makeup were skillfully done, quite elegantly, in fact.

Meg assumed that her own appearance was probably adequate, faced with the perfection of the Fritz display. She used only a bit of powder and lipstick, even though her pale eyebrows called out for mascara. Her yellow sundress with its short shoulder cape, with a faint, shaded lavender design, was perfectly suited to the summer party. Maybe she appeared too pale with her blonde hair in that color dress. She kept her posture perfect.

"We are happy that you are here, Colonel, Miss Ardmore. Miss Lowe, we believe it is high time that you learned our etiquette. Invitations are to be accepted in writing. Military protocol needs to be learned, just as rules at school do."

"Yes, Mrs. Fritz." Meg kept her tone polite although she felt a bit stung. Remember, stand straight regardless of what is implied.

The hostess continued, "Being from the Midwest, you do have an excuse for naiveté. May I present my husband, Captain Fritz, President of the School Board?"

The tall, thin officer nodded his cadaverous head weakly. Mrs. Fritz's peaches and cream complexion contrasted sharply with his yellowish pallor. The hosts turned to the next arrivals, dismissing the three who moved on into the low-ceilinged room.

Meg buzzed into Althea's ear. "I know Emily Post etiquette––I'll mail a thank you note for this party. Why does she keep making me seem as though I don't know what to do? And if she's from Illinois, that's in the Midwest, too. Quite happily, I am aware of how to behave in various situations, including any she sets before me. By the way, your diamond is indeed bigger."

"You've learned the formula: say 'arf' and role over," Althea clapped her hands softly in recognition of Meg's response to the challenges Mrs. Fritz kept throwing at her. The colonel turned around to find out why the two ladies were whispering behind him.

He said, "Let's mingle and find a delightful treat. A Fritz party is known for the variety of treats."

Meg scanned the room, remarking, "The guys all look alike in their uniforms."

Althea and Robbie, ahead of her, were moving toward a buffet table. Althea replied, "Let's see what treats are over there. One hint that works to distinguish among the officers is to pay attention to the brass on the shoulder of the dress uniforms. That tells you how to address someone if you can't recall the name. You merely address them as captain, major, and so on."

Most of the men were captains and sported campaign ribbons and medals. Only a few did not wear wedding rings, Meg noticed as an afterthought, but then only a few American wives were present.

The guests were moving through the buffet line with others, selecting a few easy-to-eat items, and taking cocktails from the bartender. Meg's choice, however, was ginger ale. She had not been inclined to spend money on any alcohol except beer during her college and teaching days. Ginger ale she knew.

A tall brown-haired woman in a tan suit who was accompanied by a taller brown-haired man in a tan civilian suit and brown bow tie approached from their backs. The lady touched Meg's shoulder. "I bet you're Margaret Lowe. I'm Sharon Sheldon, and this is my husband, Bill. Welcome aboard."

"Thank you. I'm looking forward to the year. I heard there were only a few kids last year."

"There'll be more this year. At least a few in each grade. Actually, it is fun having so much time to spend with each one. I'll probably be here through the fall semester, but we're not sure," Sharon said.

Robbie Jones asked the group a question. "How much have you seen of the town?" The group moved off to one side by a silk wallpaper wall.

Bill looked toward the colonel in a noncommittal fashion as though he had received a subtle hint. He started into describing their visit to what was left of the bombed out castle and moat, then covered their tour of the china factory, a visit to the Red Cross hospital, and a drive through the American Village.

Robbie's eyes then looked inquiringly at Meg. She hadn't been to any of those places except the American Village. Maybe Cally would take her around town. She spoke briefly of her trip to the cloisonné shop and of her street photography––without mentioning her escort. Perhaps the hint to Sheldon had been one to her, also. Ergo, why don't you tell us what you were doing yesterday when you took pictures of the bathhouse as we were exiting? She knew she had seen some signal pass between Bill and the colonel.

The Sheldons moved off, and various others circled by in approved party fashion, never drinking too much or speaking too loudly. Meg drank a second iced ginger ale, replied to general topics if directly addressed, and tried to feel comfortable but she couldn't shake an awkward feeling.

Indeed, she wondered why she had been invited. Perhaps because she was one of teaching staff?

A uniformed houseboy and two maids in layered *kimonos* shuffled around with trays of tiny crusty canapés, nothing made of rice or soy sauce. Each bite-size morsel was beautifully prepared, whether a biscuit topped with canned meat or a teeny cream puff. The pineapple chunks, offered with a toothpick stuck in each, were cold and juicy.

Instead of Western windows and doors, the house had sliding doors made of thin, dark slats of wood inset with rice paper panels, that opened to the outdoor garden. Bushes with flowers and a stone lantern could be seen in the yard close by the open door. The occasional Oriental vase, statue, or long scroll appeared elegant, each sitting alone in an alcove, drawing the eye toward it.

To Meg, the dark woods and furniture (to say nothing of the icy hosts) seemed to subdue conversation. She tuned her ears to the murmurs, softly washing over the silhouettes in the room.

Yet, the quiet, easy camaraderie of a church social also was present--people trading quips and hometown news, or observing regional differences with amusement. Intimacy was lacking, the type that existed between longtime friends. A reserve, a shell, protected each from being buffeted too severely, and here was a buffet as an additional buffer. A person could always break off from a group to replenish food or drink.

Meg jerked at an unexpected voice at her shoulder. "We're so happy you are meeting these fine young men. Captain Torleone, Lieutenant Mays: you're on either side of our new teacher, Miss Lowe," Mrs. Fritz purred and moved on.

The two men glanced at their hostess and then at Meg, who merely nodded. Articles in *Seventeen* had explained how to get boys to talk about themselves, and Meg had learned those lessons as easily as she learned history. The threesome chatted vaguely about nothing important, where their hometowns were, what travels they had done; and, then, before moving off, they laughed at a quip from *Reader's Digest* told by Lt. Mays.

Soon Althea came over to Meg standing at the buffet table and asked, "Have you seen Robbie?"

Meg looked around the room for Robbie, but she notices first the tall figure of Bill Sheldon, standing in the garden and bending near the shorter man's ear. She replied, "He's out there in the garden with Bill."

Althea turned. "Oh, all right. Bill trained as a lawyer before he became a spook. They're good friends. Robbie consults with him because he had only one year of law school before joining the Air Force. We need to circulate some more. Say so long to these gentlemen."

Meg graciously excused herself and followed Althea over to Sharon and some other guests. There the topic was the odd set of goods available at the Post Exchange. The group was laughing about some quartermaster who had neither noticed nor taken an inventory of the little general store back home. Perhaps it was leftovers from the war that dictated the way the PX was stocked for the local folks. Families shopped for a greater variety of items than single soldiers usually did.

After an appropriate interval, or due to some clue unseen by Meg, the guests declared their thanks for the hospitality and departed through the front verandah. Motors purred off into the night. Althea waved at Robbie's orderly who had driven up, signaling him to wait a minute while she collected her fiancé.

Mrs. Fritz had the last word, peering at Meg's forehead, "Miss Lowe, I trust you will be at work tomorrow without any more undignified stories. We find your flippant behavior worrisome. Good night."

Robbie assisted the two teachers into the back of the Ford and said, "I'll be a minute. I forgot to mention something to Bill."

He soon returned and climbed into the front seat, and the evening festivities officially closed. He seemed lost in thought because he only grunted when Althea mentioned how nicely the party had gone. Meg replied that it had been a gentile party. He didn't acknowledge her remark. Meg wished that she could have been in on the intense conversation between Robbie and Bill, rather than enduring the battery of small talk. Only a few other remarks were made among them as they returned to the Chiyoda Hotel.

CHAPTER FIVE

Monday morning found the sun shining through the classroom window onto Meg's head as she bent over lessons plans for one of the four history classes--plus geography--she would most likely be teaching. Mrs. Fritz showed up halfway through the morning with boxes of blackboard erasers, chalk, and rulers.

"Are we to check these items in at the end of the year?" Meg inquired in a neutral tone of voice.

Mrs. Fritz looked at her suspiciously, "We will certainly have an accounting. Sign the clipboard. Moreover, we must tell you that pedal pushers and sleeveless blouses are not appropriate attire for professionals. We expect you to dress properly from now on at our school." She proffered a pen and clipboard, and Meg signed the sheet and listed the particular items that she accepted.

Later, needing a break, Meg took the bleach downstairs to the janitor's closet and then stopped to make coffee in the lounge. The fact that the boxes with the wig and *kimonos* were gone was somewhat puzzling, but not a major concern. She'd finished with them, right enough.

She had brought two cinnamon rolls and fruit from the hotel, and she climbed upstairs to eat lunch, carrying the coffee cup. Out the east windows, the weather was beginning to look threatening. Dark grey clouds were moving in and hovering overhead. A rain would either make it unbearably humid or cleanse the air, making it simply feel like welcome summer temperatures.

She grabbed her purse and headed back to the shopping district where she had seen a big waxed paper umbrella at a store yesterday. She should have bought it then because rain seemed to appear frequently and unexpectedly. Rain began dripping as she left the store so she opened up the frame and hurried back to the school.

On opening the door of her room, she startled a young Japanese woman who was dusting a bookshelf. A bucket of rags and a small broom were at her feet, a white apron over her *kimono*.

"Excuse me and what are you doing in my classroom?" She pointed a finger at her chest and then at the girl's.

"Yamata Fumiko. I clean school." The girl bowed politely. "You see at Faddah's shop, yestehday, *ne*? Vase, *ne*?"

Thinking back, Meg asked slowly, "You were cooking in the corner?" She stirred with her hand, remembering a squat female figure in the shop's corner.

"*Hai.*"

"I'm Miss Lowe. This is my classroom. The other day, I found a dirty mop in your janitor closet. I have a friend who knows how to clean it, maybe. He's going to help me clean my sandals. You could ask him about the mop. May we see you down there later this afternoon?" She had to repeat the request in various ways, spacing words, speaking slower and slower, before Fumiko acquiesced with a bow and a smile, whether she understood the invitation or not.

Meg wanted to make her proposal clear. She stuck a pencil over her ear, motioned an invitation to the girl out of the door of her classroom and down the stairs, led the way to the janitor's closet, and picked up the bleach.

She set the jug down by the mop. Pointing at her watch, Meg pantomimed meeting Fumiko later in the afternoon with herself and a man, here, in this closet. She tapped the four and six on the dial. The girl looked interested. Meg picked up the jug again and drew a dial on the label with the hands pointing to 4:30. Pointing again at herself and the maid, she completed a trio by holding a hand high over her head and then saluting. Three fingers—one for Fumiko, one for herself, and one for a tall, saluting person—completed the scenario. The maid nodded. Meg had to assume that she had been understood, because she had no more ideas about how to communicate to the Japanese girl.

Meg next pointed at the large trap door, held up her palms, lifted her eyebrows, and shrugged her shoulders. "What's down there?"

Fumiko twirled her right hand overhead and brought both hands quickly down, saying "BOO-OOM! C'AAASSSHHHH!" She smacked her hands together.

Meg flinched at the noise. "Tornado? Typhoon? Bomb?"

At the look of incomprehension, Meg tried to lift the big wooden door, and Fumiko bent to help. Pointing down, Meg's eyebrows rose; most likely, she believed, she was looking at a bomb shelter.

The maid bowed, took off the apron, then reached between her knees from the back, pulled the front hem of her *kimono* through, and tucked it in the back of her belt, forming bloomers. She moved down the stairs and flicked a switch on the right.

Meg stepped down, eying stacks of folded cots. A tunnel ran off in the distance, dimly lit by a string of widely spaced overhead bulbs in a low ceiling. The janitor bowed and swept her arms proudly at the cots.

Meg nodded in understanding and climbed back up the steep narrow steps to the first floor. They laid the trapdoor down and parted to return to their duties.

Later in the afternoon, a tap on the classroom door announced Cally with his cap, hair, and shoulders wet. "At your command, Madam Lowe," he grinned.

"It's that late? I didn't realize. Let me straighten these things. I'll take the shoes out of my purse. I asked the janitor to be there, too, so you can teach us both something. She's the daughter of the fellow who owns the '*yen* exchange.' Where I bought the vase?"

"Really? The girl in the corner?"

"Yep."

The janitor saw them coming down the stairs and glided up, bowing, to be introduced. Meg entered the janitor's closet and dropped her shoes. "That's odd," she said to Cally as she looked at the hinges. "The dirty mop is there that I told Fumi you'd know how to clean. But it left some yarn caught in that left hinge Saturday, and I saw the strand earlier today when we were down here. Now, it's gone. Did you clean--?" She swept her hand around the floor with a questioning look.

The janitor did not reply to the question but merely eyed her gesture, and did not seem to comprehend what Meg wanted to know.

"That looks like a heavy trapdoor to a bomb shelter," Cally said. "I wonder if that's what it's for."

He turned to Fumiko, saying, "*Non desu ka*?" and pointed.

Fumiko held her hands high, and made the noise like a clap of thunder: "C'assssshhh--c'asssh!" She let her arms fall while smacking her hands together.

"Typhoon shelter, maybe? She did that same sound of crashing when I asked her before," Meg said.

"More likely a bomb shelter. I suppose it'd do for a typhoon shelter nowadays." He sounded disinterested in the subject of the shelter. Meg sat down on the floor against the wall. Fumiko squatted on the trap door, head bowed, while Cally experimented with one frond of the mop standing it over by the sink. He put water in a bucket, dropped a splash of bleach in, and, finding that the tested yarn did not lose color, Cally swished the mop around.

Meg wanted some help cleaning the huaraches and held them out toward him. "Ahem," she said. Fumiko sat there like a doorstop, not moving. Why should the janitor sit there and let them do all the work? Meg touched her on the arm and held out a shoe to her. The girl looked bewildered.

"I'll get you two started on the huaraches' spots." Cally turned to offer his expertise and handed them each a rag, demonstrating the method of cleaning the black 'measles' from the huaraches. Fumiko seemed to finally grasp why they were here: to clean a mop and clean some shoes.

They worked steadily for some minutes in the quiet, barely paying attention to the background sounds of rain hitting the outside walls, faint voices, and someone whistling. After half an hour or so, a short figure in a black raincoat, limp hat, and penny-loafers, dripping water, appeared at the door.

"We heard *voices*. What. Have. We. Here?" a stern voice inquired.

Meg looked up, experienced the same fear and awe as when, ten days ago, she'd been on deck and had seen a colossal, crested wave towering over, bearing down on the ship. It collapsed before it swamped the liner. Jumping up, with a shiver shaking her shoulders, legs ready to collapse, Meg stuttered, "T-trying to clean mildew, Mrs. Fritz."

Cally had whirled around at the sound of the voice, jerking the bucket over, blushing. Fumiko cowered.

"We gave you, and you signed, I trust, supposedly understanding, the Code of Conduct. Here we find you wearing inappropriate attire and with a soldier! And no chaperone!"

Meg hurriedly improvised an excuse, and she tossed an apologetic look at Fumi. "B-but there's another girl with us here. Fumiko is . . ."

"A chaperone means an American lady! We see that water on the floor, ruining everything with bleach, running down the typhoon shelter. We'll report this to the School Board. Your contract *will* be reviewed. Leave! Now!" she ordered, brooking no dissent. "Later, we will speak with your father, Miss Yamata."

Cally gave a perfunctory swipe with the mop toward the floor drain. He hesitated a couple of seconds before replacing the mop head in the bucket and turning back around.

"We'll clean . . ."

"*No*. Now! No more water spoiling the shelter." She was almost choking with rage.

"Very well, sir--ma'am," said Cally carefully, standing behind his fellow culprits. "'Pologize for tryin' to help Miss Lowe and the maid."

"Yes, Mrs. Fritz," Meg surrendered.

Fumiko squeaked out, "*Hai*, Miz F'itz."

Meg heard the remark as "Hi, Miss Fits". That seemed quite appropriate, and she stifled a grin.

"We see nothing amusing in this situation," Mrs. Fritz raged at her.

They wiped their hands on towels that Fumiko handed them, her body trembling all the while. Cally swiped the towel hard on the floor and that completed their swift flight preparations.

Meg grabbed her huaraches.

The Principal wheeled and marched down the hall.

Stalking off behind Meg, Cally complained in an undertone, "That was outta left-field. I don't envy you working for that tyrant of a drill sergeant."

"Agree to that depiction. Maybe I should raise my hand and ask if I can please go to my room?" she said in a sardonic tone.

Mrs. Fritz, trailing the smell of outdoors behind her, led them down the hall and yanked open the front door. With her rain-flattened hair and shapeless raincoat, she resembled the stout wide-mouthed umbrella stand beside her.

Fumiko edged out, grabbing her *geta* from the steps. The irate Principal held up a palm to stop Cally as he started to follow Meg upstairs. After taking a dignified pace up and a regal descent back down the stairs, Meg strode to the open door, her purse banging her hip. She grabbed her umbrella from the stand by the door and clasped it defensively as she edged around the woman.

After they filed out, Mrs. Fritz slammed and locked the door. "This door will remain locked after hours," declared Mrs. Fritz. She followed them around the corner toward the gate. She glowered, breathing heavily.

Cally had taken the umbrella and raised it over their heads as they hastened toward the gate to the Village. As he did so, Meg caught a peripheral view of Mrs. Fritz, still rigid and glaring after them, drizzle pasting her grey hair.

Meg whispered, "Why did she insult all of us? I can't fathom the reason why she shows such palpable antipathy toward me. What's she afraid of? Why so blown all out of proportion? Why didn't she even look at you two? Can she fire me? I think Civil Service hired me; the Fritzes didn't, did they, so she can't fire me, right? Did you see that bleach took the color from the leather and hardly touched the black measles? They don't just smell of mildew now, they're odoriferous?"

"Animal? Vegetable? Mineral?"

"What are you talking about?"

"You sound like you're playin' 'Twenty Questions.' Hush now. Quit babblin'. Lemme think."

"All right, but slow down, Cally. I have to run to keep up with you."

He appeared to be somewhere else. Eventually he said, "Ever since I was knee-high to a grasshopper, I been tinkerin' with engines ever chance I got. I fine-tune airplane engines. I listen for noises that are meshin' correctly or not. I can note them that are off. That lady is off. She was scairt bad so was mad. I've seen scairt. I've been scairt quite a few times. When we were first in that janitor's closet, didja hear voices?"

Because the rain had moved on, he shut the umbrella's stout bamboo framework and shook the drops from its oilskin top.

"Uh-huh. Sounded like a car radio or people walking by having an argument. Also, there was someone whistling by. Birds chirping. Rain dripping."

"How could the lady hear voices? We hadn't said anythin' for quite a while. Didja hear a thunk?" he asked.

She shook her head.

"Didja hear the bucket of water going down a drain?"

She lifted her shoulders and shook her head again. Was he trying to be superior? To seem more alert?

"Lemme tell you, those voices wasn't radio or outside, they was in that shelter and not happy. Plus there was a thunk. Then, she accused me of sweepin' water down the trapdoor when I heard it go down a drain."

"I don't know the answers to any of those sounds you say you heard. Are you thinking there were people in the shelter?" Meg said, skeptical. Surely Cally was simply being paranoid. Maybe he just liked conspiracies––she knew a lot of people like that back home, always finding mysteries in the plainest things. But what if he was right? She didn't know how she'd find out. If there were someone hiding down there, Mrs. Fritz would have her eyes on the shelter like a hawk now––neither one of them would get anywhere near the trapdoor. Best to let it go, keep her head down, just in case Mrs. Fritz can fire her.

"I'm shaken. Here's my bus. I'm going to go curl up with a good book, and go to bed, and have pleasant dreams."

"Well, I'm gonna spend time to think about some things that happened here just now."

"Be my guest."

"Uh, Miss Lowe, Meg, that reminds me. There's a game here tomorrow night at 1730 with a Navy team from a ship that's in port. If you can come, could you get here by yourself? I'll barely make it in time from the Ozone area."

"Yes, a game would give me a chance to scream and shout out my frustrations, Cally. I'll just stay over after work. Althea, another teacher, said Mrs. Fritz isn't here on Tuesdays, thank goodness. She runs some kind of free lunch thing." She climbed aboard the bus carrying her umbrella and olive drab purse.

Back in her room, she didn't open a good book until she had furiously rubbed some Mum into the insides of her huaraches. She set them on the desk by the window to bask in sunshine tomorrow. She opened the book, read a hundred pages, dog-eared the page, reached over to the desk, and pulled the lamp's chain. She fell into a deep sleep.

CHAPTER SIX

The next day didn't furnish morning sunshine; it merely lightened up early. Meg donned slacks and blouse after a quick shower. She picked up her huaraches and examined them, stiff and dry. Both sandals were pale across the arch with black spots remaining elsewhere.

Out the window, the day was clear. She pulled her camera from the purse and focused it on the sidewalk below. The view of black hair streaming by below looked like the picture of a blackberry bush she had taken one July back home. She clicked the shutter.

Breakfast was a stale leftover apple-turnover and orange juice that must have been made from powder. She moseyed outside the Chiyoda. The bus arrived by seven a.m., and fifteen minutes later arrived at the American Village gate.

Althea had remarked that Mrs. Fritz had duties on Tuesdays other than being in attendance in the school building. The way should be clear to do some exploring. She tossed her things in her classroom, then returned downstairs to the janitor's closet and tugged up the heavy trapdoor with some difficulty.

The stairs were a bit dusty and showed their footprints from the day before. The silence and darkness down there were creepy. But the light switch she found where she had seen Fumi flip it on, and the string of light bulbs dimly dispelled the haunting feeling.

Meg was sure she would find a radio that had broadcast those voices Cally said he heard from the shelter and prove that no one had been down in the bomb shelter below them as they worked on her shoes and the mop. The thought delighted her, because sometimes he seemed to discount her comments. Probably because she was female. Or maybe because she hadn't fought in the war. Or because she was newly arrived in Japan.

Past the stacked cots were curiously shaped boxes, with that box of kimonos and the wig-box on top of the first ones. A clipboard featured a paper with three columns (Item/ Result/Date) topped the next stack. She glanced at the pages. Several items had been crossed out. Uninteresting.

The dim light bulbs ran along the ceiling at intervals of eight feet. The lights glinted on deep red and black lacquer boxes with hinged tops. She opened several to peer at statues in ivory and wood, vases with smooth or crackly finish, jade Buddhas, snarling brass animals and tall skinny storks, gorgeously decorated cloth. The smells of sandalwood, musk, old cloth, and wood rose from them.

What were all these for? What history could they tell her? They look so old and mysterious. What dynasties and religious icons could they be? She vowed, "This year we are not going to skip the World History chapters on the Orient."

Browsing in pearl shell encrusted cases, she came across one filled with *yen* sorted into bundles that were bound by twine. How odd. She stared and stared, but forced herself on, opening and closing odd-shaped containers. An oblong box held jeweled sheaths for long and short swords, some sheaths empty. Pulling a short one up, she found the hilt also bejeweled. The sword blade had a paper-thin edge on one side that cut her finger when she tested the metal. She sucked on the finger and moved on.

In the next container, she found an old carved wood case about three inches wide and six inches long. Undoing the clasp, she contemplated a series of metal disks half-peeping from inside padded slots. Coin collection: maybe old *sen*? Those square holes in the middle looked more like they were some part of machinery. Something important. Something precious that needed special preservation in its case.

Several yards further, cartons of Uncle Ben's Converted Rice rose to the ceiling. The familiarity of the items was a surprise, but, of course, made sense for a typhoon shelter. Must be to trade––a precious sword or antique doohickey for each box of rice. Then sell the sword for cash or tobacco or some such.

Beyond the rice boxes, her eyes glimpsed open or closed pasteboard cartons that, according to the labels and pictures, contained assorted canned goods.

Also present were boxes of gauze, syringes, tape, and antiseptics. Bags of Zippos, watches; a basket of Swiss army knives; and, smaller cartons of fountain pens and inkbottles. Several boxes of C-rations plus jugs of water.

Strange to think someone had been smoking down here, or wanted to in the enclosed below ground tunnel. Cigarette cartons, some with packages missing and ends opened, sat beside a jar of cigar butts, partnered with a huge ashtray containing shreds of tobacco.

There were several mismatched shirts and trousers of GI uniforms, seven car tires, some leather billfolds, and bolts of cloth that looked like silk parachute material.

She plucked a Swiss army knife from its container and slit open a box of canned food. Would people bring can openers when they fled to shelter from a storm? It'd be hard to open a can with a knife. How can someone eat unheated soup?

As she continued along, Meg noticed her shoes slip a bit against the floor as if she'd stepped in something wet. Strange. Everything down here seemed excessively dry--better for preservation of the food, and probably why Mrs. Fritz was so upset about them spilling water yesterday.

She leaned against a stack of canned goods and inspected the bottom of her shoes. A dark smear stained her heel. She ran her finger over the spot, and it came away red. Her eyes darted around the dim space, looking for the source--a broken can of soup, perhaps. She looked around. Either drops of tomato soup or gobs of blood were congealing on the floor of the tunnel.

And then she noticed the body.

A short scream jumped from her throat, and Meg's hand went to her mouth to stifle it. Heart pounding, she took a tentative step toward the prone uniformed body, the body of an officer gripping her vision. He was flat on his back, right leg covered with blood, not moving. Meg didn't move either, for a split second.

Biting her lower lip--hard, Meg fled back to the stairs, flicked off the light, dropped the trapdoor, and made it to her classroom before she started hyperventilating. She shut the knife, shakily brushed dust from her arms and slacks, and sank into her desk chair. Meg was frightened in a way she had never been before. Talk about a surreal picture.

She didn't have many options in this strange country, knowing very few people and whom to trust. Or, who would trust her, herself, stranger to the American contingent as yet. Back home, she would have called her dad or one of his many colleagues across the law enforcement network. Nothing could keep her attention as the minutes ticked by whether it was textbooks, lesson plans, travel plans, whose birthday need a card from here, from her. She had to find someone to help with the corpse.

Hours later, the janitor knocked on the door. When she opened it, Miss Lowe waved her away, hissing, "No, no, go away." Fumi waved back, fingers and palms aimed toward the ground. Meg Lowe made pushing motions, "N-not today. Go away."

"*Hai*, okay," Fumiko said and shut the door.

When she heard Althea Ardmore go into the science lab mid-morning, Meg rose stiffly out of the desk chair and sought her colleague's attention. She desperately needed to find out how to call the police. "Where can I find a Japanese-English dictionary?"

"Oh, probably at the PX. There's an odd assortment of merchandise there. As to a where you'd find a Japanese dictionary, I'm not sure. A Mr. Yamata from a store over there taught six weeks of Japanese during the spring semester after school on Tuesdays. After 30 minutes or so, he'd look at the ceiling and start to ramble in both languages. We'd excuse ourselves, say *arigato*, leave a few *yen*, tiptoe out, and shake our heads. His daughter is that part-time janitor here, Fumi. I think she understands more English than she lets on. She has a deep bow always handy. Have you met her?"

"Yes. She said her name is 'Fumi', but you call her 'Fumiko?'"

"Yes, that's somehow a syllable added to girl's names, I think. I learned some Japanese phrases from Mr. Yamata back then. Enough to get around a city or store. What do you need?"

Meg laughed weakly, "Something like 'mayday, mayday.'"

"Can't help you there. You look pasty. Go have a cup of coffee. I'm busy running an experiment."

During a brief walk down to the shopping district and back, Meg calculated finally that Sergeant Calhoun Paley is the only one who could maybe believe her and help her. The problem was that she wasn't sure exactly where he was working. Also, she wasn't well enough acquainted with the Air Police fellows he'd introduced her to. He knows the system, been here a while.

A passerby glanced over at her talking to herself.

The day ticked slowly away. At last, at last, she saw the time had arrived for the softball game. All afternoon the rain had flicked against the window in a chilling drumbeat. Pick, flick, click. Tick, nick, sic.

With her umbrella raised and purse in hand, she ventured to the bleachers behind the chapel and hunkered down in the crowd. She managed to squeeze into a seat behind the home team's bench and behind the backstop screen. The drizzle slowed and stopped. She folded her umbrella, trying not to stab the fellow seated next to her.

Airmen and soldiers and a few civilians continued to arrive and climb onto the bleachers as the game time appeared and the teams took to the field. Some residents came out to the rear porch on their houses to watch the game in the ball field. Meg felt like an ice floe all alone and drifting helplessly in the sea of these strangers.

She and Cally had waved at each other before the game began. The team members had trotted hurriedly onto the field as they arrived from different parts of the city on buses, personnel carriers, and jeeps. She couldn't bring herself to interrupt the game by demanding Cally's attention when he returned to the bench each half inning.

The Navy team, the Giants, lost the ball game 2-12. The crowd around her cheered. Teams shook hands, and Cally walked over. His uniform, and those worn by other players, were muddy from diving to catch a ball or sliding into base.

He spoke loudly enough for her to hear over the cheering. "Did you enjoy the game?"

She smiled weakly, stalling for time while she decided how she was going to break the news to him about the dead body. She couldn't say anything in front of all these people. She did remember most of the action, so at least half of her brain had been paying attention. "Yes, your teammates Tyler to Martin to Brown were reminiscent of the 1910 poem, 'Baseball's Sad Lexicon', by F. P. Adam."

A she started to recite the poem, several of the men around her joined in with her, chanting the poem.

> *"These are the saddest of possible words:*
> *'Tinker to Evers to Chance.'*
> *Trio of bear cubs, and fleeter than birds,*
> *Tinker and Evers and Chance.*
> *Ruthlessly pricking our gonfalon bubble,*
> *Making a Giant hit into a double--*
> *Words that are heavy with nothing but*
> *trouble:*
> *'Tinker to Evers to Chance.'"*

"For your team, I'd revise it to change to the names of your teammates. I'd call it 'Softball's Sad Lexicon,' Tyler to Martin to Brown," she said. The airman seated next to her shouted, "You got it right-o, lady!"

Another joined in with a hoot and yelling, "That'll be our team cheer: Tyler to Martin to Brown!"

Two more fellows shouted toward the bench for the Navy team, "Tyler to Martin to Brown!"

Cally looked pleased. "Yeah, we'll replace the Chicago Cubs—Chance on first, Evers at second, and Tinker at shortstop where we have Tyler and Martin and Brown."

"To say nothing of your making them fan their bats and hit nothing but air, ruthlessly bursting their bubble," she murmured the compliment. The other spectators were leaving, although they were still hollering "Great job", "Good game." The jubilant comments were aimed at the American team, the Nagoya Nuggets, who were gathering their gear from the bench.

Cally smiled through the net, nodded, and made an observation that she didn't need. "Your bruised forehead is takin' on the color of motor oil. Now, wait, and I'll go change in the chapel and be right with you." He paused for a minute, studying the expression on her face before he hurried away.

The night fell quickly, unlike the long summer evenings back in Missouri. It must be because we're next to the ocean. She sat huddled, and few people were left around her when he came back.

"I didn't hear you screamin' and shoutin' to take out your frustrations," he grinned as he took the umbrella from her, folded it more tightly, and helped her up from the bleacher. He was examining her face again, and not just the bruise.

"Sergeant Paley," she began and stopped. She began to walk a few paces away from the remaining team members. She waited until they were a safe distance from anyone else who might overhear what she was about to say.

"Yes?" He started off with his sports bag and her umbrella.

"Cally," her voice wavering, she blurted, "there's a dead officer down in that tunnel where the water drained."

Cally laughed. "What's the punch-line?" He stopped and began grinning at her. "Someone ruthlessly pricking his bubble?"

The derision helped. Kicking at gravel, she stopped walking toward the gate. "I-am-not-kidding! I need help, not smart alecky remarks, and I'm scared. Understand? Scared spitless. There's a dead man in the tunnel." Meg quickly became indignant. She wanted to shake him, make him pay attention.

Also stopping, he frowned, his head bent down over her face. He seemed to change personality, right in front of her, going from a lackadaisical kidder to an alert soldier. "What? You mean you're not kidding? You really saw a dead body? A dead body under the school in that bomb shelter?"

"Yes, That is exactly what I mean. I went down the shelter this morning to see what I could see, and way down the tunnel I stepped in blood, and there is a dead officer down there!"

"Okay, ma'am, Meg. Now, now. Quiet now. You're sure? You're not joshing me?"

She nodded emphatically. "I saw it and stepped in the blood."

He looked at her in wonder and asked, "Do you know who it is? Do you know who did it?"

She shook her head, miffed. "Well, I certainly didn't have means, opportunity, or motive."

"Did the body smell?" He softened his voice. "Like if it'd been dead a while?"

"No, the tunnel tastes and feels like a root cellar––cool and snug. I was looking at cots and boxes and containers along one wall. I was all the way next to him before I realized he was there on the floor by the other wall."

"Okay. Let's get to the gate by the commissary and get calm. I better call Ty and Marty but they won't be home yet from the game. When they're there at the barracks, they can get us some AP help. We have to think, and we have enough time before curfew to do that. I have bed-check at 2400."

"I agree. I didn't know how to call any American or Japanese police to ask for help. But, shouldn't we know more? Like you seeing the body first before you call them?"

As they approached the southeast gate over the wet gravel street, he handed her the umbrella and a sack. "I was plannin' on a picnic with you although I couldn't find any bread," he said sardonically. "But, I realize someone has ta check out that shelter, and I don't know anyone I'd rather ask than my team mates. Say, do you have a flashlight in that purse-thing?"

"No. Just a couple-three flashbulbs. I do have a key to the school, if that helps."

"Good. Talk later. I'll to try to phone one a them."

He met her slow stroll, walking rapidly himself back from the gate. He took the small bag of groceries. "Let's walk around close-by the gate guards 'til they call me over."

Meg saw him decide to picnic while waiting. He took a stack of bologna and ripped off the rinds. Popping the cap from a bottle of Nehi, he nervously gulped the pop, alternating with the chow. He next removed a Baby Ruth that disappeared in two bites and then popped a stick of gum into his mouth.

"What're you thinking?" she asked. Now that she had help, she had finally settled down and peeled a somewhat old orange, daintily chewed the slices, and ate the remaining slice of sandwich meat.

"Dunno. 'Tain't fine-tunin'." Minutes dragged by. "Don't hardly know what ta do. I'm ready to go there ourselfs. Ty prob'ly woulda had to talk to higher-ups anyway. I don't think I should tell the tale to the Japanese guards on the gate.

"It's gettin' dark enough that somethin' should be done to check out your story. Lemme just tell that guard to give 'em a message when they get here, and I'll get a flashlight. I'll stash the trash."

Meg groaned. "I wish my father, a deputy sheriff, were here. He deputized me for a posse a couple of times during the war when there were not any able men around. He always knew what to do and how to proceed without being precipitous. He likes incontrovertible proof before he moves to conclude a case."

"We're here. He's not, and he'd prob'ly say, 'Go hence, explore. You've got guts, use 'em.' Be back with a flash."

Meg nodded thoughtfully at his receding back. However, Dad would have put the injunction more colorfully. She was also thinking how glad she was back then that Dad and Mom didn't always know where she went and what she explored.

Cally handed her a flashlight on his return. "I was lucky enough to find two flashlights with batteries that work. I'm sure you've enough room in that bag for yours. Anyhow, let's go in this gate, around the Village and ball field. That way we can see if there's any lights on in the schoolhouse. Don't wanna stumble on a killer."

She shuddered.

As they eased quietly through the dark outfield, he suggested, "Maybe you were right the other day about Kurt Salchow."

"What do you mean?"

"When you saw him the other day, maybe he did go into the school instead of to Nagoya Hall or a friend's house. Although why he'd hit an officer I can't imagine."

"I'd think he'd have to provoked something beyond understanding, because he seemed like such a jolly fellow when I met him Saturday."

"We'll see."

"However, I didn't mention at the time, but I also thought I saw a tiny flash of light inside the school at the time he disappeared into the Village. And, as you've jiggered my recollection, there's no telling how long that body's been there. Hey, I think if we start outside the west gate approximately where the janitor's closet is located inside the school, I can probably pace off about where I was when I found the man, if that'd help us. We'll then get to it immediately when we go downstairs."

"All right. Although, I suspect you're just trying to delay the inevitable. We do have to go look."

He was correct about that––she felt like that ice floe again, but as if it were caught anchored on the bottom, her feet having trouble moving. And she was shivering from the chill, not wanting to sail into that deep tunnel again. They stopped, and she considered the schoolhouse, then they walked outside the gate slowly as she reconstructed the layout of the shelter in her head. After about 15 yards, she halted. She stifled the icy feelings, thawing her brain by remembering the salient yardage from stairs to bloody body, and reflected, "The stairs go down about nine feet and are steep. It was at least this much farther along the shelter that I had continued examining the stuff stacked on the pallets. Before I saw *it*."

The sidewalks still flowed with pedestrians in wooden *geta* clicking slowly along, the click dulled when they strode through puddles. Neither Meg nor Cally was conscious of the other people. The vehicles chugging down the streets were mere background noise, like the sound of *geta*. As usual, most natives ignored them, although a couple of groups of boys or girls did stop to look them over, these tall, strange beings who were Americans with light colored hair and eyes.

"About here," she stopped. A cold cord ran through her torso just as it did when in grade school she was confronted by big Halloween bogeymen in masks. Trying to keep the shudder out of her voice, she replied. "About here, if I remember correctly. I had gone past a lot of storage containers and was looking in the ones with canned supplies when I saw him."

"Okay, about here; let's go back. Lemme do it, and you wait outside for the troops. Before the APs arrive, maybe I can recon."

"You're crazy. I'm going if you are. I know how to track game, too." She pulled up her mental anchor, turning it into courage, and strode forward, pulling the key from her purse, after fumbling around a bit. She simply could not stay out here alone. Action was better than words, her mom always said, particularly when she didn't want to do some chore and promised to do it later.

CHAPTER SEVEN

They moved silently silently into the schoolhouse after Meg unlocked the door. "Wipe your feet," Paley cautioned at the doorway, turning his flashlight toward the bamboo mat and then removing his shoes. Meg was surprised that she did *not* get an eerie feeling as they flashed their lights around the green walls and brown wood floor, sliding along in stocking feet on Cally's part and bare feet, on Meg's.

They crept to the janitor's closet with hooded flashlights. Inside, a brand new sign "DANGER OFF LIMITS" was tacked to the trapdoor. "That sign wasn't here this morning. I'm thinking maybe you should just 'witch' that door open. Just take a peach branch and see if what-I-saw is still down there." Meg giggled a bit nervously.

Giving her a serious look, Cally asked, "Why do you say that?"

"Don't know. I've spent all day tensed up, not sure what to do, not knowing anybody very well, not knowing where to go. Now, I'm afraid the body will be gone, and I'll have created a scene in public."

Broad strips of black tape were stuck around the edges of the trapdoor. Under the tape, on the side with the handle, were wedges made from the broken ends of a ruler. Meg pulled out the Swiss knife she'd stowed in her pocket, and Cally used it to remove the shims.

"Where'dja get this beauty?" he asked.

"There's a basket of them down there with a lot of oddments. Maybe they're to be used to dig out if there's a C'AASH? If those things down there are donations, who owns them? Milady Fritz to the manner born? Or the people who need help? But how would furnishings help feed people?" Meg knew she was babbling incoherently, quite unlike her usual staid self. But, then, her self had never stood beside a corpse before.

Cally ripped the door up, revealing the flight of steep cement stairs. "Shh," he leaned his head down, but the sub floor was too thick, causing him to place a hand on the third step in order to peer down a dark hall. "Someone's runnin'." He turned the flashlight down the long tunnel, but it was not strong enough to illuminate the length. "Sounds like he climbed some steps and opened another trapdoor and went out. Maybe your corpse did get up and leave!"

"Doubt it. Are you sure he's gone?"

Cally nodded and flipped his hand as if a fly had landed on it. "All gone."

"Okay. You better be right. Wish I had my shotgun, but this'll have to do." She shouldered the umbrella, carried the flashlight and purse, and followed his light down the stairs. Creeping down, he started edging along the left wall, looking at the floor while she swung her light over stacks of boxes on pallets on the right side.

He glanced over, saying, "Now if you haf ta talk, speak in a low voice. That won't carry as bad as whispers do."

"Like this?" she hissed. "What do you think of all this stuff?"

His answer was spoken so quietly that she had to strain to hear him. "Those cots and supplies could be emergency stuff for the school or could be storage for something else or could be black market. People barter for food. Some bartered stuff was pilfered from conquered countries--Manchuria, China, Malaya--and so the stuff doesn't mean anything that would be an ancestral treasure to the family, just souvenirs a military guy brought home, plundered or poached, and so they trade them for food."

"You mean things here were stolen from other countries?"

"Yes, it always happens during wars. Now most of these don't belong to anyone. And, when there's no money, people hereabouts are always boarding trains to the country to swap items for food."

"I can understand that," Meg spoke in her lowest tone.

Cally mused, "We've brought back thousands of brutal Sons of Nippon men from their 'Greater East Asia Co-prosperity Sphere.' Some prospered better than others during their military career. That is, while invading other countries. Here there's gonna be a while assimilating them back into the workforce. Prob'ly same with us GIs coming back to the States needing jobs." His voice was weary.

His flashlight stopped on the prone body part way down the tunnel.

"That's it," Meg exclaimed. "It's just as I left it." Meg knelt and opened her purse. Now that she was vindicated, having discovered that a body actually existed, her heartbeat settled down.

"What are you doing?" he worried.

"Putting the flash on my camera. I still have a few frames. Three to be exact. I'm going to help solve this like I helped my dad a few times."

She took one long shot and moved down several yards to take another, then placed the camera on top of a stack a third of the way down the tunnel. Tracing to where she had found the trunk of *yen* was not easy, nor to the one with jeweled swords, but she eventually found the items. Cally had indicated that no one really owned the items down here, even the malignant snarling metal lions and ceramic dragons but, anyway, those did not recapture her interest. She moseyed back to grasp her sturdy umbrella, slipped four packages from the trunk of *yen* inside the bamboo ribs. Another item joined the *yen*, that of the carved padded case of old machinery cogs or *sen* coins.

Cally was much farther down the hall, scrutinizing the dust, grunting, "There's tracks here of bare feet and *zoris*, those straw sandals; some're overlaid with about size eight leather soles, and a nine under it that limped, and also some that could be lady's or small men's or kids'. Your wedgies only go along those pallets, until you hied outta here. At least you didn't run around like a chicken with its head cut off and spoil the tracks." His light shown on the floor a couple of yards beyond the cases of canned goods.

On a trunk next to the towers of cartons of Uncle Ben's Converted Rice, Meg saw a dark covered ledger that she had missed before. Inside were columns of ideographs, page after page. The one she had spotted earlier was in English. "I've found something written in Japanese," she hissed.

"Well, give it to the cops when they get here. Didja see that can this morning?" His light fell on a can of corn about two feet from the corpse.

"Don't remember. Just skedaddled. But I noticed that there are some boxes of miscellaneous canned vegetables. Probably donations for Mrs. Fritz's Friendly Soup Kitchen."

He turned a quizzical look at her. She amended, "Well, it's more like a rice bowl kitchen that she runs on Tuesdays somewhere—like the soup kitchens during the Depression."

"Didja notice those flies around the body?"

She shook her head. "I was here a *very* brief time early this morning."

Speculating, he murmured, "Looks like the can beaned him. Mebbe he knocked hisself out fallin'. His leg was stabbed though. He's bled out."

He knelt carefully away from the corpse's head and flashed the light ahead past its feet. "Soles of a fellow about my size walked this far and ran back there. Bigger and smaller tracks under those." Because they were moving deeper into the shelter, the flashlight now revealed two steps at the end, curving to the left, while a low tunnel continued straight ahead. "More entrances. Makes sense. Good air down here, little dust. Why don't you go back up and wait for me? Nothing to do here until the APs get here."

Meg scowled at him. "I'll go up when you do. We just need to stay clear of the evidence, you know, pal. I'm no longer nervous. Move over. I'll take my last picture. I've seen blood before. Jeez Louise, quit mommying me. Do you think we could afford to buy meat when I was little? We hunted in the farmer's woods down the road. Hung the deer and eviscerated them. I've been drenched in blood several times."

He latched onto her statement. "Did some poaching, eh? Illegal, *ne*?"

"Poaching? Illegal? No one owns deer or possums. Let's put such wildlife food next to your drink of moonshine and what is the result? Each eases existence. Just as these stolen things were swapped to do." A slight grin appeared. "I do, however, most humbly apologize for preaching at you Sunday about trading cigarettes for *yen*."

She couldn't interpret the look he gave her. Was he surprised or insulted? No matter.

The flash went off, and she wound up the roll. "Isn't that the captain from the commissary? I was too startled when I first saw him to look closely, and my flash just brightened up his face."

"Yes'm, Cap'n Archer, I knew that right away . . . and he bled out. Maggots are gonna be settin' in. Let's get outta here. I need to call Ty again. First, I'll scoot along the wall to those steps and see where's they lead. Play your flashlight at an angle across the footprints, Meg."

He moved quietly, eyes sweeping the floor. "The guy is my size, I reckon." After disappearing up the steps, he returned to her side to mutter, "It's another trap door where the runner went, and some kinda arguments goin' on above it. Smells like wet leaves."

"Wait." He held up his hand. "There's footsteps." He clicked off his flashlight. The sound of boots echoed through the shelter. Meg guessed the person they belonged to was walking toward the trapdoor overhead.

"I heard them. Praise the Lord, and here's some ammunition. I'm glad I slit a box open this morning." Meg reacted swiftly, moving back past cartons of Camels and Lucky Strikes to the box of soup cans. She tossed two cans to Cally, motioned toward the open carton, armed herself, and doused her flashlight. They shrank back against opposite walls, cocking their arms.

Crisply starched khaki pants and spit-shined shoes came carefully down three steps, and the overhead lights flicked on. "Is that you, Marty?" Cally yelled.

Meg wasn't going to be sure it wasn't a murderer until she saw a face so she kept her arm cocked, prepared to strike someone out if need be so.

"Meg Lowe is here with me. And, there's a dead body here. There's a bunch of boxes." He tossed his cans back into the carton and moved toward the closet stairs.

AP Phil Tyler quickly strode down the remaining steps and aimed his revolver at Meg. Another similarly armed AP followed him and also the Japanese cop, then came Col. Robbie Jones and WAF Sgt. Laura Duncan, armed only with a notepad and pencil.

A radio squealed in the AP's belt attachment.

Col. Jones looked past them at the prone, still, bloody body and barked, "Call the medics and ambulance."

Meg and Cally held their hands high.

"We didn't do anything," Meg protested to AP Tyler who hadn't taken the revolver from its aim at her face.

Col. Jones stepped over and relieved her of her camera, snapping off the flash attachment, and handing that part back. "And you were down here with a dead body, but why? I'm assuming you took pictures of the body, heh? I'll return any pictures not needed for evidence from last Saturday and whenever," he said. "Maybe, to start with, Sergeant, you could explain why you two have interrupted our surveillance of this place?"

Clumping footsteps announced company from the other end of the shelter. The colonel looked beyond them as more men with AP armbands, and one without, clambered down the steps at the far end. Sgt. Kurt Salchow appeared--he was the one without the AP armband--and, behind him, were two APs who seemed to be guarding him. Behind them, Japanese cops pushed the Yamata father and daughter forward.

One AP saluted the colonel. "We finally chased down the sarge. He ran outta their shop just as our shift was changing causing us a bit of confusion in the rain. The local Metropolitan cops with us arrested those other two."

Meg and Cally had half-turned at the intrusion, and she saw him glance at Salchow's shoes. Salchow was protesting, breathing heavily. Mr. Yamata and his daughter stood stiffly between two Japanese policemen. The Yamatas showed no expression. The Yamatas did not bow the way Meg had noticed Japanese doing to other people.

Most of the newcomers glanced at the body on the floor––curious, revolted, impassive reactions.

"Stay back there," growled the colonel to the newcomers, turning to confront the two he identified as the miscreants. "I asked you to explain yourselves."

"We––ah––we––have no excuse, sir," Cally said.

"We do, too," Meg said firmly. "We were trying to find out what was going on down here is all. No sin in that, is there? Why are you arresting me?"

"You're not under arrest––yet," was the reply. He limped by Cally to peer at the body. "Poor impatient guy," he breathed. "I guess I told you too much about the progress of our investigation."

Meg noticed that Cally was studying the colonel's uneven footprints where he had limped down alongside the left-hand wall. The colonel was moving back toward the closet stairs as more footsteps sounded on the floor in the janitor's closet.

"Just what is going on here?" a familiar voice demanded as Mrs. Fritz and her husband tripped down the stairs. "Why, Colonel Robbie Jones, what are you doing here? This is where we store emergency supplies. A friend called us from the Village and said people were storming the Bastille!"

"We are investigating a series of crimes, including a murder," he replied.

She looked shocked. "But what are you doing *here*?"

He gestured. She looked toward the body, swayed. Her husband put a comforting arm around her back. Taking deep breaths, she patted her chest, and indicated Meg and Cally. "And that girl and that boy--they are the guilty ones! We know! They were snooping around yesterday afternoon after suppertime. We heard them plotting. We made them leave and forbade them to return except during regular hours. Look how they followed our orders."

The colonel looked from Mrs. Fritz toward Meg and Cally but then he turned his whole attention back to her.

She continued her diatribe. "And I left a note to the janitor at the shop this morning to post an Off Limits to Unauthorized Personnel sign on the trapdoor up there. I assume she did it while I carried on my work at the Food Kitchen. The sign and tape are now all over the floor. Only thieves would do that sort of damage." The principal snorted in disgust.

Two men, carrying a stretcher, and a medic, a caduceus on his collar and gold leaves on his shoulders, edged past the Fritzes. A soldier with a lot of stripes on his shoulder followed.

"May I put my arms down," Meg begged.

Col. Jones nodded at her as he motioned the newcomers toward the body. "The temperature here is pretty steady so can you tell when he was killed?" he asked the medic.

"Perhaps," was the laconic answer.

"Now, Mrs. Fritz, your accusations are made in front of a lot of witnesses. Go more slowly. First of all, what did you mean about Miss Lowe and the sergeant snooping around earlier? And, why do you suspect her of murder so quickly?"

Meg interrupted, "First, It wasn't after supper time when she ejected us--it was late afternoon. At least she's correct about our talking a bit earlier, but not plotting, except how to de-stink mold and remove spots from shoes. And, she accusing me of things right and left out of clear space all the time."

Mrs. Fritz ignored Meg and replied to the colonel. "Look at the supplies we have thoughtfully stored. Why did I suspect them? They were planning to steal these from the mouths of the starving! Or from children who are escaping a typhoon or earthquake. We caught them by that trap door up there in close cahoots yesterday."

"Yessirreebob––you mean kids can survive on these *kimonos*, cigarettes, old vases, and statues for lunch?" Meg's ironic tone resulted in another intake of quick breath on Mrs. Fritz's part.

"What unmitigated gall! We have no idea what you are raving about. Or even why you say such things. You shouldn't speak of what you don't understand. Dear, do you know what she's suggesting?" Capt. Fritz looked as bewildered as Mrs. Fritz did. "Miss Lowe, the President of the School Board has now seen your behavior, and *something will be done*. See, Colonel, how cold-blooded she is. Quite capable of murder."

Meg swept an arm at the lacquer chests, and then marched over to pick up the ledger and clipboard. She waved them. "*We* kept an accounting of *our* intake of many types of wares? In the counting house, counting out *our* money? Squeezing bloody relics from Japanese families?" she asked in her firm classroom voice. The Fritzes looked confused. Meg gave the ledger and clipboard to the colonel who handed them and the camera to the WAF.

Col. Jones began issuing orders to the gathering of people. "Captain Fritz, you and the missus go up to her office. I'll summon you later. AP Tyler will go with you.

"Let's all go upstairs. The police will guard you and keep you from talking to each other until after I've finished interviewing everyone. I'll choose a classroom for you to wait in and another one for taking preliminary identifications," Jones ordered. He called to the other end to the police and their prisoners, "The rest of you go back out of the bathhouse or Yamata store to let the medics and technicians work down here. You men then bring the people in around the west gate to the school."

CHAPTER EIGHT

Meg rescued her umbrella from the side of a pallet and, placing the flash attachment and flashlight into her purse, took her purse from the bottom stair. Everyone was moving up the stairs in single file.

"Hah, so that's where the other entrance came out--straight into the Yamata shop," Cally noted behind her as they climbed. "It's old prints of the colonel's shoes, 'cause he limps, like those I said that go down that far tunnel hall. And prob'ly Salchow was the one running out--those steps that I heard after I opened the trap door. His shoes matched the footprints."

"Oh boy, oh boy! Did you notice that the Yamatas actually *were* inscrutable?" she whispered back to Cally.

He snorted a small laugh. "Yes, most Japs are pretty lively--not poker-faced like we were told durin' the war."

Walking over to the front door as an AP there stiffened, she placed her umbrella in the hall's ceramic stand. She heard Cally asking the colonel to call his barracks if matters ran long and excuse him from bed check because of the investigation.

"May I wash my face?" she returned to ask Col. Jones. He had taken over the schoolhouse.

"Yes, Sergeant Duncan will accompany you in a minute," he replied. He summoned the Fritzes from the principal's office and dictated orders to the gathering. "You all will sit separately, not speaking, in that classroom, and I'll see you each over here in this small room." He gestured for Sgt. Laura Duncan to go off with Meg to the restroom.

Meg looked back over her shoulder at the motley group. The policemen herded the other people into the grade school classroom. She knew that separate desks and chairs gradually increased in size from the first row to the fourth against the rear wall. The men who were there under the colonel's order would have trouble fitting into the small chairs. Both Cally and Kurt Salchow had sturdy builds, as did the APs. The Yamatas were both small and slim and seemed distant. She wondered how Capt. Fritz felt about all that raving his wife was doing.

On the walk back from the girls' restroom, Meg spied Major "Medic" and the multi-striped sergeant, holding two bags, going over to Col. Jones in the teachers' lounge, while two stretcher-bearers took a shrouded body out the front door. She gave a little shudder.

Catching a staccato delivery, she slowed her steps with her head down trying to hear the medic's and sergeant's reports to the colonel. ". . . right femoral; . . . yester . . . " The two men finished giving their report, came out of the room Col. Jones had chosen for his interviews, and headed to the front door.

Col. Jones followed Meg and Sgt. Laura Duncan into the classroom. He spoke softly, but his voice seemed to thunder. "Obviously an investigation into major infractions of the Occupation Rules regarding disposal of commodities has been underway for some time. The legal issues involve various infractions regarding thefts, conversion of wares and food, and the black market. Moreover, any absence of tax exemption certificates being obtained for acquiring local antiquities is another infraction.

"The Air Police will file Delinquency Reports concerning the American Occupation people identified as involved. These DRs will be forwarded to the Commanding Officer here in Nagoya. Major infractions will result in appropriate disciplinary action."

Someone in the classroom gasped. Meg held her breath. Had she committed a crime? These Occupation laws would clearly be different from those promulgated by her father. It was time to study military law.

Col. Jones continued his lecture to the classroom of civilians and military personnel. "Legal assistance is available from the Base Legal Office in the Hospital Building if you should so desire. I will take depositions tomorrow pending availability of such assistance if you insist.

"Our investigations of the black market, the sales and thefts of goods by fake repairmen and others have been completed; perhaps stolen objects from other countries are involved. Add to this an innocent murder victim. Please think carefully over your activities and observations: who, what, when, where, why, and how.

"Sergeant Tyler will call you next door for an interview. Please have your Identification Pass available. If you do wish to volunteer any observations, those will be typed up for your signature when you are scheduled to appear at my HQ office. We'll dispense with the preliminaries here rather than dragging everyone to headquarters. Civilians will be interviewed first, returned here, and without any conversation amongst you before or after the interview. Clear? All right, Mrs. Fritz, please come."

She pursed her lips, looking indignant, as if affronted, and followed. She set out under a full head of steam, as it were. The three APs and two Japanese policemen stationed themselves around the room, ever watchful.

Meg and Cally had been placed two desks apart on the last row. Meg frowned, head resting on her fist, elbow on the desk, deep in thought. Cally sat at attention, as did the Yamatas, father and daughter, Capt. Fritz, and Sgt. Salchow.

Mrs. Fritz, stern-faced, came back after a short time, although to Meg the short time had seemed stretched out like taffy.

AP Phil Tyler, stone-faced, beckoned Meg into the colonel's presence. That meant time speeded up, as did her blood pressure.

"May I please make some coffee?" Col. Jones nodded at her request, saying nothing but she felt his eyes studying her movements at the hot plate. Nervous, she felt a need to explain something, not exactly sure what would be appropriate. "I suppose Sergeant Tyler has reported on me? About my prank scaring the guys the other night?"

No one replied. The silence did nothing to ease her anxiety.

After the coffee had perked, she slowly served him and Duncan. The colonel motioned for her to take a cup for herself. Then he ordered, "Let Sergeant Duncan have your Identification. If you wish to volunteer something, let's start with your recalling the pictures you have taken. I need background on those you have on this roll of film before you came upon Captain Archer's body."

Surprised not to be asked how she had discovered the body in the tunnel, she began a slow recollection. "The first one I took was of the Seattle port as we left and the second, of that dreary Adak Island in the Aleutians. I remember taking one of a lifeboat, and after that I was seasick for days. The only good day was when we hit a storm, and I opened a door to a wind so strong I was unable to breathe. Glorious. That night I put in a flashbulb and took a photograph of Slim Jane pretzel sticks peering over my hammock up high. That one will be funny. I don't remember any others. I vaguely remember landing and being escorted down here on that long train trip, but from then on I was sleeping and staggering to the little cafeteria between going to get my Identification and Ration Passes." She shrugged. "I'm still tired."

She put a sugar cube in the cup and took a sip of the tepid coffee. "I finally woke up enough to call the number of Principal Mrs. Fritz. Do you think she can fire me? I shouldn't have sassed her down there."

He said, "Go on."

Her eyes went out of focus as she thought back while furiously trying to figure out why he was listening to all this but giving few reactions to her responses. "She told me to come over at one o'clock Saturday. Have I been here only a week? My shoes had black measles--what you'd call mildew, mold, fungi, etc. I called for a taxi and came over to the American Village. I met her and Althea and then went to find a remedy for my shoes at the commissary. I saw that fellow--who passed over in the tunnel?--having a temper tantrum. Cally--Sergeant--Paley there in the store offered some advice and walked me to the school. Later, after I, er, met him again that evening, he also offered to walk around with me Sunday afternoon. I bumped my head on a stick." She yawned. "Long, long day. I took I don't know how many pictures I took on our walk outside the Village. Maybe three."

Her eyes refocused on him. "Ah. You were the officer with the civilian--was that Bill Sheldon?--from the bathhouse who were staring at me Sunday afternoon! Were you after the little man who ran out? Does the bomb shelter go that far underground to the bathhouse?"

He showed no reaction. "Go on."

"I met you that night with Althea. The next day the Yamata girl showed me the cellar or shelter, I don't know what it's called, with the stacked cots. Cally––Sergeant Paley–– came over at the end of the day about five p.m. to show us how to clean my huaraches. About 30 or 45 minutes later, She-Who-Must-Be-Obeyed showed up and threw us out. Cally said she sounded scared. I didn't believe him, because he was young, and we were young, and she's powerful. I thought she was just plain ornery. Her hair dripped, her raincoat drooped, but her shoulders were ramrod straight, and she snarled at us."

That encounter with Principal Fritz she recited with fervor, adding, "She's been snapping at me ever since I met her Saturday here. I cannot understand what I've done wrong."

"Go on. I merely want to know about the snapshots you took."

Another sip of bad liquid, and she went on, heedless of his attempt to steer her in a particular direction. "Cally said he'd heard voices downstairs while we were working. I argued with him, and I said it was people outside or a radio we had heard."

"Go on."

Sighing, she closed her eyes. "This morning I rushed over here early to prove Cally wrong. Smart-aleck guy. I'd chortle if there was a radio so it would be possible that he had heard radio voices, rather than their being from outside the school, either one as I had said, radio or outside, not under us. Fumiko had showed me the light switch yesterday; is this still Tuesday?"

As usual, he didn't answer her question.

Meg talked. "The bulbs down the shelter's length were dim and spread out so that it was somewhat hard to see so I looked in a lot of trunks and boxes at all the artifacts and so tried to imagine the history they could recite. I kept moving down them marveling and finally came to the groceries and bandages. I kept looking inside boxes, and then I slipped."

She raised her foot and showed the heel of her shoe. "It was blood. There on the floor was a dead body it came from. That scared the bejeezus outta me so I ran back to my classroom where I huddled all day waiting for Cally's ball game, because he was the only one I knew somewhat, and I didn't speak Japanese so I couldn't call the police. I'd know what to do back home where my dad's a deputy sheriff."

Meg paused a second before she asked a question. "Althea said you were with headquarters; did she mean what we civvies call 'police headquarters?'"

"Go on."

She knew she was spewing out her explanation but also knew she always reacted like that when confronted by unfathomable events. "The Navy lost the game, and I told Cally what I found. He laughed at first and mocked me, and then when I convinced him, he tried to call his AP buddies, Tyler and Martin. It was too soon after the game for them to answer immediately so he left a message. Then we decided to check out the footprints on the floor, so he borrowed flashlights. I took two pictures of the pallet goods, and one of the captain who had passed over. I'm actually not queasy or swoony about blood. And that's it. Now, may I please be excused? I'm groggy because I'm so very tired. And I'm probably a bit incoherent."

He picked up the camera, twisted the roll of film a couple of times to make sure it was all on the end roll, and removed the film from the back. He gave her the camera. He then nodded and said, "The photographs that you took Saturday on your walk, as well as those from tonight, may have to be retained by my office for evidence. You will receive the others back."

Her lengthy absence must have been intriguing, for the group eyed her with curiosity as she drifted back to her seat. Mr. Yamata was called, and a Japanese policeman was beckoned to follow him into the lounge.

The AP with the radio was also summoned from the room.

Meg shrugged at Cally and returned to her thoughtful posture: head resting on fist, drowsily reviewing what she had told Jones, and shifting off into a kaleidoscope of colors. Red crew cut and brown eyes; brown eyes and pink dimples; black measles and dark rain clouds; mauve dress and purple bruise; garish signs, campaign ribbons; white clouds of hair and white embroidered *obi*; deep blue cloisonné, deep blue *kimono*; red lacquer chests with gold designs, red Swiss army knives . . .

After a short period, Yamata reentered, and Fumiko was called by a voice that Meg heard faintly. She forced a replay of events to focus on one person: Mrs. Fritz.

Meg's eyeballs quit moving behind her closed eyelids; she slowly sat up. She rummaged in her purse and extracted the red knife. Meg calmly started clipping her nails with the scissors she pulled out of the knife hilt. An AP reacted at first, starting toward her with a frown, but a trembling Capt. Fritz drew his attention.

"Oh, someone, we need a glass of water for the malaria pills. We need it now," Mrs. Fritz implored. One AP left the room.

Meg put her hands in her lap and waved her fingers until Cally's eyes glanced sideways at her. She looked down at her lap, and his eyes followed. Meg tapped her left hand, used it to mimic stabbing her right thigh with the knife, and pointed her right thumb at Mrs. Fritz. He kept looking, and she repeated the gestures three times. He looked straight ahead for a while, a small frown between his eyes, then winked his left eye and dipped a slight downward movement of his firm, freckled chin.

The girl also was gone a while, and next Capt. Fritz was helped out, a glass of water in his trembling hand both when he was going and when he was returning.

Cally was called next. When he marched back to the room after several, to Meg unusually long, minutes, he gave Meg another wink and nod before he sat back down in the classroom. She knew he had passed her conclusions about Mrs. Fritz to the colonel.

Sgt. Kurt Salchow was still sweating heavily. He was gone longest of all. Meg looked at her watch, shaking her head when she found out it was already after midnight. She put her head on her arms and fell asleep.

Trailing Sgt. Salchow by a few minutes, Col. Jones and a newcomer, Bill Sheldon, appeared in the doorway. The noise of everyone stirring at the men's appearance woke Meg.

"Mr. Bill Sheldon! We are so glad to see you. Perhaps you will finalize this tedious interrogation, and we can leave. Captain Fritz must get to bed immediately." Mrs. Fritz stood, smiled, and poked her husband.

Col. Jones walked to the front of the classroom and leaned his hands on the desk. His eyes seemed to be able to watch everyone in the room, Meg noticed. Mr. Sheldon moved next to him and also looked at the seated people with a searching eye.

Sheldon had a sack that he upended on the teacher's desk with a thump. "Mrs. Fritz. People. We have been looking through the Yamata store this evening. Do any of you recognize these?" He shook from the sack a black raincoat that was followed by a pair of penny loafers. "First, tell me if you've seen these things before."

"Where did you get--say you got those things from?" Mrs. Fritz asked looking up at him with a perplexed expression on her face, a face that turned livid.

She whirled suddenly on Yamata-san. "How could you? Why didn't--"

"Silence! Say no more than that now," barked Mr. Sheldon. He pushed up the pocket of the raincoat, and a red Swiss knife tumbled out. "Is this a blood stain here inside the pocket, perhaps?"

Mrs. Fritz screamed, pointed her hand at the coat, her hand shaking so hard that the diamond wedding rings trembled, and then shouted, "You lie! They're not mine!" and toppled forward onto her desk. (Meg told Althea a few days later that when Mrs. Fritz reacted so strongly it was a reprise of the melting of the Wicked Witch of the West.)

Capt. Fritz shrank back, with a horrified look at his wife. Meg, Cally, and Fumiko jumped up.

"*Ah so desu*, I see," Col. Robbie Jones said. "I called Mr. Sheldon to follow up on information gleaned here tonight. Then, I ordered some jeeps from the motor pool to take you to your billets. However, some of your quarters will be different than the ones you were in last night."

"*Hai!* High time and no written thank-you note needed, Mrs. Fritz," Meg murmured sarcastically.

Sheldon put the evidence back in the sack. "Mrs. Fritz, you will be questioned for your knowledge of the following items: murder of Captain Archer, lack of tax exemption licenses, stealing, and black marketing. You will come with me and Sergeant Duncan."

Capt. Fritz had his mouth open in shock.

Col. Jones stated, "Captain Fritz, you should go straight to the Base Hospital. Servants who admitted repairmen who had fake papers into your home and/or work or into the homes of other Americans will be interrogated concerning collusion in theft of property. Also the employees at the PX and commissary will be questioned."

The colonel studied the Yamatas. "You two are to be questioned about operations in this matter, and your police will take care of that with the liaison AP. First, you must procure your Identification Passes and License from your shop."

Col. Jones looked at Kurt Salchow. "And you will be questioned for your knowledge of theft, shoplifting, and conversion of property. The APs will take you to GHQ.

"Paley and Lowe are excused until signing of their statements requires their presence."

The group filed out under their various escorts. Meg Lowe carried her purse and collected her umbrella, walking into the night beside Cally.

All he said was, "Yep, you were right. Southpaw pitcher beaned 'im in the forehead--as I did ta you, come ta think of it. Then she took him outta the game completely by taggin' him out on his right leg. Nothin' but trouble, she is."

The AP at the front door motioned the couple toward a personnel carrier. Meg and Cally both climbed up into the back and leaned back wearily on the bench. The driver followed at the end of the line of the vehicles moving from the American Village School.

"You know I agree with you about her. Too, I'm deeply grateful for your strength and astute help, Sarge Cally. If you hadn't had that sensitive ear for fine-tuning and your recon experience, you wouldn't have believed me about the body. Probably wouldn't have noticed she was left-handed just like I did when she was carrying things or directing us out the door or shouting admonitions at us. Waving her left hand did her in. The blood came from the wound in his right leg from when she threw that knife. I'll never forget this easy camaraderie we've had."

She said slowly, "That meeting was almost like a Rex Stout book using Nero Wolfe and his sidekick Archie. Jones and Sheldon revealed the solution in front of all the suspects. I'm surprised they did all that in front of everybody."

"Perhaps, Meg, Mr. Sheldon was there for the five civilians because he knows civvy law. But Colonel Jones is the *chief* law enforcement officer for the two civilians who are Japanese-Americans, the three Americans civilians in the Occupation Forces, which means you, and us two military. Think about it. What else could they do that was any better and more efficient? They're good at reading reactions."

"I'm too tired to consider it right now. I'll put attention to the details sometime. All I can think about right now is that I'll have to sign tonight's statement for Colonel Jones at his office. As soon as that's over, I'm going to take one of those Special Services trips through southern Japan," she remarked. "I'll be gone several days, and you'll probably be gone to the Yokohama port by the time I'm back. Write me when you get Stateside, will you? Then I can write back and tell you if I did comprehend the nuances of that meeting."

"Sure will." He yawned.

"I'm going to wear my huaraches proudly with the unusual pattern––part bleached blond leather, part tan streaks, black measles, and all. They'll remind me of you."

She grew silent. Sitting with her body turned toward Cally Paley, she next commented, "I know you know 'The *band is playing somewhere, somewhere hearts are light*, etc. etc., *but there's no joy in Mudville*'? Here, there's no joy in Fritz' ville."

"Yeah, ma'am. Mighty Lady had struck out."

"That's the way I feel. It's sad, but over. She must have seen somewhere that my father's in law enforcement. Somehow she felt I threatened her dealings. That's the only way her animosity toward me makes sense. Why she slew the captain of the commissary in her treasure hold. Ergo, I'll leave it at that. I'm not going to worry about what happened."

"Me, neither," he replied, taking her hand and squeezing it. That felt comforting after the past few hours.

The sky was lighting up in pale blue and shredded white, the hues that a pair of washed out jeans had after a hard life.

"Do you play poker or craps? Gamble?" Meg murmured.

"Yeah. That's a strange question, but then that means you're up to somethin'. Why?"

They pulled in front of the Chiyoda Hotel. She placed the umbrella against his knee. "Well, you gamble, and thus you are *ever* about to *tinker* with *chance*, my dear pitcher. You have a stash in this umbrella--don't throw this out: have a *yen* for souvenirs, and let the container of metal things run home to be appraised . . . when you figure out how to get a tax free exemption for it. Remember me."

The driver climbed down and opened the tailgate. Meg tapped the umbrella against the sergeant's knee, patted Cal's cheek, swung her legs out of the back, waved over her shoulder, and disappeared indoors.

PART TWO

Go Fish

CHAPTER NINE

"Hello," Meg said hoarsely, clearing her throat. She'd been stiffly alert every time she jerked awake during the wee hours of the morning, trying to sleep with questions pounding in her brain about what she had seen last night. Her immediate memory was a dream of a flashbulb shining on dark blood and khaki pants.

"Junichiro Ina at the front desk here. A box and a trunk have arrived for you," reported the Chiyoda Hotel clerk.

"Give me a few minutes. I'll call down for them to be delivered." Meg hung up the phone.

"Oh, steamy Nagoya. Rise and shine!" Meg Lowe, sweaty from the heat and humidity in the room, groaned. "I seem to have overslept." Lunch service would be over soon. Get a move on. She would force herself to shake them legs and step out smartly.

She walked to the window, fanning the skirt of her cotton nightgown, raised the blinds, and was then able to open a window by clicking a latch on the side. No breeze came in, but the fresh air helped liven up the room. This particular fresh air had something, maybe sea salt, in it. It wasn't as "fresh" as the air back home, come to think of it.

Scenes from the days before flicked through her mind like the three-second scenes from movie reels people had shown her, scenes such as racing cars going by, or five cheerleaders leading the crowd's joy after a touchdown, or a baby crawling across a floor.

Glancing around the room at the two brown overstuffed chairs, thick green Army blanket thrown on the floor beside her bed, the steam radiator on one wall, and the desk under the window, she sighed. She figured it looks like a bear's lair, or even more, like a bare lair. She scolded herself: "I need to spruce up this room. Make it homey, some pictures, a nice bedspread. First, I'd better hurry to get something to eat. Also, I have to put my laundry together for the maid. Now, a call to Colonel Jones to start the day."

After looking up the office for investigator Col. Robbie Jones, Meg dialed, and a quiet voice answered, "Private First Class Brooks, HQ office."

"Miss Margaret Lowe here. I need an appointment to sign a statement for Colonel Jones."

"Yes, ma'am, 0730 hours tomorrow; I'll put that down," was the soft reply.

"Oops. I forgot that everyone starts work that early. But okay," she replied.

Back in her room after eating at the Chiyoda Hotel mess, Meg reviewed the chores––strip the sheets, sort laundry for the maid, unpack the trunk just being brought in, put film in the camera, but, first, delve into the box of favorite books. She hefted out the maroon Will Durant book on the Orient and placed it within easy reach.

A nose-and-eye-stinging bag of mothballs that her mom had inserted in the trunk to "keep the creepy, crawly doohickeys moving away, away" had broken. The odor on the clothes and grey cotton interior of the trunk, making her eyes water and her nose burn, would go away––with time. Meg heaped the clothes from the trunk onto her bed and tossed the smelly mothball bag into the trash. Leaving the room hastily, she turned to shut the door behind her and bumped into another gal in the hall.

"I'm sorry. I had to get away from the smell of mothballs," she explained to a short, curly-haired brunette in a white uniform.

"Oh, that I can understand. I'm Betty Carnahan next door. I've seen you around. Meg Lowe, isn't it? Where are you going with that purse-thing?"

"Shopping and work––at the school."

"Myself, I have to get back to work, too, at the Base Hospital. This evening, though, I'm going to a movie at Nagoya Hall. Would you like to go with me?"

"This dress is the only one that is halfway decent; I'm afraid I'd embarrass you." Meg looked at her new acquaintance with regret because, truthfully, she would enjoy going with her.

"*No* one looks cool, calm, and collected in this humidity. Is that a yes, no, or maybe?"

"I'd love to go with you. What time does the movie start?"

"At 1930 hours."

"Great idea. I'll meet you in the lobby about 7:00."

Meg put a hand out to stop Betty from moving away too fast. "Say, is there somewhere near here where I can get a quick haircut and shampoo? My hair looks greasy from all the heat and humidity. And, I need to buy some clothes."

"The beauty salon is behind the elevators on the first floor. It's open all day, unlike the PX that opens today at 1100 for five hours. That's where some clothes are. You can still get to both," Betty informed her crisply as she slowed down and walked down the stairs with her.

"Thanks for the information. I'll see you later," Meg said, going round the corner of the lobby.

The hairdresser gave her a short haircut and refreshing shampoo, massaging her scalp. She sat under the dryer for a bit, but she knew the humidity would dampen her hair as she ventured forth.

The Post Exchange was a small department store but shoes? Nope. Clothes? None. Meg fingered a strand of graduated pearls and bought the necklace to wear to the school. A Japanese dictionary in small print and a package of Red Hots were her final purchases.

As she meandered over the uneven pavement of the streets to the school, she ruminated on a number of things she needed to check later. First, she needed to rid herself of the folders of last year's lesson plans. Second, she would take care of the errands she had planned and make arrangements to see some of Japan.

Meg felt her stomach tighten as she walked toward the front door of the school. Would last night's chaos still be creating a tense clamor? Would Mrs. Fritz's shriek echo down the empty halls?

"Hi, there," she called to the science teacher, as she mounted the stairs and walked onto the second floor hallway. "Why are you the only teacher that I've met?"

"Some others haven't arrived yet. We didn't have many students last year but there are a few more this year because more families are arriving."

"I thought it was odd to see so few ladies."

"Yes, it feels like a great weight when there's not a whole group of us yet."

"Another question on another topic is about local history. Althea, did you ever see that mirror of the goddess

Amaterasu over at Ise or the Sacred Sword at the Atsuta Shrine here in Nagoya?"

Althea answered as if distracted by some experiment pending completion, turning from the doorway to her lab room. Her attention focused away somewhere else. She took a minute to register Meg's question. She answered impatiently, "Well, that one came out of the blue. I'm rather surprised that you are interested in history lessons this morning rather that what activities you've been engaged in here at the school."

"I'm always interested in history. I teach it, make dramatic scenes." Meg laughed shakily. She wasn't going to discuss any activities. She wanted to forget yesterday. "I teach it, remember."

"Yes, I know that's what you're *supposed* to do. To answer your inquiries, there're two 'no, ma'ams' to your question about the sites. No one except the Emperor of Japan or his representative can get anywhere near the relics. All that anyone else sees is a series of fences at Ise and a representation at Atsuta Shrine here, all with entry forbidden to every other mortal. So, no, I have not. Why do you ask?"

"Oh, I've been leafing through the Durant section on Japan. Surely there is a lot of purported symbolism in this country among the various beliefs. I'm beginning to think that the Shinto beliefs are not quite so mysterious as they are similar to those of other religions, particularly ancient ones."

Althea nodded in agreement, her attention caught for the moment by Meg's assumption. "The factitious beginnings of *homo sapiens* arriving on earth as explained in any ancient language are off-center. Darwin brilliantly developed that proof in his *On the Origin of the Species.*"

Meg said, "I have faint acquaintance with that science of *yours*. I read *HMS Beagle* describing his tour through Patagonia, Chile, Galapagos Island, and the South Pacific.

What confuses me is that Christianity has its statues, paintings, and sacred artifacts. Unlike this Japanese religion, we are allowed to see those to enhance our spiritual beliefs, beliefs that are a source of strength to many people, regardless of the various ways to reach heaven."

Althea shrugged impatiently, turning away again. "Here's a belief you can chew on. Don't toss your cookies––I'm the new Principal, only part-time, though, until a new one arrives. It appears that Mrs. Fritz is returning Stateside with her ill husband, and I've become the chosen one. That means I will teach only two or three science classes. That also leaves math classes for the high school without a teacher. Can you pick up algebra or geometry? We have to get things scheduled before September. I'm not sure what the incoming teachers specialized in."

Meg felt a shiver as she wondered how much Althea knew about why she had been elevated to the principal's job. Meg chose not to, not to say *anything* about what had occurred last night. Unless Althea brought it up. Who could guess how much Col. Jones shared with his fiancée? Or, if he'd had time to? She had to think a second to understand the question that had just been directed at her. "I'm not qualified to teach math. I'm preparing for 9th-12th grade social studies and geography. I can do English or gym classes in a pinch. Would either help?"

Meg tried to concentrate on what classes she could teach but her mind kept returning to the sight of the stretcher-bearers carrying the body out of the front door of the school. She gave a shake to her head to clear the image.

"Probably English in junior high. Too, I'll have to see if any dependant women have teaching certificates, look through the dossiers the military keep on wives of officers. We have enough money from the Monte Carlo funds to spring for a part-time teacher if I can find one willing to pitch in at this school now."

"I beg your pardon. What funds?"

"Oh, money for the teachers and school the past two years have been raised by some officers putting on a Monte Carlo night––games of chance. People having a great time betting and contributing at a party."

"So that is where my pay comes from?"

"That is what I just said."

"Seems curious, but it'll do if that's the way it is. When are we paid?"

"Your first check will be paid four weeks after the beginning of the semester in September."

"I see. I'll be fine 'til then. See you later," Meg said to Althea––who was in the process of shutting her lab room door. Meg walked into her own classroom to unload her handbag of the mostly useless folders from last year, check them against new lesson plans, revise where possible based upon what was at hand from the boxes of donated books. None of the texts she had used in previous years matched the ones that had been collected for the next year's work here. Good thing she had already outlined most of the lessons.

She tried to bore deep into her work to help her forget those tense moments less than twenty-four hours ago. Strange how the dead body of a military man, a man used to war and casualties, should disturb her. Helping her deputy dad discuss murders hadn't affected her the same way. Perhaps the problem was being a stranger in two strange cultures, the foreign Japanese one and the American military one. Had Cally mentioned something about Japanese Americans? But it was an American killing an American and was an old-fashioned Western starring perhaps, Roy Rogers or Gene Autry, alias Col. Jones or Mr. Sheldon. Confusing that a female did it. Meg felt maybe a few hours of sleep would be needed instead of work. Here she's without an emotional crutch of support from family or long-time friends. That hypothesis about two cultures soothed her tension, like a bath in Epsom salts soothed aching muscles.

She focused on work once more. The tasks kept her attention for the next few hours. She concentrated on the work with only an occasional jolt of last night's memory having to be stifled. A little after noon, she stopped, put down her pen and texts, and studied the room.

Also, things that needed to be corrected, in addition to her old lesson plans, were the globe and huge wall map, both outdated because of boundary changes for countries following the Second World War. Perhaps the geography class could do a class project drawing the new boundaries and coloring a new map of Europe and Eurasia.

CHAPTER TEN

On the return walk to the Hotel, she stepped into a store when a short, smiling Japanese storekeeper beckoned to her. The lady's nice smile, deep bow, and friendly look seemed a welcome change from the stressful hours Meg had spent during the week already. The lady offered her a cushion on the floor, which Meg accepted, and a cup of tea, which she turned down. Three embroidered *kimonos* were then spread for her inspection.

Meg studied the way a straight piece of cloth became a sleeve. Cloth was folded over with edges sewn together, placed into a gap in the upper seamed sides of long lengths of cloth, those that formed half of the front and one side of the back. The cloth on the sleeve hung down, creating a pocket in the end of each sleeve.

The dark blue *kimono* seemed more for a man while the others were a turquoise, thin silk robe with painted flowers, and a heavily decorated, thicker gown of deep blue silk. The silk was soft as milkweed or cottonwood fluff. She chose the royal blue robe featuring tufted flowers appliquéd or cleverly woven into the skirt and upper back. Meg's mom, who was shorter than Meg and had the same blond hair color, would have to shorten it quite a bit, but the remnants might be enough to make a jacket. The blue color would match Mom's eyes.

The storekeeper, extending each finger as she counted off numbers, said, "*Ichi, ni, san, shi, go, roku, shichi, hachi,*" and then made three zeros with her thumb and forefinger, indicating that she wanted 8,000 yen.

Meg shook her head and wrote "3,000" on a slip of paper. Cally had told her she needed to bargain rather than paying the sum first mentioned, as she had done for the vase at the Yamata shop.

The lady shook her head in return and held up seven fingers. Thus bargaining back and forth, Miss Lowe experienced her first successful negotiation when she said "no" to each offer of "*shichi, roku, go*" and three zeros. Finally, Meg said "*hai*" to a cost of "*shi*" and three zeros, i.e., 4,000 *yen*, for the *kimono*. About thirteen bucks for a gift for her mom was really extravagant, but satisfying all the same.

For an additional delight on this day, as she neared the intersection, a parade of dancing girls inched up the street. The smallest ones (some with confusion in their dark eyes) were leading girls of increasing height.

"Oh, for elegant," Meg breathed.

"Do you always mutter out loud? I hear you next door all the time."

Meg, startled, looked to her side and greeted her new acquaintance. "Hi, Betty. That's how I used to memorize homework: out loud; sinks into my memory that way. Didn't know it would disturb you. Didn't realize I was doing it. I'll try to be quiet from now on. Are you done with work?"

"Yes, another day, another *yen*. I'm walking home because it's so nice outside. What are you doing here?"

Meg snapped a picture. "I've been working, shopping, and looking around. I'm beginning to differentiate tall, straight-shouldered people in khaki military uniforms from each other, and small, black-haired, black-eyed Japanese from each other. I just look at people's faces and ears now. This gorgeous parade was coming down the street when I turned the corner."

"Those girls were sold by their families to *geisha* houses," Betty said with disgust.

"Some writers say they were sent as apprentices to the entertainment industry in return for a little cash to the family. Being trained as hostesses and musicians."

"Well, that's the same thing in my opinion. I wish I could help them somehow. Maybe the new Constitution'll help them have some rights, but they are trained from the cradle to be subservient and humble before men," she said mournfully. "A Shinto priest in Kyoto told us that people don't tithe to the temples but, when money is needed, the temple opens a *geisha* house."

"That for sure is different from our tent revivals. Although sometimes livestock is given the reverend in payment. Ouch. That's too close a comparison to make me feel comfortable. Wish I hadn't thought of it." Meg shook her head.

"Well, I heard you. No matter. I'm going home to change clothes. See you later." Betty ambled off down the street toward the Chiyoda.

A male dance instructor faced the female troupe, modeling gestures and movements to the reverse side of theirs. Small girls around six to eight years old were positioned in the front phalanx, their features covered with white rice-powder that made them seem like a troupe of mechanical dolls. They were sheathed mostly in pink *kimonos,* beautifully decorated; their robes were tied with sashes. Long sleeves wafted delicately with the fluttering motions of the dance; feet stepped to one side and then to the other. The flowers on the silk garments waved as if a soft breeze were anointing a field of mountain flowers. The girls wore identical haircuts--Dutch bobs with bangs.

As the older girls and women moved slowly toward her, Meg saw hints of gold and silver thread among the blue, violet, and green woven cloth robes. The hair ornaments varied from fancy ribbons tied in multiple bows to fake satin flowers on lacquer combs to wispy balls on long hairpins.

That observation furnished Meg with a great idea. She could lighten her felt winter toque to wear for summer events by sewing some fake satin flowers to the sides. For all those occasions demanding a hat, she had nothing suitable. She had both black and white gloves to choose from to complete any outfit. She had always wasted very little time shopping in any season. Now here, her school tasks almost completed, there was little else to do--other than take pictures. She paid closer attention to the garments wending their way toward her.

Next down the street came women garbed similarly in luxurious silk cloth. The oldest girls and women, however, had elaborate wigs or hairstyles, not Dutch bobs or mere hair ornaments. Thick, black hair was looped up, out, and back on the topside, drawn into large high chignons that stood stiffly styled to serve as a backdrop for hair ornaments. Their *kimonos* were arranged so as to bare the backs of their necks.

Dancing with a step, turn, step, turn in their gleaming white split-toed *tabi* and shiny black lacquer shoes, they glided forward. Each turn to a side was accompanied by a fluttering fan on the other side, held flat, or, turned in unison with the other girls', to the same angle. One hand would gracefully lift the long sleeve on the opposite arm, concealing, revealing. Throughout the parade, their fingers all undulated in precisely the same fluid motions.

A rhythmic beat of wooden clappers and a faint tinkle of strident music on long-necked, guitar-like instruments both paced the parade. The tapping sound had a rhythm that was unlike drumbeats of Western dance bands or the marching bands at her educational institutions.

Meg took quick snapshots of the dancers and returned to her shopping. Most stores seemed to feature only one type of wares. Such as clothing or baskets or china or lacquerware.

A store with tiny statues carved of wood or ivory received some of her business, as did an art dealer who offered lovely woodblock prints he had made and displayed around his store. In a shop full of decorated fans, she bought both a silk one and a heavy paper one, mounted on a bamboo framework, for her mom.

A small brocade purse caught her eye at a kiosk and went into the collection of small items she was putting in the olive drab satchel. Her last purchase was a straw, cone-shaped hat such as she had seen workers wearing in the rice paddies on the way down from the Yokohama port when she had arrived the previous week. The hat, whether worn in rain or sunshine, would leave her hands free. Right now, her hands were encumbered. She plunked the sack with the *kimono* and the fans into the straw hat and used it as a basket tilted up against her chest.

As she crossed a canal going back to the hotel, she put the packages down to take two shots of youngsters swimming in the water. The kids obligingly jumped up to the road and lined up, grinning at her. Unlike the parade of dancers packaged in gay *kimonos*, these girls (and boys) were nearly naked. The barnyard stink from the canal they were jumping into made her cough, though she tried to be discrete about it by coughing behind her hand. What she really wanted to do was pinch her nostrils together, but she didn't want to act as though she were criticizing the children for the sewer odors.

Actually, these children looked cool and happy. The scene was a contrast to the solemn girls in the parade who were immersed in *kimonos*. The only cool parts of their bodies would be the waving hands and the napes of their necks where the *kimonos* were positioned a few inches back.

Meg arrived back in her room and piled the purchases for her mom into the trunk. Soon, she would find out how to ship the presents home. Some local items needed to be found to send to her dad and twin brothers, too.

She lifted her huaraches from the desk under the windowsill and sniffed. They were rather oddly colored but no longer smelled mildewy because of the Mum she had rubbed into them. She replaced her black wedgies with the clean sandals, splashed water on her face, and made her way to the mess for supper.

Afterwards, Meg flipped through the English-Japanese dictionary. The foreign words seemed easier to pronounce now that she had heard the sound and pace of the language. Plus, all those Oriental names in the Durant history book would stick with her more easily. With a laugh, she thought Cally would have known some Japanese cuss words that were *not* in her dictionary.

\#

Betty was already in the lobby when Meg came down. They took a bus to Nagoya Hall. Meg felt as though she was riding in a grand carriage above the crowds. They came into a large, elegant park covered in flowering bushes and sweeping lawns. The driveways were wide and paved; a stone gazebo, or maybe it was a fountain, struck its pose further on.

"I like your pearl necklace," Betty said. "I have one from Mikimoto's Pearl Farm. That trip was fascinating. I tried to hold my breath as long as the pearling girls were under water, but I couldn't hold it anywhere nearly as long. They filled their lungs and made a strange squeaky sound breathing through their mouths. After diving down with baskets of oysters, ones that have had a little bitty irritant inserted, they hook these basket crates close to whatever's down there. You simply have to see that place working so hard all day. The men sit in the boats, just sit. The girls do all the work. White cloth outfits and odd masks on their heads. They work in the quiet bay, except when there's a hurricane, of course. Interesting place."

"I've never heard of a job like pearling, much less one with the strain of being under dark seawater a long time. Where I come from, the water is generally clear, except after a heavy rain. Plus I usually swim in pools. For sure, I'm going to treasure my pearls all the more, knowing some girls plucked them from the sea."

"That's a nice thought." Betty looked at her with a smile.

"And, what a peaceful place this is," Meg exclaimed. "What are those squatting ladies doing to the grass?"

"Oh, those are our lawnmowers, a blade at a time," Betty laughed, her brown eyes twinkling, her head shaking her curls from side to side. "We gals think we have fine motor skills from knitting and crocheting, but to be able to sit on their haunches and precisely clip each blade with tiny scissors bests any skill that I have."

Their carriage carried them up to the door of a beautiful building.

Nagoya Hall was enormous, four stories of white stone, imposing as an American county courthouse in an affluent town, firmly settled in its regal splendor. Around the grounds were splendid beds of shrubs with colors as dazzling as those on the robes of the *geisha* dancers. American and Japanese people moved toward the stairways and aisles. The lofty hall created a cave-like echo of the mixture of languages and accents.

Betty remarked, "I know this sounds odd when you're just getting used to the rhythm of the Japanese language, but the Japanese also have regional accents, just as the Americans do."

"I am surprised. I'll find a way to take some Japanese language lessons soon."

Posters regarding various coming attractions or health warnings were pasted on the high ceilinged halls. "What's V.D.?" she inquired, indicating one poster.

Betty chuckled, round face faintly reddened. "Haven't you heard of the woman who named her daughters Ganora and Safillis?"

Meg choked, "Ah." Her own fair complexion turned incarnadine.

Japanese and Americans continued to stroll into the building's halls, some stopping to gaze into display cases of artifacts that lined the entrance hall.

"I forgot Wednesday nights are for performances, not movies. Earlier this year I saw *Carmen* by the Fujiwara Opera Company. That one was extra fine. I saw in the paper when I got home that the Tokyo Orchestra would be playing tonight. I'm sure it will be excellent," Betty whispered. "We should go up to the lower balcony," she gestured toward a staircase.

She continued, "One time I went to a *Noh* theater in Tokyo. It was a long eerie play with blank masks and elegant robes on the three actors––plus I didn't comprehend either their movements or the songs by the chorus. I left at intermission when some relief skits came on the stage."

"Myself, I like all kinds of music––Big Band music, swing music, concert music, operetta, and opera music. And I'm even beginning to like the country-western songs that I had never liked before, but they're all that's on Armed Forces radio, and they're catchy. I don't know how one would dance the Lindy to it, but the tunes are easy on the ears," Meg replied. "So, I'm ready to hear a concert. My folks took me to one in St. Louis when I was little, but this is the first time since then that I've had the privilege of attending one. I'm glad you invited me here this evening. I can hardly wait to describe it to my folks. Plus this Nagoya Hall auditorium is magnificent."

#

After the hour and a half concert, applause was ringing in their ears as they themselves finished clapping hard for the musicians' excellent performance. Meg had found herself totally caught up in the splendiferous compositions by Mozart. Edging out of their seats toward the aisle, Meg and Betty discussed going to the Chiyoda Club in the PX Building for a snack.

"Stop, please, ma'am," commanded an Air Policeman as they descended the stairs feeling relaxed from having heard the melodies.

A cordon of APs blocked their exit on the lowest step with uplifted hands.

Meg and Betty glanced around and saw that exits in every aisle and stairway had halted. Meg raised an eyebrow at Betty who shook her head in response.

Japanese police uniforms were mixed in with those of APs and, moreover, MPs could be seen out in the lobby.

"Sorry, ma'am, but I have to search your purse." Betty handed over her purse.

"What's wrong, officer? Why all the police?" Betty asked. She retrieved her purse from his search, then stood on her toes, peered over his shoulder. Meg gave him hers, too, and watched as he pawed through the interior, her purse so very roomy compared to Betty's small evening bag. He handed Meg's back, and they pushed through a throng of bodies pressing around the doorway. The two curious girls edged next to a young military police officer as Betty asked her questions again.

"Burglary, ma'am. Some antiques loaned by a museum have been heisted. In broad daylight, too. It's almost a classic example of Houdini legerdemain."

"What was stolen?"

"A couple of small weapon things. Move along."

As they waited at the curb for the bus, they speculated about what might compose, might define, "small weapon things." Betty wondered if these were more secret weapons like the A-bomb. Meg scoffed a bit and put a comforting hand on Betty's shoulder. "Nope. I bet it's some bamboo darts or such," Meg suggested. "We're not under threat. Sounded more like they were artifacts of some value. Thefts bring out the police."

"Why do you know?"

"My dad's a deputy sheriff in Missoura, and we talk about his work."

"You make this sound like a radio program like 'Mr. District Attorney.'"

"Something like that, exactly. Good observation, Betty. And, not our concern. They'll take care of solving it as police always do."

The Chiyoda Club was not crowded, and the iced coffee was good after the warm day and, later, the close air in the auditorium. Another bus delivered them back to their quarters.

Marvelously, Meg's bed had clean sheets. Earlier she had smoothed out a pair of slacks under the mattress-- one college roommate had taught her that tactic that would relieve some wrinkles without using an ironing board. She had learned more in college than just history and political science and economics. A spray of cologne would help for tomorrow's outfit because she didn't have time to wash out any clothes. She also didn't want to pay to send them out to the laundry. She retired, feeling relaxed and soothed by the evening's music and memory of the flowering gardens at the Hall. She barely remembered the small weapons robbery.

CHAPTER ELEVEN

Early Thursday morning Meg caught the bus to the Headquarters Building and found her way to Col. Robbie Jones' office. "I'm Miss Margaret Lowe," she announced to a young private who sprang up from a desk inside the door. On a second desk, under glass, was a photograph of a female sergeant being promoted as she received additional stripes from an officer.

Meg was motioned to a seat by the enlisted man. "I'm here for an appointment with Mr. Jones."

"He is S.C.A.P.––in Tokyo," he said in a quiet voice.

Puzzled, she repeated slowly, *sotto voce*, as though it were a secret, "He's e-s-c-a-p-i-n-g Tokyo?"

The private gave her a strange look. "No, ma'am. He was called to the General Headquarters of the Supreme Command of the Allied Powers in Tokyo."

"Oh, boy, I see. More initials," she sighed. "When will he be back?"

"Monday." The private spoke in a wispy voice that matched his thin figure. A hurricane wind would probably knock him over.

"I was supposed to sign something for Mr. Jones today. Do you have it?"

"No, ma'am. **Colonel**" (*ouch, slap my fingers with a ruler*) "Jones did not leave anything with me for you to sign."

"What happened to the Sultan of Swat?" she asked, as if little interested.

"I think he died a few months back."

"Not Babe Ruth. I meant Mrs. Fritz." Meg sat up because she could not conceal her interest a second longer.

"Don't know, ma'am."

"Or, won't say?" Her voice was pitched to be a gentle tease behind the words, wheedling perhaps an answer.

No response was offered, and a closed look replaced a friendly face.

A door opened, "Miss Lowe, please come here."

"Lieutenant. Um, Lieutenant Mays. I didn't know you worked here. I met you at Captain and Mrs. Fritz's party the other night. You are Lieutenant Mays; am I correct? We chatted with Captain Torleone for a while." Meg walked toward him with a smile of greeting.

She entered and, in a glance, saw that the office was decorated mainly with family photographs of a blonde woman and two towheaded children. The office furniture was wood, and the desk was clean, except for a walkie-talkie. The private in the outer office could be heard whistling. Lt. Mays pushed a button to shut off the sound.

"Correct, ma'am. No, we didn't talk much about my work that night." He pointed to a wooden chair.

"Does Captain Torleone work here, too?" Meg asked.

"No, his office is down another floor, directly below us."

"So how *are* the Fritzes faring?" She asked, interested in their welfare. "That poor man." By asking about them, she indicated that she knew he had heard her question on the walkie-talkie tuned to the outer office.

He did not smile. He ignored the question and turned the subject back to her. "Colonel Jones asked me to tell you he needs some additional information."

"Oh? Regarding what? Does he doubt my veracity?" she asked indignantly. "Think I omitted something? It was a long interview, and I'll admit I was tired."

"He didn't tell me any particulars. Just had some clarification to do with your report."

She bit her lip, then inquired, "What about Sergeant Paley? Did he sign his report?"

"Yesterday."

"Well, if there is no information to render today, I'll come by Monday morning. Now I'm going over to the Special Services office to see if I can reserve a space for a tour of Kyoto this weekend. That's why I won't have time to see him tomorrow."

"That trip's probably filled. It's very popular, and you need reservations weeks ahead of time." He looked at her a minute. "Say, I have a reservation for cormorant fishing tonight with my friend, Johnny Hills, but I have to mind the store and can't go. You probably met him at the Fritz's party. Would you like to take my place?"

"I don't remember him. But, I like to fish. Is a cormorant a bass or a trout?"

Lt. Mays eyed her, looked at the wall over her head for a full minute, and looked at her again while reciting:

"A great big bird is a cormorant
His beak holds what e'er his belly cahn't.
A ring on its neck
Keeps big fish in check
And, kid, there's more'n Ah'd ever want."

Laughing out loud, Meg said, "A cormorant is a bird, like a pelican? Please repeat that. I'm going to write Mom and Dad tomorrow and tell them that limerick. They'll laugh."

He obliged by repeating it and then explained, "Yes. The birds are roped to a boat. A basket of fire hangs up over the side, attracting the fish called *ayu,* a kind of smelt or trout. The handlers are sensitive to the amount a bird has scooped up and, when the beak is filled, empty the bird's beak into a basket."

Meg said, "Having birds swallow and regurgitate the fish sounds dreadfully unappetizing. And messy. We do gigging back home." She swallowed a sudden lump in her throat at the thought of home. Catching herself being homesick, she quelled the memories and hurried on. "We carry a gasoline lantern or firebox with lighted pine knots over the side of a boat. A fellow with a pointed pole spears fish, and sometimes frogs, in one of our multitude of clear Ozarks streams."

"Tourists are on separate boats, not the fishing boats."

"Sounds somewhat different than anything I've ever experienced in fishing. How do I get there?"

"A busload of families will be going to Gifu--it's about an hour away. The river is nearby a park."

"I'd like to meet some families," she replied. "I'll meet your friend, Johnny, introduce myself if he doesn't remember me. When do we depart and when do we return? Tell me how to take your place."

He picked up the phone and dialed the number for Special Services, changed the reservation, and told her to obtain authorization at the DAFC office.

"*Hai!*" she exclaimed, "I know that one--Department of Air Force Civilians."

As she was leaving, Lt. Mays reminded her to return to see Col. Jones first thing Monday morning. Thinking about it as she walked to the DAFC office, she decided his tone of voice was more like an admonishment, although she wasn't the one who wasn't on hand for the appointment with Jones today.

She found the Special Services office in the Yamato Building and, being a teacher, grinned at being given a signed "permission slip" to deliver to the tour office (expenses responsibility of the traveler).

When she asked about a tour to Kyoto, she found out all the tours were booked through September. "Is there anything else yet this summer––on weekends, preferably?"

"In August, there're trips to climb Mt. Fuji."

"I have only three pairs of shoes. None would have the purchase to get my feet up Fuji." She shook her head at the offer.

"The FP 47, a boat on the bay, goes out on Saturday, and there's a trip to Mikimoto's Pearl Farm on Sunday. You can swim in the bay from the FP 47. That trip lasts about three hours. You can also swim in the North Pool that's shown on the back of that booklet I just gave you."

"Yes, I'd like to have some relief from this heat. I'll go swim on the bay first and take in the swimming pool during the early mornings next week. I've never swum in a bay of salt water, but I certainly augmented the flotsam and jetsam in the Pacific Ocean when I was seasick. Do I need more permission from DAFC?"

"Yes."

She signed, "And a Pearl Farm, you said. I've heard about that, although I already bought a strand for myself."

"That tour leaves early Sunday. Train and bus. It's pretty interesting."

"Do we return Sunday? I have a meeting Monday."

"Well, sometimes."

"All right. I can't afford to miss my appointment Monday so the pearl farm is out. I'll do the boat on the bay as well as the cormorant trip. Thus, I'll have to make only one more run to the authorization office."

"Roger." He warned that the evening on the river might be chilly and that the bus this evening would not return before the 2300 hours curfew. She hurried to the DAFC for another permission slip and, next, back to her room to see if her leisure clothes had returned from the laundry.

As she entered the Chiyoda Hotel, Althea Ardmore hailed her to talk about the shower Meg had agreed to host. She'd almost forgotten about it. "I'd like to invite an assortment of ladies," she said, "so a neutral location would be best. I was thinking the chapel recreation room. Is that all right with you? I am inviting my tennis partner, Sharon Sheldon, our stalwart opponents, Corporal Donna Aldrich and Sergeant Laura Duncan, a couple of other GI Jills, officers' wives, and civilian girls."

"The chapel room is a great idea, Althea, although I haven't seen it. I could type up your invitations on a stencil and mimeograph them. I doubt any engraved ones are available."

"Oh, no, no mimeographs. They have to be handwritten. Protocol, you know. I will give you the envelopes with names and addresses. You'll have to find some paper to fit or cut it to fit the envelopes. On second thought, you can type them, but not mimeograph them. There are 20 or so to do. I'll give you the names of a couple of high school kids who would probably deliver them for a quarter. The wedding is in a month, and that means the shower should take place about two weeks before it."

"Any ideas on refreshments? I know enough party games to suffice." Meg had been to any number of bridal showers for her high school and college friends and relatives.

"The commissary has a fine bakery. That's where I'm ordering my cake. The chapel has a big coffee urn and dishes enough. Tables and chairs and some white tablecloths of some thick material. Probably some napkins of the same material."

"Do I tell people you'd like Japanese things for the house?"

"No need. Whatever they choose for a gift is fine, and, if they ask me, I'll mention the Japanese wares. As I told you earlier, we'll be moving into the Kanko Hotel unless a house becomes available for the fall semester."

"I hear your fiancé is out of town at GHQ at SCAP in Tokyo."

Althea turned away, chuckling, "I heard that, too; don't worry––he always comes back on a wing and my prayer. I'll be right back upstairs in a minute, and then I'll bring the envelopes to your room."

Meg answered the knock on her door and took the information from Althea.

"I'll type them tomorrow morning," she promised the bride, "and order the refreshments for the chapel."

"My tennis partner, Sharon Sheldon, is chagrined that she didn't think of holding a shower. She'd like to help."

"I'll give her a call. We three can meet and greet, serve and circulate."

"Her phone is listed under William Sheldon." She turned away again, seeming distracted. Taking on the school's administrative job on top of teaching would totally capture anyone's attention.

After Althea left, Meg saw Betty, in her white uniform, who seemed to be in a hurry. "Do you have anything I can wear this afternoon? My clothes haven't returned from the laundry, and I want to saunter around the streets to take pictures. These slacks are too hot."

"I'm in a hurry, but I have some things. I bought a pair of those baggy pantaloons the peasants wear and some of those socks and sandals that your big toe splits off the side on. I found out they hurt my feet so I use them for decorations. I also have a happy coat I don't have use for; you'll need a belt to keep it closed. I don't know what the crest on the back of the coat means. I hope it's benign and not an advertisement for fertilizer. I'll toss them to you and then skedaddle back to work."

"Thanks. The cooler clothes will make my afternoon more bearable. I'll settle up later."

Meg donned the clothes and hung her cone hat on her back. Tying a belt around her waist, she slipped her Identification Pass, money, and Red Hots into the brocade purse and secured it to the belt with a large safety pin. Carrying her camera, she set out by a different route to the American Village than that usually taken by the bus. A few blocks later, she noticed that the Yamata store, where she had bought a vase for the bridal shower, was closed, as if it has been shuttered permanently.

Easing around a waist-high stack of 2'x 4' pallets and curious about where the store's trapdoor to the bomb shelter was located, she tiptoed inside, saw the large trapdoor propped against the wall. An opening about three feet square yawned in front of the door that slanted back. That heavy door has to be for an entrance leading to the underground bomb shelter. She knelt and peeked down.

An AP was sitting on the curve of the stairs, reading by the dim bulb on the ceiling, his white spats gleaming in the dim light. He looked like her younger twin brother, David, from the back, when he concentrated on a Rover Boys' tale. Instead of studying his textbook.

Meg couldn't resist teasing the AP. It would be like being back home, getting one up on a brother. She whispered hoarsely, "Ancay ouyay earhay emay?" in pig Latin just as she had done to her brother. She fled out of the store when the AP jumped and started to turn around. She fled north past the bath house and to a grassy spot on the corner, hunched down with her camera tucked in on her tummy, pulled the hat closely over her head, giggled, and waited. Pretending to work the blades of grass, she heard the sound of footsteps and of men speaking English.

Cautiously looking over her shoulder, she saw the irate AP standing in the Yamata shop doorway. A short fellow in the shop between Yamata's and the bathhouse vanished inside the doorway as the AP stepped to one side.

Men, khaki clad, carried out lacquer boxes, wooden trunks and chests, and cardboard cartons, and placed them carefully in an Army truck. An additional pallet of small boxes was loaded. Finished with the work, most of the men climbed into a personnel carrier that she hadn't noticed earlier.

Two men rolled several car tires out of the door and lay them down on the center floor of the carrier between the rows of men, which aroused some vociferous objections. Those two climbed into the drivers' seats of the two vehicles and drove away, leaving empty pallets outside the store.

The short man exited the store and scampered down the sidewalk toward her. He was wearing a gray robe and had a grey face. Maybe his little building had access to the bomb shelter, too, and he had been watching to make sure nothing was taken that belonged to him—or that he had hidden there.

To the east, over her other shoulder, Meg saw two young American boys with binoculars scanning the sky. Her thigh was starting to cramp, forcing her to stand carefully and massage the ache. She kept the hat on, low over her face because she felt somewhat silly now, especially with two boys nearby who might be in her history classes in a few weeks. At least, they couldn't be reporting her outlandish dress to that awful Mrs. Fritz, but to the awesome Miss Ardmore. Better not even take that chance.

Along the block, the grey man slowed as he came to a terra cotta colored tile wall backed by dense green shrubbery. He glanced above the wall toward a house. The roof of cedar shingles that she could see was barely visible behind the wall and plantings. The wooden beam at the end of each row of shingles carried a round embossed crest.

The pale-faced man slipped through the gate. An inside door evidently slid open, because half a block away, Meg could see the top of the man's head as he bent and straightened, shedding his shoes.

The boys stopped by the tile wall. As one boy aimed his binoculars high, he exclaimed, "I tell you it is a kingfisher. I bet you that it's prob'ly going to dive after a *koi* in one of those garden ponds Japanese houses like this have." He turned to grab the edge of the wall and boosted himself up, pulling himself into the "Kilroy was here" pose--nose and eyes above the wall, framed by fingers of both hands. Meg snapped a photograph of this profile before he dropped from the wall.

Meg heard faint voices from behind the wall around the house. The boy was contemplating a knurled tree a little way down the wall. After studying the thick-leafed branches hanging over the wall around the house, he took hold of a limb and without a noticeable rustle, hauled himself prone. He pointed his binoculars toward the sky, followed a trajectory down into the yard, fell out of the tree, and cried out in pain, holding his arm.

Meg tracked the boy through her camera lens while he pointed his binoculars at the house. Just as she was snapping the picture, however, the boy fell, hitting the ground with a cry and rolled over holding his arm. At the instance of the cry, the grey-faced man had been coming back out of the gate, but hurriedly reentered it, perhaps to seek assistance for the lad.

Spotting a jeep with the familiar white Air Police stripe across the hood, Meg hailed it over, no longer worried about concealing her identity from the boys. The two APs were sergeants Tyler and Martin, whom she remembered from Cally's softball team. The Japanese police officer was their regular companion, Sgt. Hagikawa according to his nametag.

"What scene are you dramatizing now? An Okie fleeing from wrathful grapes?" inquired Tyler. "I need your ID Pass."

"A boy over there fell and is hurt. He's an American. He was watching a kingfisher, and it dived into a pond, and he fell from a tree."

"You certainly have a penchant for observing the insignificant," Tyler muttered, and then called, "Boys, come here; we'll notify your folks to meet us at the hospital."

"I read about your latest softball game in *The Nagoya Nugget*," Meg said as the boys edged around a horse pulling a cart and its owner walking alongside it.

"Wowzee! She can read!" Sgt. Phil Tyler opened his mouth in mock surprise, handing back her ID Pass after scratching notes on a form.

Meg looked back toward the intersection with the avenue. The buses, automobiles, trucks, horse-drawn carts, and streetcars made a counterpoint to the trudging crowds in bare feet, wooden clogs, or Western shoes streaming slowly alongside them. The populace wore shabby clothes or white shirts and black trousers or uniforms. A few Americans strolling the sidewalks were dressed neatly in cotton uniforms or civilian suits.

The two boys were helped into the jeep and driven off. Retracing her path, Meg decided The Grey Kimono Man had come from the shop by Yamata's to tell another guy about the soldiers removing goods from the underground shelter. Arrogant fellow had not tried to help the kid. He might even be part of the thieves. Too bad she hadn't noticed if he were left-handed. Might be a secret sign among them to shake left hands. If Hopalong Cassidy could beat the forty thieves in that movie about a rigged election, she should be able to beat more thieves, having already got Miz Fits. Malarky! Meg scolded herself for letting her imagination cast a couple of poor defeated natives as criminals.

Her big toes were beginning to burn, what with being forced to one side as well as rubbed raw by the short split-toed socks. Time to go prepare for the fishing trip and get back into her comfortable huaraches. Those sandals wouldn't hurt her.

CHAPTER TWELVE

Two buses of the Allied Occupation folks left for the Nagara River at Gifu Thursday evening. A picnic supper was included in the plans (and cost), plus the opportunity to visit a shrine. The air was so hot that, even with the open window next to her seat, Meg had to dispose of her wool sweater that she'd been carrying because that wool was sticking to her hands. She rolled it tightly, stowed it into her purse-cum-satchel with her loaded camera and flash on top of it. Her striped seersucker blouse dealt with the humidity satisfactorily.

Her handbag held credentials and make-up essentials, plus a small canteen of water. Her handkerchief was soon soaked with sweat. Thus, it seemed not to matter that she was still wearing the same dark blue slacks she'd worn twice already in the heat.

The bus driver, as usual on the wrong side of the road to Americans' right-side preference, took them through a countryside of rice paddies, people looking up from calf-deep muddy fields on the left, with steep hillsides on the right, crammed with green trees.

"Not much arable land with those steep hills in the middle of the island," her seatmate muttered. Sitting two rows back from the driver, they could see out front through the windshield as well as through their open window.

"No cotton plantations to be bolled over, no wheat waiting to waft in the wind, no rye rustling in the breeze that I've noticed." Meg talked softly, watching the scenery go by. The hillsides were the same colors as the Ozark hills, south of the farm her folks owned. The rice paddies resembled no acreage that she had ever seen before.

She thanked her seatmate––a tall, shorthaired, brunette sergeant named Billie-Jo Gorman––for the occasional use of her colorful silk fan. The lady talked a lot about her family and mentioned her work.

"My folks wanted a boy to be named either Billy or Joe. Mom insisted on dropping the final 'e' on Joe and adding 'ie' to Bill so that I'd have a girl's name. My younger brothers are named Joey and Willy. You could easily guess that Billie-Jo, Joey, and Willy are very probably related. I usually answer to 'B-J,'" she explained. "I work as the supply sergeant, or quartermaster, whichever title you prefer, out at Komaki Airdrome and the Ozone area. We're vetting our replacements that didn't receive much training Stateside. I mean, the three weeks of training that they get now leaves a lot to be learned. People back home are screaming for all the wartime soldiers to be returned to civilian life. Of course, the GIs overseas are screaming to be returned home, too."

Meg could hardly get a word in edgewise, but she finally managed to ask, "Do you know a Sergeant Calhoun Paley?"

"Sure. He had received his orders to ZI yesterday. He'll leave with some other guys in a few days. He was elated at being demobbed Stateside and was rushing around seeing if he needed export licenses for some bitty souvenirs from Matzusakaya Department store. Bet his dad won't know what to make of little bowls and dolls at his store on Route 66," she laughed. "Paley was chewing gum like no tomorrow."

Meg snorted. "I really don't like people who chew gum, especially in my classes. I read that people from other countries think we look like cows chewing a cud." A stick of gum Sgt. Paley had given her still resided in her handbag, she remembered.

Billie-Jo responded, "I'll admit to an occasional 'moo chew.' We didn't have money for such a luxury as gum except in the Christmas stockings. My dad was gone during the war. He was a Seabee and now is working on the building of Levittown in Long Island. The crews specialize in different trades and follow one another. When I had leave before I was posted here, I wrestled supplies into the framework houses for his crew. Mom brought out food for us.

"Back during the war, my mom worked in a munitions factory, like Rosie the Riveter; I worked on an Army Air Corps base; my grandfolks took care of my brothers."

Meg warbled a parody of the *Showboat* song, "Summertime", "So your Daddy's fit from your Momma's good cookin'. Fish are jumpin' but the cotton ain't nigh." She hesitated a bit, then modified the parody to "though the rice's sure high."

Meg admired the Gorman's contributions to the victories. Because she had spent the Second World War in college or teaching, she hadn't been able to do much herself.

The scenery caught Meg's attention again when she caught sight of a lone woman squatting in a ditch. "What was that poor old woman doing in the ditch?" wondered Meg aloud as she craned her neck to look back.

"Just contributing some local fertilizer, probably. The gooks squat and void. The ditch is their crapper. Honey buckets collect it for the fields."

"Americans back home use outhouses, and embattled military use latrines. She probably just didn't make it home to hers," observed Meg.

"Wrong, dear. They do their eliminating outside when the urge comes. That is why we don't eat rice cultivated here, because of human waste used as fertilizer."

"Just eat Uncle Ben's from stateside paddies fertilized by animal waste, I guess."

While swapping the fan back and forth, always waving it in front of both heads, they composed fanciful language imitating so-th'n belles ala Scarlett and Melanie with mint juleps in their canteens.

"Needs ice, Ah declare," Meg commented.

"Didja hear how Herbert Hoover said, 'Franklin, dear sir, I won't give you a dam?'"

"Frankly amusing. Far more Rhettorically, as my folks would quip." At B-J's blank look, Meg spelled out "Rhettorically."

"Oh, ha. Yore a hootenanny yoreself. Oh, mah soul: ain't julep Ah drinkin' here. But, if I had some mint from the States, Ah'd have here a *mint d'eau*."

"Mint dough? As in dough from the U. S. Mint? You mean counterfeiting? Or, cookie dough?" A thought flickered of a packet of *yen* in an umbrella.

"My French grammar is rusty, but I'm not talking about baking money or making it. I mean the French word for water, *eau*. Mint with water or some such. *Creme de menthe*—I probably should have said *l'eau de menthe* or *avec menthe*. It's been over ten years since I had high school French."

Meg's mind skittered back to wonder what The Colonel wanted her to explain. She nodded and replied, "I get it. I had Latin in high school and a course of Greek and Latin equivalents in English in college. No languages that I could speak in any country today. All dead ones, as the saying goes."

They discussed various movies, actors, and favorite novels, some (featuring Hope and Crosby) of which they disagreed about as worthy of merit. Meg thought the duo was funny, but B-J didn't.

The idea of fishing with birds was new to both. The lady sergeant said, "I read a brochure that said the birds catch *ayu* in their beaks. I wonder what that is."

Meg used her classroom lecture voice. "It's smelt––"

Sergeant B-J Gorman reared back, chin out, and sniffed, "Well, you've been sweating as long as I have, for Lord's sake."

"––a type of trout or salmon. My dad used to fish for them in southwest Missouri at Roaring River. But then, gas rationing came in. Hey, looks like we're here at a park but I don't see the river that I expected."

"I expected to see buildings leveled like in Nagoya and that I saw from the train on the way down from the Yokohama Bay. The war's been over four years, and I was surprised that so much devastation still existed."

"Wal, honey, they's gotta lotta problems with money. Every dang thang was poured into the military. Takes a while to adjust." B. J. stood but bent down to peer out the window by Meg's side. "Humph. We're the only ones here."

The other bus was not in sight; only the sergeant in charge seemed worried about that. The tourists ("disbussed, not disembarked," Billie-Jo, B-J, commented) straggled off from the picnic grounds to see what could be seen.

Some airmen started climbing a steep wooded hill but gave up after struggling upwards several minutes. One fellow hung a handkerchief on a tree limb so that the distance climbed could be judged from below. For some reason he also yelled triumphantly, "And that's also for the Communists to see what we can accomplish!" People clapped their hands, to the puzzlement of some little Japanese children watching the Americans.

"What did that signify?" Meg was likewise puzzled. The path was hardened dirt and sloped gently upwards.

"The airmen are very proud that Russia backed down from the Berlin blockade in May, although we're still flying in. I'm sure you know that our planes and the Limeys and Frogs have flown supplies into Tempelhof Airport for over a year for the local Krauts. Some Yanks even dropped little balloons with candy to the kids. We lost only one plane the whole time––and that airport approach is narrow."

Meg lifted her damp bangs and stepped away a bit. "I don't want to sound like a supercilious snob, but why do you use such nicknames for our Allies?"

Surprised, Billie-Jo stopped and explained, "You're silly all right. Everyone does. Use nicknames. Although if a Limey calls you a 'bloody' Yank, that's an insult. I don't know why, but it's fighting words. We're all Allies, even the Krauts, at least those in West Germany. The Russky's are our enemies now. Have you seen the movie *Stage Door Canteen*?"

At Meg's nod, she continued, "I keep thinking of the friends of America that the Russian lady and man submariners were supposed to be in that picture. Now look at the Russians."

"Turnabout, left friend in, left friend out, that's the hokey-pokey, and that's what it's all about," Meg sang. "They certainly changed sides a lot during the war."

"Plus they didn't declare war on Japan until two days after Hiroshima," B-J informed Meg. She looked up and back at the handkerchief on the hillside.

Meg took a photograph of the hill, doubting that the white flag would show up. She would remember what it was, however.

"Here's a joke I just heard. There's a little Japanese dog that likes to jump on people to nip-on-knees." Sergeant Gorman grinned. "Get it?" She spelled 'nipponese.'

"Yes. I heard you." Not laughing, Meg turned at the sound of giggling as they started down the little rise. Approaching them were two little smiling girls. Meg greeted them, "*Konnichi-wa.*" They giggled again behind their hands. Both ladies handed the kids some Lifesavers.

Another little girl on a bicycle, a few years older than the others, pedaled up and asked where they were from. Surprised at the English, they chatted a bit, finding out she meant what city in Japan, Nagoya. She giggled and said, "Of course" when Meg first replied "America."

The small girls came running back from a shabby house, holding out a little doll for each woman. The American visitors, smiling broadly, repeated, "Thank you and thank you and *arigato gozaimasu.*" Meg pointed at her camera and at them and asked Billie-Jo to stand between them while they held their dolls aloft.

"Takee picture, *ne?*"

The girls giggled, "*Hai, hai,*" and followed the pantomimed instructions.

"These might be comparable to the elaborate dolls that are displayed on the Dolls' Festival day in March," Billie-Jo conjectured, examining hers carefully as they strolled onward. "Those dolls are treasured. It's quite a formal ceremony within a family. On Boys' Day, colored balloons shaped like carp are flown in various sizes outside the houses. The sizes represent the ages of the sons. You'll notice a lot of holiday celebrations around here. Very colorful ones, not just the Japanese flag of the rising sun being marched down the street behind a band in a parade of floats as we do with our flag in celebrations."

The one-story temple they passed was dark, dim, and dank. They peered in the doors but chose not to enter. Meg had Billie-Jo take her picture on the low steps and reciprocated. The air remained muggy and still, not giving up the slightest breeze. Oppressive air, oppressive trees hunching over them, oppressive twilight. Meg shook herself. She walked a little faster.

"Some shrines had machine shops beneath them," grumbled Billie-Jo. "Colonel Jimmy Doolittle honored the religious shrines in Ise by not bombing them in the early '40s, although he did a good job on Tokyo in '42. The Nips thought he was afraid to disturb the spirits in the temples. That gave them the idea of hiding their factories under the temples. My dad and his Seabees built ramps and air bases for the U. S. military troops above ground right *in plain sight* all across the Pacific. Thumbed his nose at danger. He told me that back then he was sure they were going to invade Japan from the south in the late fall. Then, blooey! That atomic bomb and unconditional surrender within a week!"

Meg's feet, still sore from the uncomfortable items she had worn earlier in the afternoon, steered her back toward the bench. The group returned to the picnic site to find the other bus had arrived. (The driver had taken a wrong turn.) A lieutenant came searching for Miss Meg Lowe and introduced himself as Lt. Mays' friend, Lt. Johnny Hills. He was short and built tightly; his dark glasses concealed his eyes while his grin revealed brilliantly white teeth.

"May I join you ladies?" He sat down on the picnic bench across the table.

A family with a teenage girl and younger boy joined them. The straight shouldered father introduced himself as Major Worth (8th Army patch), his tall, thin wife as Mrs. Worth, his daughter as Janie, and his son as Josh. It turned out that Janie would be in Miss Lowe's 11th grade class while Josh was in ninth grade. The boy kept looking at her throughout the introductions and greetings. He lifted his bandaged arm and said, "Didn't you help me this afternoon, ma'am?"

"You were bird-watching––following a kingfisher––and fell from a tree?" she greeted him with a smile.

"Yes, ma'am. I wish I hadn't cried. I've been the man of the house all the time Father was gone."

The parents looked on him proudly; Mrs. Worth's head nodded up and down, up and down.

"Anyone who is shocked by pain will have a few tears leak out. I guess now you'll have time to be a boy of the house," Meg said softly.

"I'm already a Boy Scout. I'll have earned quite a few badges. Going for Eagle Scout if there's a troop here."

"Great job, Josh. I'd like to see the badges. Scout troops provide a wonderful experience," she said as she smiled at him. He nodded and wandered off after his sister.

The parents looked at her uncertainly as though she were speaking a foreign language to their son and excused themselves to mingle.

Sgt. Gorman turned to Lt. Hills and asked, "Aren't you the lieutenant with Railroad Transportation? I think you worked with the Japanese police to retrieve my *materiel* requisition that was stolen from a train? I'm Sergeant Billie-Jo Gorman."

"Yes, I did," the man replied. "It was found outside the building that some Commies rent. Probably going to swap for weapons or food."

"I did remember to send you a letter thanking you and the local police. Did you receive it?"

"I sure did. Passing along compliments is good policy." He saluted B-J, and she returned the salute, smiling happily.

"I heard you were with the 442nd Regiment," B-J commented, curiosity in her voice.

"That I was. I was posted here a couple of years ago." He said nothing else, and B-J seemed to take that as a signal not to push for further information, Meg noticed.

They turned to others at the table and shared comments on the weather and the country. The military people had been stationed in various places during the war years and were mostly putting in time until their twenty years were up, and they would retire.

After being served a picnic of frankfurters and beans, the tour group roasted the familiar campfire marshmallows until the gooey blackened treats were edible. They pulled them off the sticks, ate them, and licked their fingers clean. They chatted away the warm, waning hours of the afternoon. Sweat slid from under sunglasses and was wiped away with damp handkerchiefs.

CHAPTER THIRTEEN

As the sky darkened, people boarded the buses for a trip across the Nagara River bridge. The tourist boats were drawn up alongside the riverbanks. On arriving, the Americans climbed into the two pleasure boats awaiting them.

Half of the party was guided into a boat down by the river several yards away, while Meg and others were waved onto one closer by. Their low-slung boat was shoved hard by two men but wouldn't budge. The load of Americans was evidently heavier than the Japanese men were used to moving. They called to another boat for help, and two small, muscular men trotted over to help. They tugged, stumbled, tugged, pushed, and finally sent the boat into the river water.

In the far distance in the evening darkness, three boats, each with a fiery basket at one side, could be seen. A Japanese man on Meg's boat began explaining about cormorant fishing in almost the same words that Lt. Mays had used when she was in his office, except for the limerick he had composed on the spot. The narrator stood at the prow while gesturing to emphasize activities he was describing. One boatman was behind him working on steering the craft.

Meg's eyes wandered over the people seated on the opposite bench and then toward the stern. Occasionally, she would twist her head to peer at the cormorant fishing boats that were slowly approaching the tourist boats.

At the other end of the boat, she saw that Lt. Johnny Hills talking to a short Japanese girl wearing pantaloons and a happy coat. On his other side, a boatman in baggy clothes with his head lowered seemed to be whispering intently. A man in black trousers and white shirt and a girl in a long, light colored outfit, who was waving a fan desultorily and speaking occasionally, flanked the man and listened to his whispering.

The girl Johnny was talking with looked familiar; she was eating something from a bowl, shoveling food into her mouth with chopsticks, it looked like. However, the scene was hazy in the lantern lights, creating an out of focus sensation, and Meg shut her eyes briefly before looking back at the narrator.

The guide's voice droned on. ". . . Four men manage the boat: one at the stern guides it; another tends the fiery brazier, dazzling the fish, keeping up a vocal racket, ready to give aid. The second in command handles four birds amidships; and, the master, at the bow, distinguished by an ancient headdress and grass skirt, handed down through the centuries, cares for twelve birds, holding cords with left hand, manipulating cords with his right. When the bird's beak is full, it raises its head and is pulled into the boat.

"This great awkward bird is raised and lowered by a small band of whalebone on the middle of the back, attached to the thin cord of spruce 12 feet long and pliable enough to prevent entanglement. Fish are emptied into a basket; small fish go past the neck ring and comprise the bird's nourishment."

As the narrator dramatically finished describing the attributes of cormorant fishermen and the harvest from the river, Meg's attention stiffened. Fumiko, the school janitor, wearing the baggy pants and happy coat, was the female with whom Lt. Hills was talking.

". . . and the bird is lifted from the water. I forgot to say that the costume that the master wears is modeled on the one from the 11th century," the guide finished. "Here comes a fishing boat. The master will bring a bird on board later to demonstrate the retrieval of the fish from its gullet."

Fumiko Yamata waved a hand at Meg, which caused the other three Japanese to look at her with a start. Then, they looked toward where Fumiko was directing her fingers, and followed hastily as she and Lt. Hills sauntered toward Meg and B-J.

Meg rose. "Fumiko? What are you doing here?"

"My dad's cousins has boat. I help move things." She bobbed her head as she spoke. Fumiko waved toward the other members, introducing them in broken English. Meg couldn't understand the names and didn't ask for them to be repeated. The other girl was odd-looking: a white powdered face, no eyebrows, cropped hair, big knuckled hand with an elegant fan constantly weaving back and forth in front of her dark eyes.

Meg, in turn, introduced them as "the Yamatas" to Sgt. Gorman standing behind her. B-J, taller than Meg, was a full head taller than the Japanese that Fumiko had introduced, and she simply nodded hello. Her uniform was enough to identify her, Meg realized.

They all turned to face out as people started pointing behind them across the water. The Americans around Meg were commenting loudly in excited voices about the boat approaching their side.

Brazier fire from the cormorant boat came slowly over the water as Meg raised her camera, took a flash picture, ejected the bulb, and pulled another from her purse that she had placed on the deck. Fearful that the bright light from the burning basket might ruin that picture, she pointed the lens down at the birds as the boat neared.

Out of the corner of her eye, Meg sees Johnny Hills reach for Fumiko's hand. The gesture barely registers because the boat is dipping up and down.

Every tourist moved over to their side of the boat, and it tilted alarmingly, water sloshing over the rail. Meg hauled up the big olive green purse and handed it to B-J behind her who slung the strap around her own neck.

The Special Services sergeant hollered, "Please, people, take turns. Move back to where you sat." His voice became frantic as the boat lurched again. "Move back. Move back now. We'll take turns for your picture taking and viewing of the operation. He will bring the bird on board to demonstrate the recovery of fish after you've seen how the outfit works."

But, he spoke too late. The sudden weight shift caused both Meg and Fumiko's male cousin to fall to the deck. While falling, Meg snatched her camera to her chest to prevent the resultant spray from harming it.

She struggled to get up, feeling a sharp object under her knee. "My flashbulb," she muttered and stuck it in her pocket. She stood gingerly, braced her knees back against the bench, and took aim again at the approaching boat and birds.

With the tourist boat's lanterns now to her back, she shielded the camera lens somewhat from the brazier firelight by continuing to aim the camera down toward the water. She glanced down and saw blood on the deck just before she set off the flash toward the birds.

Fumiko's cousin, she realized, hadn't gotten back up as she had. Meg knelt again beside him, her camera in her left hand.

"He's bleeding," she yelled for help for the injured person, the boat owner.

Standing again, she handed the camera to Billie-Jo, and she backed up to permit a lady who called out that she was a nurse to maneuver near the boatman. Her uniform boasted lieutenant's bars on the shoulders plus an insignia that Meg did not recognize.

The guests swarmed again once they saw the downed man. Some tried to help. Most just wanted a better look—and Meg just wanted away. She pressed herself as close to the railing as possible, jumping as someone's elbow knocked into her chin. Over the din she could hear the sergeant shouting orders to the crowd, but to no avail. Soon the boat lurched down in her direction. Meg saw Fumiko and the two other people she had introduced tumble forward, right over the injured man. She reached out as if to stop them, but the boat tipped further. She was losing her balance, falling over the railing. She grabbed for an arm, a shirt, thin air. And then she pitched, head first, into the Nagara River.

She automatically held her breath as she fell into the cold water just as she did when her brothers pushed her off the lake raft back home. Reflex action. It was dark down under, and she kicked her feet to turn right side up. Kicked again, hoped she was right side up. She was. She spit a bit of bad taste from her mouth out when her head was free, and her eyes saw the boat.

"Gadzooks! Here, here, help me," Billie-Jo loudly demanded. She hastily stashed the camera inside the purse, swung the bag to her back, leaned over the rail, put her arm under Meg's arm, and then grabbed her hair, and tried heaving her back over the rail into the boat.

Lt. Hills had helped the two Japanese up off the deck from atop the fallen boatman and pushed them away hard.

He reached over the side to grab Meg's other arm and helped lift her clear, dumping her over Billie-Jo's knee. She pounded Meg's back. Water and food flew out onto the boat deck.

The Special Services sergeant and the nurse had knelt on the bleeding guy's other side from where Meg vomited more water and stomach refuse.

"Aim her away from this man," ordered the sergeant sternly.

The nurse lieutenant hissed, pointing, "Go away, go away."

Maj. Worth kept his buffed shoes away from the mess on the deck as he bent his head to peer at Meg. "Go back to the pier. We need an ambulance for that bleeding fellow," He ordered. "Are you all right, miss?" Meg looked at him blearily, but she nodded as if she comprehended his question.

She really had barely heard him through the cacophony around her. Tourists were exclaiming, the brazier keeper was bellowing, and scared children were crying and wailing.

"Oh, no, if we go back to the river bank with all this mess, we'll be here all night. I can't be late for work tonight," Sgt. Billie-Jo Gorman fretted, stood, and pulled Meg away from the injured fellow by her shoulders.

The cormorant boat had moved frantically away when Meg fell near it. Compared to how slowly the oars were usually worked, the boat was moving rapidly; the birds were flustered but seemed adequately controlled by ropes held taut in the hands of the headman and the number two man. The fishermen sent heated language toward the tour boat.

The commotion and barked orders on the tour boat itself increased the confusion. B-J wiped Meg's mouth with a napkin and sat back, looking for some way to get things moving. The boat moved very, very slowly back the way it had come. B-J stood with her hands on her hips, wanting to command some action.

Parents gathered their children close, everyone taking up belongings they had brought and checking that nothing was left behind, eager to go. Meg slumped in a puddle on the deck.

CHAPTER FOURTEEN

"Whereabouts do you live?" asked Lt. Hills, bending down toward the pair, noting Sgt. Billie-Jo Gorman's look of frustration as well as Miss Meg Lowe's haggard demeanor. Speaking in a confidential but urgent tone, Lt. Hills said, "I missed the bus and drove down in a jeep. I'll take you girls home."

They both eyed him, Meg somewhat blurrily, and replied simultaneously, B-J saying, "You know I work at Komaki. How do you rate a jeep?"

Meg weakly gulped, "I'm at the Chiyoda."

"As you well know, Sergeant Gorman, I'm in charge of Railroad Transportation. I monitor jeeps; schedule goods and folks by train; and, so forth. I have transportation when I want it. Let me talk with the Special Services sergeant," Hills said stiffly to B-J.

Meg was still lying below most of the cacophony on the deck. She heard the trace of wounded pride in his voice as he spoke to B-J, as he crouched over them.

Sgt. Billie-Jo Gorman stiffened, saluted him, and gave a quick reply. "Yes, sir. Certainly, sir."

Hills wended his way through the crowd. He talked in bursts of disjointed conversation with the distracted Special Services sergeant who finally nodded agreement, waving him away impatiently. B-J gave the description in a running story of the action to Meg, speaking animatedly, trying to keep her awake because her eyes were trying to close.

After the tourist boat was, at long last, propelled back to the original mooring site, people were helped out. The threesome who were going back by jeep climbed over the shallow rail with a bit of help and immediately separated from the throng. The second boat had also arrived back at the bank.

Hills led the two ladies up the rough riverbank and across the road, Meg stumbling once with B-J grabbing her arm to steady her. The path they took was then up a terraced hill of rock and brush. The brambles caught at their wet clothes and their ankles as they angled along a half overgrown path behind the shrine, and then paced along a flat plat of land.

Meg had the purse slung back on her own chest with the strap from one shoulder crosswise to under the arm on the opposite side. She kept gagging. That terrible taste of river water remained in her mouth. Her hair was plastered with river detritus. Soggy clothes dripped unfamiliar river smells from her body.

Lt. Hills held up his hand and moved around to face them. "My jeep is parked back at Gifu, but I know a shortcut so that we don't have to walk a couple of miles, Meg, with you in your depleted state. Come on, I'll show you."

Lt. Hills ducked his head into a black void as big as a highway culvert and stooped low, bidding them to follow. He flicked his lighter to indicate the height inside a cave.

"This was constructed to be used either as a bomb shelter or a machine-gun nest. People also lived in these caves, just as they did in urban bomb-shelters during the war. A group of us scouted these places out when we first arrived. The ceiling gets low back in there. I'm going to light a torch. At one place a huge rock is on our left side of a narrow ledge, and the ledge has a small stream on the other side. I'll go all the way across the ledge and hold the torch so that you can work your way across. You might want to keep your hand along a wall on the left in here until I say to stop."

The torch flame hit their eyes before he thrust it around in front, he was being sure of foot because he led with the light. His two female passengers stumbled over uneven blocks of stone and rocks that comprised the slippery surface, sight obscured by the clammy darkness. Meg, feeling groggy, feet squishing in her wet shoes, followed the torch. B-J kept her steady by placing a hand lightly on her right shoulder.

Tunnels led off to the sides, the entrances marked by zigzag emblems, or maybe ideograms, resembling lightning streaks or wisps of steam. These were weirdly visible in the spotty air throwing off flickers of light that came over Lt. Hills' shoulder.

The women hesitated as they heard the sound of water, stopped short when he commanded, and halted while he was moving ahead over the ledge between the rock and water. With the torch turned toward them, he beckoned, and the ladies moved carefully over toward him.

"Hubba hubba," he urged. As he turned forward again, faint sounds of laughter and conversation came into the air.

"Behold," he laughed, "the jeep is out by that restaurant. Meantime, we enjoyed unusual cuisine, dining in a green canopy of trees and grass. We have had a minor adventure tour this evening and a nice swim. We trust the trip was delightful." He bowed.

Billie-Jo Gorman laughed. She could hear commotion by the restaurant as well as back toward the river. "What happened to that boat fellow? I saw the blood before I was helping Meg but couldn't tell where it was coming from because those other three people fell on top of him. Probably the blood was from his head if he hit it on the bench. Wonder what the girl's boat uncles will do if it gets around that the trips are dangerous."

"Oh, he'll recover. And, I'm sure the fishing trips will continue. They'll manage all right. That branch of the family always did," the lieutenant croaked, gesturing Meg into the back seat of the jeep. He explained, although Meg didn't comprehend much, just following orders, "Sergeant Gorman gets out first, so she rides in the front, and then you'll have to switch."

"You know the Yamata family?" Meg heard Billie-Jo ask as they drove off into the night.

Meg didn't hear the answer. They bumped through the dark countryside on the uneven roadbed. She was rocked to sleep by the motion of the jeep.

#

A voice called urgently, "Miss Lowe! Miss Lowe!"

Another said, "Meg! Margaret. Meg, wake up. We're approaching the Komaki Air Base, and you'll need to show your Identification Pass at the gate."

Meg groaned as she woke with a crick in her neck and fumbled in her purse to find her wallet. She pulled out her wool sweater first and drew it around her wet shoulders because she was chilled. She fumbled around, found the billfold with her pass, and held it up to the window when they stopped at the gate. The guard's flashlight went back and forth several times from the ID picture to her face, framed now by wet hair unlike the way it was in the photo. After viewing her several times, they were permitted in.

After B-J climbed out and walked into a Quonset hut, Meg moved into the front seat. The jeep moved back out of the gate and turned onto the dark road.

"I think you have something that belongs to me," Lt. Johnny Hills said in a low tone.

"I do?"

"Um hmm. You picked something up from the deck when you first fell. It's a doll. Let me have it, please."

"Nonsense. I remember that I picked up a flashbulb, although I do have a doll a little girl gave me. I must have pulled it out with the flashbulb. Ouch, I have a charley horse in my neck. Here is the doll, see?" It was next to the billfold in her satchel.

He pulled to the side of the road and stopped. She held up the little Japanese doll, turned toward him, and winced.

"Ow, my neck hurts." She grunted, digging at her shoulder, and dropping the doll back into the handbag when he shook his head in disappointment.

"Here--I'll help." He massaged her left shoulder with his right hand. Somehow his thumb also started pressing her windpipe as he stared at her face. It was as if he were seeking to know if he could trust her explanation.

Intuitively, Meg responded to the threat of superior muscle power with the acting sensitivity she used so effectively in the classroom. She became historical Anne Boleyn, young wife out of favor with King Henry the VIII, innocent and unrepentant, arrogant and unafraid, placing her head on the block, lovely neck stretched forward to be chopped off. Meg lifted her chin, bravely exposing more of her neck.

She was luckier than Anne Boleyn.

The lieutenant drew back with a pat on her shoulder and then started the vehicle.

She was also now more alert than she'd been a minute earlier. Meg's heart thudded in her chest. She could feel her pulse throb in her throat where the lieutenant had pressed his thumb. Her mind shed most of the fog.

"How does that particular Yamata branch always win?" she inquired, pulling the sweater tighter, moving as close to her passenger side door as she could. "I didn't hear what you told Sergeant Gorman when she asked."

He replied in a monotone. "Those local boatmen of *that* branch always had enough to eat during famines, scarce sources for goods, and war times. However, in contrast, the Yamata father and little daughter had it bad because they are Americans, descended from the first Issei who emigrated in the 1880's. They came to visit Japan in 1940 and first sought their distant Christian relatives in Nagasaki, trying to find some family mementos."

"Jiminy cricket. They really picked a bad location to visit." Meg shook her head.

"Luckily, they had come north before the August bomb in '45. Relatives here had hidden them (somewhat unwillingly) in those caves--those by where we just came out--for going on a year. The old man was found out about a year after they came north by the authorities and was assigned to the unclean class--that's those dealing with nasty tasks, butchering, cleaning latrines. And dear Fumiko was taken away to be a *geisha* or actress, concubine, something like that. The police let them survive in those roles, most likely chuckling at the American Yamatas' humiliations."

"Doubled down on bad luck, seems to me. Poor Yamatas. I wonder why they're still here. Do you know?"

"No, I said I didn't know them. Meanwhile, during the war, the Japanese-Americans in the United States of America were imprisoned in bad settings. Derelict camps, unfinished shelters, in several obscure locations, in several states. Hence, that kind of luck. Those boatmen here thrived because they could furnish food to the military––as well as feed themselves."

He suddenly struck the steering wheel hard.

"I don't understand. Were you talking to Fumiko about something special?" Meg was intrigued by his vehemence.

"I was showing Fumiko Yamata my family heirloom like the ones they had been seeking when they sailed into Nagasaki. I was speaking in English, but Fumiko did some translating for the other female, an impersonator who became bored and moved around to my other side, where the men were. Behind me, I heard some of the argument going on."

"You mean when the one fella was whispering to the others? I think it was the boatman whispering."

"Yes, it was. The gist from one man and that odd-looking impersonator was an order, politely, of course, to the boat owner who disagreed, politely, of course, to transport stuff to Tokyo, and something mumbled about the American Village. 'It would be very difficult,' Fumiko's cousin who owned the boat said, and if they kept pressuring him, 'maybe the Americans would pay to know about such a plan.'"

"Plan?"

"To transport stuff: I'm going to report that to my officer. However, the boat owner argued that they were making good money working with the American tourists, were getting old, didn't need the grief of getting involved in transporting black market stuff, and were quite satisfied with the way things were. I think Fumiko was listening to the argument more than to me.

"Their visitor was then saying that he would relieve me of my statue, not only because it could be worth a lot of money, but also would threaten the fishing tour contract with *gaijin* Special Services. Then Fumiko took off with my little trinket before I could take it back, and you know what happened next."

"No, I don't remember anything except the haze of lights and voices and almost coughing my guts up."

"I lost my heirloom. That's what happened."

His bitter tone shut her up. They drove in silence the rest of the way and separated in front of the Chiyoda Hotel. She squashed her way wearily up the stairs.

CHAPTER FIFTEEN

A huge, bulbous, gooey, green marshmallow threatened to engulf her, oozing inexorably down a hill toward her, bits of charred matter scattered over its pulsing surface, a tiny white flag in the middle of the vertiginous, verdant mass, she herself unable to move toward the safety of a visible culvert because her feet were stuck in a muddy ditch--and she woke up.

Meg crawled out of bed, heart pounding in her temples, and breath coming in short gasps. She peeled off the blouse and under garments she'd been wearing the since the night before, she stripped the dirty sheets, and set them aside for the maid. Energy was surging through her every molecule from the memory of the frightening dream. Drained, she collapsed on the stuffed chair. Duty called.

She would have to phone the front desk to ask for the maid to come because the sheets were changed only once a week, not twice, which required a small additional fee. Laundry of white clothes and colored garments needed doing. Mayhap the maid would pound in a couple of nails for the woodblock prints and thus freshen up the drab room, too. That way, she'd only have to pay a single extra fee.

Meg'd left the slacks, still damp, hanging on the closet doorknob. They were too damp to put under the mattress that she used all the time as an alternative to ironing. Doesn't even dare put them in with the other clothes because she'd get more mildew, more black spots.

"I can't tolerate these nasty, musty clothes," she exclaimed. Suddenly she laughed, "And I thought the only thing I was intolerant of was intolerance itself. Get yourself together." She shook her head at herself. Hopefully Betty didn't hear her raving.

Running hot bath water into the tub, she sank down blissfully, rubbed Ivory soap into her hair, rinsed her head under the faucet, rubbed Lifebuoy soap into her hair, rinsed her head under the faucet. The water was pretty murky by that time, so she emptied the tub and refilled it for a good, relaxing bath.

Her black wool sweater she dunked up and down in the tub after the water-cooled, wrung it out in a towel, and spread it on the trunk on another towel.

Today, Friday, had showed up with calming low humidity and bright sunshine that she could see outside her window. Meg recalled that she faced the chore of typing bridal shower invitations at the school. After dressing, taking her time, she wandered the streets, finishing the roll of film with two pictures and inserting another roll.

The local police officer directing traffic at an intersection of Hirokoji-dori Avenue was performing his famous ballet leaps gracefully, his white-gloved hands waving like ripened cotton bolls in a breeze. Past him, Meg leapfrogged over puddles. A woman had thrown water near the entrance of Matzusakaya Department Store to settle dust, and, as she swept the sidewalk clean, she sent dirty water following in Meg's footsteps, maybe deliberately.

As Meg ambled back up a block toward the American Village, she spotted a few more things she would like to buy. Nearing her destination, she noticed that the Yamata shop was still empty; the pallets were gone, maybe stolen to make a shack to live in somewhere. People did that after their home had been bombed out or been blown aside by a typhoon or been collapsed by an earthquake. Meg had noticed some tiny homes that reminded her of the deliciously hidden duck blind that her mom had taken her to during elementary school. That's where she learned to trace and shoot the flying Canada geese or mallards. These rebuilt homes are as dark and secretive as the nested place in the reeds by the stream back home.

Meg looked up from her reverie. Japanese guards she hadn't seen before waved her into the American Village gate by the school. She would have to use the typewriter in the teachers' lounge where, as a nice incentive, the percolator was located.

#

A few hours later, she had typed most of the required invitations when she was startled to see one addressed to Mrs. Fritz. Better be diplomatic about how I mention this to Althea, she thought, placing that invitation in her purse. Don't know how much Robbie's told her. Or is even allowed to tell her.

Around noon, she finished typing and phoned Josh Worth to see if he and another boy would deliver the invitations. They quickly arrived, and for a quarter each in script, set off to the various addresses. She set off for the Chiyoda Hotel for lunch.

Across the lobby of the hotel the clerk beckoned to her before handing her a bouquet of camellias in a green vase with a note attached.

I want to see you again.
Love,
Johnny Hills, Lt.

Resisting the temptation to toss the flowers into a wastebasket, she took them up with her in the elevator and into her room, placing them on the desk. He should not have been such a downhearted person to be around last night. She still wasn't sure but what he had been threatening her when he massaged her neck. Perhaps it was her imagination, the panic and fear of drowning catching up to her several hours later.

Sighing, she sought out Althea down the hotel hall, but she didn't answer the knock on her door. Meg returned to her own room and counted out some *yen* for another shopping expedition. She heard Betty Carnahan turn on the radio next door so Meg left her room and tapped on the next door.

"Betty, I want to buy those peasant clothes from you. I couldn't find anything at the PX."

"Oh, they cost me all of 35 *sen*," Betty laughed. "You must borrow my Penney's catalog, pick out some yard goods, and when they come, I'll introduce you to a fine seamstress. She doesn't even need a pattern––she can work from a picture of anything you want her to make."

"Here are the coins." Meg sorted them out from the coin purse she pulled from her satchel.

"What's the matter with your palm?"

"I discovered that cut this morning. I must have hurt it on the fishing trip last night when I went over the side of the boat into the river."

Betty said, "Are you saying you hurt that hand last night and haven't treated it for infection?"

"Correct."

"I have to hurry back to the hospital, but you take this hydrogen peroxide, gauze, and tape," Betty said as she whirled around her room gathering the supplies. "Wash your hands with soap and water, then douse the palm, and bandage it. I'll look at it again tonight. Don't hesitate."

The instructions followed, although the liquid hurt something awful, Meg tumbled onto clean sheets and fell asleep, choosing to forego both lunch and another tour of the shops.

Hours later, Betty interrupted her afternoon sleep by banging on the door. She said she had come to apply some additional antiseptic to the injured hand.

"Now, you take care of this tomorrow, Meg," she ordered. "Cleanse, salve, gauze."

"Going swimming from the FP 47," Meg mumbled sleepily.

"Oh, no, who knows what lurks in the bay?"

"The Shadow knows," she gurgled.

A moment of hesitation. "Lamont Cranston, The Shadow, knows what lurks in the hearts of men, not what microorganisms lurk in the bay," Betty retorted.

"'S'okay. You wound the gauze around a wound. Those're heteronyms, didja know that?"

"I'm surely pleased to hear about them. I trust they are not microorganisms." Betty started to slip away from Meg's bedside and said, "I have rubber gloves you can wear if you insist on swimming in that filthy water."

"No, thanks. I'll be good. I've had enough shots to make me immune, to save me from everything the bay waters hold."

Betty said darkly, "I tell you that slimy worms with slimy germs doth squirm beneath the slimy sea. That's a *Rime*. Let me see your hand tomorrow evening."

Betty had brought along a Penney's catalog that she slapped on the bed. She said it was there so that Meg could put in an order. Before Meg could open the book, Morpheus reclaimed her.

Saturday, Meg awoke to the phone ringing with an acceptance of the shower invitation from one of Althea's friends. Two other ladies called acceptance soon afterwards. Billie-Jo Gorman called then, merely to check on her after the adventure Thursday evening. Meg indicated that she was fine and going swimming, at which signal, B-J said she was going to join her on the FP 47 if she could get a reservation and hung up.

Meg really doesn't like B-J's crude, vulgar comments, but she did pull her from the drink. She supposed she could bear an afternoon with the girl. She opened the catalog and filled out an order blank for dress materials and some low-heeled shoes. She'd put in a money order from the APO office and mail in the order on Monday next.

Sharon Sheldon called to offer help with the shower and agreed to meet her Monday at 1400 hours at the PX.

Downstairs, after eating a late breakfast, available only on Saturdays, she took a cheap envelope from her mailbox. Meg found an awkwardly worded note inside.

> *Please to advice you to Cousin's wakes*
> *ate the Catholic Church. 1800-200 hours*
> *thursday evening. Please to come*
> > *Yamata Family*

Meg returned to her room, put on the least rumpled blouse she had remaining, and took down the slacks she had hung on the door knob to dry Thursday night. A tiny, dark wood object fell on the floor. Picking it up, she was astounded at the delicate, perfect carving of a bearded man in a robe. Even the soles of the feet were carved with a symbol that seemed faintly familiar. She rubbed the statue with toilet paper and put it on the desk.

"Oh, boy," she groaned, "This must be the heirloom doll that the lieutenant thought I had. Wonder why it was worth threatening, yes, threatening me over? Well, I'll give it back to him and that's that."

With her purse now containing her swimsuit and swimming cap in addition to its regular load, she walked downstairs. The clerk called her over. "This bonsai tree came for you, Miss Lowe."

"I think it'd look lovely on the reception desk. Or, I'll put it over there by the entrance. Is that all right?"

"Certainly, Miss Lowe."

A card was tucked into one side of the tortured tree's low ceramic container.

> **You are so cute.**
> **I'd love to scoop you into my arms the way I did from the Nagara River.**
> **Love, J. Hills**

He's not capable of netting me––but he is nettling me, Meg growled to herself. Then the front door of the Chiyoda opened and in he walked, removing his sunglasses. She experienced a quirk of fear. Why must he keep hounding her?

He strode to her and took her hand. "You've received my cards and flowers?"

Taking her hand back, "Yes, I'm putting that potted plant here." She placed it firmly on the table. The clunk made the desk clerk turn to watch them.

"That's a fine place to display it. I came to get you to go places and see people and do things." He looked pleased.

"I'm already engaged for the day," Meg said, choosing her words deliberately, "and it's private." No need to provoke him into anger. The clerk rests his hands on the desk, sending an occasional curious glance their way while ostensibly reading the register.

This was the first time she had seen his narrow eyes in daylight. Inwardly she was reminded of the dead-soul eyes of a student who had been in her 10th and 11th grade classes, until he thankfully turned 18 years old and joined the military. He had worn his shirt unbuttoned halfway down his chest, displaying acne that continued from his face, and glared at her all through class. Once he had said, "I hate you," as he walked by her in the hall. Daring her to flunk him, he had completed the bare minimum of her assignments required to pass. Everyone knew that his mother, who taught third grade, sported facial bruises delivered by his abusive father. The lad was developing in the paternal mode.

And now, here were similar inhuman eyes gazing at her.

"I can take you to wherever you're going," he insisted.

"No. Why don't you just go row a boat over the River Styx?"

He grinned to show that he caught the allusion but said casually, shrugging with amusement, "I don't monitor that kind of transportation. How about tomorrow? It's supposed to be a gorgeous day."

"I'm busy all day tomorrow, too."

"My, my. We could go to a movie Monday night."

"Why don't you just go fly a kite?"

"Unfortunately, that's a type of transportation I can't commandeer." He gave a bark of laughter. "Why don't you tell me where you're going, and I'll catch up with you."

"There isn't room for you, and you've not been invited."

"You could invite me."

"What do you not understand about the word N-O?"

"Aw, c'mon, I really want to see you, other than over a marshmallow roast, river dunk, dead fish, and a private cave. Bet your friends would like to know about us in that cave."

"Goodbye. I'm not going to go anywhere with you."

"Your wet hair looked like melted butter covered with molasses after we pulled you out," he remembered in a mocking, dreamy tone. "Uh-huh. Uh-huh. I'll bet you'll change your mind, Meg, Margaret, Miss Lowe, asleep in my jeep."

He finally left without a scintilla of defeat on his face, putting back on his hat and sunglasses. His eyes had shown no emotion at all during their brief exchange.

She gave him a few deep breaths for a head start before following him out the door. Concealed in the doorway, she watched him parade march down the street until he disappeared into his jeep and drove off. Satisfied that he wouldn't be following her, she ventured out, going in the opposite direction and taking the long way around to the Special Services building and Snack Shack.

Meg took the Special Services bus from its stop by the Snack Shack down to the pier on the bay. Anticipating the afternoon on the FP 47 boat had provided a relief from the recent stresses, and the reality developed into relaxation.

The boat was a long slender one with cabins for changing clothes and a cheerful crew of local people. A sergeant with a rakish air welcomed the party aboard and showed them around.

B-J Gorman pointed out a low-slung 'Roosky' ship in the harbor as the crew steered the boat from the pier. "Hope they see that hanky we left on the hill by Gifu," she said menacingly.

After an hour's cruise around the sunlit bay, the boat anchored. Several people changed into swimsuits and dived into the water. Swimming in water with waves was a lot more difficult than swimming in a languid lake, as Meg discovered. She soon climbed out of the water, quite a while before the others were "piped" on board for a snack.

Billie-Jo reached the ladder before her and said, "You go up first. I'll be able to *push* you over the railing this time. I wish I had seen the *cormorant* disgorge stuff on the tour boat deck instead of the way you did!"

"It wasn't an experience I'd care to repeat, either."

After donning her clothes, wringing out her swimsuit, stuffing it in the swim cap, and both of those stuffed into her purse, she washed the scratch on her palm that had swollen in the salty water.

Meg returned to the aft deck, twirling her hair in both hands. "You said that Lieutenant Hills was in something-- the 440th something. What was that?"

"442th. The Japanese American troops in Europe. Really famous."

"How so?"

"Rather than being sent to an internment camp in the States, he enlisted. Japanese Americans were sent to Europe with the 'Go for Broke' 442nd Regimental Combat Team. They were the most decorated unit in the war. Pulled some hard action under terrible combat conditions; rescued troops."

"Pretty impressive, I must say," Meg allowed, now somewhat ashamed of the way she had been thinking of him, because it was confusing to hear of heroics. He looked cold eyes at her, cold unnerving eyes. She shrugged off the disparate pieces of information and changed the subject "Did he say how he knew the Yamatas?"

"Lieutenant Hills said, if I am remembering correctly, 'All our families were sent to prison camps in the States. Yamata's family, those members who had chosen not to come on the trip to Japan, rented his land to a neighbor rather than having to sell it.' In contrast, Hills' own parents had to sell their property at a loss when they were interned.

"He helped me drag you out of the river." Billie-Jo took a drink of tea and sighed, "He's an admirable man; if only he were taller, I'd make a play for him."

"Is he here because he speaks Japanese?" Meg ignored B-J's side comment and asked her another question. She still didn't quite understand where he was coming from, his background, and his history.

"Yes, of course. He was brevetted to first lieutenant when he arrived. In case you don't know, that means raised up in rank but not in pay."

"Is he related to the Yamatas? I mean the girl on the boat. She is a janitor at the American school, and her father owns a store around the corner from the American Village."

"I'm not sure about that. I think he may have talked with them on the boat, but I didn't really notice. He certainly knew their history. How well do you know them?"

Meg related a bit of the connections with the Yamatas to B-J: the school, where she and the Yamata daughter had met and rubbed mildew from her huaraches; the vase, purchased at the father's shop for a bridal shower she was hostessing; and, a little excitement involving both her and them at her school earlier in the week.

B-J settled down and listened but asked nothing else. Once she murmured something about the seagulls resembling strafing planes. Both she and Meg were drowsy.

On the return trip, they took a good, leisurely hour going around the opposite side of the bay. The long boat ironed its way across the crinkled waves, leaving a long v-shaped wake smoothed out aft.

People had changed back into uniforms or civvies. They sat on the deck under the canvas top. Hot tea, tuna fish sandwiches, and croissants were a perfect ending to a relaxing and refreshing day.

"Now hear this!" Billie-Jo suddenly sounded like an announcer on a ship's public address system, cupping her hands around her mouth in imitation of a megaphone. "Two types of fish you do *not* want to eat." She aimed her sandwich at Meg. "Canned tuna is okay. But beware. *Sashimi* is raw tuna from these waters, and pufferfish is poison unless prepared correctly. Then here we have those *koi* that are not edible but are valuable. We're well advised to eat in approved establishments only. Too much muckety-muck in this country for our stomachs. You may, however, eat canned salmon or that shad roe, made into canned caviar. Don't go fishing, just remember these *go* fish––get it, *five* fish?" B-J exploded with laughter. "I'm teaching you about this. Listen up."

"I heard you. I'm not deaf. You informed everyone on the deck about that little joke, in fact," Meg said sharply, yes, rudely even. She disliked being jolted awake, enjoyed being drowsy, feeling the restful swaying of the boat. Her Mom had often told her that a lady is never *unintentionally* rude.

Sometimes Billie-Jo was too much of a know-it-all show-off, something Meg knew she herself also became with her knowledge and love of history. On one hand this is useful when trying to keep high school students engaged. She performed quick snap demonstrations such as the Burr-Hamilton duel or dramatic recitations of Roosevelt's Four Freedoms: "of speech and expression, of worship and from want and from fear."

Sitting back to watch the golden sunlight shimmering across the waters, the sea breeze gentle on her skin, she relaxed again. She would clean her left palm again when she arrived home, shuddering to think of infections that could sprout from germs she couldn't see.

#

More acceptance responses for the bridal shower arrived Saturday night. She received the rest on Sunday afternoon, except for one to Mrs. Fritz's invitation--the one she had silently handed to Althea to dispose of--and also she had not heard from Mrs. Worth, for an unknown reason.

While at the chapel that Sunday morning, she had made an appointment to see the chaplain's assistant Monday afternoon. She and Sharon needed to arrange the bridal shower setup.

Then the one refusal came Sunday evening from Mrs. Worth. She gushed her remarks in a wispy, high-pitched voice that must have been entrancing in her teens, with an up tilt at the end of every sentence. "I am so very, very, dreadfully sorry and regret so awfully that I cannot make the shower, but my husband is a field grade officer, and I must be careful with who I mix with? You just run by my house here and pick up the present that is, that is, I bought, a bunch of trinkets from a creepy little man who came by my house when the maids and houseboy were gone? I'm so awfully bad at arithmetic like all us girls that I don't even know how much I gave him, given the exchange rate for that awful *yen* and *sen*? Now, see, I'm over near Castle Heights? How about Monday afternoon? I'll leave the box by the front door for the maid to give you? I dasn't touch it--it might have radiation in it, you know? You'll tell dear, dear Althea that I am so sorry to miss the festivities? That's a good little girl, dearie." The phone disconnected.

"Yes, ma'am, no, ma'am, no excuse, ma'am?" Meg mocked the dead phone. "I'll make the trip tomorrow be worthwhile, dearie? I dasn't disobey? I'll do it by taking a taxi, carrying out that assignment given me by you, and then meeting Sharon at the PX."

The singsong voice she imitated ended with her shuddering at the idea of a grown lady mewling.

CHAPTER SIXTEEN

onday morning, Miss Margaret Lowe took the bus ride to Col. Jones' office just as she had done the previous Thursday. The same quiet-voiced Pvt. Brooks was at the desk nearest the door, and Althea's friend, Sgt. Laura Duncan, was at the desk that had the phone and glass top over snapshots of herself receiving another rocker or maybe it was called a chevron.

"Just knock on the door," Duncan said, gesturing to the right hand one.

"Good morning, Robbie, I mean Colonel," Meg said, opening the door after his voice barked "enter."

"I'm here to sign my statement." She glanced at a picture of a P-38 and another one of Althea Ardmore on the cabinet.

He beckoned her to the side of his desk. "A few things need going over. Here, look at your pictures. You show several chests and several boxes of American goods, with the floor showing footprints. The one of Captain Archer has him lying on the floor with his head toward the school stairway. Yet, his feet have scraped the floor as though he pulled back to sit up. His left hand is over his stomach. Is that how you first saw him?"

"I was a wee bit frightened at the time, but the odds are that he was lying there like that. I qualify that by stating that when Cally and I went down there with flashlights, I did not notice anything different. I probably would've noticed because my dad taught me how to track in the darkened hours of night."

"I trust you're being perceptive in this case, for sure. Statements from the other participants last Tuesday have cleared up some matters. Now, this weekend Mr. Yamata and I skimmed through his inventory and the Fritz one for the soup kitchen and found that several packs of yen, medical supplies, cigarettes, canned goods and other food items, a small coin chest, and some dolls are missing."

"What?!" Her surprise was genuine.

"Did you notice anything like those items?"

"Oh, my. Would the doll be this? I picked it up from the floor of the cormorant boat, thinking it was a used flash bulb," unwrapping it as she spoke.

"I do not know if it is or not," he answered. "He didn't provide a description of them but I think he meant they are girls' dolls. In *kimonos*. Girls' *kimonos*."

"Look, this one is a miniature man in dark wood--long hair, long beard, long robe--tiny toes. Must have stepped on a fish because there's one carved on his sole and four ideograms on his other foot. I used my Japanese dictionary trying to decipher the marks, and I can only see one that might be *ri*, but I wouldn't even swear to that. I think I've seen something like those marks somewhere. Anyway, see, there's an odd hole in his back. How I ended up with this is a long story.

"To be brief: there was an accident on the tour boat, and Sergeant Billie-Jo Gorman, Lieutenant Johnny Hills, and I took a short-cut through a cave over to his jeep rather than wait for the bus. She had to be at work that night, and I was tired and soaking wet, but that's another story.

"After we dropped B-J Gorman off at Komaki, I climbed into the front seat. We drove on a bit, and Johnny, Lieutenant Hills, demanded that I give him a doll. The only one that I knew

I had was one a little girl gave me that afternoon. I showed him that. He pulled off the road, and he pretended to rub a charley horse in my neck but pressed my windpipe rather too much. I had given him no provocation to pressure me in any manner whatsoever. I did not like that squeeze play."

"Hmmm. He tried to choke you?"

"I don't think he really meant to do me arm," Meg said, although she was reluctant to give any sympathy to Hills. "But he was quite . . .threatening, menacing--I'm not quite sure how to describe it."

"Perhaps you misread the situation, after your frightful night on the boat?"

Meg hesitated. "Maybe. He seemed to be trying to hint he could strangle me."

"I think you're being a teensy bit dramatic, Meg. He's an officer and a gentleman. Plus highly decorated. Intelligent."

"And, I know what I surmised, sir. I wasn't groggy after he did that, after that happened, no, sir, believe me."

"Go on." He dismissed her comments.

Meg was insistent on making a point of her feeling of threat. "I discovered Saturday that I did have this doll; it was stuck in the wet slacks I had worn that night. Today I am carrying it in my bag to give back to him if I see him. Saturday I became irritated because he sent flowers twice with inappropriate remarks on the gift cards. Saturday noontime he had even shown up at my hotel and pressured me to date him. His eyes have not a trace of feeling in them. I forgot about the little statue because I became angry."

"For your enlightenment, if you'd been through the war he has, being shot at for years, having buddies die in your arms, you too might have a different expression in your eyes. But, go on." It sounded like Col. Jones was scolding her, Meg judged, with a slight stiffening of her backbone.

"That's all I can tell you. I fell on a hard object when the boat tilted. I thought it was my flash bulb. I didn't know the fellow who fell forward and hit his head when the boat tilted. That's the last thing I remember until we left off Sergeant Gorman at Komaki, and I woke up in the jeep."

"The fellow who fell forward 'passed over,' as you so quaintly describe death."

"What?"

"The report says that at the time you went kerplunk into the Nagara River, three people fell on the injured man who was a co-owner of the boat. Of those who fell, one was a woman who accidentally stabbed him with a bamboo piece from her fan. You seem to have a habit of entering a crime scene like a Greek inside a Trojan horse, although you, in a bit of contrast to those warriors, are visibly present and accounted for."

"Thanks for the compliment, sir--I think."

"I have the list of people on the tour, but not who was on each boat. Perhaps you can remember some names?"

"One person who surprised me was the school janitor, Fumiko Yamata--she said her dad's cousins owned the boat. Must have been one of them who died?"

"Hmm, Yamata girl's not on the list. Of course, I was given the list only of personnel and tourists." He ignored her question.

She waited a second and then continued. "Then there were Major Worth and his wife with two children; the daughter is Janie and the son, Josh. Josh had his wrist in a splint. But, that, too, is another story. Both children will be in my classes next year. There were three airmen--one had an accordion, and we sang songs to drown out the *sake* party on another boat with Japanese tourists. I think the musician's name was Jeff. Four women were together, and I'd guess they are wives. Mrs. Enders, Mrs. Holman, Mrs.

Ranger, and Mrs. Cohen. Then there were two captains with their wives and little girls––the Concords and Byrnes.

"I have the list of addresses if you want them, because I promised to send them their pictures. I took pictures of the cormorant boat, but it was quite a ways away, and they may not come out clearly. As I said, I don't remember much after that. Memories of the remainder of the evening evanesce."

"And that means?"

"I don't remember much is what it means."

"Please, Meg, may I have the latest roll of film?"

"Colonel, I have it ready to mail to my mom, to have it developed because I want two sets of 3x5 pictures for the other tourists on the cormorant trip. Also, the next day, to finish the roll, I walked around taking pictures here in town. Kids were swimming nearly bare-naked in the canal. In contrast, tiny girls were dancing down the street sheathed in heavy *kimonos* in this heat. Mom will enjoy those snapshots. She can have a whole role for the scrapbook."

He held his hand out. "I'll give you two copies after I check them for relevance to the boat incident."

She pulled the yellow Kodak mailer from her purse and handed it over with a sigh. "May I have the little doll back?"

"I'll check it with Yamata-san first. He said the dolls are part of the Dolls' Festival set he had purchased for his daughter, Fumiko. Hmm. This wooden one is more a statue than a doll––it could be a *netsuke*, one of those things that men hang over the sash of the *kimono* to balance the *inro*, a small storage box. Are you sure you did not notice any dolls in a quilted box last week when you were in the school's underground shelter?"

"I did not see any that I remember. There were just too many things I hadn't seen before, and the light bulbs are pretty dim down there."

"If you do remember, kindly let me know immediately."

"I don't like being sidetracked while I'm preparing for the classes I'll teach. Moreover, Colonel, I'm trying to put together a shower for your lovely fiancée, Althea, who is also now my favorite school principal. Meanwhile, what I am wishing to see are Japanese places while there's still time before school starts." Besides the *yen* is spent, and the old coins are Stateside; that leaves only the other things that are missing. Not my problem.

"Where are the Fritzes?" she asked suddenly.

"Transferred home to a VA hospital." He stood and motioned for her to sit. "I'm going to hit a high fly to you in left field. The autopsy results on Captain Archer indicate that he was stabbed with a long, slender two-sided blade, one that is not found on a Swiss Army knife, but more likely on a stiletto. Confronted with this, rather than insisting that she had had no part in any way, shape, or form with his misfortunes, Mrs. Fritz finally admitted that she had thrown a can at him, causing him to topple backwards and hit his head. Also she flicked open a Swiss knife and threw it. But she says he simply told her to go away and leave him alone."

"But why didn't she call the APs and report it?"

"I don't have an answer to that question. She maintains that she might be charged with assault but can appeal on grounds of self-protection, because he frightened her mightily, suddenly appearing in her eyesight and causing her to think, incorrectly, that he was stealing. Consequently, she is being escorted home on a hospital ship with her husband. The civil arm of the military will assume her case. All told, you were half-right in that particular instance."

"My, oh, my. And Sergeant Salchow?"

"Transferred to Osaka."

"Where are the Yamatas now? They haven't been transferred, because I saw Fumiko on the boat. Yet I noticed their store is empty and dark."

"Why don't you ask them? I know you've heard the talk about their probably involvement in the black market but so far we have no definite proof. And before you keep on, let me tell you that in Osaka, a whole long block of black market stalls line a wide boulevard. It has been reported in the papers with several follow-up articles. That Osaka street of booths is a giant 'swap meet.' However, what we have been investigating could be titled a 'swipe meet': artifacts, jewelry, supplies are stolen and moved surreptitiously out of the country. Rich guys swagger around, murders happen. You probably read in *Life* and *Look* about egregious art thefts in Europe back during the war. Here it is more like thieves sneaking them out under their coats. China and Manchuria are involved because many of their treasures were looted by the Japanese and brought here. Ponder that. But don't ask me why I'm giving you that much information, because all of that which I'm revealing from readily available news is simply to quiet your suspicions and keep you quiet about events you've inadvertently stumbled into."

"Actually, more obfuscation than information," she scoffed. "Would this, perchance, have something to do with the robbery at Nagoya Hall last Wednesday night?"

He reared back. "How do you know about that?"

"I was there with a friend to see the concert."

"Go on."

"Come on, I don't know anything about what was taken. Was it related to this swiping for the black market?"

"I see." The colonel took a long breath, studying her. "Umm. I have nothing to share about that. Let's go to another subject. I received a report from the APs about you from last

Thursday. Tell me why were you wandering around dressed like a peasant when you helped that boy?" he ordered sternly.

"A pal loaned me some clothes, and I was doing this and that."

"Go on."

"I wish you would quit saying that, sir."

"Go on." He seemed to be enjoying putting her through these paces.

Sighing, she continued, "I went into the Yamata shop and spoke nonsense down the stairway at the AP and then ran out, and I next pretended to be a lawn mower."

He raised one eyebrow. "Meaning?"

"That is, sitting hunched down, working each blade of grass. Thus I became inconspicuous as a flower. The AP ran up the stairs and stood by the shop while some men were loading things from the tunnel. They hauled stuff through the Yamata's shop out onto a truck.

"Down the street to my right, I noticed two boys and a grey-faced kimono-clad fellow who had earlier been in a shop by the bathhouse. I watched the kids who were bird watching, and one climbed a tree, fell, and hurt his arm just as I took a picture of the boys."

"Of course you did."

"The Grey Kimono Man had gone into an expensive looking house. He was coming out just as the kid let out a scream, and went quickly back inside through the house gate. He might have gone for help, but an AP jeep going by saw my frantic wave and agreed to take the boys to the hospital, what with notifying their parents, *et cetera*. I recognized the APs from the softball team. QED, I'm here ready to sign both reports."

He looked at her thoughtfully and brushed a hand over his crew cut. "All right for now. Here are your *first* statement and your *second* statement. I will tell you some conflicting descriptions have arisen. Therefore, be sure these reports are what you've related. If you want a legal opinion, I'll tell you where to go." He laughed suddenly at the way his final remark could be interpreted and turned to his work.

"Oh, pshaw. I'm betting the sergeants all have every word spelled correctly."

"Use the chair over there by the table. I'm doing some reports."

Rising from the chair a few minutes later, she walked over to hand in the signed reports. "They are accurate statements," she said. "Did the APs supervise everything taken from the shelter--except I think the cots were left there?"

He leaned back and commented, "Yes, they did. Things in this black market investigation are still unclear and cannot be subjected to the harmful gossip that you girls--"

"I'll have you know that I do not gossip. My folks taught me not even the cost of the electric bill should be discussed with the next-door neighbors," she interrupted sharply.

"--do so well. I can't give you any official version. What are you going to do about Lieutenant Hills?"

"Ugh. I think he's too pushy. Chilling. I'd prefer to keep away from him. It's unconscionable to think such things of me as he imports."

"If you do see him, just be your usual acerbic self. That attitude of yours is quite a protection. I noted your father's police career. Please realize that the Articles of War regarding military justice differ considerably from civilian laws. Just call me if you ever need to seek advice about relevant matters."

"I have not the slightest idea about what would be relevant but I'll keep that in mind." She sighed. "You're sitting in the catbird seat and, as you stated, I'm out here in left field. I am very reluctant about complying with your suggestion to date Hills, because I am circumspect when it comes to dating. I'll let you know later what I decide about seeing that lieutenant socially."

"I'll have Private Brooks call you to retrieve any pictures and negatives from your film that I don't need for the investigation." He waved her from the room.

Meg left the colonel's office and headed instinctively to her bus stop. It wasn't until her bus was pulling to the curb that she remembered her other errands for the day. It was hard to think about putting on Althea's bridal shower when her thoughts were filled with murder and black market sales. She pulled the cord and exited near the office buildings. The Snack Shack was nearby and offered pretty good hamburgers and root beer.

Eating slowly, Meg pondered the events and then called for a taxi to drive to the Castle Heights house to pick up the shower gift from Mrs. Worth. A maid handed her a brown carton. The woman hadn't even wrapped the gift!

Back in her room, Meg fished around inside the box to see if anything were worth wrapping for the bridal shower. The box contained some nice little lidded lacquer bowls that she placed on the lamp table. A dozen engraved ivory chopsticks were unearthed next, plus she found a brass stork with a missing leg swathed in dark cloth. A porcelain dog sitting upright with a lifted paw (and a missing ear) was next. Mainly, it looked like a box of trash. She touched a thick bundle of old brocade on the bottom, put things back into the box, and went to meet with Sharon Sheldon at the PX. Following that, they'd go off to the Village chapel to discuss the shower with the chaplain's assistant.

CHAPTER SEVENTEEN

For the next three days, Meg and Sharon Sheldon designed the bridal shower and sought items to buy for decorations and teatime. Sharon had informed Meg that the exchange rate could go up and down and that she had traded a hundred dollars at the Y350 current rate. Meg had also been given that rate; the costs would be split between them. Nothing at the PX caught their eyes as being pertinent to a bridal shower. Sharon agreed they should visit the chapel first before purchasing anything. Along the way to the chapel, Sharon commented, "Bill said Sergeant Calhoun Paley told him what you concluded and that it helped solve a crime. He said it was good work."

"Um-hmm," Meg muttered, pushing at the door into the front hall.

Given that nineteen ladies, including themselves, would be attending the shower, the seating and placement of tables were a bit difficult. The chaplain's assistant suggested that the big recreation room be arranged with two sets of chairs, set in a "U" shape, with side tables between every other chair. A larger table would serve as the crosspiece at the juncture of the two sides. That end one would hold gifts.

Althea could be perched at the table in a cushioned chair. The treats and drinks would be placed strategically beside each guest, and the low tables also had room for flower arrangements.

The food would consist of tea and coffee, cream, sugar, lemon slices, small cream puffs, sheet cake, cookies, and small scones from the commissary that they would visit after seeing to the arrangements in the chapel recreation room. When they left the chapel and entered the commissary, the smell of baking goods was wonderful. The baker at the commissary showed them some delicate mint candy flowers in assorted colors, and these were added to the menu. Two-dozen bakery goods should suffice, with the large cake to boot.

As they walked out of the commissary, Sharon joked, "Let's go to the local five and dime––or, to be accurate, the *go-sen* and *ju-sen,* Matzusakaya Department Store, and see what's there. I haven't bought a shower gift yet."

"*Hai, hai.*" Meg laughed at Sharon's translation.

Roaming the shops, they traded *yen* and *sen* for party favors and decorations. For favors, moving from one shop to another, they found small, varicolored silk fans, tiny Imari-ware cups, and plump, palm-sized red pincushions. Red is the color of joy in Japan, they were told at three different shops.

Most of the Japanese stores specialized in certain products. In one, they selected three Japanese dolls, posed upright in individual glass display boxes, for the winners of the afternoon's bridal shower games. The favors they purchased would grace individual place settings. Even after dividing up all their parcels, the two were quite loaded down.

"Well, we've covered all the bases, Sharon. Let's meet at the recreation room two hours before the shower starts. We have to make sure everything is in place," Meg suggested.

"All right. I'll see you at noon in ten days," Sharon replied

Meg had asked the chaplain's assistant, Cpl. Mitch Holland, if it were permissible for her to attend a funeral at the Japanese Catholic Church. He looked surprised and replied that the American and Japanese churches frequently traded choir performances and charity events. Churches were not off-limits: Occupation Forces were welcome at Japanese churches. She hesitated to ask him about how Christianity, Buddhism, and Shintoism coexisted in the Japanese culture. Then a vague memory of Lt. Hills stating that the Yamatas had sought their Christian relatives in Nagasaki before the war came to mind. Christianity had been here all the time but she'd failed to be aware of it. She just hadn't noticed church spires anywhere around town.

Until she received the invitation to the funeral for the boatman, Meg hadn't realized where the Catholic Church was located here in Nagoya, and there it appeared in front of the taxi she hired Thursday night. As Meg leaned over to sign the guest book inside the foyer to write "sorry for your loss," she had a sudden recollection of a wartime poster. It depicted a vicious Gen. Tojo, grinning evilly, shouting "SO SOLLY" (although she thought the Japanese pronounced the double "r" sound in "sorry" more like "sordy" than "solly").

She chose instead to write her name and "my sympathy to the family" before joining the people going through the family members' reception line. The women were standing behind the men and kept their eyes lowered while peeking at her. Fumiko did not acknowledge her presence.

The family members, when every guest was seated, walked to the front pews and were followed by an altar boy waving incense, a priest, and the casket being trundled in. Because the service was conducted in Latin, Meg spent her time looking at old dark paintings of Jesus on the cross, wobbling under the cross, being helped with the cross.

After the service, refreshments in another room were offered. There, more paintings of Jesus were displayed, speaking to children, handing out the five loaves and fishes to a multitude, curing Lazarus. They were the same pictures she had seen in Sunday school when she was little.

The mourners greeted her prettily; several men she hadn't known existed were presented to her, all bowing deeply. The man from the boat (the one arguing with the boatman who died) presented a bland smile and barely nodded. A taller man in a dark, elegant *kimono* was next to him. Neither Fumiko nor the oddly dressed woman from the cormorant trip appeared at the reception.

Mr. Yamata approached and quietly stated that the fried food on the table wouldn't make her sick. She tasted two items and declined a drink of tea as Mr. Yamata explained that this cathedral was in Aichi Prefecture, but the burial ground was in Gifu Prefecture where the boatman had lived. Hence, they were not following the hearse to the graveyard. He introduced her to the priest, Father Osaya, a portly, short round-faced man with thinning black hair.

"Fumiko seems withdrawn," Meg remarked. The men nodded.

Her father replied, his eyes downcast, "She is like a sumo wrestler stamping one foot and the other, but her feet are not sure which culture to land in--Japanese or American. We've been here nine years, all during the Japanese war with the U. S. but are now recovering and helping with solutions to some Occupation problems."

Meg nodded. "I'm certain we are grateful for such help, sir. May I use a telephone to call a taxi?"

"Let me give you our telephone number, too. If you have time, please call my daughter. I think she would like to get to know you better." He wrote both numbers on a paper program. She took it and was led to an office where she phoned for transportation.

Later that evening, the next unexpected invitation was a call from Sgt. Martin. "I'm on full round-the-clock duty this week, but next week I don't have evening duty. Would you like to go to the Brass Pile with me some evening next week?"

"Is that a nightclub?"

He chuckled. "No, it's a pile of brass household things that were collected for the war effort, to make ammunition and so on."

"Oh, like the newspapers and used grease my brothers collected. Wonder what happened to that stuff. Probably on a trash pile somewhere."

"Don't know. But here, people are allowed to scrounge in the brass for souvenirs. Have to wear old clothes and gloves; I'll bring gloves. How about Thursday night next week about 1800? We can grab a bite at the Snack Shack before we get dirty.

"Unusual idea but fascinating, too. I'll be ready, Marty."

CHAPTER EIGHTEEN

Her palm was no longer red and had scabbed over nicely. Betty Carnahan had stopped by one evening. She knocked just as Meg was shoving the wedge shaped top of a mucilage bottle against her left palm, trying to force the top slit open. It worked suddenly: a glob of glue squirted onto her palm. Meg answered the door holding her palm up.

Betty paled when her eyes saw the palm and gasped, "That's a horrible infection! We need to get you to the hospital pronto."

Meg laughed at her shocked expression, "No, no, see here." Picking up a piece of paper from the desk, she rubbed the mucilage from her hand.

"Oh, my. That threw a scare into my very bones," Betty said, fanning herself in an exaggerated manner with her own palm as she was sitting down. "Don't do that to me again, you hear?"

Meg promised that she wouldn't but had an amused smile every time she remembered the event. Healed, she visited the North Pool every morning the next week, going early to avoid sunburn as much as possible. The dependant children frequented the pool so she often waved to Janie and Josh Worth. Josh couldn't swim due to his wrist cast, but he did his best to pester Janie from the shallow end. In turn, Janie would splash water on him as she stroked by.

On the first Wednesday in August, Janie and Josh Worth approached her as she sat at the poolside. They were tanned and wet. She was freckled and dry.

"Should you be getting that cast wet?" she teased Josh with a grin.

"I'm getting it replaced this afternoon at the hospital so it doesn't matter. Father said so."

Janie said, "Miss Lowe, you remember that Lieutenant Johnny Hills we were talking with on the cormorant trip?"

"Yes."

"Yesterday evening, my father took us to eat at the field-grade officer's hotel, the Kanko Hotel."

"I've heard of a 'farmer out standing in his field,' but I never heard of field grade officers. Are they outstanding officers? Oh, I remember that your mother did mention that term."

Helpfully, Janie replied, "Just officers who are majors, light colonels, and bird colonels."

"I see, I think." Meg backed off the teasing. Perhaps Mrs. Worth had trained them to conform politely and without humor. She'd have to tread carefully around these dependant children of the military.

Janie spoke, "Afterwards, Josh and I went to the little ham radio station at the top of the hotel. We have to be quiet, but we can listen."

Josh raised his fist in front of his mouth and called, "Jig Two Roger Oboe Charlie, Roger, over and out."

Janie continued, "The ham radio fellow kept calling into the microphone. We stayed quiet in chairs along the wall and heard a return call passed along from various ham operators that originated from a town in California. When that Stateside ham operator found out that we were in Nagoya, his message to our radio operator was that Lieutenant Hills' parents had died in a car accident that very day."

"Miss Lowe?" Josh asked, concern in his voice, as Meg closed her eyes and put her hand over them.

"I am sorry to hear that," she replied slowly. The two students looked at her with troubled eyes, nodded in agreement, and wandered back to their friends.

Saddened by the news, gloomy thoughts chased themselves around her brain for the remainder of the day. She had been wrong to judge the Worth children too quickly as a bit uncaring. She had been wrong to summarily reject Lt. Johnny Hills even though the possibility that his stroking of her neck could have been lethal still made her shudder when she remembered that night after the dunking.

Jumping out of bed on Thursday morning, recalling that, during the prior evening's hypnagogic state, prior to falling completely asleep, suddenly the realizations, some certain conclusions, had sprung up. She concluded, to wit:

- the little wooden statue was of Jesus;
- the etching on its foot was a fish;
- yes, the fish symbol on his foot was exactly that which had been used by the harassed Roman sect of Christians and, likely, copied by the harassed Christians in Nagasaki;
- in addition, the "wisps of steam in the cave" she had hazily seen were probably the fish symbol;
- and, she had hurt her palm scraping it along the cave wall.

The wooden heirloom could date back to the time when Christians were expelled from Nagasaki in 1587 and went underground. Or, maybe from centuries later, when Christianity was allowed back in during the Meiji Empire. Surely it was Johnny's heirloom she had in her handkerchief.

And, the items in the box from Mrs. Worth might be from Mr. Yamata's inventory. She put the box on the lamp table and went through it again. That bundle of old brocade she had dismissed earlier turned out to be wrappings for four lovely Japanese dolls––maybe Mr. Yamata's Dolls' Festival items. The missing things that had been mentioned by Jones were general categories except for these dolls. She called for a taxi.

"Driver," she ordered quickly when the taxi arrived, "take me to the Headquarters Building. And then wait. I need to go to the commissary."

Racing inside the G2 office, she started trotting toward Col. Robbie Jones' door when Sgt. Duncan blocked her path. "Halt!" she ordered Meg.

"Look what I found, Laura," Meg cried.

"Place the box on the table and keep your hands where I can see them," came the clear orders.

The two noncoms looked on as Meg delved into the box. "Robbie, er, Colonel Jones must see these. Aren't these what Yamata-san is looking for, maybe?"

Pvt. Brooks started commenting, "Those look like the missing . . ."

Sgt. Duncan snapped, "Quiet, Private Brooks."

Col. Jones came from his office. "What is this commotion? Ah, you again. Your Lieutenant Hills came in a couple of hours after you left last time. He was able to give a better description than you did of the cormorant boat mishap. He described an argument he had overheard."

Meg held up her hand, palm out, and closed her eyes for a few seconds. "Yes, he told me about the threats as we drove home. It's a slippery memory. Some things I heard as I fell asleep in the back of the jeep, I guess. Seems the conversations going on behind his back had caught his attention, but he didn't know the people, other than just introducing himself to Fumiko and her cousin. Fumiko faced the railing with her back to him, eating a bowl of rice, placed it in a shelf and the chopsticks down her sleeves, and turned to him when he offered to show her a family heirloom. She had it in her hand when she saw me and waved."

She paused.

"Go on."

"He firmly believed that threats were directed at the boatman cousin about running things down the river. One fellow had demanded that the boat owner do something like that, and he responded that he could get an award from the Americans if that threat were reported to them."

"Why didn't you report that to me? That they tried to force the boatman into helping move stolen and black market goods on the waterways."

She shook her head. "Colonel, I had vague memories of what went on after I took a dunk in the drink. I told you that. I heard B-J and Lieutenant Hills mention how he had stopped thefts on the trains."

She grinned and changed the subject as she displayed the four little dolls in their brocade wrappings. "Here now, I've found something. These dolls are all elegant. Could they be what Mr. Yamata was missing?"

"Could be," Col. Jones said slowly. "Sergeant Duncan, would you see if that fishing trip film has been processed?"

She returned with a sheaf of photographs.

Col. Jones said, "These two pictures are from the boat. I wonder if you know the faces in the picture here? Lieutenant Hills reported that he didn't know anyone beforehand."

"I got them!" Meg crowed, paying no attention to the others as she examined the photographs; she was extremely excited and elated. The pictures had come out much better than she had hoped for with all that uneven lighting.

Three heads snapped toward her. "Got who?"

"The birds in the water. See? I didn't remember that I took that. Oh, goody goody for me."

"I asked about the faces, Miss Lowe," the colonel said.

She looked harder at the profiles on the left side. "This is Fumiko's uncle; he's the one who fell; this other thin faced man was visiting, I think, or he could also partly own the boat. This partly concealed face was that of a girl with a strange white face, white painted on eyebrows, and dark hair clipped off short, waving around an elegant fan. Name started with a 'K.'"

"She's a he."

Meg raised an eyebrow. Thinking "I can do that, too, see, mister Colonel Jones?"

He added, "Not a girl; Kikuyo-san is an actor with the Tokyo *Noh* Theater––plays female roles. He's been questioned about being involved in involuntary manslaughter, because his bamboo fan pierced the uncle's neck when everyone fell according to the Japanese police; he's probably out on bail."

"Nonsense. Bamboo? Not on your life. She-he-it didn't have a bamboo fan. It was an elaborate one unlike any I had seen before. Here, look, you can see silvery ribbing where he-she-it laid the fan over her-his-its right forearm as we all turned to watch the cormorant boat a-comin' in. Fumiko's hand is partly on it, too.

"At the time, I didn't notice that the fan looks silver in part. Also, I don't think now that thin-face partly owned the boat. He's dressed wrong, resembles the fellow who owns that shop by the Yamata's, the noodle shop, the shop flanked by theirs and the bathhouse. I noticed him when the bomb shelter/tunnel was being emptied week before last. He had melted back into his shop and then hurried up the street to that gated house. I told you about that when I explained how Josh Worth was injured."

"How can you be sure of such an identification? Distinguish these people?"

"My dad taught me to identify differences in the environment when we went hunting. Observe things. Be quiet. Wait. Set out decoys. Use a quacker."

Col. Jones pushed back his chair, rubbed his leg, rose, and limped to the window. "Sergeant Duncan, see if you can locate Sergeant Hagikawa to demand an autopsy report on the boatman. And, ask Lieutenant Mays to come here.

"We'll check out the actor and the Yamata daughter again. Miss Lowe, I have to keep these two pictures and negatives. I'm sure you can buy a postcard or a picture of cormorant birds somewhere. Moreover, I have kept the bomb shelter/tunnel pictures and negatives, but the rest of that roll is on Sergeant Duncan's desk for you," he said abruptly.

"All right, I took one out of my second story window that looked down on the street full of people streaming both ways. Back home, they'll think all the dark heads look like the branches of a blackberry bush!"

He waved toward the door.

She fumed at his lack of response but then chattered on. "I've been busy. I attended the funeral for Fumiko's boatman cousin at the Catholic Church. I had received an invitation, but Fumiko ignored me for some reason, wouldn't even meet my eye. She was grieving, I suppose. I didn't see the odd-looking actor, whom you said is an actress there, but that grey-faced man from the boat was there, and a lot of people I didn't know. We all signed a guest book; maybe you can have Mr. Yamata identify everyone from that." She gave him a sharp nod.

"Go on."

"Plus, Sharon and I have been busy with the shower plans. And then, Josh and Janie Worth told me that Lieutenant Hills' parents died. Had you heard?"

"No."

"What are you going to do with the items in the box I brought in? Mrs. Worth gave them to me for Althea's shower."

"I'll call Yamata-san to see if they match anything in the inventories. He was supposed to bring a list by yesterday. The little wooden *netsuke* is not his. Private Brooks, will you give the little wood statue and the earlier photographs to her as she leaves?"

Meg heard the dismissal and walked stiffly out to pick up the items and return to the taxicab. If he didn't want to hear about her activities leading up to her conclusion that the tiny statue was of Jesus, he could remain in ignorance.

She saw Cpl. Donna Aldrich in an office on the lower floor and poked her head in the door. "Hi, Donna. When do you take a break for lunch?"

"How about right now?"

"Fine idea. I have a taxi waiting. You name the place."

"Dismiss the taxi. We can eat pretty tasty stuff at the Snack Shack," Donna replied.

As they strolled toward the lunchroom, Meg commented, "I notice Laura Duncan wears a wedding ring but never says anything about her husband."

"It's sad. He went missing in the Pacific war in February 1945. I think he was a bombardier. A couple of months back some callous guy remarked that her hubby was probably having tea on some island with Amelia Earhart. Laura turned white, the only time I've seen her lose her composure, and slapped the guy. He promptly apologized. No one has asked her about him since, that I know of. The war was so close to being over when he disappeared. She still hopes even now, even though it's four years later."

"I see. I understand her better. Let's have a vanilla milkshake here at the Shack. I heard that when someone asked General MacArthur what kind of milkshake he'd like, he said, 'I'll take Manila.'"

"It is still too recent, though, to really laugh, Meg, about those jokes. I have trouble with the Willie and Joe cartoons that Mauldin draws, although I get them right here in my heart. Maybe in a few years my revulsion about flippancy will heal," Donna said, patting her chestnut hair down before replacing her hat. Her unusual blue eyes, flecked with darker, sapphire blue, were somber.

#

Back to the Chiyoda after lunch and a quick stop to buy some oranges, she shuddered as she alighted from the taxi. There was Lt. Johnny Hills leaning against a jeep, a white lily in a slender green vase in his hand. "Hiya, dear, I thought you'd be back by now. C'mon, I'll take you to dinner and a movie."

"I'm going to change clothes, and I'll put this flower on my desk. I already have a date tonight. And, Lieutenant, I'm uncomfortable going out in the evening with a fellow I hardly know."

He straightened and started for his jeep. "I see, Miss Lowe. I certainly understand. You've been here so many years that you already are acquainted with a lot of boys, heh?" He looked at her almost with disdain, if she read him correctly.

When she returned to the Chiyoda Hotel front door at 1800, Sgt. Martin was waiting for her with a Japanese taxi. A few feet down the street, she saw Lt. Hills sitting in his jeep, watching. His sunglasses hid his eyes, but his lip curled as he threw a salute in her direction.

"Wait a minute, Marty. I'll be right back." She remarked, looked at the jeep a minute. Then she ran over to the lieutenant's jeep and leaned down while digging in her purse.

"Johnny, I heard about your parents, and I'm so sorry."

"I was going to tell you about that tonight."

"Here, wait, here, is the heirloom doll I think you were looking for. It was caught in my clothes when I fell in the river that night," she explained, handing over the statue in its handkerchief wrapping. "I didn't find it right away, not until I was going to have my clothes laundered. When I saw you later, I didn't have it with me, because I gave it to Colonel Jones to see if it were the Yamata Doll's festival thing that had gone missing. Am I right? Is this the one you were looking for?"

Lt. Hills' hand trembled as he took hold of it. Unwrapping the cloth slowly, he stared, and immediately tears surged into his eyes, coursing down on either side of his sharp nose, running down his tan cheeks, from under the sunglasses.

"This is the only thing--the only thing in my side of the family . . . carved in Nagasaki in the last century . . . it was the only thing Grandma got from Great-grandpa when she was given to an Indian brave. Her brothers got everything

191

else in the Oregon ranch. Dad gave it to me to protect me through the war. And, it did."

He wiped his eyes on her handkerchief without apologizing for the unmanly breakdown. "I'm leaving in two days for my folks' funeral, and then I'll leave the Army for good and go back home to Oregon. Goodbye!!!" He yelled the last word; tossed her hanky out the window, surprising her, ground the gears, and took off.

#

"Here we go," Marty said, opening the door and ushering her out of the door gingerly as they left the Snack Shack. He had said little throughout the meal, asked no questions. He was evidently sensitive enough to notice that she was a little shaken emotionally by her confrontation with the fellow in the jeep.

He handed her some green gloves from a briefcase, opened the door of an old black Japanese taxi for her, climbed in the other side, and gave a map to the driver with the route marked. Wearing khakis and his holstered gun, he seemed at ease with their destination for the evening, although she still could not imagine what a Brass Pile would be.

Then it appeared, a tall heap of junk. The pile of smeared golden and greenish metal was still warm from the day's temperature. Marty stood with his hands on his hips surveying the junk, looking for something that was still intact and worthy of salvage.

Searching the Brass Pile perimeter, she found a tiny metal bowl with tripod legs and a lid. "What would this be for, do you think?"

"Oh, it looks like an incense burner."

"I was surprised you asked me for a date out of the blue, Marty," she said off hand. "I met you only a couple of times."

"I just thought we'd have a good time exploring. You know, the only reason you weren't shot when you did that ghostly *kimono* thing at the softball diamond is that the Japanese have a lot of ferocious looking characters. We've been taught to be careful how we react. You're still learning about the background here, I bet. Colonel Jones thought it was a good idea for me to ask you out."

She had a slight, knowing smile as she sat down to wait for Marty to finish sorting through the brass pile. So Jones had chosen someone to watch over me--or watch me? "I smelt that," Meg Lowe held the incense burner close to her nose.

PART THREE

DAI SECTION

CHAPTER NINETEEN

On Saturday, August 6, Sharon and Meg arrived at the chapel assembly room at noon and began setting out the chinaware, utensils, and food. Guests would be served first with coffee or tea in a cup on a saucer. The place cards were set on the low tables between the chairs, a lady's place at each side of the table.

The long serving tables each had a folded tablecloth ready to smooth and drape over the scarred wood surface. The commissary had delivered all the refreshments.

The angel food sheet cake was cut into 32 pieces. The icing featured a red heart enclosing the initials "R. J." and "A. A." Along the tablecloth were the little baked refreshments arranged neatly on platters with a flat fork nearby to use to pick them up to place on the cake plate each guest would be carrying.

"I didn't like those tacky flower arrangements the florist sent, and I'm going to complain. Putting three little flowers, one straight up, one on its side, and one leaning over. What kind of party bouquet is that?" Meg said.

"You simply must take a flower arranging class. The flower positions represent heaven, earth, and man. Very appropriate." Sharon glanced at the closest vase with approval.

"I'm still going to complain. I gave them a picture of what I wanted."

"Not worth it. The florist did a traditional arrangement on those pretty little flat vases. We'll each get four vases when we toss the flowers. You're still back home with the traditional way you've done things. Think local, think Japan."

"Sometimes that doesn't fit comfortably, I'll admit. Sometimes things are simply too strange, exotic, unusual, what you will."

"Here they come," Sharon said and moved toward the door to welcome Althea and two other ladies.

Hatted and gloved, suited and heeled, the guests arrived. Meg wondered how so many pretty hats had survived being stuffed in luggage. The servicewomen Sgt. Duncan and Cpl. Aldrich looked poised with their straight postures, pressed khakis, and overseas caps.

Each guest, after finding her name on a place card on the low tables and depositing a purse on the chair designated by the card's location, chose to mingle. Eventually, before sitting down for the bridal games and opening of gifts, each lady lined up for a coffee refill and for a piece of cake.

The bridal shower progressed as planned, with ladies circulating, gossiping about––no, make that discussing, *not* gossiping, *mister* Colonel Jones, sir––the murder of the commissary captain and the thefts, the black market. After guests had first taken a cup of coffee, a saucer, and a paper napkin, Meg shagged bits of information as she passed around the group with a tray of tiny cream puffs. She had loved those at Mrs. Fritz's party and was pleased that the cook who made them was still stationed at the commissary. The information she picked up was mostly about the thefts or servants.

The ladies were talking about the revelation of thieves in their midst.

"... my maid was dismissed, and I had to train a new ..."

"... all the Fritz servants were involved in the ..."

". . . that school janitor who was working at the commissary mornings, always fouling up the prices, and trying to cheat me out of money as though I can't add."

". . . I kept wondering why I couldn't find my gold earrings ..."

"... decided I left the little Darumi carving in the taxi ..."

Meg paid little attention to the comments near Althea. As Althea moved from each lady to greet the next, the conversation shifted to her wedding. Meg vaguely overheard comments such as "Congratulations" "Best wishes." "The Colonel's such an elegant man." "Are you going Stateside soon?" "Where's your honeymoon going to be?"

Meg moved around to the edge of the group to hear more gossip, that is, *discussion* of current events.

"In New York, we had cat burglars climbing in windows. These thieves had the effrontery to *live* in our houses?"

"Not many servants were organized in the houses located in the Villages, probably because of the gatekeepers."

"No, not all of the thieves were servants--some were just fake electricians and such taking little things out in their tool bags, like I lost my diamond pin."

". . . Captain Archer was stabbed and bloody in the school house."

"Ooh, where did you hear that? Don't tell me such gory tales! My kids have to have classes there. I'd like to ask Althea about that but this doesn't seem the proper setting to do so. I'll catch her later this week."

"The thieves were pretty well organized. Didn't steal worthless ..."

And some of the talk was directed with admiration at Cpl. Aldrich and Sgt. Duncan as they circulated. They were treated with the esteem given to warriors; the WAC and WAF were not ignored as though they were waifs, as Meg had feared, having observed that a severe protocol governed the military hierarchy. Duncan and Aldrich responded proudly to questions about their careers, although Laura said little about her work with Col. Jones.

Sharon Sheldon bade the ladies select cake and other refreshments and refill coffee cups before sitting down to play some games. They worked themselves into seats beside the tables. The conversations continued around the tables as they nibbled on the treats. But soon everyone quieted down as Sharon passed pencils and paper to the guests. Meg and Sharon seated themselves on either side of Althea at a long table in the loop of the "U" of chairs. They also took up pencil and paper and demonstrated instructions, as needed, for the bridal shower games.

Mrs. Leonard won the first contest. She had made the most anagrams from the names "Althea Ardmore Jones" printed at the top of individual cards. She had re-arranged the names in telegraphese words.

> Dear handsome Rajah, 'sole' mate, enamored dreamer.
> Thee and me adore as one heart,
>
> Eros

The group applauded and laughed. Mrs. Leonard bowed, opened her prize, and presented the doll in the glass case to Althea. The winners of the other two bridal shower games also presented the bride with their dolls. These dolls were standing up, clad in embroidered silk *kimonos* and *obis* and had elaborate hair-dos.

Althea opened her gifts and thanked each lady for her taste and thoughtfulness. Sharon kept a list of the gifts by the person's name, while Meg pulled the ribbons through a hole in a paper plate, ending up with a fake bouquet for Althea.

Meg's gift of the cloisonné vase brought oohs and aahs. Her admiration for the school principal had grown over the past few months, so Meg was happy that she had splurged on the vase when she first arrived. Running short of money now, she'd replaced Mrs. Worth's big box of "irradiated items" with two small linen handkerchiefs. A few days earlier, Meg had called Mrs. Worth to tell her the box ––not mentioning that it was mostly junk as far as she could tell––had been confiscated by the police. That revelation drew a frightened gasp from the woman, but Meg soothed her by saying that she'd replaced it with a gift of linen, "linen" being a nice term that covered a lot of possibilities. Mrs. Worth sent over Josh with two script dollars and her thanks. He had worn his Boy Scout badges to show Miss Lowe.

The two hostesses helped Althea Ardmore load the gifts into a taxi, replying to her effusive comments and gratitude with grins, and returned to clean up the room. Althea had joked,

"Off to be a wife,

Dealing with cooking and strife,

I have my new life!

That's a *haiku* for yo-u-u-u two!"

"What's a high-queue?" Meg asked.

"It's usually a *sublime* poem, mostly about nature or meditation. Has 17 syllables. Spelled *haiku*."

Meg dried the dishes while Sharon washed them. They were pleased with the afternoon's party––for the most part. When they had exhausted all shower talk, Meg found herself telling Sharon of her adventures during and after the cormorant trip. Sharon proved a good audience, gasping and exclaiming her disbelief. In response, Meg dramatized every grisly detail.

Sharon only stopped her when she finished the part about hurting her palm in the cave. She exclaimed, "You and I need a vacation after all the excitement. Bill and I and some others are going to climb Mt. Fuji next weekend. Why don't you come, too?"

"I'm really not into hiking and don't have shoes for it, but thanks. I like swimming." She wouldn't admit that the extra laundry bill, the buying of treats and favors for the shower, the *kimono* and fans for her mom, all had her pinching pennies, as if pennies were used here. Stingy spending *sen,* that was it. Already had been using the budget for the first week of August. No, anyway, climbing a mountain didn't sound like fun.

"We'll have you over to see the slides then, when we can. We're leaving for the States in late September," Sharon said.

"I keep seeing snapshots of that evening I fell off the boat, like a chimerical slide show, in my mind's eye. There were side tunnels marked with the Christian fish symbol. I thought at first they were wisps of steam. I also found that very fish mark on the bottom of a little statue that belonged to the lieutenant, and I gave it to him."

"Bill said that cave is marked Off-Limits."

"Well, Lieutenant Hills said he had explored it before."

"It was being used for black market goods recently, and the officers shut it down because of what Hills saw the night he took you and Sergeant. Gorman through it."

"Oh, you know all about it," Meg sounded disappointed. "Did Hills say anything to Bill about the Yamata girl? I have a sense something Hills told me might be important. I can't get a good grip on the memory. A lady this afternoon said something about a janitor working at the commissary."

"Don't know."

"Something funny happened with that Mrs. Worth I met on the trip. She tossed a box of junk at me for this bridal shower. She turns every sentence into a question? She said the box could be 'radiated?' and told me to come pick it up?" Meg laughed. "I took it to Colonel Jones' office and substituted those two linen handkerchiefs as her gift. That woman's skittish as a quail trying to keep danger away from a nest."

"Um, we don't use that word."

"Junk? Danger? Oh, radiated, irradiated. Pshaw! May we mention Pearl Harbor?" Meg said cynically.

"Hush!" Sharon scolded. "Things are censored, Meg. A friend of ours took two reels of movie film during a visit to Hiroshima and never received them back. It's necessary to be careful."

Meg's cheeks burned with anger--both at the thought of censorship and at being hushed. She bit back her retorts, however, not wanting to press her luck with Sharon's friendship. She steadied her voice to ask, "What happened to the Four Freedoms? FDR enunciated them as freedom of speech and expression, freedom of worship, freedom from want, and freedom from fear."

"Hush. We're dealing with diplomacy here and now in the Occupation."

An uncomfortable silence fell over the kitchen broken only by the sound of water splashing and china clanking and silverware clinking.

Sharon cleared her throat after a few minutes and broke the tension with a mild tone of voice saying, "To change the subject, you know that Bill and I are standing up with

Althea and Robbie two weeks from today. August is going to be busy so we need to do the tourist things in the next few weeks." She added, "Have you heard the Japanese proverb that those who have never climbed Mt. Fuji and those who have climbed it more than once fall into the category of fools." Sharon first admonished Meg in a severe tone--and then laughed at her expression of bewilderment.

Meg shook her head. She conveyed her visceral reaction in her stiff tone of voice, conveyed that the comment had not been met with amusement. "No problem there with that category--Colonel Jones already implied that I'm not intelligent enough to be let in on very much of what's happening. I know I'm not with the investigators. But, I'm floundering around at sea in the events without knowing what I'm diving for. Do I know something important about the thefts? The murder of Captain Archer? Am I really a fool? Enough of my whining. Now, I'll change the subject. You mentioned during our shopping spree that the exchange rate varies. Why is that?"

"I'll bet you took Economics 101 and 102." Meg nodded at Sharon's remark. "What you should have taken was Finance 101. Look at the kitchen appliances here by Mitsubishi. I have them also in my kitchen. Manufacturing is going great guns. I'm sure you've noticed all the bamboo scaffolding around town as reconstruction continues. As the local economy recovers, Japanese money will be worth more against the dollar. I look for it to be 250 *yen*, instead of 350, to the dollar anytime now. Eventually maybe on par with the dollar."

Meg nodded again. "It would be wise to exchange money now, I see." She muttered, "As if I had any to spare. Maybe I could get my cigarette ration and exchange Lucky Strikes for a *samurai* sword for Dad."

Sharon surveyed the commissary goods and remarked, "I'm surprised no one wanted tea. I can use these lemons, if you don't mind, Meg. Let's divide up the leftovers."

Meg replied, "You take more food, because there're two of you."

She'd just finished drying her hands when Cpl. Mitch Holland, the chaplain's assistant, came into the kitchen scolding, "You ladies didn't have to do the dishes. We have a janitor."

Sharon dried her hands on a towel and drained the sink. "Hello. I know you have a meeting here tonight, and there weren't all that many dishes. We're just about to split up the leftover food. Meg will take one of each, I'll take two, and you can have the rest to share with your staff. Could you use the tea?"

He nodded.

"Good. Now, let's fold up the chairs and put the tables back against the wall." Sharon moved toward the door.

"Oh, my," he rolled his eyes as he took a piece of cake. "That is tasty."

"What is the meeting tonight?" Meg asked.

"The Young People's group is meeting here--we're going to Gamagori Inn for a *sukiyaki* supper. Why don't you two come along? We have a big bus for the dozen or so young airmen and about fifteen teenage dependants. It'll be my treat--to repay your help and generosity."

Meg had been ready to decline, but if the corporal were going to pay . . . "I'd like that. I'd like to meet my students before the year starts."

Sharon paused a minute and then asked, "May I use your phone to call my husband? I don't know if he's available tonight."

She returned shortly and said Bill was free to go on the evening excursion.

"Didn't I see you and your husband on a float at the Fourth of July parade?" the corporal asked her.

"Yes, I was the Statue of Liberty. Boy, did my right arm get tired! My husband was one of the huddled masses yearning to be free."

"The food and fireworks were perfect. All that red, white and blue," Holland said.

"The float that won was really a work of art. Those frilly paper flowers the men had made covering the frame on the truck. And the entertainment was perfect––the booths, games, skits, music."

He agreed, saying, "The Japanese have so many festivals roaming the streets that it was extra fine to have one of our own. Even the crowning of a Queen, I forget that wife's name, was a charming ceremony. I liked the drum corps, too, although I'm glad I don't have to march anymore."

"Oh, Corporal. You should have seen the mess we almost piled into at the beginning. We assembled half a block outside of Nagoya Hall Park. The local policemen agreed to clear the street a block ahead as our two-block long parade moved, also they would be stopping cross-street traffic. My float was just behind the color guard at front; the drum corps was behind me. Unfortunately, just as we started off, a single-file stretch of pedi-cabs carrying gorgeous *geishas,* glancing languidly at the gawkers, were headed directly toward us."

Meg and Mitch grinned at the picture being described.

"People along the sidewalk stopped and swerved their heads left and right, watching the interesting dilemma, prepared to laugh. The color guard in front stopped and marched in place. I wiggled my left hand behind me, holding the Book of Laws, at the drum major, who caught on that something was wrong and trilled his whistle in a signal to his musicians."

"And did you avoid having to crash and crush them?" Meg asked.

"Yes. The head pedi-cab cycler, luckily, noticed us in time and swung into a narrow lane half a block ahead of us, followed by the entourage of wheeled *geishas*. You remember that our parade was as wide as the whole street. We weren't able to run narrowly through traffic like those Japanese boys who hoist palanquins over their shoulders, racing down the street howling."

Mitch said, "Whew, that had to have been a close call between the American parade and the Japanese column of *geishas* sailing by. I had not heard about but I can picture it. Pretty funny in retrospect, though. I bet you all laughed like crazy when you were breaking down the parade in the park. I'm glad we have some festivals like that to keep up our spirits."

Meg and Sharon left the chapel after thanking him for the use of the rec hall, waving good-bye, and promising to be back at 1800 hours.

CHAPTER TWENTY

That evening, Meg stood with the chapel's youth group and the Sheldons waiting to board the bus. Meg searched for something to say to the taciturn man. "Sharon said you're going home in September. Is your work all wound up?"

He eyed her. "The Tokyo War Crime Trials were over last year. The somewhat convoluted black market investigation is nearing finish. The Occupation Forces have done a lot for the population--extending the offshore limits for fishing, turning acreage of munitions' plants into farms, offering food rations, bringing back millions of men. The Russians were supposed to repatriate Japanese soldiers but have been lax plus we suspect they've taken some thousands of prisoners to their country."

"I wonder what the purpose of that is. Slave labor?"

He skirted the question. "Possibly. Leningrad has to be rebuilt. Russia lost a lot of men during the war even as it tried to pick the side of the victors."

"Yes, I've read that."

"And, a new form of Japanese government has been installed with a new constitution, and life has been returned to peaceful endeavors as much as it is possible for Occupation Forces to encourage. That's what we do."

Meg kidded, "I understand America's work here. But the first time I saw you was when you and Robbie Jones came out of the bathhouse behind those people who were so scared. Sometimes in southern Missouri or northern Arkansas, one sees wild turkeys flying into trees over the gravel banks of the White River. Their flight is one of nature's aerodynamic mysteries––their heavy bottoms hanging low, long necks stretched in front, some necks with wattles red and wrinkled, wings arrogantly out flung. That is exactly how those frightened Japanese looked, defying gravity as they levitated out the doors, streaming cloth behind them. You simply strolled out, fully clothed, from the bath house."

He merely nodded, stifling a yawn. "Probably." He waved to a couple of teenage boys who waved back.

Meg saw that one boy was Josh Worth. She spoke to Bill Sheldon again. "I took a picture as the activity erupted into the street, and it isn't in the packet Colonel Jones gave me back." She waited for his response. "Did it turn out?"

"It had some people in it none of our photographers had caught."

"Moreover," Meg added, "I took a picture of Sergeant Salchow counting his money, and that snapshot wasn't returned to me, either. I agreed only that the colonel could keep the pictures from down in the tunnel."

"No, Miss Lowe. It's part of our investigation." He turned to the group of kids and asked about their career plans.

Josh Worth came up and said hello. He introduced his fellow bird-watcher, Tory Torleone. Meg chatted about bird watching and asked Josh if he had seen the kingfisher before he fell from the tree.

"It was diving when a man appeared on the porch and handed something in a dark cloth to an old man sitting on a cushion. Whatever it was, the older man threw it in the pond, and the kingfisher veered away."

"Too bad. At least you guessed right about the type of bird it was. How's the wrist now?"

"Doing fine. I got a tan at the pool so my arm isn't so ghostly looking. The doctor said that I had just cracked a bone, but when he took the cast off it looked bad. The cast left the skin wrinkled and my muscles stiff."

"Swimming has helped, then even your hair is sunburned."

His eyes sparkled. "Yes, ma'am. Your hair looks different, too. Oops, Mother said I should not make personal remarks about ladies."

"Let's just say that we exchanged compliments. I don't mind telling you that I let my bangs grow out because they were too hot hanging over my forehead, that's all." She took her headband from her thick blonde hair, pulled a handful over her right eye, and asked him, "Think I could be a movie star?"

"You mean like Veronica Lake?"

"Um-hmm."

He snickered. "Oh, my yes. Well, we'll see you in school after Labor Day."

Another lad was gesturing to them; Josh introduced him as Sam Enders, and they sauntered off. Janie Worth came over to say hello and introduced two girls who had graduated the previous spring. Dressed in jeans and blouses, they looked like the college freshmen they would be in the fall. From their remarks, Meg concluded that no seniors would be enrolled in the high school this fall; ninth grade would be the biggest class with seven students.

Everybody boarded the bus, and the young people sang "ninety-nine bottles of beer on the wall" all the way through to a sad drawn-out "no more bottles" ending as they drew up in front of the inn. Meg hummed along and grinned as college memories surfaced in her mind––her party pals used to sing the same song. The singers must have timed the lyrics on an earlier trip for it to end as the bus braked to a halt.

Gamagori Hotel was located on Atsumi Bay. A few boats were out on the water, but the busload of Americans emptied quickly into the garden, some of them glancing at the boats lazily drifting.

The group from the chapel next entered a large foyer, after removing their shoes outside on the verandah. Cotton socks were provided for their feet. The dining room was austere, compared with the only Japanese dwelling she had been in––that is, compared with the Fritz's living room. No decorations or flowers were to be seen.

The floor had plump, dark colored cushions arranged on woven *tatami* mats around low tables; each table had a *hibachi* pot in the middle. Meg lowered herself to the cushion opposite Cpl. Holland while the Sheldons took the other two sides. Meg tried sitting on her knees, then her crossed legs in front . . . but that put her too far back from the low table. Neither position worked. She finally stretched her legs sideways, bent at the knees. Then looking around, she saw that the other Americans had pretty much copied that final pose.

Soon the *kimono*-clad cooks arrived, knelt at separate tables, and placed vegetables, strips of beef, and some soy sauce into a pan in each *hibachi*. A tub of rice was brought in for the cooks to allot among the guests' bowls. Glasses of water and cups of tea were offered. The chopsticks were made of pale wood.

Sharon demonstrated how to use the chopsticks and Meg did her best to follow her example, though she couldn't seem to keep the food clutched long enough to get it into her mouth. Sharon then gave verbal instructions. "Bottom one kept flat, top one manipulated up and down by the forefinger to be able to pick up a vegetable or to shove rice into your mouth."

Meg commented, "Not only is this the first time I have used chopsticks, but the first time in my life that I've eaten rice. Odd texture, no taste. I don't believe I've tasted soy sauce before, either. I'm used to sweet potatoes with brown sugar and spices or white Idaho potatoes with butter, salt, and pepper. I like those white ones raw sometimes, too."

"Always something touristy to experience here in Asia that I've never done before either," replied Cpl. Holland.

One airman, wearing khaki trousers and a white tee shirt, had brought in a portable record player. He strung a cord over to his table while his friend brought in a box of 78 speed vinyl records to play softly throughout the meal. The group of Americans ate and conversed, shifting around on the cushions trying to be comfortable. The meal went quickly.

The young people and Cpl. Holland streamed out of the room toward the piano in the lobby where there were sofas and chairs. The youngsters commenced harmonizing on Big Band songs. Someone played the piano accompaniment.

The adults--Sheldons and Meg--remained on their pillows. Meg stretched out her legs to one side, took off the white socks they had all been given to replace their shoes and wiggled her toes, bright red toenail polish glistening.

Sharon looked at Meg's feet. "Your feet are as small as my daughter's. She left some boots here that you could use to climb Fuji. It won't cost more than five dollars to go next weekend."

The *kimono*-clad cook seemed to pay no attention to them; however, she took longer to clean up their meal than those cooks at the other tables. She had no expression on her face nor did she look at them as she kept her head down, then finally rose and departed with the dishes. Cups, a teapot, and water bottles were left for the three at the low table.

"No, thank you. I'll just go on being in the category of fools. I appreciate the offer, but I don't go hiking unless I'm seeking a deer."

"And have you found a d-e-a-r?"

"My cat is named 'Dearie.' She always followed me around. Brought me mice. Mom says the cat actually misses me. As to a human dear, I correspond weekly with a fellow who started college the year I finished my undergraduate degree. He was wounded in the Pacific Theater but stayed in the Reserves at Ft. Leonard Wood and is now in St. Louis in law school. He has his eye on JAG, you know what that is?"

They nodded.

"I send him the *Pacific Stars and Stripes*. We're developing our Rules of Engagement," Meg smiled. "I told him I wanted to explore the Pacific Theater, and here I am, although I haven't seen a local Japanese *theater* show, as it were. Haven't been to the shrines or historic places, just cormorant fishing and on a trip around the bay."

"Too bad."

Bill turned to her, and inquired, "You did some hunting with your father?"

"Yes, sir, we went after game. I was even on a couple of posses because all the young men were off to war. That was scary. But what I really enjoyed was playing games like Monopoly and Chinese checkers. Unfortunately, my little brothers took the marbles outside and fired them at coons and squirrels. Something happened to the pieces of other games, too. We used wood chips painted different colors for houses and hotels. Never could find anything that would fit in the Chinese checkerboard. On the other side, of course, the board was regular checkers, thus we had one game that was still in good shape."

"Did your father ever discuss his cases with you?"

"Only if my twin brothers, Jeffrey and David, had gone outside to play. He brought up obscure circumstances in a case now and then and listened to Mom and me comment, suggest, question, point out aberrations."

"When you'd heard conversations from people around you gossiping about the case?"

"Yes, sir. Or maybe we noticed some discrepancy in his recital of events. It's hard to explain unless you've been there."

He laughed. "You might say I've been there and *am* there. Have you noticed any more southpaws in your perambulations since you saw Mrs. Fritz?"

"See, one of my brothers, David, is ambidextrous. He is left-handed, but teachers made him write with his right hand. The Japanese seem ambidextrous to a great extent, flipping fans and sleeves from hand to hand. I'd be hard put to say that a particular one is left-handed exclusively."

"Colonel Jones described what you and Lieutenant Hills had reported from the cormorant trip. By the way, Hills remembered a lot more than you did."

"I was half-conscious and sopping wet." Meg begged off. She'd had enough of people praising Hills' memory over hers.

"The cave is Off-Limits. Hills noticed that the side passages had been stacked with boxes. We raided the site; lo and behold, the boxes were full of black market goods, expensive artifacts, and food, probably all stolen."

Meg pondered and looked down. "I guess we were in a bit more danger than just getting drowned and messy."

"Yes, ma'am."

"Is that why Colonel Jones suggested that Sergeant Martin squire me around, carrying a pistol at his hip?"

"Yes, Meg. You could apply for a firearm but would be restricted in when and where you used it. You're caught up in a network investigation that you can't be told much about. Be very watchful until we have the deaths cleared up, as well as the black market thefts cleared up, too."

"I thought Captain Archer's and the boatman's deaths had been solved with Mrs. Fritz's admission about tossing a knife and that actor's arrest."

Sharon exclaimed, "Haven't you heard about what she's done?"

"No. Whom do you mean? What?"

Bill Sheldon sighed and curled his lips. "Mrs. Fritz has been telling everyone in hearing range that she was arrested falsely. She admits tossing the knife but left him alive and groaning. Mrs. Fritz was escorted to ZI, Stateside. She'll have a civilian defense attorney because she had the gall to get her Senator involved in what should be the military jurisdiction."

"No, I hadn't heard that. Well, is the actor arrested for the boatman's death?"

"Don't know. The boatman, too, was stabbed but obviously Mrs. Fritz didn't do that one either. That investigation by the Japanese police is ongoing, and we have only an ancillary role."

"Colonel Jones said the boatman was pierced with a piece of bamboo."

Laughter from the parlor interrupted them. Applause drowned out Bill's comment, but she saw his frown come and go quickly.

Sharon noticed his expression, also, and changed the subject. "Both our children are in college, and we need to be there for the huge family Thanksgiving celebration at my parents' farm. I'm taking some of the Japanese recipes for everyone to try. I love *tempura* and *sukiyaki* and rice and soy sauce."

Meg sipped from her cup. Something Johnny Hills had said about Fumiko was teasing her memory. "I remember," she exclaimed. "Lieutenant Hills said Fumiko Yamata was eating a bowl of rice with her back turned to us. She put her chopsticks into her sleeve. Could the stab have been done with a chopstick? They do seem to me to be rather too blunt and unwieldy, as I discovered this evening."

Bill Sheldon smoothed his face into a noncommittal expression. "I'll pass that tidbit along."

"A lady today mentioned something about the school janitor working in the commissary on Saturday mornings. Is that so?"

"Why do you ask?"

"It just popped into my head. After all, Fumiko Yamata is the only person other than myself who was around both murders, and she is the school janitor."

"We checked everyone thoroughly before we offered them jobs. Be careful what you say about where you were," he warned.

Meg took a sip of tea. "I'm always careful. I'm not a dumb blonde."

Sharon laughed and said, "One up on you, Bill."

Meg was silent as she ruminated a couple of minutes. "No, she wasn't working with Captain Archer that Saturday when I saw him at the commissary because that clerk put her hand over her mouth when she laughed, and Fumiko doesn't do that. I wasn't used to recognizing Japanese people back then, but I do remember that gesture when she made a mistake on the cash register."

"Don't know."

Meg prodded. "Wasn't Fumiko a *geisha* or something?"

"Where did you hear that?"

"Lieutenant Hills said she was forced into some *geisha* or acting job during the war years."

"Well, that's correct. Ended up, er, a concubine, you could say, of a high-ranking Japanese officer who's been found guilty and hanged. She was rescued in 1945 and returned to her father."

"No fooling? Fancy that."

"I don't mean to scoff, but you simply don't understand the terror dynamics that were present in war time Japan. It was a police state. You mustn't condemn them. We interviewed her after you and Lieutenant Hills mentioned she was on the cormorant boat, and she gave up the names of the two Japanese visitors. She seemed rather taken aback that both of you had revealed that she was on the boat. You yourself were the only American on the trip she had been acquainted with beforehand."

"What about Lieutenant Hills?"

"He'd stayed away from Gifu until that night . . . then thought maybe it was time he'd meet his male shirttail relations. She was introduced to him by them."

Meg said slowly, "I think Johnny also mentioned something about Mr. Yamata causing trouble for his relations by moving up to this area from Nagasaki just after the war with the United States started. Was he consigned to slavery, doing 'untouchable' jobs, being a pariah?"

"Yes. When we came into the area, he staggered into the Red Cross Hospital in nothing but a filthy little loin cloth, having been starved into skin and bones, looking nothing like the 1940 passport picture he shoved at the nurse before he collapsed. The passport picture, of course, had both his and his daughter's picture from years before pasted into it. He was fed and treated until he gained strength. He offered to help with translation, built himself a shack, sold rags, tore down the shack, built a store, made money, taught Japanese to Americans and English to Japanese, and bought a house near the store."

Cpl. Holland appeared to announce, "About time to go, folks. We like to be back in Nagoya by 2100 hours."

Meg persisted as they rose from the cushions, "But why was Mrs. Fritz dealing with the black market?"

Sharon responded, "Mrs. Fritz was stretched thin, what with all her activities and a sick husband."

Meg had an unkind thought, picturing the lady as being more like a concrete pillar than stretchable like an elastic girdle. "What happened to the things she took for food, and what happened to the food in the shelter? I'll bet she sold them through Mr. Yamata's shop and gave him a percentage."

"Most likely. However, Mrs. Fritz said that she intended to have the Japanese items she received sold at a silent auction on Monte Carlo night to help the school. Right now, we're keeping them under stout lock and key until her case is finished in the courts." Bill added, "Some of the donated food is going back into the shelter under the school. The source of those unopened cartons of cans remains unexplained, as does that of other American items."

Sharon argued, "Hold on now. You make it sound like a bad thing. First, she never saw it as dealing with the black market. Second, because the economy is picking up, we have decided to shut down the Food Bank. Elderly women are virtually the only ones who come by nowadays. The three of us who have been at the counter the last couple of weeks agree that it is wrong to have people swap valuable things. It would be better for us to simply hand out the boxes of rice, and let them make their own meals. Third, next Tuesday is the last day we're open. Any legitimate donations that are leftover we'll give to the orphanage and the Red Cross; and, we'll post a sign that the customers may seek help at the latter. Fourth, some of the food that is appropriate for an emergency, such as a typhoon or earthquake when children are in school, of course, we will retain and replace from time to time. Fifth, Yamata has claim on certain items that will soon be released to him but I don't know if Mrs. Fritz is due money from their sale."

Bill's face softened, for the first time since Meg met him, and he looked at his wife. "You teachers do know how to lecture."

Sharon looked at him in the same kind of glow, saying, "You betchum, Red Ryder."

Meg felt like an urchin with her face pressed to the window of a bakery shop, eying a wonderful confection, sugary affection. She cleared her throat. "We used to take venison, squirrel, rabbit to the orphanage or the insane asylum after we cleaned the meat."

Bill, paying no attention to her interjection, more resigned than irritated by Sharon's revelations, added to Meg, "Some of the items in the box you turned into Robbie were Yamata's. That broken eared dog with the upright paw he had taken because he felt sorry for the poor widowed mother--her husband died when their store had collapsed into rubble after an air raid.

"For most things, Yamata says he never asked for the provenance, just estimated the worth, noted name, and sent a voucher to Mrs. Fritz at the stall," Bill revealed. "When we moved the tunnel items to a warehouse, there were items that he maintains he had never seen before, and things of value he was missing. He was somewhat vague, unusually so, given the circumstances. That led us to scrutinize local people who worked in various American homes or offices. We still don't know how the black market underground messages and wares are conveyed, especially around and out of the American Village and Castle Heights housing areas."

Meg said, "Sergeant Paley, Fumiko Yamata, and I heard what sounded like a radio going by when we were in the janitor's closet the day Captain Archer was killed. Maybe it was a walkie-talkie. Or maybe it was somebody stringing a cord between two paper cups the way my friend across the street and I did in elementary school."

Sharon laughed in recognition of the childhood telephone system.

Bill wasn't amused. "Your humor continues to be misplaced. We have two deaths and many thefts. Any servant who had been given clearance earlier and was subsequently identified from Yamata-san's inventory list, was then dismissed forthwith after being fined. One American from the motor pool was IDed, but we still don't have the organizer of the local gang," Bill said. Then he insinuated blame by noting, "Your fingerprints were on several chests and boxes."

"I always admitted that I'd looked into things when I first went into the bomb shelter. I expect they'd be on everything I'd moved by until I stumbled on the body. I've been meaning to ask, was Sergeant Salchow involved?"

"*No.*"

"All right. Now from what y'all have described, I understand how the swap meet shenanigans work. Thanks for the clarification of what Colonel Jones had mentioned a while back. I discern that some of those items––medical supplies, tires--weren't swapped, but swiped, as Colonel. Jones calls it. But, how paid? How communicated? How transported? Why don't you call Sergeant Billie-Jo Gorman at Komaki and ask her how Lieutenant Hills found the stuff that was stolen from her?" Meg said, lifting her blond bangs and blinking in perturbation.

"PEOPLE!" called Holland in a bellow that did catch their attention.

Bill Sheldon glanced at Meg as they walked outside, stretched his lanky body over, and held Sharon's hand.

Back in the bus to listen to "ninety-nine bottles of beer" all the way to the American Village. Sigh. Meg hummed along while she was sorting out her impressions of the evening's conversation. Apparently, things had quieted down in regard to thefts, the black market, movements of stolen property, and the two deaths.

CHAPTER TWENTY-ONE

On Sunday morning, her next-door neighbor, Betty Carnahan, knocked gently on the door and said, "Wake up! It's time to go to church."

"Give me 15 minutes," Meg replied, stretching her arms and rising from the crumpled sheets.

She ran the bath water as she peeled an orange, then brushed her teeth and combed her hair. After bathing, she put on clothing already worn a couple of times. Dressed in her chintz blouse and skirt and hose and wedgies, she tapped on Betty's door. Betty had a big smile when she answered the door and beamed, "My husband is being transferred here from the Philippines next week. I'm so happy." She grabbed Meg's shoulders and hugged her.

"I had noticed your wedding ring, the one with the huge diamond that's digging into my neck."

Betty laughed at her jibe and explained. "We knew he would be stationed somewhere in Japan, and that's why I came over from the States. We didn't expect he would be assigned to the Nagoya Base Hospital. Thought I'd be the one who'd have to move. I'll apply for dependant housing here. Hope we get a Japanese rehab." Her dimples flashed. "Let's go thank God."

After the service, they strolled back toward the hotel chatting about the Japanese surroundings they were passing. After a pause, Meg yawned.

"What have you been doing? How's your palm?" Betty inquired.

"Oh, I forgot to return your antiseptic compound that worked so well. The scratch did fester a bit after I swam in the bay. Oh, and I've remembered where I hurt myself. I was touching my hand along the wall of a cave."

Startled, Betty said, "Bats leave droppings, guano, all over. It's fortuitous that we started treating it right away. You were on that cormorant trip when the Japanese fellow was murdered, weren't you? The nurse on that trip, Lieutenant Wanda Norton, works with me and mentioned that an American girl fell into the river and caught a ride home, but she didn't know your name. You welcomed slimy things in that river, too, my friend."

"Yes, and thanks to you, and more thanks to you, no worse infection occurred in my wound that you wound with a dressing. And, now I heard the cave is a storehouse for black market stuff. Rumors about stolen stuff, too. Stolen from Americans."

"Oh, that black market problem. Although we thought the hospital supplies were secure, some have gone missing. Don't worry about what I gave you. I am allowed to check out the items I used on your hand. We heard the rumors, too, and have installed better locks on the supply closet."

Betty waved the black market problem away with a gesture and changed the subject. "Let's have lunch, then I'm going to take a nap and write to Dean, Dizzy Dean I call him. He is a humorous fellow for such a busy physician. Tell me, what is a 'heteronym'? I can't find it in my little dictionary."

"Well, you need two words that are spelled the same but are pronounced differently and have different meetings. I mentioned 'wound' and 'wound.' There's, say, 'I would consummate the deal if the other guy weren't such a consummate liar.' Or, I might be in a 'pique if you don't admire my *pique* dress.'"

"That's hilarious. I'll write that to Dean."

Meg insisted on stopping by the florist, having the clerk pull out the picture of a bouquets she had left with them days earlier on the bridal shower shopping trip, and registered her complaint concerning what they had actually delivered. The clerk was flustered. Betty stayed back a bit embarrassed: she thought the flowers had been charming.

Meg, later that afternoon, curled up in a chair with a notepad and pencil. With a grin lighting up her face, she considered making up titles that she hoped would mess with the black market murdering scoundrels, get their goat. She tapped the eraser against her lip and started composing *The Lowe-down on the Wisenheimer Kids' Ichi-ban Book List:*

"Sixteen Yen on a Dead Man's Chest"

"The Woman in the Black Shoppe"

"Man of Seven Fables"

"Grim Ferry Tales"

"Two Down and Out"

"Statue of Limitations"

"The Case of Aichi Fingers"

"Noh Mask, No Gain"

"Eight Views of Fumiyamata"

"Bomb Shelters and Peacetime Uses"

"What Goes Down Must Come Up" (especially if one plunges into a river).

As soon as she had finished, Meg composed a letter home. If censors were reading mail, a big "if" admittedly, she would be elliptical in asking for advice.

> *Dear Folks and the twin menaces,*
>
> *The weather is great but I have Fibber McGee's closet with the contents collapsing, and the world keeps on trucking. Post-war living reminds me of using our black ration coupons for food at that market, White Buyers.*
>
> *I can picture Tom and Jerry going after each other, as usual. Certain fat cats are certain to be around, like here.*
>
> *Am enclosing a selection of books they should read for amusement, and I want to know if they have any suggestions for additional reading.*
>
> *Love to all,*
> *Margaret*

The salutation and signature were signals for "attention, please"; the hints were of black marketeering; the opening comment indicated being smothered by events; giving her brothers the names of cartoon characters allowed for more hints about people being chased.

Before sealing the book list into her weekly letter home, she made three copies with her fountain pen, refilled the pen, leaving her inkbottle close to empty. Have to remember to buy both black and blue ink. She tucked one list into the little brocade purse and another into her olive-green satchel. The third she left on her desk under the phone. The telephone rang just as she was replacing the receiver, making her jump.

"Hello, Meg, this is B-J, Sergeant Billie-Jo Gorman. I won't be seeing you for a while. I'm going TDY to Tachikawa Air Base, help them out. Get some *materiel* organized."

"Oh." Meg frowned at the phone, although she knew B-J would ignore her expression if she could see it.

The sergeant plowed ahead cheerily. "I'm sorry I haven't called earlier after our adventures over hill, over dale, over river and bay. A Colonel Jones called me the other day and wanted to know who fell in what order on top of the boatman. I shut my eyes and recalled that the two women fell on his body crosswise, and that a man fell on the poor guy's arm. What's going on?"

"The boatman died, and it isn't clear why."

"You don't say? Anyway, here's what's really curious. The other day I was on a bus and I saw you and I swear I saw that lady with the shaved eyebrows––the same lady who fell on top of the deceased boatman––following you."

"When did you see me?" Meg asked.

"Oh, a day or two ago. You were with a gal wearing a pompadour as her hair-do. Doesn't she realize that hairstyle went out years ago? We're way past the short skirts, padded shoulders, and pompadours of the war years."

Meg said stiffly, "I'm certain she is quite comfortable with herself."

"Sure she is. Cheese and crackers got all muddy. Take it easy! I bet you still use pin curls and get a Toni permanent. I've told you a short haircut like mine is the easiest fashion to take care of. Anyway, when you left a store, she this lady–– the one from the boat, not the one with the pompadour–– she moved after you from the front of a stall, then stopped in front of another store when you went into one further down the street, as if she were waiting for you. I don't know; it could be nothing. Maybe she wanted some hints on how to use cosmetics? Or a Toni? My bus was stopped at the intersection, and I was watching for you to look my way, but you didn't." B-J Gorman laughed. "Maybe worse, you need to watch out, Yank, the rebs is a'coming' after youse, Scarlett."

A twinge of terror threw Meg for a second. "I'll watch for her and give her some pointers, mayhap includin' mah rifle," she managed to joke. "Have a good time down sou-uth at Tara."

Disconnecting the phone, Meg pondered the information. Maybe the cautions she'd been receiving did have some merit. Looking around the room, she suddenly sensed that items were not where she had left them yesterday. She turned to the closet and, indeed, some clothes were in reverse order of what she preferred. Nothing seemed different in the bureau drawers but there was other evidence someone had gone through some of her things. But why?

The trunk that held items for her mom had also been disarranged a little. One of the ornate fans was missing. Too late, she dug out a key and locked the trunk. Were people looking for the little trinket that belonged to Lt. Hills? If so, too bad.

The ringing telephone caught her again. She grabbed the receiver. "Hello!" Maybe she could ask that arrogant B-J what to do but it wasn't B-J calling this time.

"Hi, Meg, Marty here. I'm off next Tuesday and Wednesday during the day times. Would you like to go to the zoo?"

Meg was still caught in B-J's revelations about that shaved-eyebrow lady and had to re-capture her attention to respond to the unexpected voice. She took a deep breath and then replied slowly, "I have a meeting at the American School on Tuesday morning at 0800. It'll be over by noon. Yes, let's do that zoo Tuesday afternoon. I'll be ready at the

hotel by 1300 hours. Ha, I'm talking military times again."
She hoped she sounded more pleasant than she felt.

She put down the phone and remembered a phone call she needed to make. Digging in her purse, she located the slip of paper that Mr. Yamata had written his phone number on, and she dialed.

"*Mosh moshi.*"

"This is Miss Lowe. Is Fumiko there?"

"No Miss Dowe here." The phone slammed down.

Thinking perhaps she had misdialed, she tried 45-555 again, but the same answer was given. She shrugged and tossed the paper into the wastebasket.

#

Before Meg left for the schoolhouse early Tuesday morning, she slipped a scrap of paper into the door latch. If the paper were gone when she returned, she would know someone had been in her room uninvited because the maid service was not scheduled on Tuesdays. She wished she could set a real trap for the snoops and had tried to figure out how to rig up something to trigger her camera when they opened the door, but engineering had never been her strongest subject. Her brothers could figure something out for sure as they had caught her in many a trap.

Classes were drawing closer, and so Miss Margaret Lowe lugged her Durant book to the school. At her desk, she read about the way Japanese artisans manufactured their lacquer ware, cloisonné, silk cloth, and fans. On the way to her classroom, she had retrieved some glue from the supply closet along with a packet of paper (signing the items out on the inventory sheet, naturally).

At eight o'clock, she left the book open at the description of lacquer trees (which, surprising to her, were tapped for sap like maple trees were) and went down to the meeting in the lounge. She placed her purse in the bottom drawer and shoved it in to lock it. She had been doing that since Althea showed her how to lock it by pulling out the top drawer first and pushing the top drawer in last.

Miss Ardmore introduced the President of the School Board, Colonel Smithson, Fifth Air Force, as the person who had arranged the Monte Carlo nights during the previous years. He was a pleasant fellow and, in turn, introduced another Fifth Air Force colonel, Blythe, and an Eighth Army major, Warson, as the other members of the School Board.

Smithson reported, "We will have about forty-four seventh through eleventh high school students next year, more than twice that in elementary grades, and a total of fifty-two so far in the morning/afternoon kindergartens, located in Quonset huts on the grounds." He finished his short speech with an accolade on the greatness and importance of their institution and invited the teachers to introduce themselves.

Temporary principal and science teacher, Miss Althea Ardmore (who would be Mrs. Jones before school starts, she smiled) handed out the schedule of classes and called on each teacher in turn.

Journalism, speech, English: Miss Arvada Nordstad

Physical Education, incoming principal: Mr. Lewis Hines

Latin, trig, algebra: Miss Matilda Patrick

History, English, geography: Miss Margaret Lowe

Temporary Substitute teacher: Mrs. Sharon Sheldon

Grades 1-6 or kindergarten: Mrs. Cynthia Ranger, Mrs. Felicity Enders, Mr. Vernon Lloyd, Miss Tamara Talbot, Mrs. Zelda Down, and Miss Chloe Volker.

On the cormorant trip, Meg had met the first two elementary school teachers who were introduced. She had seen the other single ladies at the Chiyoda Hotel dining room.

Col. Smithson smiled at each teacher, as did the other people in the room. He announced that the dedication of the Nagoya American School would be in November. Chuckling, he noted that two years ago, when the school first opened and organizing was frantic and messy, Coca Cola had donated a gross of pencils, and the principal scrounged paper the Navy had deposited––and abandoned––on the docks of Nagoya Harbor. They had about two-dozen students in junior and senior high school that first year of the Nagoya American School.

This year, he was going to donate his copies of *National Geographic* to the geography department and launch another drive for book donations. The drive was being announced in the *Nagoya Nugget*. Moreover, the school already had ample supplies because money had been left over from last year's funds.

Mr. Hines would become principal while Miss Ardmore filled in at first.

Next, the Japanese helpers were introduced: secretary, librarian, two janitors (Fumiko was not one of them), and caretaker for the grounds. They and the faculty were all dismissed with best wishes for the school year as well as the remaining days of summer vacation. The two principals remained behind for a closed session on the budget.

Not having known a man who taught elementary children, Meg greeted Vernon Lloyd over coffee served in the teachers' lounge. "Your training for elementary school education is unusual," she said.

"I'm working on my dissertation. The subject will be describing the rote and recitation methods by which Japanese children learn nearly two thousand ideographs by the sixth grade. Our American schools likewise utilize rote learning in a few subjects. I have the comparative data for those. I spent an extra year learning formal Japanese. I'm pretty sure that I can move into the daily argot."

"Let me know if I can help. I don't have their language, but I can type English."

"That I will remember. Thank you."

Meg had met the rest of the high school teachers in her journeys to the school and found them charismatic for the most part. With the years of teaching experience represented in this group, a fine year of pedagogy loomed ahead. A support group of like-minded professionals in education, she realized, was similar to that shared by the members of a military unit. If you want some guys to charge a machine-gun nest, you don't want the plan debated, the guys sniping or smiting each other, but the duties executed by a unified front.

Upstairs, Meg stood with her hands on her hips and stared at the purse in her desk drawer. It had been flipped over. Meg shook her head, removed it and walked downstairs. Meg pulled Sharon aside on the front walk and showed her the letter she'd received from the florist the day before:

Madam:

 We appreciate you kindly give us order for flower yesterday Saturday. We trie our best and that's all we could. Earnestly looking forward to your further orders.

Flowers Store

Sharon signaled, "Now, now, student," with an admonishing finger wave and said she thought Meg had been wrong to complain, but she grinned at the letter. Indeed, she was going to have Althea order the wedding flowers from that sweet, polite storeowner.

Meg hurried to catch up with the other single ladies and continue the conversations about achievements of earlier classes they had led. For the moment, she completely forgot about black market doings and bodily harm to men she'd been near. This group of teachers was articulate and did promise to offer a great year of adventure and companionship.

The slip of paper was still in the door latch. No one had entered her private space.

CHAPTER TWENTY-TWO

Marty arrived with the ubiquitous holster on his belt and smiled when he saw her wearing her usual blouse and pedal pushers and huaraches and carrying her satchel.

Higashiyama Park Zoo covered several acres with the usual animals––monkeys, lions, elephants––cloistered in areas separated by groves of trees. The weather was extra fine, Meg thought, as she and Marty walked the hundreds of feet between exhibits with the flowing crowds of families.

Japanese children crowded around a cage featuring an "English Pig." "I guess that isn't *really* meant to be an insult," Marty said, "although they could have used the scientific name. English Swine, of course, would have been somewhat worse."

Marty related that when the Salt Lake City Zoo had contributed a lion, signs sprang up all over the city saying, "WELCOME RION." For weeks before the lion's arrival, streetcars were decorated with streamers and placards in the "rion's" honor.

At an enclosure, five young boys in dark school uniforms sat atop an elephant, clutching on the grey hide, trying not to fall off. Two other elephants were doing tricks, walking across small low stools. One stopped, took its left front foot and right back foot off a stool, and balanced. After placing all four feet back on the stool, it then lifted its two back feet into the air.

Meg backed up to take pictures of the elephants for her brothers and bumped into a Japanese couple behind her. "I'm sorry," she apologized. They sauntered away as Meg called Marty over to hold her satchel purse.

"I've never seen an act like that before. Those elephants have been well trained. I wonder where they spent the war," Meg said.

"I heard almost all of the animals were eaten, and the zoo has been gradually building the population back up."

"I bet elephant meat has a lot of fat in it, like possums we ate back home. Wonder if it is tough like dried jerky. All that muscle having to move a ton of flesh around."

"I never heard and don't want to find out by trying it. I wish they had a cotton-candy machine. Maybe I should buy one of those barbecued grasshoppers from that vendor over there."

Meg laughed and said, "I brought some desserts left over from a bridal shower Saturday. Let's go sit on a bench."

"That seat looks too dirty to sit on."

"I have a scarf; I'll spread it on the bench." She dismissed his complaint with a little shake of her head and produced the scarf, spreading it with a regal flourish on the bench.

The bag of food provided an excuse for a welcome interlude after they'd walked for the better part of two hours deep into the zoo grounds. They watched the crowds go by on the way to the merry-go-round or to other animal exhibits.

"Where are you from?" asked Meg.

"My dad died when I was little and my mom moved us from Moberly, Missouri. We moved to Minnesota, across the Red River from Fargo. Her family lived there. I loved it when I was young––ice-skating and hockey, tobogganing and cross-country skiing all winter long."

"Weren't you lucky to find joy in that long winter? Where I come from, we get a coupla snowballs in winter––and a coupla sunburns in the summer. Not months of a single kind of weather."

Marty nodded. "As I said, I was young. Too, we had great teachers at school although probably not as good as you," he teased.

Meg punched him in the shoulder.

"I liked every class, including art, but I haven't studied much of anything since then except military manuals. I really wish I could take some of those six-week classes at night, but we APs move through three five-day shifts over 15 days. I do go on my off-duty hours to the craft shop by the Comet Club. I like to work with wood and plastic and clay."

"What kinds of things do you make?"

"Mainly, jigsaw puzzles to amuse my grandparents during the long winter. After I was drafted, I was stationed in camps in warm areas like southern California. I'm not sure I would like those winters much any more."

He took a bite of cake and a sip from the canteen of water. He asked, "Where is Nagoya in relation to the U. S.? It's nice here."

"We're straight across the Pacific Ocean, a little north from the Los Angeles area on the west coast." She waved her hand in the general direction of North America.

Marty reminisced, "I left from Long Beach, a town by Los Angeles. While I was waiting to be shipped out, I took a tour of MGM studios. It reminded of the buildings back home that are situated on the flat plains; they resemble stage sets, a Potemkin village. Now that I've lived in climates that are warmer in more months of the year, I don't think I'd enjoy blizzards. Huge snowstorms come from September through May while we huddled in those houses, or tried to beat a storm back into the house. I do miss being able to see for miles, unlike the opposite, being cooped up in something like these tiny Japanese gardens. The teeny pond, stepping stone paths winding around a lantern, leave me wanting to beat it out of the place.

"My girlfriend and I are going to move to southern Iowa and grow corn when I get out in 14 years. She's blonde like you but taller. Her name's Ingrid Gjervold. I gave her my high school ring when I was drafted after I graduated in '44. Our prom was exactly a month before D-Day as it turned out. She was just in 10th grade. She wears my ring around her neck," he chuckled, adding, "although when the Red River floods their farm, she's afraid she'll lose it putting up sandbags, so she fastens it to the post in the hayloft."

He was lost in "rememory" for a minute, smiling, staring off into space.

"My guy's in law school," Meg said. "His name is Walt Raleigh. Before you ask, yes, his first name is Walter; he's originally from Winston-Salem in North Carolina. He didn't like Wally or Walter, and prevailed with just plain Walt. I signed up for two years here, because he can finish law school while I'm gone. We're not engaged yet, just promised."

"Where did you grow up?" he asked.

"The Show-me State, Missouri. And, that means I can ask for clarification about any and everything, because you have to *show* me it's correct."

"Why do you call it 'Missoura?'"

"I think it depends on where you were from, what part of the state, and when you lived there. What is Harry Truman's favorite piano piece?" Meg teased.

236

"*The Missoura Waltz*. Oh, I get it. Well, my mom pronounces it Missouri, and so shall I."

"Back to asking for how things work. For example, I don't understand how you APs and Colonel Jones work together?" Meg wondered, interest lighting up her face.

"There's law enforcement, and there're investigators. Our work frequently coincides."

Meg commented, "I haven't seen Phillip lately."

"You mean Phil Tyler? His first name is Theophilus, not Phillip. When he was little, kids would make rhymes such as 'Theophilus is marvelous but looks like an octopus.' That did not make him happy. Now, my first name is Marvin. The chant would be 'Marvin isn't starvin', he's down in Eden's garden.' That infuriated my mother who is a staunch Lutheran. Obvious therefore why we both prefer our nicknames. I can't imagine that anyone could make up a rhyme to go with Margaret, but Meg would be easy . . ."

"Don't even try, buddy. I wondered about him because he sneers at me for some reason. Now I have another question for you. I think my hotel room has been searched. What should I do?"

"Don't you lock it?"

"Of course. But the front desk has a key, and the maid has a key. I don't always lock it when I go down to lunch or supper or when I'm in it. This morning I put my purse in my schoolroom desk drawer that opens only if I pull out the top drawer first. I came back for it after the meeting. It wasn't placed the way I had left it. I didn't see anyone in the school except our staff. We were meeting each other in a downstairs room."

"Is anything missing from your purse?"

"No, but you people seem to think I'm being followed for some reason or in danger, correct? Or is it just maids dusting my things that are moving things around?"

"Well, now, Meg, if I were you I wouldn't go anywhere alone, strolling the streets in weird outfits, taking pictures without noticing what's going on around you." His voice took on a commanding tone. His shoulders pulled back at attention.

"I have another more likely reason why they seek me out. I'm followed because they think I'm cute as a bug's ear. Marty, I'm always aware of my surroundings. I used to go hunting with Dad for wild, sometimes dangerous, animals. I think I'll get a weapon and go to the hunting park."

"You're welcome to try to qualify, but I wouldn't bet on it. And hunting season is only in midwinter." Now his voice was somewhat haughty, superior.

"I'll bet you a *yen* I would qualify for a permit." She wrapped up the paper bag and put it in her satchel. She tried to capture the earlier ease she had felt in his presence. "I really like the two brass storks you found at the Brass Pile and gave to me. They polished up pretty well, even though a leg is missing on one and a bit of the head on the other."

"They're cranes. Symbolize long life, like turtles and such in Japanese folklore. Lucky for long life."

"I put them on my desk. This noon I noticed they were not where I'd placed them."

"Just someone dusting the desk, probably. I'll mention these intrusions to Colonel Jones."

"I don't mind if you do."

"All right now. This is my afternoon off. Would you rather take a boat and go for a row around the lake or go see the statues of dinosaurs?"

"Let's go row a boat. Which direction is the lake?"

"On the other side of grove, that-a-way. Let's take a short-cut through the forest."

He started off through the grass and trees, pushed aside tree limbs and held back bush twigs for Meg to walk through, but he suddenly stopped. As he turned around, Meg saw that his face had hardened, looked grim and stern, and her heart speeded up with fear as he spoke.

"Turn around and go back quickly. There's an unexploded bomb in there." His military training was back in high gear. She obeyed with alacrity.

Back at the path, he looked both directions, sited their location on the path, by look of particular shapes of nearby trees, requested her green headband and placed it on a tree limb, behind the trunk.

Meg felt her feet tremble and stumbled. "Did the bomb go off?" she squeaked.

"No. I think we just had an earthquake tremor. The town of Fujiya had a bad earthquake about fourteen months ago, and we couldn't fail to recognize an earthquake after what we felt clear over here in Nagoya that time."

Her first earthquake––she'd been warned about them and had expected something a bit worse––like throwing her flat on the ground. She wondered what it would feel like from inside the earth, or inside the tunnels under the school perhaps.

He interrupted her musing. "We need to find a phone, and I don't remember seeing any; did you?"

Meg said, "No. Whom would you need to call?"

"Bomb disposal, of course," he replied, preternaturally calm. "Let's hit the road. The evening comes on fast here, and this has to be done quietly and safely. I've heard you spoken of as being discreet. Act that way about this, okay?"

Walking swiftly, they reached the street and took a jam-packed tram to the central area. He signaled to a taxi and gave directions to the Chiyoda Hotel and AP office, saying, "I'll take care of this. Anything you want to do tomorrow?"

She considered. "What is going to happen about the bomb? Is it going to go off when the ordinance people find it?"

"I doubt it. Not your problem. About tomorrow?"

She stilled her heart and eventually responded, "I'd like to visit the cloisonné, Noritake China, and silkworm factories."

"I'll check if there're any tours tomorrow. I'll find out what days they are held, if not tomorrow and see if we'd have the same schedule." He was determined to keep her mind away from the bomb, Meg figured.

"That'd be great." She gagged. "What's that awful smell?"

"It's that honey-bucket cart over there." Marty gestured to an oxen cart with wooden buckets on it, led by a straw-sandaled man. "Human waste. Night soil, it's called."

Meg still felt rattled and began babbling. "Honestly! Back home, on the far side of our fields, we have an outhouse for when we're working far from our bathroom, but we put lime down the holes to smother the smell. When it's too full, we dismantle the outhouse and bury the hole. Bury it well away from the little creek, of course. We use up a number of Penney's catalogs there, too."

She looked sideways to see if he understood her reference to the use of the catalogs. He nodded, and she continued, "We also have a garbage pit that we shove dirt over when it's full and dig another one. My brothers love to drive the front-end plow. I don't see why the Japanese people don't die of disease if they put human waste on their fields."

"I suspect, like with most human-susceptible germs, if the people survive those while eating their crops, they're immune," he answered.

The taxi moved into traffic and away from the fetid odor. She exited the taxi at the Chiyoda and waved goodbye.

An hour later he called to say the only factory tour was on Thursday, and he was on duty during the daytime then. She suggested substituting shopping for a ceremonial sword for her father tomorrow, although she couldn't be buying it yet.

She also offered to tell him tomorrow about the manufacturing processes she had read about in the Durant book and in tourist brochures. Sgt. Martin was agreeable and said, in turn, that he would relate what had transpired regarding the dud bomb. He also said he wasn't much interested in silkworms of any kind.

CHAPTER TWENTY-THREE

Meg was at the PX again, this time looking at jewelry. She had already bought dangling silver honey-bucket earrings and was holding up a black and silver damascene bracelet and earring set to the light, wondering if she had enough spare change to buy it. Meg noticed a familiar tune being whistled near her and turned. "Why, Kurt Salchow! What are you doing here?" He smelled of sweat and Old Spice.

He turned his strong body in a circle, looked up at the ceiling and down at the floor. "Wherever I am, there I am; I think, therefore I am. Let's see. I met you before. Margaret O'Brien? Did I meet you in St. Louis? No, you're Cally's dolly, Margaret Lowe––I'm so slow. What are you doing here? That is your echo in here, isn't it?"

"Another teacher and I are trying to buy indelible ink or order it for class projects. School starts after Labor Day."

"Still on vacation, huh? No more pencils, no more books, no more teacher's dirty looks."

She laughed in complicity. "Um-hmm. I thought you were in Osaka cleaning up the black market."

He looked stunned for a second. "Guess our big cross section's not so secret anymore. Army, Navy, Air Force. Oops! Forgot to call in the Marines! You keeping up with our doings?"

"Truthfully, I don't know anything much."

Salchow said, "Down in Osaka, I was on a bit of R and R. Just diddling around down there. Now our alphabet soup is cooking with G1, G2, G3, G4, that's the team I'm rooting for. Plus, CID, CIC, CIB, CIA. C-i-a-ty, wonderful c-i-a-ty, you're the only group that I adore. When the moonshine's down in the mess hall, I'll be serving a-a- a-at the mess hall door," he sang. Then he gave her the V for victory sign and said, "One two, buckle your shoe; three four, lock your door . . ."

Meg's amused smile turned into a frown. That certainly wasn't how the song went.

". . . five six, hit with sticks; seven eight, you're the bait . . ."

"Bait? Now what exactly do you mean by that?" Meg demanded.

". . . nine, ten, I need *sen!*" Salchow finished with a flourish. "What, you haven't heard that version before?" he asked, still smiling. "Say, have you seen Fumiko Yamata––I can't find her anywhere."

"No, I saw her once, no, twice, on a boat trip and at a funeral. I tried to call her but must've had the wrong number. She's not working at the school anymore."

"Her dad says she's in seclusion."

"News to me. Wait a minute," Meg said. "What did you mean about my being bait?"

"Wear your wedgies, wear your pumps; then you'll never get some lumps. It all fits, you see."

Tamara Talbot, the teacher Meg had come here with, found them then and came over, her auburn hair frizzy in the humid air. "Meg, they had one bottle of ink, and I ordered four more."

"Great. Let me introduce you to Sergeant Kurt Salchow. This is Miss Tamara Talbot."

He swept off his overseas cap, "Pleased to meet you, Tamara. I'm ripe for another stripe. I'm looking forward to having you sew it on." He started singing again, "Tam Tam Tammy, good bye, Tam Tam Tammy don't cry. Watch for my call; we'll have a ball, if you don't hear it ringing from me, I've had a fall." He looked at her soulfully and asked, "You at the Chiyoda?"

"Yes." He gave a deep bow, turned toward the exit, and was swiftly gone.

"He's crazy," Tamara said, though her hazel eyes were glinting as they tracked his departure all the way out of sight.

"I wonder," Meg said gravely.

"I hope he calls. What do you know about him?"

"Not much. He seems to be with some investigation group in the Eighth Army collaborating with the Nagoya Metropolitan police and the Fifth Air Force. But, don't quote me on that, because I'm not sure."

#

Wednesday afternoon, Meg and Marty, in their usual garb, started out along the walk in front of the Chiyoda. Moving into one shop after the other, they could not find a store with swords on the first avenue and turned onto the intersecting street.

"This is getting frustrating. I saw a lot of fancy swords down in the schoolhouse tunnel so I know that there are some. Maybe those were all that still exist after the years of war." Meg sighed and stopped, pulled out a fan, waved it in front of her face and then Marty's. She glanced around. "Look, over there, what are those little boys carrying in the bamboo cages? I couldn't see anything in them."

"They like singing insects, like crickets. Look halfway down the block there. I'm going to get my fortune read."

"On our farm, we didn't like crickets, locusts, or grasshoppers. They're a plague. Ruin crops and all the income."

They came up to a man with a shoulder high contraption that held a birdcage on one side, a verandah and tiny temple on the other side. Marty handed the man some money.

A black bird was released. It hopped over to the temple, clicked open a door with its beak, and retrieved a little folded paper. The bird snapped open a paper ribbon with a twist of its beak, and the man handed Marty the paper.

"I've heard of Chinese fortune cookies, but not that. Can you read it?"

"No, but I'll have Sergeant Hagikawa translate it tomorrow."

They strolled by several more shops selling everything except swords, to Meg's disappointment.

She commented, glancing around, "For a city that was virtually flattened, these streets are laid out elegantly. The buildings, though, are definitely old shanty town, roofs touching the ground."

Marty answered like a proud tourist guide. "It was the American engineers who designed the layout after the war. The main streets with the tramcars and local buses served for the beginning of construction of neat blocks of stores and buildings. Between earthquakes and bombings in the war, the Japanese have had to rebuild their wooden places over and over. I think even the *Daibutsu, the Great Buddha,* is said to be from the 12th century but has had its body, arms, and head replaced now and then."

"I don't believe you. That's like 'Tyler to Martin to Brown' or 'Tinker to Evers to Chance'." Meg, noticing a man and a woman who constantly appeared in her peripheral vision when she stopped to look in a store, quickened her step. "Come on, I'm pulling a prank on some people I'm teasing."

"What did you just say? What don't you believe? Why did you give our chant? Prank on who? Wait up." He sounded shocked, and his face and body instantly assumed that Air Police demeanor he wore when in action.

She dodged around two pedestrians and slid ahead. "Just play along." She shook her closed fist at him and moved faster alongside the curb.

"What did you say? Are you going crazy?" He sounded exasperated.

She suddenly crossed over in front of him and hissed, "Tag up. Follow me," as she entered a small shop with some metallic things displayed in a small glass counter.

"Meg, what's wrong?" He sounded incredulous, even had a tiny tremor in his voice.

"We're being followed. I took a leadoff walk as though I were angry. Got you on base behind me. I kept seeing a lady and a tall man, both in Western clothes, every time we came out of a store. First one of them, then the other. See if there's a way you can sneak a peek sideways, outside at the street. There'll be a man loitering, not as tall as I, while everyone else is moving along."

The short storeowner appeared from behind a curtain, a Camel held in his fingers and smoke drifting from his mouth.

"Good day," he said. He examined them after they both recoiled and then bowed his head politely, waiting for an answer––or an explanation.

Marty then ignored him, poked his head out the door for a few seconds, then pulled it back in, looking grave! "Blue pants, black shoes, bow-tie." His report was delivered briskly.

"That's the guy. I saw the same couple in different clothes walk by us yesterday at the zoo. While we were eating, they walked by both ways and glanced sideways at us. I think it is also the couple I backed into when I was lining up the elephant shot and called you over. They're probably going to play a trick on me but I'll beat them to it." She laughed.

"Yes, I noticed them, too. That they glanced at us."

"May you buy?" the owner interjected.

"No, sorry, sir." Turning to Marty, Meg said, "Now, when we leave, I'm going to be looking for something in my bag, and I will accidentally drop this little brocade purse with a book list––I'm dropping the ball, you see. Deliberately. Like I've thrown the game."

"What do you mean? I'm not following," he whispered.

"I'll show you a copy of my list when we go for a snack, which I recommend we do right after this point. Get out of sight of them. You keep your head turned to me as though you're apologizing, and see if you can spot a woman in a blue skirt and long sleeved white blouse following us, too. Let's hurry."

"Gotcha, as you said when Cally Paley threw you a curve on the chapel's ball-field."

She strode from the store as though she were angry, tore a handkerchief and the brocade coin purse from her bag, wiped her eyes, and hustled up the street toward the Snack Shack. Again striding through a sea of black hair––hair on heads on shoulders a good four inches below hers––she ignored the flowing crowd as they did her.

"I made both of them," Marty said when he caught up to her, "The man picked up the coin purse. Go into that store and buy something."

"What?" She hesitated before moving into the store.

Marty stood with his hands on his hips and stared after the man walking swiftly away. A woman glanced up, turned, and went the other way, disappeared into the crowd like a drop of water absorbed into a sponge. The stream of pedestrians flowed carefully around Marty.

He looked back at the crumbled sidewalk, spied the brocade purse, and brought it to Meg as she came out, fumbling in her satchel as though she'd just discovered the coin purse was gone.

"What do you guess is going on? The man took out the contents and dropped the purse." Meg watched Marty's eyes float around the crowd, as if he might find the answer to the mystery there. "What have you gotten yourself into?"

"I'm still trying to figure that out myself. That's what this decoy was for." She held up the purse. "I don't suppose we could find a bite to eat in the mean time? I'm starving. I get hungry when I'm nervous. Let's go get something to eat."

He hailed a Japanese coal-burning taxi to take them to the eatery.

Their short ride passed through streets that had no sidewalks but plenty of traffic, wheeled or walked. Destroyed buildings still appeared in some blocks, left over from the bombings that ended four years before. She would no longer tergiversate: she trusted she no longer floundered around in military protocol and/or procedures. Her confidence in investigating crime heightened.

"I simply don't know exactly what's going on. I may know something I don't know I know, but my take is that they think I've something in my possession they want. Maybe they just want to spook me." It was either the packet of metal rings/coins (now with Cally) or the little statue (now with Hills) if they were after something she'd had in her hands. Or maybe she'd irritated one of the little spirits that abounded in Shinto teachings. She grinned as they chose a table and set down their drinks. "Marty, now I've pretty much revealed all that's relevant because I trust you. Here's a copy of my Book List that I hope will cause the dust to settle."

"What does this book list mean?" He smiled over a couple of the titles.

"I was cogitating about the black market that's causing Colonel Jones so much worry when he should be focusing on the wedding. I've heard a few things here and there that made me think the valuable black market items that are swiped are being ferried out of the country after traveling to a selection of sites. Plus, I think a Japanese *Noh* actor is messed up in it and maybe Fumiko Yamata."

"An actor? What makes you think that?"

"On the cormorant boat there was a man, one who takes women's parts in *Noh* plays. He might've been trying to talk the boatman into sailing stuff down the river. Another sergeant, B-J-Gorman, earlier told me she saw a shaved eyebrow lady following me. The actor had shaved eyebrows like the lady that B-J Gorman described as following me the other day. So, he's an *actor*. Being an *actress*. Follow?"

"Yes. I'm following your suspicions all right."

She continued describing elements contributing to her suspicions. "Trains have already been made secure. But if a river by a big city, such as the Kiso near here––the so-called Rhine of Japan––is connected to another one that runs to a bay or, say, to Lake Biwa, what does that suggest? Boats and barges float. There are airports throughout the islands, too. Look at a map."

He shook his head. "Too much to determine without proof. Sheer speculation. Airports're under S. C. A. P. Those people that the Occupation hired have been vetted. Although the actor, I heard, is under indictment for involuntary manslaughter."

He thought a bit more while Meg watched his face, finally offering another topic. "How about 'Tokyo, Rose of Jeer-lawney?'"

"Or how about, 'Tokyo Fell! *Tokyo Rose*,'" she countered.

"Pretty Boy Floyd Sails Into The Void."

"Bonnie and Clyde Go Out With The Tide."

"Nancy Drew Sees a Clue." He grinned and pointed at her.

"Rover Boys Always Swim Over." She pointed back.

He chuckled. "We'll see if you've opened Pandora's box."

"No. *They* did. I just revealed the evils. Wanted to flush 'em out into the open and pick 'em off."

"You have to tell us when you have specific information, not guesswork, not senses merely alert just from being in a strange culture. You're smart enough to know the difference. Now it appears that you're pushing against this little threat by upping your--sometimes misplaced--humor. Meg, this's not amusing."

"Perhaps." Her fingers still felt tight, and she flexed them again. That tightness was her old symptom of stress, and she knew it even as she played down any reaction.

He looked straight at her for a solemn minute. "Can I have this list for the investigators?"

"You may, but if the other copy I have in my room is gone, I'll need that back. I already sent one home. I wrote some cryptic notes in our family shorthand. From a distant, different perspective, they might be able to fill in some angles."

She took a sip of her milkshake and almost choked as the cool drink entered her throat. She gurgled out, "What were those people doing shuffling and clapping in a circle around that bear down the block?"

"They're Ainu from Hokkaido. Having a bear festival."

"Ah. 'I knew' that. Sorry, couldn't resist. Too bad it isn't a beer festival. Ah, well. I read that the Ainu were the first inhabitants of Japan. Did you know that once all the continents were squeezed together to form a land called Pangaea? Here we are in latter-day Pangaea opening Pandora's box without pandering to a . . . ?"

"Panda, patsy, parliament . . . panic?" His teasing voice was back.

"Okay, I'm relaxed. Say, Marty, on another subject. My classes start soon. I wonder, because of your experience in craftwork, if you could help me figure out how to fit a new Mercator map around the globe in my classroom? I'll need it later in the semester. I've already decided to have geography students redraw both that and the big map with new country boundaries. I'm not sure how to proceed."

"That shouldn't be very hard. I can do a Mercator projection replica in the hobby shop when I'm working a night or day shift and have the evening off. Let's go measure it."

#

When they entered the classroom, Meg snapped on the light switch. Something seemed wrong, but a swift perusal didn't reveal what the something could be.

Marty called her over and had her hold a cloth measuring tape, evidently produced from in his pocket, while he made notes, moved it, and had her hold it again. "Of course the earth isn't completely round," he muttered, "but the globe being so makes it easier to calculate circumference. When I was in grade school, I made drawings of animals from the shapes of States. Florida was a skinny green krait, a really poisonous snake; Kentucky was a porcupine; Wisconsin, a rabbit."

Meg said, "I start off the geography class by teaching about the International Date Line, Greenwich Mean Time, and longitude. *Around the World in Eighty Days* is the first book report assigned, a great illustration to help students remember. Of course, we in the Occupation all passed over the International Date Line when we came across the Pacific. The whole assignment goes well. Next, I do latitudes. After that, they'll be reworking the map and globe."

He moved her hand onto another place with the measuring tape stretched between his hands, still stopping to make notes.

"Oh, oh, Miss Lowe," cried a voice as a girl staggered into the room with a dog on a leash. "There's a dead body--oh, Miss Lowe--body by the elementary school Quonset huts. Mother said I could walk out with Cory Torleone because his Father's on The Promotion List. We were walking Stilwell on his leash with a flashlight around the Village when we saw this body and bloo . . ."

Meg ran over and held the girl's shoulders as she gagged. "Calm, Janie, be calm."

Janie Worth twisted, bent, and threw up into the wastebasket. She gasped in between words as she rattled off an explanation. "It's by the front walk, by the school door. Cory's dog Stillwell dragged me to it. It's bleeding all over the grass. I think, I think that it's the man who sold Mother the radiation trash and scared her. I-I was by our pond and saw him knock on our door days ago."

She vomited again.

"Where's a phone?" tersely asked Marty.

"Principal's office, end of hall, first floor. Why didn't we see it when we came in?" said Meg but Marty had already run down the stairs. Meg kept patting the girl on the back and wiping at the sobbing face with a handkerchief--the one she had kept Hills' trinket in. The dog was watching everything Meg did as it sat near the door.

"There, there, Janie." Miss Lowe stroked the girl's hair. The girl clung to her with one hand and took the handkerchief in the other.

A boy came trotting upstairs. "Miss Lowe? I'm Cory Torleone. That sergeant came out and said he'd stay by the corpse until the APs come and that I should come take Janie back to my house. Can we stay up here and watch from your windows?"

"I think not. It's too dark to see anything and could take a while. I need to clean up, um um, some trash. You people scoot on home with Stilwell, and let the police do their work. You've both been very brave. I'll give them your names so that they can contact you while you're with your parents."

And, after washing the wastebasket downstairs in the janitor's closet, maybe it would be time to see if the earthquake tremor yesterday had disturbed the supplies in the tunnel.

Marty came bounding up the stairs behind her as she climbed from the faculty washroom. "Time to go. I'm sure keeping various units busy this week when I'm supposed to be off-duty."

"Did the bleeding soldier trip over something that fell during the quake yesterday?"

He took the wastebasket and set it inside the classroom door, turning off the light. Meg walked out of her door. He reported, "Not a soldier, it is an Oriental guy. The guy was stabbed. Deliberately. It must have happened right after we came in because the blood is still hot and flowing. Terrible sight, all slashed up."

"Dreadful, absolutely wrong, to happen by a school building. Janie is really shaken. Her folks will not be happy at what she's been through. She threw up a lot in my wastebasket."

"That thing smelled like bleach when I brought it upstairs, not like barf."

"I rinsed it out several times and dumped the mess down a toilet, then went to the janitor's closet, but all I could find was the bleach I left days ago. I left it in that closet to dry. Bleach did rather ruin the look of the wastebasket's insides, but I assure you, sir, that it smelled worse before."

"Is there a light switch down on the first floor for the hall here upstairs?"

"Yes. While we're here, shouldn't we check the tunnel to see if it survived the tremor we felt at the zoo? There might actually be things people would trip over there or in the school."

"No time tonight. Anyway, isn't that the principal's duty or the School Board's?"

"I suppose yes, except the principal is planning her wedding. I guess you're right. They've probably already done it. If not, I'll find out tomorrow and do it."

"Into the tunnel in a solo game went dangerous Margaret Lowe

And watching her go was a hapless gent, the AP she kept in tow."

Meg poked him. "You like reading Robert Service, *ne?* He wrote wonderful tales about the northern most part of America."

"Hai. I read a lot of the paperback books that were sent out from the States. Books fit right in a guy's pocket and

helped pass the times of sheer boredom, before those of sheer terror."

"Walk me home?"

"We'll have to be interviewed a bit by the police officers working around the dead body in the yard. After that, we can take the bus at the stop outside the gate."

"Do you know who it was that was killed? Was it a Japanese policeman?"

"No." His short answer, his very tone, was one of dismissal, as though he wasn't going to answer any of her questions.

"Wonder who it was. Let's go. We can cross over to the other side of the street. So they can come over and interview us about what we know which is nothing."

They glanced at the activity in the schoolyard. APs, MPs, and Metropolitan police were busy. An AP came over and found out that they, indeed, knew nothing about the body lying in the schoolyard.

Marty distracted her from the scene by touching her arm and saying, "Let's go home. Too bad we didn't find a shop that sold swords today."

"Oh well, we will sooner or later." She shook herself. "I know that I'm not in Missoura right now, but I felt a jolt when I saw that body lying there. My dad and I helped during a car accident outside our farm one time when the driver was hurt. *But* he struggled to his feet. That man over there won't."

He nodded agreement and held out his hand. "Hey, you don't need to struggle with this thing happening in your schoolyard. Take this rabbit's foot to guarantee you luck and a long life, in addition to that due to the brass cranes."

"I'm happy to oblige, believe me. Thank you. Oh, it feels soft, like my cat, Dearie, cat named Dearie, not you as dearie.

I'll keep it with me all the time," Meg grinned and slipped it in her purse. "I could also use a four-leaf clover if you find one."

He added, "I don't know where it would grow in Japan. Sorry. By the way, the dud was removed successfully yesterday. It's good we found it when we did; we're probably in for bigger shaking."

"How do I prepare for a quake?"

"Try diving quickly under a table or into a doorway. It'll become second nature."

"Roger, over and out. Here's the bus for my trip home to a hotel! See you next week."

CHAPTER TWENTY-FOUR

The package from J. C. Penney with the yard goods and flat black shoes arrived on the afternoon of Monday the 15th of August. Considering the order had gone across the ocean and the package had come back over the ocean, it hadn't taken all that long.

Meg examined the goods; surely seemed as though she'd laid out too much money for such a small parcel. Blue and white waffle weave cotton was there as well as plain green cotton and maroon corduroy for a skirt, slacks, and jacket from all three types of cloth. Flat black shoes. Okay, everything was there. Maybe it cost less to mail when wrapped as small as possible, although she thought things were charged by weight, not size.

Meg set the items to one side and wandered to the window. Looking down at the street, she saw a honey-bucket wagon. *Ugh. Wonder how the garbage is collected. There's the Brass Pile for metals, but I haven't seen a City Dump mentioned.* She turned away and went back to the cloth, smoothing out the wrinkles and holding the different colors to her face before a mirror.

At supper in the Chiyoda dining room, she asked Betty where to find a dressmaker.

"There're three tailor shops in our buildings but I use a dressmaker some of us found last spring. I'll take you over after supper. Do you have a pattern picked out?"

Meg shook her head. "I don't know where to find one."

"I told you earlier. You can borrow some magazines and catalogs, and scrutinize them. I tell you, she can make anything after she takes your measurements," Betty advised.

"Hard to imagine how she can do that after making shapeless Japanese garments."

"Don't worry; she'll do well. I suggest you pick one dress pattern that has a jacket but is made in cotton, because some days start off hot and end a bit chilly."

"End up chilly? That's hard to believe in this 80 degree weather."

"We even have snow in the winter, Meg."

"Then I'll have Mom send me my winter coat and boots. She always maintained that we should 'Use it up, wear it out, make it do or do without.' 'Waste not, want not.' Those bits of advice I actually follow."

"Wise, very wise. Left over from the Depression and rationing in the war years. Wise today, too," Betty said.

"What's a ball park figure on the cost?"

"Oh, a few hundred *yen*," Betty replied.

"Guess the seamstress'll have to tell me the score. I'll go borrow some magazines. I still have your catalog that I can check for ideas, too. See you about 1900 hours."

In her mailbox later that afternoon, "Miss Margaret Lowe, BSEd, MSEd, APO 710" found a letter from her parents with pictures of the twins and her cat, all grinning at her––yes, even the cat. She smiled at the address and the 5 cent red airmail stamp with a one-cent stamp beside it. The message was as cryptic as her latest letter home had been.

Dear Hunny-bunny,

Enjoy getting your weekly letters. Jerry figures the mouse gets the cheese and that it is Limburger, not Swiss with holes, so hold your nose. Tom notes that he himself likes to bat around a mess of strings that are twisted into each other with his paw. Meanwhile, Mom says "Remember, into each little upturned nose some rain must fall." What a bunch of wits--or at least half-- . . .

In the midst of squalor, you have helping hands that are reaping a great crop, I believe.

I say, you've got a mess on your hands, so you should wash them. And, McCoy, watch out for a Hatfield. Had fun with your reading list.

Love, Dad

Working the items over in her mind, Meg decided that her ideas about there being a lucrative black market smelled correctly, without holes. Moreover, she could leave solving the black market organization to the authorities. Or else she simply had to put the right interpretation on identifying the culprits if she didn't mind some dire result from sticking her nose where it didn't belong. She wandered to the window and watched the traffic gliding by below, endless traffic.

Suddenly, her head filled with longing to see her two bratty twin brothers, now in college at Mizzou. How odd to become homesick for them! Her parents hadn't tried to discourage her applying to teach here, but her brothers had mocked her mercilessly, miming WW Two propaganda as in "So solly you be gone." Yet, they were the ones that she missed. Of course, she'd never let them know that.

#

On the way to the seamstress, Betty stopped at a kiosk. "Look, Meg, there's a picture of the ancient *Noh* staging I mentioned. Those three actors in the luxurious robes and plain masks kept sliding across the stage, talking, talking singsong. The men seated on their knees at the side were a chorus. I left when that long scene was over, and some other actors appeared at the front of the stage to provide a skit that had people chuckling."

"I think I'd rather see a *Kabuki* play or the *Takarasuka* Girls' Opera," Meg said, awakened from her running thoughts on the letter from her dad. She and Betty moved on through the stream of pedestrians. "Those productions seem more up-to-date, understandable."

Betty gestured at a dark storefront. "Here we are. She'll take your measurements quickly. Does really good work."

Despite Betty's warning, Meg was still surprised by how quickly the dressmaker worked. The woman kept talking in Japanese during the session. "Is she saying 'DIE' at me? Or is it 'dye'?" Meg straightened her shoulders and looked at Betty to explain, figuring that the dressmaker didn't speak much English.

"Neither. She's saying '*dai*'—you know that means 'great'. You have big shoulders and long arms and are tall."

Meg blinked. "Oh, I see what she means. Like the *Dai-ichi* Building in Tokyo, *DaiButsu, Great Buddha,* in Nara. This fall I'll go tour Kyoto and Nara if I can get on a tour. I feel *too* tall here in Japan, and awkward, although I'm only 5'2". I bet you don't feel it as much, given how petite you are."

"No, I hadn't thought about height differences much. The dressmaker also said '*sukoshi*' when she measured your waist and upper legs. That means 'small'. For example, if I ask you if you want some more 's'kyaki,' you say, 's'koshi.' The words are not spelled the way that they are pronounced, in case you hadn't guessed."

Meg repeated the words, exclaiming, "The GIs on campus would say 'give me a *skosh*' when they wanted more food."

"That's another adaptation for '*su-ko-shi*' that Americans use."

"Got it."

"I think you should buy some raw silk and have a dressy suit made out of it. From what I've observed, the students' parents offer quite a few parties at the Kanko Hotel or their homes. You could change off the blouse and vary the outfit if your silk is a neutral color."

"I appreciate that idea. It's great. I'm going to tour the silkworm factory next week and will bring the silk cloth back here. No, maybe I'll do that tour tomorrow if I can find someone to go with me. Maybe I'll find some lighter, thinner colored silk for a blouse or two. Are we ready to go home? I mean, back to the Chiyoda?"

Betty nodded, and Meg made arrangements to return for a fitting.

Settled back in their rooms, they turned to their own tasks. Meg called Sharon to see if she was free to go on the factory tour the next day. As she dialed, she thought if not Sharon, then one of the other teachers in the hotel might go with her. Receiving no answer on the Sheldons' phone, Meg walked upstairs and knocked on Talbot's door. The strong-shouldered teacher clapped her soft, white hands with delight and suggested they ask Volker, Patrick, and Norstad. Norstad was unable to join the entourage because she had a dental appointment.

Back in her room, a slight quake froze Meg for a second, then she dived to the floor under the desk, heard the brass cranes toppling, and a swish as the woodblock print fell onto the bed, accompanying her down. She kept her arms clenched tight over her head a few seconds more but nothing else happened.

She stood up, glad that Marty had told her most hotels and big buildings were on rollers, permitting the tremors to shake, but not break, the walls. She set the cranes upright and knelt on the bed to hang the woodblock print back up, a picture of a stone lantern under a sprig of pink blossoms.

#

The teachers took a taxi to meet up with the tour bus at the silk factory the next morning. Not wishing to visit the other factories, they had made an appointment with Special Services for an adjunct tour at just this one.

Viewing the silkworms, before purchasing silk, was a mandatory part of the tour. Because the little worms had been fed with mulberry leaves two months before and placed in a straw nest, they saw the stage where the worm became a chrysalis within the cocoon. The moths would emerge shortly and be killed inside the chrysalis by high temperatures--except for the moths that were allowed to lay eggs first. Meg thought about how different the chicks emerged on her folks' farm. Her brothers would come up with some witty comparison if they could see these silk worms.

Next they observed pictures of the reels of the filaments that, after being softened in hot water, were being spun into raw silk. They were led to the weaving and drying rooms. At last, the purpose for which the troupe had visited the silk factory was realized: they entered a retail store that featured bolts of many colors of cloth.

Meg was a bit disappointed that the tour was over. She had peeked into a room along the way where men and ladies alike were engaged with needlework, following intricate patterns outlined on the silk. They worked as quickly as machines, and Meg hoped they'd learn more about that process on the tour, but they never returned to that room, and their guide never mentioned anything about it. And, here at hand, for purchase, was the magnificent outlay of that meticulous work, beauty to buy.

Plain silk included satin, chiffon, and crepe. The decorated silks were damask, brocade, or figured satin. Some silks were dyed; others were striped, embroidered, patterned, foiled, or dappled from the different colored threads woven in intricate patterns.

Matilda Patrick, perhaps because of her height, took three yards each of neutral colors, dark blue and tan, closely woven silk. Her profile resembled the sandstone bust of Nofretete, Amenhotep IV's, i.e., Ikhnaton's, queen in Egypt. Not only that, she often said "tut tut" in admonishment. Nofretete had been Tutankhamen's half-sister, Meg remembered from her Durant book, and almost giggled at the thought. Nofretete, long neck, dark hair, wide, dark eyes, smooth nose, and tapered chin.

Tamara Talbot bought flowered crepe for a blouse and enough silk in a subtle green, intricate design for a suit. Meg wished she had such an eye for proper colors that would enhance her own blond and blue-eyed appearance.

Because thin silk wrinkles badly, Meg eschewed that particular offering leaving her with enough money to buy yellow and blue flowered chiffon for a blouse.

Chloe Volker chose black and white patterned brocade.

Meg reveled in the excitement of shopping with friends. Purchases took a good hour. After they left, chattering about the garments to be made, her mind settled on more conspiratorial thoughts again. She lost track of the chatter. "Say, maybe we should stop by the school," she said suddenly. "I wonder if those quakes yesterday did any damage to the tunnel shelter."

"What difference does it make?" asked Chloe.

"Well, we might have a hurricane and have to get the kids down in there in a hurry. You know those storms last hours."

"As I live and breathe, that's frightening," Chloe said, putting a hand over her heart in fake terror.

"Yes, yes," said Arvada. "I've read about the terrible storms that come off of the ocean. Another of the reasons I don't feel safe here." She bit at a fingernail. "Maybe the tunnel will collapse on us if we go down there."

Meg sighed. "No, Arvada, don't be scared. We'll stop if anything has collapsed but, if there are just cracks, we should tell the engineers to repair them. Let's take a taxi because that'll be easier and quicker. I'll pay the fare because I have some *yen* left over."

Meg actually was curious about what remained of the supplies and swap/swipe goods after seeing so many things hauled away a few days ago. But she now had an excuse . . . they could check out the tunnel for damage from the short earthquake. All piled into the taxi with their bundles and were driven off to school.

Inside the schoolhouse, they deposited their packages in the lounge and followed Meg downstairs. She carried her purse and, after heaving up the trap door, led the way down the stairs, flipping on the lights. Her skirt caught on the top of the banister, and she turned to free it.

Chloe chanted, 'I see London, I see France."

"Do be quiet," Matilda admonished as Meg grinned, remembering the childhood chant and replied, "You see my underpants."

No part of the ceiling or walls had collapsed as Meg carefully pointed out to Arvada. Cots and supplies, however, were covered with fine dust from the quake. Matilda ran back upstairs and brought rags for the teachers to use. Handing a terry cloth remnant to plump, brunette Chloe, she showed her how to lift the top cot, dust it, and check the ones below for damage and dirt without having to move the whole stack.

Meg told them she wanted to take photographs of the tunnel in order that any cracks could be repaired. First she had two of her colleagues stand down along the wall in order that the photographed dimensions could be clearer. Engineers were going to have to look at the shelter with keen eyes, and she wanted to support her plea for assistance.

While the dusting proceeded, Meg wandered down the tunnel, saying she thought it was connected to another, and she needed to check for damage around the corner. Correct in her assumption, she wandered past the stairs up to the old Yamata store and those to the bathhouse to find that the tunnel turned another corner to the east. The tunnels, just as she had suspected, developed into a series of below ground shelters.

She took a couple of snapshots, put her camera down, and foraged in her purse for something to ease her mouth that had become dry. She unearthed the Red Hots and also the stick of gum Sgt. Cally Paley had given her weeks before. Finishing off the candy and trying to chew the brittle gum, she leaned back against the wall and felt a slight nudge on her back. Unaware that the tunnel had more outlets, she turned around to discover what the protrusion was and was surprised to find a small doorknob.

Picking up her camera from the purse on the floor, she nudged the door open. Inside were several closet doors and, between the walls of doors, a staircase. Lifting the camera, she took a quick picture of the room, releasing the flashbulb into her hand, just as a voice exclaimed, "Well, well. Welcome, Miss Lowe, to our humble abode."

Frozen in place for a second, she stiffened more when she saw Mr. Yamata coming down the stairs. She involuntarily retreated a step because he had a sharp, long knife, a thin stiletto, in his hands. "Don't be frightened. I'm cleaning this little jewel, because I just recovered it from my *koi* pond. A colleague found it in Nagoya Hall. Myself, I don't know how it came to be there in a glass case. He turned out to be a Judas who stole Dolls' Day festival toys and other items from me; he won't be working for me any more.

"This jeweled stiletto matches another I have acquired, although I don't know where I put it. These implements have been heated and beaten over and over to become strong and beautiful, forged better than Vulcan could do. Would you like to test how sharp it is?"

He moved toward her, the weapon in one hand, a sheath in the other. "No? Myself, I like things to be as sharp as I am."

Meg moved back another step as he waved it in front of her.

He stopped at her glare and bragged, "I'm not jaded about jade, either. I'm building up quite a collection of antiques. Unlike the Olympians, I am going for the gold metal, not medal. No 'D' grade, Miss Lowe. I no longer have to manage a store because I am the *ichiban* consultant and teacher to the Occupation Forces . . . that's a nice living."

Meg backed up another step, disturbed by the way he was rambling. She had never known him to do that. Then she remembered Althea telling her weeks ago about how he would begin rambling during their English classes last year.

He grinned and said, "I don't want to be nosy, but just what are you doing here? We have no celebrations that are imminent. The *O-Bon* Buddhist Festival for the Dead was last month, although I could show you how it transpires. It includes spiritual meditation and regard for the dead. We have to wait until next year to remember my cousin, because he died after the ceremony this year. I have quite a lovely Shinto and Buddhist shrine upstairs. Along with the Catholic church membership, the gods are smiling on me."

His spiel somehow was hypnotizing her. His use of English was mixed with Japanese expressions that made her concentrate, such as dumping "*ne*?" or "*ah so*" into the middle of a sentence. She was trying to figure out where he was going with this meandering among topics. His rambling lighted on festivals and, at last, about his daughter, Fumiko. Meg had been wondering what happened to her.

He began repeating his statements. "I don't open the shoji screens until Moon-viewing next month: that particular festival includes 15 rice-dumplings, fruits, vegetables, and lots of *sake*; poem improvisation, singing, eating. At this moment, Fumiko is out with––" his head turned to the stairs, and then turned back toward her, "the troupes whom I'm sure she'd like you to meet. She seems to have a bad taste in her mouth when she mentions you. She's having trouble getting over my cousin's death."

He breathed heavily after his rambling discourse and changed hands for the stiletto and sheath.

"Did you say 'out with the t-r-o-o-p-s' or 'the t-r-o-u-p-e-s'?" Meg asked, her voice shaking.

"Take your pick. I'm sure something could be arranged upstairs for your entertainment. May I see that camera?" He took her arm and urged her toward the stairs. She tried to tug free.

"Meg! Meg! Where are you?" Matilda Patrick came calling, her footsteps sounding down the hall.

His eyes widened, his body went still, the unctuous smile disappeared from his face. "There are others here?"

"Teachers, checking supplies."

"I'm afraid I don't have tea to offer so many. Perhaps another time?" He gave her arm a hard pinch, pushed the door against her, and forced her out of the room while taking a key from a chain he had pulled out of his robe's neckline. After he shut the door, she waited until she heard a lock turn before she stuck her gum in the keyhole. Her brothers had done that to her bedroom door once after she stuck salt in their breakfast milk––ha, they had taught her something of revenge.

"Stuck-up guy, by gumption, you're stuck up now." Meg giggled nervously.

"Wonder if I should report my encounter with Yamata to Colonel Jones?" she muttered after a second of thinking.

"Did I hear a door slam?" Matilda called. A few seconds later, her tall dark-haired figure appeared looking down the hall.

"Yes, I had opened it, and a Japanese man came down the stairs, and," Meg put a sinister note in her voice, "waved a knife at me. He pushed me out and slammed it when he heard you call."

They walked back toward the stairs. Matilda patted Meg's arm to calm her down and demanded to know exactly what had happened.

The other teachers had turned around at Matilda's exclamation of alarm, "What happened, Meg?"

"Let's go have some coffee in the teachers' lounge, and I'll explain. A little."

The group trooped upstairs and returned to the lounge where they had placed their purchases. Matilda prepared the percolator, and Chloe set out the cups.

"Tell us what is going on!" clamored the teachers, plopping on the chairs, spooning sugar into their cups, ready for the coffee to be poured, and studying Meg.

"A guy waved a knife at me just now."

"Are we going in danger up here in our classrooms?"

"What was Matilda exclaiming about? I don't understand."

"Makes me wonder if I should've come here last month to take this teaching job," timid, blonde Arvada said. "Maybe my grandmother was prophetic––this *is* a land of heathens, of savages."

"No, no, Arvada. The whole episode is simply about an enigmatic, confused man. He seems a bit out of his mind. He's an American, by the way."

"Well, I'll be hornswoggled!" said Tamara.

"Frost my buttons!" cried Chloe.

Meg glanced at their surprised looks. "Yes, third generation American, as am I, incidentally. He's Japanese-American. Turns out that this father and his daughter came to visit the old country in 1940 and were caught up here because of the hostilities between Japan and us. The dad suffered horribly, labeled as an outcast and forced to do nasty, filthy work. The daughter was sent to Tokyo to be an entertainer . . . also called concubine, comfort girl."

"But then what was all this brouhaha about?" asked Arvada.

Meg lowered her voice dramatically. "There have been thefts going on in the Village and buildings. He might have had something to do with them, because I saw some storage closets in there by his stairway. Maybe he hides stolen goods there." This story was becoming an antidote to the fear Meg had felt, and she began freely to enlarge upon her observations.

"I heard about those burglaries. I keep my jewelry locked up." Chloe nodded.

Meg said more firmly than she had been doing before, "Earlier this week, I considered how I would move messages and stolen goods secretly around town and the Prefecture. It could be with garbage removal, honey bucket carts, garbage barges, see? That was when I made up a book list of fictitious titles and happened to say *Fumiyamata*, his daughter's name, in one title. I dropped the list off a couple of places where I had noticed her friends. Evidently I got his attention."

"But, I can't see why a book list would make someone murderous," argued Tamara. Tamara then threw in a diverting anecdote. "You are just kidding us, I bet. Sounds not quite as mild a soap opera such as *Backstage Wife*, more like one of those strange *Inner Sanctum* radio shows. One evening when I was a kid, I listened to *Inner Sanctum*; remember that squeaking door that opened the show? The plot was that someone with a metal finger of some icy substance was killing people. While I listened, I was reading about ghosts at a Girl Scout Camp. After I closed the book and turned off the radio, I walked up to my bedroom. My brother jumped out and yelled 'boo', and I burst into tears. He was torn between laughing and being apologetic. So, don't any of you say 'boo' right now; I might burst into tears. Now, continue your explanation, Meg. Don't leave anything out."

"Part of what happened was that I met the old fellow a couple of times." Meg was furiously trying to censor the story. Tamara's recital had given her time to figure out a diversion. Stories about a criminal investigation should not be bandied about, she knew from working with her father and from the AP's hints. She quickly shifted the path of her tale.

"I bought a bridal shower vase from him, the father's shop for Althea Jones, our principal? I ran into him at a funeral and somewhere else. That daughter of his is around now and then? I don't know if she'd been married to a noble or is just a kept woman? She'd been dating that American soldier, Kurt Salchow, but maybe he was just investigating the family? The father was really threatening just now, might also have put out a vendetta aimed at me, because for a while people were following me around, the same people, a man and a woman. So, maybe that is why he's mad at me?"

Meg kept raising her voice at the end of sentences, creating questions as though she weren't sure, although she was positive how things had transpired. Suddenly she realized that she sounded like Mrs. Worth with that irritating habit of sounding so very girlish with her way of speaking. Distasteful to realize.

"Let's go back to the hotel and have some afternoon tea, shall we?" She stood and looked at them with raised eyebrows. They nodded as she shook her shoulders, took her satchel and parcel, and walked swiftly to the door. All the teachers followed suit, gathering their bundles, and left the schoolhouse for the bus stop. They chattered about the Yamata chap, his experiences that were outside their experience, and what his daughter's life must have been like. Meg let them ramble even though most of what they guessed was wrong, colored by their American backgrounds.

CHAPTER TWENTY-FIVE

Saturday, August 20, was a perfect day for a wedding. In the chapel, flowers and candles presented a lovely setting. One of Althea's friends monitored the guest book as the small crowd arrived promptly. At the altar, Sharon and Bill Sheldon attended the couple.

The bride wore a white silk dress with a small hat made of ropes of white silk. She carried a bridal bouquet of baby's breath, white carnations, and other white blossoms that resembled orchids, and green fern. Sharon had on a pale pink silk dress with the same type of hat in matching color, perched behind her pompadour, and carried carnations. Bill wore a bespoke civilian suit with his usual bow tie while Col. Robbie Jones was in full dress uniform.

Meg studied the wedding party. At last, someone older than she herself was is getting married. Back home, all her high school friends had married years ago. Now they dangled kids on their knees. Meg's throat tightened in nostalgia. These people here she had known for only a few weeks but felt just as close to as those high school friends seldom seen in the past few years.

Following the ceremony, guests were served punch and cake in the chapel assembly room. After the newly married couple had cut the wedding cake with a small sword drawn from an elaborate sheath, Sgt. Laura Duncan and

Cpl. Donna Aldrich served the guests a second cup of tea, circulating with the chapel's coffeepots, their dress uniforms worn proudly. Meg loved her own new summer suit and the blue and yellow material in the new chiffon blouse reflected her coloring. The mirror had showed her that her tan and little freckles complemented the summery outfit so she had not powdered her face.

One slight problem happened when Sharon started to cut the rest of the wedding cake. Her finger slipped against the knife and bled. She had just handed a piece of cake to Meg, and thankfully not someone else, because the bloody streak ran down her particular piece of cake, centered as it was on the middle of the little plate, the red stripe almost blinding in the surrounding whiteness of cake and plate. Meg stared at the crimson marking while her mind blinked back over the three male bodies she'd seen decorated with streaks of blood. Plus a stiletto had been brandished at her. She could've puddled blood that day under Yamata's house. She shook her head a bit frantically. It's Sharon who needs help just like David, her twin brother, did when he tried to whittle a whistle and started howling at his "owie." Meg had wrapped his finger in Mom's apron.

"I'll spell you, while you wash that cut and put something on it," Meg blinked and then whispered harshly to Sharon, put the plate with the affected cake on a chair behind her, and stripped off her white gloves. Sharon edged away toward the hall to the ladies' room.

Betty walked up and offered to help. Meg nodded gratefully and suggested that she take the five gifts people had brought to the chapel over to Col. Jones' rooms at the Kanko Hotel. Betty asked a couple that had a car to help, and the gifts left in safe hands.

A couple approached, carrying a child, and the mother slipped behind Meg, putting the child smack down on the injured slice of cake Meg had placed out of sight on the chair. The wail from the little girl grabbed the father's attention. He picked up the child, cuddling it--and found himself with white icing, the blood not visible in the mess--it must have mingled in with the decorative part of the icing--and cake all over his uniform and the child's dress. The couple left hastily through the door behind Meg through the kitchen, and they motioned her to keep quiet about the disaster as they departed. No need to spoil the wedding. Nice people.

Not one of the guests even turned a hair toward the child's cry. They were all gathered around Robbie Jones, talking, joking, and waiting for Althea's return.

The bride had forgotten to toss her bouquet, rushed as she was to doff the silk wedding gown and don traveling clothes. Most of the females present were already married so it didn't really matter. Meg guessed that the bouquet was still in the ladies' restroom. When Sunday school children arrived early the next morning, they could play at moving step by step down an aisle to Mendelssohn's *Wedding March*.

The new Mrs. Althea Jones was effervescent as a soap bubble when she returned to the vestry of the chapel. People peppered the couple with rice as they ran from the chapel to Col. Jones' chauffeured sedan, off for a honeymoon at Lake Biwa.

Cpl. Donna Aldrich and Miss Margaret Lowe left for the Castle Area Ball Park shortly afterwards to watch the Nagoya Comets. Meg stuffed her knit hat and gloves into her satchel. She was a bit dressed up in her nylons and heels, but people did wear dresses to ball games sometimes.

Seated in the bus, looking out the window as they passed a huge *torii*, Donna remarked, "Did you hear what happened last Halloween here at Castle Heights? A couple was hosting a party and intended to have a scavenger hunt. They left clues with the guard at the gate. Several of the invited couples had never visited their house before and stopped at the gate to ask directions. Imagine their surprise when they were given the following slips of paper which actually were the clues: 'Find it in stone lantern;' 'Locate rose bush, look underneath;' 'Four bricks down and three over on entrance path.'"

"That is too funny," Meg chuckled. "I'm going to write my Dad about that set of clues. He'll love it. Say, do you think the Nagoya Comets will finally pull off a win?"

Donna snorted. "Doubt it. The team they're playing is undefeated."

"It's a Japanese team, isn't it? I thought maybe they wouldn't be as good."

"You'd be surprised," Donna said. "Baseball's been growing here a lot since the surrender. Before even that, a newspaper owner brought Babe Ruth here in the mid-30s, drawing large crowds. Of course, everything turned toward the war effort later."

"I'd not known that bit of lore. I used to play softball. I ran into some men from the softball team here who play in the American Village field." Meg looked out the window before she continued. "I really like the cheers the crowd has for our batters––who do pretty well––but the fielding needs improvement. I've been to Nagoya Nugget softball games in the Village, the team I'm rooting for that plays mostly other local teams. It's more like intramurals.

Donna's prediction about the final score was correct. The Comets lost big time. Because the evening was deepening quickly in this seaport town, the game was called after the seventh inning.

Donna and Meg were still dressed in their wedding reception outfits, although Donna's was the typical uniform of a corporal. She and Meg edged carefully down the bleacher steps.

On the bottom step, Meg's left heel caught on the back of the step, and she lurched forward, trying to grab the rail. Her pearl necklace swung from her neck, and her thumb snagged the string and broke it. A strong arm kept her from falling.

"Careful, Meg," said Sgt. Tyler. "I'll get your shoe free if you step out of it now. You sit down on the bleacher. Why are you so dressed up for a ball game anyway? Why do you go from one extreme to the other--wearing peasant clothes for strolling the streets, dressed to kill for a ball game? You must read a very strange fashion magazine in your spare time."

Meg ignored him at first, struggling out of her shoe and looking with distress at where her pearls had disappeared. Then she reacted to his tone of voice. "Just what's available to wear, sergeant. You and your uniform don't have that problem, I am sure." She could be snippy, too. She sat down with his arm still holding her arm. He then turned to watch Donna who squatted on the ground trying to find the pearls in the gravel.

"Oh, no," moaned Meg, watching her. "My lovely pearls."

Donna said, "I found a lot of them. Do you have anything to put them in besides just dumping them into that large bag of yours? They'll get lost and never be found. Might as well leave them in the gravel." She held out two handfuls.

Meg pulled out the brocade bag. "Here, put them in my coin purse."

AP Phil Tyler had managed to loosen her heel from the step. She slipped the shoe back on. "Thanks so much," she said in an even tone.

He too knelt, to her surprise, and found four more pearls under the step. The dark evening shadows stymied the duo's ability to find any more.

"Thanks to you both. Donna, this is Phil Tyler. Phil, Donna Aldrich." They shook hands and smiled at each other. "I'll have the pearls restrung. Maybe have to buy some more graduated ones for those you couldn't see."

"I'll tell the groundskeepers to look for them in better light tomorrow," Tyler offered. "They clean up the park starting at dawn's early light."

"I'd appreciate that." Meg nodded her thanks and looked beyond him. The bus was pulling up at the gate. "We better get going, Donna."

As the bus rambled toward downtown, Donna poked Meg's shoulder. "Do you play tennis?"

"Huh uh. Never learned. Didn't see anyone I knew playing it, either." Meg lifted the hair from the back of her neck because there was no breeze alleviating the heat. She was just noticing that the chiffon was sticking to her back under the jacket.

"Let us gals teach you tennis–Althea's going to be dropping out of our doubles. It's a great sport. We can play even when the ball games, swimming pools, and golf course are closed in the late autumn."

"All right. Thanks. I'd love to learn something that will get me exercising in the fall. I've been swimming a lot but didn't have any idea of what I could do for exercise during the winter around here. Tell me where to get equipment and when to show for lessons, okay?"

"Tomorrow afternoon, after church, about 1400 hours in the Village. The rest of us have lots of equipment to start you off. I'll outfit you before when I drop by the Chiyoda first."

Meg could run, Meg could hit a ball, but she couldn't do both at the same time--a talent required by tennis, as she discovered the following afternoon. A ball traveling fast at her was soon reduced to a reasonably paced sphere, much like a softball, if quite a bit smaller. Yet she wanted it to be coming toward her, not somewhere else on the court.

"That was a fine workout and a half," Meg exclaimed as the players wiped their faces and arms with small khaki towels before changing partners. She groaned, "But I'm always missing the ball. I can't get to it in time."

"You're getting the hang of it. Just don't stop dead like you've been doing before you take a swing. It'll all come together," Laura advised. "We have time for one more set before our hour is up."

Donna added, "Pretend you're in the outfield, Meg, running to catch a high fly while you calculate its trajectory and the speed, and you run *to* it with your glove held so, and swat at it with your racket." She was acting out the movements as she spoke, running in place, eyes out, racket back.

Meg's leather shoes slipped twice on the court in the last set, almost causing her to fall, but she caught herself, although she missed the ball. On the third try, she hit the ball so hard, with a swell landing clearly inside the line on the opposite court, that the other three stopped and looked at her.

"Could have gone right through my tummy like grape shot ammunition," blurted Sharon.

"That was super," exclaimed Meg's partner Donna gleefully. "Your arms are so strong you could throw Kong off the Empire State Building."

After those remarks, Meg felt much better about playing. She still missed plenty, but every now and then she would swing her racket just right and land another impossibly perfect shot, and boy, did that feel good.

"You've learned quickly," Donna said, her hand raising a "V" for victory sign.

"Aw, 'tweren't nuttin', to use my brother's favorite expression. Sharon showed me how to hold the racket at an angle with both hands on the handle. And, you showed me how to gauge where the ball's a-comin' in. I finally understood how to run in from left field and hit the ball, rather than stop to catch it. The outfielder analogy worked."

CHAPTER TWENTY-SIX

Two weeks before Labor Day, Sharon Sheldon called. "Meg, would you be able to come over tomorrow evening? Captain Torleone's wife is in the hospital with their new baby girl, but the Jones couple and Mays and his wife Cora are going to come. I've made my famous lemon cake to bribe you guys into watching our pictures of the Mt. Fuji expedition."

"Sounds like fun. What time?"

"I'll have Bill pick you up at 2000 hours. We're in Castle Heights. Dress is casual."

The Japanese dressmaker had skillfully sewn her garments; *dai* shoulders and *s'koshi* waist fit well. The night of the party, having chosen the blue and white checked waffle-weave sundress and jacket, Meg added earrings. Solvent again this month on her mid-August budget, she'd bought pearl clip earrings to match the ivory colors of the necklace, which had yet to be restrung.

Meg eyed herself in the mirror. Her hair was pulled back under a blue headband that tied at the back of her neck. Her bangs had grown as long as the rest of her hair, and her forehead was as tan as her cheeks.

Amusing herself while waiting, she speculated that with the Torleone's boys being named Tory and Cory, this baby girl would be Dorrie or Laurie. (Meg bet herself a *cent* on

Dorrie and a *sen* on Laurie.) Tory was probably a nickname for Salvatore. Cory: no clue.

She waited for a glimpse of Bill's car arriving in front, glanced idly out of the window that faced the street, watched traffic move and pedestrians dodge. Men plodded down the main street leading oxen pulling carts of grain, bundles of this and that, honey buckets. She spied the Sheldon's Chevy coupe pulling up, grabbed her satchel, and locked the door behind her.

Outside the hotel, she waved as he moved to open the car door for her. After he returned to the driver's seat, she said, "Bill, sir, I have taken some pictures of the school's underground shelter. Three teachers and I went down to check it out after the earthquake tremors. If I give them to you, could you have engineers look at them and check out the place?"

"Be happy to."

They rode in silence down the street as Meg pondered how to broach the subject of the Yamata door. She said dreamily, "When I was fifteen, my brothers stuck gum on each side of my head."

"Riveting. So? Then what?"

"I ran crying to Mom to have her cut it out. All she did was put ice cubes on the gum until she could pick it out. The reason I brought that up is that I have a picture to show you of something I found. In the far reaches of the tunnel is a small doorknob in the wall on the right hand side. I opened the door to a room lined with doors for either closets or cabinets and a stairway was going up the middle into a room.

"I took a photograph and, suddenly, that weird Mr. Yamata was coming down the stairs with a jeweled gilded knife in his hand. He made some curious remarks and, when the other teachers called me, he went still and shoved me out the door, locking it. After he locked it, I stuck gum in the keyhole. I suggest if you want to investigate the closets, you take a few ice-cubes with you."

"Meg. Meg. Will you ever learn not to go poking around things that are none of your business? Didn't you ever learn to knock at a door to see if someone was home? If a front door swung open, didn't you call, 'Anybody home?' before you went into a house in Missouri?" he groaned. "That explains why Yamata-san is demanding an apology from you, somewhat incoherently, but now it makes sense. You better write him a nice note and stay out of his sight. This I'm telling you in private before we arrive at the house. Take some lessons in Japanese etiquette; learn to say 'please' and 'thank-you' to local people. No matter what you think happened, he could have simply found the knife that was stolen from Nagoya Hall and was trying to tell you that," he mused.

"No, the theft--and I had never heard what was taken-- was *after* I heard what Josh Worth saw before he fell out of the tree, that a man tossed something into a *koi* pond. That knife must be the knife Yamata was brandishing because he said he had just pulled it from a pool. But, too, he bragged that it made a matched pair. He also muttered something about one from Nagoya Hall. He was confusing, threatening. Follow me?"

"Now you know that you're creating a maze and expecting someone to recognize the torturous path you've designed. Yesterday, Sergeant Kurt Salchow went down to repair that door, because Yamata demanded he be the one to do so. Someone with a sword took a swing at Salchow, and ended up cutting the electric cord overhead, smashing the light bulbs. Kurt took a bad cut on his arm, but survived."

"That's terrible news. My friend is dating him. I bet she doesn't know."

"Fortunately, three engineers with flashlights were working by the school steps at the other end of the tunnel. They said there were chunks of ice on the floor as well as shattered bulbs, hanging wire, and a prostrate sergeant. They had him hauled to the hospital. They didn't see who caused the damage."

Meg winced. "I'm sorry to hear that. Evidently someone else knows about using ice to remove gum. Wonder why Yamata demanded him in particular."

"If he loses his arm, being cut badly, needing to be dissected, Yamata's edict will hardly make much difference to him. He'll be crippled."

They were both silent before Meg said, "On another topic, Marty said he'd turn over my book list to you. I was trying to be funny. I hope it wasn't a catalyst. And Mr. Yamata made some remark about Fumiko's friends really wanting to meet me. My take is that they think I have Johnny Hills' valuable heirloom. Somehow I have to get word out that I don't, that he has it, and it is long gone. These casualties are somehow inextricably intertwined." She decided not to mention Cally's possession of the packet of metal objects. No one could possibly know that she'd taken those from the display down under.

"All right. Let it go. We're doing our work; you stick to yours. Lady, I'm really going to be glad to go Stateside and be rid of you. J. Edgar Hoover will be a breeze to deal with in comparison."

"Ha, so you are CIA. Dad told me that while the OSS was a thorn in Hoover's behind, he is breaking out in a rash over the CIA."

"No comment. MacArthur doesn't allow CIA here. I'm merely Sharon's dependant," he claimed loftily, grinning. He parked the car, walked around the hood, opened the door for her, and led the way to the front door.

Entering the Sheldon's ranch style house, she struggled to turn off the spy plot unraveling in her imagination. It wasn't until after exchanging greetings and enduring an awkward silence, during which Sharon couldn't stop touching her brown hair, that Meg noticed she had cut it. It was now the same style as Althea's brunette pageboy. There was an ash blonde lady in the room whom newly promoted Capt. Mays introduced as his wife, Cora.

Bill had put a screen in front of the dining table before he came after her at the Chiyoda. Meg greeted everyone and, gesturing to her hair and that of the other ladies, asked, "Captain Torleone, is your wife blonde or brunette?"

"Like Little Orphan Annie, red hair, freckles, and blue eyes, and what a temper! Old Scots-Irish, as you'll hear from her brogue when you meet her," he replied. "And call me Harry."

"Annie Laurie?"

"That's her name, all right. We named the baby Laurie Ann."

Meg mentally lost a *cent*, paid herself a *sen*.

Sharon served everyone after directing each to a sofa or cushioned armchair. She chatted about the train trip to Okitsu where they spent the night at the Minaguchiya Inn.

Describing their evening before the climb, she chuckled, "We passed one inn when we went on a walk after a supper of C-ration frankfurters and beans."

Meg groaned, remembering the picnic at Gifu by the Nagara River.

"The inn was marked 'OFF LIMITS'. Inside the front entrance was a sign, 'GIS PLEASE ADVISED TO PUT SHOES HERE,'" Cora Mays added.

Sharon nodded and laughed. "Before we retired, the ladies were assigned use of a big bathroom with a huge vat of hot water. First, though, a maid directed us to sit on small stools and have a sponge bath with soap and water from a little bucket. Only then did we climb into the big tub. There we were in our altogether when a Japanese man slid open the *shoji* screen and smiled. One woman held her wash cloth in front of her body, not covering up very much, and screeched 'goawaygetoutget out *sayonara* get out.' He backed out still grinning. That little scenario broke the ice in our group for sure. We were warm friends before we even started the climb up the mountainside.

"Our bedroom was little––only a few *tatami* mats wide. Bedrolls had been opened on the floor, and I was surprised how comfortable they were. Mosquito netting was provided, but Bill and I didn't use it because the room, even with the sliding door open, was really too hot.

"More coffee anyone? Bill's ready. I need to turn off the lights."

Bill explained, "These first few I'll show quickly. We took a bus from the inn to the first station rather than climb from the bottom, because we were to be staying at the top station Saturday night. That way, we'd be in position to see the sun rise over the top of Mt. Fuji Sunday morning."

"Why else would anyone climb Fuji? Oh, of course, so you're NOT a fool," joked Althea.

Bill saluted her and showed the next slide of the baggy pants coolies hired to carry the luggage to the top of the first trail and then down the Gotemba trail on Sunday.

Sharon explained, "We kept our canteens and salt pills and cookies with us. Bought straw hats and staffs. At each way-station, for ten *yen,* our staffs were given a unique mark with a wood-burning tool; we could also buy hot tea. Now,

Bill, go more slowly and show our group straggling along and also some scenery of the mountainside. Trees grew here at the lower level, not higher."

At a slide of a seated woman in a straw hat frowning at her feet, Sharon interjected, "Meg, that's Cora here hidden by the hat. I loaned Cora my daughter's boots and four pairs of socks as I had suggested I could do for you when we were at Gamagori. At first she grumbled that they were too hot and heavy. On Sunday night, though, she hugged me for insisting."

Bill picked up his narrative, "Sharon and I climbed steadily, having a sit-down and drink of water at every station and way-station and sometimes in-between stations when we needed to breathe. Three teenage dependants on the trip had to stop at an early station for a couple of hours, because they put too many salt pills in their canteens and became sick."

He took a sip of coffee and clicked the next slide. "Their being delayed caused us to have problems holding back our train car the next night until they came down. They were badly sunburned, too. But back to our climb."

The slides were beautiful, revealing vast distances and close up detail at the tree line, then ascending the sparser vegetation, still green, with brown twigs intertwined. The distant farms were spread out like a patchwork quilt pattern down the slopes on cleared land. Snowcaps on those mountains in the distance resembled clouds or perhaps were clouds.

"Our group, those who were this far along, posed here to give an idea of the vastness. Up we go, and I'll click these along as we progress."

Several slides later, he remarked, "Even our group didn't make it to the top––where, as I said earlier, our clothes and supper were. At first, we hunkered down in a hut at the seventh station, having been led to it in the dark by a sergeant waving a flashlight and urging us up, up along the mountain path. Then we moved outside, although a hut somewhere up top had been reserved for us, this sure wasn't it. This one was full of sleeping strangers. We shivered outside, but a Special Service sergeant had stayed back from the top with some extra blankets for us. In the morning, we found out we had been sleeping on top of a *benzyo*, a latrine, all night. Here's Sharon on the spot over the pot."

The group laughed at his droll tone.

"Here's a view of the top, and the next three are of our group at the top. The caldera doesn't seem very deep for all the publicity. Disgusting that souvenir stands were there as they are everywhere tourists go––even though it's supposed to be a sacred mountain.

"Breakfast wasn't very appetizing. More C-rations. We chose hamburger and gravy––cold. This is the start of our racing, sliding, falling down Gotemba trail. The trail was made of lava gravel. In some places, the depth of the lava was shallow, and we'd stumble and slide a bit. Then it would turn suddenly to gravel and dirt that our feet sank into. There, see the patches of snow? One fellow took off his shirt and slid down some snow, until he fell. At one hut, we were able to buy some straw slippers to put under our shoes that helped with traction. Sharon's showing her shoe in this slide. And thus ended our pilgrimage in order to defer becoming fools."

He clicked off the slide projector. Sharon came in with a full coffee pot, clicked on a table lamp and refilled their cups.

Capt. Torleone refused the coffee, stood, and said, "Thanks for the evening show. I need to get home to the boys. I'll let myself out."

"See you tomorrow," Robbie Jones said.

The men stood and shook hands with the captain before he took his cap from a hall table and went out the front door.

Bill returned to his task of removing the carousel of slides from the machine and, looking skyward, queried the group, "Notice anything peculiar in these pictures?"

While everyone else had been oohing and aahing over the beautiful scenery, Meg had leaned forward and squinted her eyes, searching every picture for a certain man's face. Bill glanced at her a few times, but she ignored him.

Now she could articulate her uneasiness. Kind of him to notice her intensity during the showing. "Yes, Bill," She turned to Col. Robbie Jones who was sitting down by Althea on the couch. "Robbie. One man looks like the one who was trailing after Sergeant Martin and me until Marty put his hands on his hips and stared at him and his girlfriend. The guy had picked up my brocade coin purse that had the book list in it. In some of your slides, he's looking carefully at American females, particularly Cora, at first anyway."

"Yes. We wondered about that. You may have noticed that she has your coloring."

Meg gave a start and frowned. "Now I see it. We're both blond, same size."

Sharon interposed, "That guy stayed well away from me and Bill but I'm glad Bill caught him a few times tracking ladies. He seemed to be looking for someone. You notice that he came down at the same time as the laggards in our group?"

"Yes, the shadows from the trees were much longer than those in the slide of you and your friend by the bus, waiting for the rest to descend Fuji."

"And so we eventually returned to Nagoya."

CHAPTER TWENTY-SEVEN

Sharon passed around the room filling coffee cups as the group quietly pondered the purpose served by someone trailing an American lady. Bill removed slides from the tray and put them into a slender box. Cora and her husband sipped their coffee. Althea and Robbie patted hands.

Robbie lazily changed the subject. "On another topic, When you were describing Josh Worth's accident one time earlier, you mentioned that a grey-faced man had gone into a Japanese house?"

"Yes, and, oh, Josh said the visitor gave something to a guy seated just inside a room, and the guy threw it into a *koi* pond, scaring away the kingfisher. Robbie, I was just re-telling that story in the car to Bill. That's because Mr. Yamata and I had an encounter where he wielded a knife under my nose. He said he'd retrieved the weapon from a pond."

Sharon and Althea both looked at her, appearing startled at her comments.

Robbie said brusquely, "This is another connection, Meg: the grey-faced man is also the last person who burst from the bathhouse in your earlier photograph. I didn't show it to you, because we didn't know which of the flying bodies in front of us had been the one we were trailing down the tunnel," Robbie Jones added.

Bill said, "We'll have someone check out that address. It looked somewhat like Yamata's house if I remember the photo correctly. I believe we have the description from your second report of the visitor that came from the store near Yamata's, the report about Josh Worth's injury."

Meg looked at the men with surprise. She had tried to find out if they shared things with their wives, and now she knew that they did. Talking openly about something she'd been warned to keep hush-hush obviously didn't apply when they themselves were involved.

"Then there's a murdered grey-faced man . . . looked Korean, long face, pale complexion," Loren Mays contributed. "His store is unoccupied now, because he was killed, stabbed, one night by the American Village School. I'd bet he was brought over here from Korea as a prisoner during the war. By the way," Mays said, his voice suddenly dark, "he had a note in his pocket that Sergeant Hagikawa translated for me. It read 'miss megdowe nagoya school.'"

Meg was glad the room was still dim because her body reacted with another jerk, turned cold. "He was coming to see me?"

"However you want to interpret it, is fine," said Robbie. "For example, was he after you or coming to visit you?"

After collecting her thoughts, she remarked, "I'm unsure. They're maybe trailing me and Cora, because they can't figure out why we have blond hair . . . I haven't seen them lately. I don't think I'm in danger, especially because your investigation of thefts is not connected to me, not pertinent to my career or experiences.

"Now that I'm trying to connect events, I think, too, that the Japanese house could link up to the bomb shelter tunnel. I hadn't run far when I saw that the boys were bird watching there. Did you check out the far reaches down in the shelter?" Meg asked, a faraway look in her eyes, seeing none of them, as though they were invisible, outside the house walls; she studied the white movie screen at the far end, thoughts cueing each other, coalescing.

She was brought back by Robbie's reply. "We did and do. We inspect it all the time. You stay away, missy. The local robbery system is out of business, and you do seem to be an ancillary issue. Right now, the thefts have ceased as though the communication and transportation systems are shut down, from Nagoya to Osaka. The black market for food will continue as long as farmers receive more compensation that way than if they provided the government with the produce as they're supposed to."

"Thus the bogus repairmen, supervisors, and garbage collectors are no longer sending scows down river and over the waves because of your investigation?" she asked.

Bill looked at her. "You'd not be far wrong if you thought that a couple of GIs are facing court-martial and a one-way trip to the maximum security prison at Ft. Leavenworth; they are both pretty scared of something or someone, as are their collaborative local garbage men. We just need the boss to tumble out of hiding."

Sharon rolled up the movie screen and tucked the implement away in a hall closet. That seemed to signal the end of the evening. Meg now knew the meaning of the phrase "felt a sense of disquietude." No one else seemed relaxed, either, as good-byes and thanks were being exchanged with the host and hostess in subdued tones.

"Ah, Bill, sir? I'm ready," Meg said politely, standing up, "and I enjoyed visiting with you-all again. Are you driving me home?"

Col. Jones sighed, "We will." The Mays couple followed them out to the cars.

The colonel opened the back door for Meg and his wife, then climbed in next to his driver. As the car started up, he turned toward the back seat saying, "I didn't tell you, Meg, but I'd already told the others when you arrived at the Sheldons'. I've received my separation papers."

Meg 's jaw dropped. "You're getting divorced?"

Robbie and Althea hooted. "No, separation from the service! My points added up well. My flight plan has been filed. I have a job awaiting me at an aircraft plant on the West Coast. We'll be leaving in a couple of weeks."

"He's teaching me how to pack our suitcases efficiently–– like he does B-4 bags."

Meg was struck by an idea. "Must be great to be moving on, and, Althea, may I buy your hats?"

Althea turned to look at her. "I saw that knit thing you've been wearing. Not very summery looking even with that silk flower sewn on the side. I'll give you my hats. I doubt they could travel well any more. You might also ask Sharon; she and Bill are leaving about the time we are."

"That leaves the school in a pickle," Meg said.

"Cora is taking over my three science classes; her boys will be in school. Sharon was just substituting this year. Hines will have Smithson go over the officers' wives' dossiers to find replacements that have college degrees. I've already cued him in on the principal's duties here," Althea said.

"The interservice investigation into the thefts is over, or stale-mated. Captain Mays is taking over my job," Col. Jones added. "We'll leave your adventures to him to figure out."

"I don't mention my hypotheses to anyone who isn't married to law enforcement," Meg retorted from the back seat. "Hear me? I was with Sergeant Martin at the school when the grey-faced man was stabbed. We'd been shopping all afternoon."

Col. Jones replied, "You're saying to me, friend, that you could have done it while he was looking at shorts or shirts and thought, simple child that he is, that you'd merely moved out of sight from embarrassment? Actually, you were stabbing someone?"

"You would have had me handcuffed by now if you believed that script. Dismissing your jibes, let me interpolate the similarity in the murders and attack on Sergeant Salchow. Sharp instrument, always used, events always occurring around the same people––people in addition to myself."

"Go on." Then Robbie Jones snapped, "I suppose you think it's time to round up the *unusual* suspects."

Meg raised a finger, "Ah, these *are* usual, one a suspect shadow who knows what flows from the ways of men. Think, students, before replying about 'why' it happened. There's a person who is invisible even in front of us, knows Americans and Japanese, can deliver and manage an organization as though following someone else's orders, can slip a knife into men. It's a purloined letter mystery: someone right in plain sight."

She purred, "I have a question and some observations. Think of the synchronicity. Question: 'Who would benefit if certain people were murdered? Those being Captain Archer, Yamata's cousin––the boatman, and a grey-faced storeowner. And who perpetrated an attack when Kurt was ordered to, ah, to repair, ah, the lock?"

"All right, I'll bite. Who?" Althea asked.

"Let's examine the characters that have been on our stage. See who should be cut from the cast or who should be cast as a killer and/or leader of the swipe meet:

First we have Yamata once had a successful store and also was once in the despised class, because he was assigned to unclean tasks, like garbage disposal; now he's proud of his riches;

Then there's a couple, one on the fritz, and sailing out-of-town, knew both Yamatas:

The unknown variable is one Fumiko Yamata who is incommunicado and once was a janitor in the American Village;

And, finally, a Japanese female impersonator who is mysteriously involved.

We know where and when the assaults happened: three in the American Village, one on a boat. We know how––the men were penetrated with a slim knife, three got it in a vein, and I don't know where Kurt was hit on the arm, but was stabbed in vain (he he).

"That leaves why, why? Tell me something, please. Why was Kurt originally arrested with the Yamatas that night?"

Jones snapped, "We didn't want anyone to know he was working with our team. He was able to visit the Yamatas that way."

"Why haven't the Yamatas been arrested?"

"For one, he is *non compos mentis*."

"And she's not guilty because she's a *girl*? Like Lizzy Borden and Lucretia Borgia?"

"Quit bugging me. I don't know why you've got a bug in your ear about events. We and Mrs. Fritz proved that she was not involved in the black market thefts. We're still working on unraveling the organization," Robbie urged.

"Sure she wasn't; some day let me know the exculpatory evidence, please," Meg murmured.

"She didn't murder Captain Archer, either, although she did hurt him. The Aichi and Gifu Prefectures are in charge of the other two murder cases. We're merely consultants because both happened on temporary American property.

Mr. Yamata suffered terribly during the war and had no reason for lashing out."

"Probably not. But that leaves someone who can slip under the radar, demurely deliver instructions to an organization as though the orders came from a man, or be strong enough to slip a knife into one American and two Japanese men, strike at an old American boyfriend, or be dismissed as critical to an investigation because she/he is a Japanese female, of no importance in this society––or in yours? Of course, females don't murder people, either."

Althea spoke to Robbie, "I told you once I thought Fumiko-san could speak and understand English better than she pretended. Sly girl. She was like a chemist hunched over a beaker steaming over an Etna burner, mixing up poisonous, noxious things from vials. I wouldn't let her into my lab."

Col. Jones ended the evening saying, "Althea, you know how it works in this society, men are head of the family, and girls are taught from infancy to be obedient," Robbie said as the driver pulled up in front of the Chiyoda Hotel. "Here you are, Meg. Be a honey, be obedient, and tend to your own beeswax. I'll not need any more of your help; you're out of my sight, Meg. Good night. Don't let the bed bugs bite." He let her let herself out of the back seat.

"Clichés! Clichés!" Meg commented as she entered the hotel, shaking her head in frustration as she went upstairs.

Because Tamara had hinted she was dating "that crazy guy from the PX," she knocked on Tamara's door. "I have to give you bad news. I just heard that Kurt Salchow had been stabbed yesterday and is in the hospital."

"Oh, my Lord. How did it happen? Who did it? Is he dying?"

"I know little about it. We'll have to ask him."

"Let's go see him. We have to see him, Meg. Can we go tonight?"

"I doubt we'd be able to. You can go pound on Betty's door, wake her up, and ask her. But. It. Will. Irritate. Her. Let's go first thing tomorrow."

"I'm not going to sleep well, worrying about him."

"I know. Maybe it's not so bad. Be calm, Tamara."

"Not likely. Wake up time will be 0700 hours!"

Meg waved off frantic disconnected questions, turned, and left for her own room, having no patience this evening for speculating, much less commiserating, about something else that she knew little about.

PART FOUR

GETA GRIP

CHAPTER TWENTY-EIGHT

Meg Lowe accompanied Tamara Talbot to the hospital to visit Sgt. Salchow at 0830 the next morning. Tamara described in disjointed detail her two movie dates with him. She was deeply shocked to find out about his injury. Meg didn't tell her about the ice-cubes in the far tunnel.

The confrontation that Meg had described to her colleagues, after the door slammed in the tunnel, had taken a vicious turn now. Meg knew that Kurt was injured partly because of her gum revenge on Yamata. Tamara, a city-bred girl, was not used to blood and guts and might become angry with her. There were tears coursing down Tamara's cheeks now as she gulped. Meg was a bit torn by the need to conceal her part in the events, perhaps with the gum in the keyhole, the provocation of her effrontery, her encounters with an enigmatic Fumiko, she had been the catalyst for the injury.

On the way to the hospital, Tamara finally said the injury sounded strange, her assumption being that Salchow worked for a newspaper, writing about events around them, relating stories that were amusing to Americans, trying to be a song writer and musician in his spare time.

"Why would someone try to hurt a guy zany as he is?" she wondered aloud to Meg. Meg shook her head in answer. So what if once upon a time, he had been seeing a baby-san.

And the baby-san's father had set him up to be punished. Let Kurt explain that to Tamara if he wanted to.

Pulling out a sheet of paper with fancy handwriting on it, Tamara revealed that Kurt had asked for her opinion on a poem. After all, she had lived in Nashville, home of country music. She handed the sheet to Meg. "I know little about music even though I love dancing. What do you think I should tell Kurt about this being a likely candidate for a popular song here in Japan?"

Because of the popular recordings of the Japanese song "Nagoya *Bugi-Wugi*" and of the translation of "My Blue Heaven" into "*Watashi-no Aoi Sora*", Kurt wanted to capitalize on the timeliness of his own composition. He was sure it would be amusing to members of the Occupation Forces, Tamara reported, but she herself despaired of the poem's meter and asked for a frank opinion from Meg. He was aiming to make it into lyrics for a swing dance band. Maybe it would cheer him up to have them enthusiastic about its possibilities.

Keeping a bouquet of flowers in her far hand, Tamara craned her neck to look at the paper as Meg was reading it. Meg noticed the elegant handwriting, almost like a scribe might use. It was nicer than being printed in elite type. But, she had no knowledge of how to compose either lyrics or music. Nevertheless, she found herself drawn into the project.

> KYUSHU CHOO CHOO
> By Kurt Salchow, MSGT
> Hark, all you 'Occ' Forces
> This gypsy endorses
> A spot of which you should learn.
> Though to you 'fat catters'

The one thing that matters
Is 'home', your only concern--

Just crawl in the 'Dixie',
The train-clerk can fixie,
--Check out for several days.
The train trip is real nice,
U. S. stands the meal price,
And head for Kyushu's blue bays.

It'll land you down there,
'Fore you're hardly aware,
This crack Allied 'Dixie' train.
And, remember this, Phil,
You'll sure get a thrill
Beholding Kyushu's terrain.

The sea breezes blow
Not to keep off the snow,
-To cool the Florida clime!
There's Unzen and also,
Fukuoka, Mt. Aso,
Ashiya, of ancestral time.

You'll bask in the hot sun,
Swig gin, have great fun,
No cares or worries, you bet!
Uniform for the day
Is to yell, 'Anone!
Three more, before you forget!'

If you hanker to roam
Before sailing home,

This Yellowstone hot spa's your trip.
Just crawl on the "Dixie",
The train-clerk can fixie,
And restore your whole verve and zip.

Meg handed the lyrics back, and said, "It isn't the rhymes or meter but what the melody would be, because the singer can elide over an syllabic stress that is a bit off. For example, sing 'Fuk'o-ka', not 'Fu-ku-o-ka.' It might work. Let's see if he has started on the music part. Also, Kurt needs a chorus that repeats––the lyrics do that only on the last stanza. Had better have four stanzas than six, maybe. Cut it down so that it's easier to remember it all."

"Yes, I get what you're saying. I've been tapping out the rhythm but nothing works. With your correction to that town's name, I believe a 3/4 beat could work," Tamara replied thoughtfully as the taxi rolled to a stop.

Entering the room, recoiling at the sharp, unpleasant hospital smells, Tamara carrying a vase of flowers they'd bought on the street, they tried to conceal their reactions to his bandaged hand, arm, and shoulder. His strong body looked as if it had grown sideways with all the wrappings and tape around his side.

"Hi, soldier. How're you doing?" Tamara bent toward him solicitously, trying to conceal the choking sound in her voice.

He was sedated, barely able to acknowledge her, but his eyes opened to slits. Then, in a weak voice, with apparent effort, he said, "Hardhearted Tammy, the vamp of Japanah?"

Tamara laughed. "Yes. What happened to you?"

He mumbled a description. ". . . like soda fountain. Lights go out. Swore. Damn. Swivel stool, fall on butt, drop ice drink. Guy afraid face me. Dark. Swished, sliced, diced.

Sorer than a hound's tooth. Goodnight, sweetheart, time to go. Sleepy."

A nurse entered and shooed them from the room saying he needed to rest.

The ladies tiptoed from the room. Tamara said, "He's hallucinating, poor guy. I don't want him to go gently into that good night, Meg. I like him, and I want to work with him forever. No use talking to him about the lyrics and music today, I guess. If his right side is badly damaged, he'll not be playing the piano or saxophone anytime soon, if ever. Would they tell us what his injuries are?"

"I doubt it. We're not family. But maybe would say how serious it is. Go ask that nurse when she comes from the room."

Tamara stationed herself outside the door. The nurse said that it was not life threatening but was a serious injury. She told them to return at afternoon visiting hours.

Meg commented as they walked down the stairs, "It did looked pretty bad. At least the doctors and nurses here have a lot of experience in treating severe wounds. He described it was though he twirled like a weather vane, but the assailant struck at his vein in vain. Homophones."

"It's not a time to be showing off your vocabulary, being flippant." Tamara was irritated. "Although those are also homonyms in some definitions. Well, I'll remember your homophones to tell him because those are rather humorous. Sorry I was grouchy there for a second, but I was shaken because he looks terrible. I wonder what really happened."

"Maybe he doesn't know although he mumbled that description. Sometimes trauma seems to erase the memories immediately surrounding an event. That I know well; it happened when I fell in a river last month. I couldn't recall anything until later, and then things came back together from the bits and pieces. I'm still not sure that I remember everything."

Tamara gave a tiny moan. "Wish I could do something to help him get better. I really like him. In fact, I have my cap set for him. You can stand up with us, and he can choose his best man when he's better. I'm going to take him back home to Nashville where I went to college at Vanderbilt. I just know he would love it there. So much opportunity and music start-ups. Too, the school was founded and funded by a crotchety ole man who drove a paddle wheel up and down the Mississippi and called himself a 'Commodore'. There's lots of good music coming from that there town––I'm sure you've heard of The Grand Ole Op'ry?"

"Oh, yes, of course. Armed Forces Radio mentions it and so have you before."

"And the Maxwell House is a hotel there. You've heard of the coffee named for it? During the Civil War the stairs up each side of the lobby to the balcony were used as beds for wounded soldiers. I wish we didn't have wars. Just coffee and music. Sip and sway and sing on the steam boats."

Meg said, "Here's an idea that just occurred to me while you were conjecturing up a dreamy future. A lot of popular songs use a theme from a classical music piece. For instance, 'I'm Always Chasing Rainbows' is from the middle part of Chopin's *Fantasy Impromptu*. My folks had a record player, and we frequently listened to major works while we read or worked on making something with our hands.

"Earlier, I noticed a record store somewhere around here. Let's see if a clerk could help us find a cheery piece of music that would fit his rhyming scheme. Something from a quick Chopin composition or a Strauss waltz or whatever we can unearth. How serendipitous if something would fit his lyrics, *ne*? Something perky for the vacation bound, or someone *longing* to be on a vacation."

"We could serenade him outside the window. No, maybe softly during visiting hours," Tamara said gleefully. "I hope you're familiar with composers."

"I recognize some when I hear a melody." Meg lifted her sunglasses and peered across the boulevard at a record store. She held her nose at the stench from the honey-bucket cart trailing down the street behind two oxen and fingered her earrings.

"Where did you find those earrings that look like silver honey-buckets?" asked Tamara, peering at Meg's ear lobes as they stood waiting at the corner for a signal from the traffic cop. He was waving his arms to direct traffic from his dais at the center of the intersection.

"At the PX last week," Meg responded. "I thought Kurt would be amused at the sight, but he couldn't even lift his head. A little wad of cotton with a dab of cologne fits inside the earrings; that gives a better fragrance than those honey-buckets have."

"I am enchanted by them. I'll look for a pair for myself. I'm sure he'd make some outlandish remark. I devoutly wish I were not going to Kyoto this coming weekend because I'm concerned about Kurt. I want to be by him as he recovers."

Meg stopped dead on the sidewalk, causing an elderly lady walking by who was carrying one egg in her palm, to bring it protectively to her chest.

"Hey, I'll give you the earrings if I can take your place on the trip. It was full when I checked with Special Services, and I was really disappointed. I feel a need to get out of town and do some exploring of Japanese culture."

"Oh, you don't have to give me those, but I'll accept," she said holding out her hand as Meg unscrewed the earrings.

"Perfect exchange. I can amuse him with two things, these and music. If we can find some music, I mean. I'll hunt down a record player to determine how well some selections match his rhymes with the rhythm.

"It's a three day trip there to Kyoto and back, Friday through Sunday, Meg. Allowing for success on finding possible music, I'll have some choices for you to hear when you return. Moreover, staying here, I can see him every day and find out how extensive the injuries are."

"The chaplain's assistant, Mitch Holland, would know the name of the fellow who brought a record player to a supper party at Gamagori," Meg suggested.

Tamara screwed the earrings on her lobes, took out a compact, and admired her ears in the mirror. "I'll never ever have pierced ears. After I read how Rose had hers done in *Eight Cousins*, I felt nauseous. That reminds me, you should have heard Kurt object when I told him he would be my guest at the movie *Little Women* playing at the Asahi Press building. That's why he called me hardhearted Tamara like the song about the vamp of Savannah. It turned out to be a good movie, so he's just putting on a show."

Browsing through the records in the store was difficult because the labels were garbled versions of the Western names of conductors or soloists or titles. The resulting names were conflated by translations that had evidently been drafted into Japanese and then translated back into English. The air in the store was filled, however, with the raucous sound of *samisens* plinking to no recognizable melody and drums dully throbbing thunk-thunk-thunk to no recognizable beat.

"I'll look up some words in my dictionary tonight and study how to pronounce them and come back here after I visit him tomorrow morning," Tamara said. "Let's go to Special Services, DAFC office, and get you routed to Kyoto."

CHAPTER TWENTY-NINE

S gt. Marvin Martin reported in to Meg Wednesday night. He'd finished a globe prototype. In fact, he had made two of them and would meet her at the American Village ball field Thursday night after his softball game. If it were all right, he'd assume she could get there by herself.

Following the Thursday game, Meg said, "I need to explain why I changed the word 'right'--that I usually use to agree with you--to the word 'correct' when you said for me to meet you at the game. I caused a snafu last Tuesday."

She led the way to the schoolhouse, unlocked the door, and waved him inside. She turned on the hall and stairwell lights before they started up to her classroom.

Marty said, "I'll believe whatever you tell me about it, for sure. I think you, in particular would have snafus frequently, a normal 'situation all fouled up,' to use the polite definition."

Meg ignored his comment. "The other night Colonel Jones and his wife were taking me to the hotel from a party at the Sheldons' house. He wanted to look at a Japanese house I had mentioned. He asked, 'Is this the street?' I said, 'Right,' and he signaled and turned right into a narrow street. I asked why he had turned; he told me what I had said. I replied that I meant 'correct,' that his question about the street we *had* been on was correct. He couldn't back up because a coal-burning truck was behind us. We wandered around a bit and finally were back on track. That was a grammar lesson I learned." She laughed.

She added, "Tonight, Marty, I was looking forward to seeing you and Phil Tyler play softball again. He helped me when my shoe caught in the bleachers at the baseball park, and I broke my pearl necklace. I need to thank him sometime."

"Yes, he told me. He went back but no more pearls were found. Have you restrung them yet?"

"Have to find some heavy thread."

"I'll look at the craft shop," Marty offered.

"Oh, thanks. That'll help. Tell me about the bird's fortune telling? Did Hagikawa translate your fortune from that envelope the raven undid the ribbon on?"

"He said it said, 'The future is ahead.'"

They both chuckled. "Can't prognosticate anything in addition to that one," Meg said, as they went into her classroom.

"Not exactly Nostradamus," agreed Marty. "Can't predict what's already happening to one's self, much less what's in the future."

"I had a letter from my boyfriend, Walt, in St. Louis. He's curious about what's already happened here because I've slipped some generalities into my letters to him. I feel I can't tell him anything definitive about this month's events. It's all murky. But, he'd be sure to tell my fortune from off the top of his head if I hinted at the murders I know about."

Meg swept her eyes around the room, sensing something wrong, something out of kilter, just as Marty exclaimed, "Look here! Some kids have cut the United States from the globe. Sounds as though the piece fell inside. When I twist the hole toward you, see if your fingers can reach inside and extract it. Maybe we can repair it."

He held the globe shoulder high as Meg tried to maneuver the piece inside to the outside. She pulled out a small card featuring an evil face, as phantasmagoric as those on the statues guarding the gate to a shrine.

"Some jokers," she said angrily. "Oh, oh, let's check the big map rolled above the blackboard."

"This may be deliberate damage, directed at you, Meg," Marty said. "I doubt dependant children would do this. It must be someone who has access to the school and doesn't like you, however, who would and could do it. Do you hear me?"

"People keep saying 'now hear this' to me as if they were talking at me through those megaphones used at ball games. I hear, I hear." She groaned when she pulled down the five-foot wide map and saw that the middle portion was sagging where the United States had been scissored out of North America.

"Definitely deliberate. Look at how closely they followed the border lines," Marty said, running his fingers along the shorn edges. "But weren't you were planning on revising both the globe and map anyway? Wouldn't that be something if they ended up doing you a favor by speeding things along?"

Meg tried to laugh. "Well, yes, but I don't like this type of favor, Marty."

"Let's go to work, then, ourselves. I didn't try to measure that wall map the other day and wouldn't have measured the States anyway. They haven't changed boundaries since 1912, and although we'll probably be adding two more states soon, that won't affect the contiguous states," Marty said, hands on his hips, surveying the vandalism.

"I'll get a ruler, and you make notes again," she offered. "I know what else is wrong. My reference book on the Orient is missing. I'm pretty sure I left it open on my desk before the

School Board meeting last Tuesday week. And I had some glue on the desk, too, to do the map and globe makeovers. I'd decided to have the American History class re-do the wall map. Maybe I was prescient in my planning, now that it is obviously necessary."

She took a ruler from her center desk drawer, handed some paper and a pencil over to Marty and started trying to position the ruler sideways and lengthwise where he indicated. It was a lot harder to position than the tape measure had been, and when the ruler slipped from her hand for the third time, she simply gave up and tossed it over her shoulder.

Marty flinched when it clattered against the floor. "Do you notice anything else that's been tampered with?" he asked after a moment.

"All this is quite enough," she said sadly. She shuddered at the invasion of her territory: not being able to confront an antagonist was unsettling. She'd have to set up rules the way Althea had for the science lab––meaning that no one is permitted to enter without approval each time. She began to wonder if it would be permissible to lock the door to her classroom. Althea was able to keep intruders out of the science lab; why could she not from a social science classroom?

"I wonder if the janitor took my Durante book to the teachers' lounge or the storm shelter. And why would she? None of the textbooks seem to have been disturbed, dust has accumulated on the tops and thus not been wiped off," she remarked, eying the bookshelves with a searching glare. "We should check downstairs."

Marty abruptly rejected the idea of going to check the storm shelter with a vehement shake of his head. "The lounge, okay, we can check. But we're not going down there to the below ground tunnel. It'd be dangerous after an earthquake until the engineers check it out and make any repairs."

"But a group of us already looked. It was just dusty. Maybe we could take just a peek down the stairs to where the cots are? After I check out the teacher's lounge?" she wheedled. "I won't go any farther. See if my book's somewhere."

"All right, a peek." He sounded as if he finally realized that she was worried about her tome.

Marty needed to bring his tape measure for the wall map because it was too big to be able to gauge things with the foot-long ruler. After settling the second Mercator projection on the globe to discover the better fit of the two, they went down to the teacher's lounge but found nothing resembling a book. Next, they walked to the janitor's closet to find the trap door had been raised. A lantern gleamed from the hole.

Meg saw the same transformation in his demeanor as when he discovered the bomb in Higashiyama Park: calm, serious, intent in his manner. Without a sound, Marty drew his gun. She drew back two steps to lean against a wall.

"Hold it right there!" he barked at a man at the bottom of the stairs.

"Don't shoot, fellow. I'm an electrician!" begged an American, stammering as he shot his hands in the air like a Fourth of July rocket and turning so that they could see his Army patch.

"All right." Marty holstered his pistol. "Why are you down there this time of night?"

"Some engineers found that the light bulbs had been shattered, bits of sharp glass like confetti all over the floor around the corner, and the electric wire cut. I hope who ever cut the wire got shocked to his toes. It's a mess, and I'm not a housekeeper. I just do wiring, bulbs."

Meg came forward and stooped over the stairwell beside Marty. "Do you see any books down there?" she asked.

"Lady, I'm not looking for books." He glanced down the hall over his shoulder. "No books. No librarians. Can I get back to work?"

"Of course," Marty said, standing upright and taking her arm. "We're leaving. We had an incident involving a death here last month, and that's made us jittery."

"You've just heard about another more recent incident that'd make anyone jittery," the GI replied snidely. "Might say this one was a real shocker." He laughed.

The couple left the school, pondering the various types of damage that were occurring. As they walked out through the west gate, Meg said, "Actually, there was a third incident that I know of." She recounted her encounter with Mr. Yamata. "Then the other teachers called me, and he literally shoved me out into the hall, and he locked the door. I put gum in the lock."

"You did? Why?" Marty stopped dead and stared at her.

"If I wanted to get back in, I'd just hold ice against the gum and dig it out. I told Mr. Sheldon about this, but he already knew. Yamata had complained about me. I'm going to have to write Yamata a letter of apology saying I regretted disturbing his 'p-i-e-c-e' of mind. I think I can get away with the misspelling."

Marty said, "I doubt that you can be so insulting and not be found out. He teaches Japanese to English speaking people. He must have a pretty good vocabulary to do that. Plus he'd understand the difference between *peace* and *piece*."

Meg was focused on relating her scary experience and paid no attention to Marty's demurral. "Yamata also demanded that Kurt Salchow repair the lock. He was trying to do so when someone swung a sword that broke the electric light wiring last Friday evening and slashed Kurt on the arm, too. The electrician didn't include that little anecdote in his recital of what he called the more recent incident down there."

"I had not heard of this either. Any idea why Yamata asked for Kurt especially?"

"Maybe because Kurt doesn't date Fumiko any more. He hasn't been able to find her––at least that's what Kurt said–– and, therefore, her dad's trying to get them back together. Maybe after I gummed up the works, her dad thought that Kurt ungumming them would help the couple chew the fat again."

Sgt. Martin swung around and, for the first time, frowned at her. "What impression do you, a member of the Occupation Forces, make upon the Japanese? You are a member of the *Occupation Forces,* and you are acting like we're on a college campus ripe for high jinks. Your years of education should have prepared you for fitting into a different culture easily. I was drafted when I graduated high school in '44, but young as I am, I know how to be dignified in America's best interests here. Especially now, you are aware that there are delicate, serious matters under investigation."

She sank back from his anger, his glare, but kept her chin up stiffly as she replied in an even, somewhat amused, voice, "Marty, I keep my history classes engaged in a 'dead subject' by being dramatic and humorous. You should see me act out the Hamilton-Burr duel! As if I need an etiquette lesson here. Why don't you admit that the informal, easy-going manners of folksy-wolksy Missourians are more pleasant? Or else why don't you get me copies of *General Emily Post's Military Etiquette Book For Occupation Forces* or maybe *Bill Maudlin's Book of Jokes For Asia* and give me a test on them? I think the Americans are already seen as kindly and pleasant. The atmosphere here is benign."

"That's because we *are* friendly. We're as tired of war as the general population is. We're even careful not to shoot at their frightening masked characters, as you may remember. That's why you didn't get shot the night I first met you when you were being that *kimono* ghost."

"What amuses them, if not practical jokes? Remember my occupational specialty, Marty--teacher? A teacher could not survive in the classroom day after day without having a humorous outlook with which to respond to high school students."

"How would I know what you're asking about that amuses an Oriental mind? Maybe practical jokes amuse kids in Missouri but what do you know about the high schoolers here? Also ask someone else who knows what amuses the Japanese. Cripes, I'm tired of escorting you around. I'm exhausted, and I have to pull double shifts for a while. And, I'm tired of being kidded about being a teacher's pet because I've been assigned to escort you around town. Please tell me you've made some tour plans. I hope so."

"Yes. I'm going to Kyoto on Friday."

"Thank goodness. Learn something about Japan first hand from the Japanese, not just from books. Say 'Nagoya, *sayonara*.'"

"I haven't been to Nara yet or Nikko to hear no evil, see no evil, speak no evil." Meg accompanied the words with her hands over her ears, eyes, and mouth, in turn, as she tried to kid him out of his funk. Suddenly she slapped her left hand and then held her nose.

"What're you doing?" he asked warily.

"Touch no evil, smell no evil."

At last, she elicited a small laugh out of him though it was quickly followed by a sigh. "You're taking everything light heartedly. I guess that's one way to cope. I'm pleased you're going to go do a tourist trip, get out of town for a bit. Be *out* of touch. Can't *stink up* the investigation, either."

"Yes, all right, I hear that, got it, and I'll get to see more of the cultural background that made this nation." At least, he opted not to mention that she might've *gummed up the works*.

Marty looked back at the American Village. "Myself, I'm scheduled back at work for those double shifts. I told Ingrid how I was helping you with the maps, but now I must apologize because I have to postpone that work for a while. I'm worn thin as an old shoe."

"Oh, I have time before I need those maps. I believe you about the seriousness of the investigations and my demeanor. I'll be an obedient little girl, go enjoy myself, and wait for the denouement. Good night. And, Marty, I am grateful for all you've done. I'll let you know when I'm back in town, and we can finish making copies of the globe projection blanks and those on the wall map.

"Even my Walt Raleigh had written that I was rather acting as though I were on an exotic island, like the Galapagos with Darwin, populated by nothing except visiting Americans observing the local fauna. Which I have been doing, admittedly."

"That's rather self-centered, Meg. Do some good; or, yes, at least, find out what the local life is like. I'll have the globe Mercator finished in about a month after I'm relieved from double duty."

"We can't see the cloisonné and Noritake factories?"

"Go see them in some other town or with somebody else," Marty said softly.

"Yes, sir, laddie. I'm ready to go to the hotel. Shall I call us a taxi from the principal's office?"

"Yes. It's getting late. After I let you off, I'll take these rough outlines of the map back to the Ozone barracks. I probably won't get to make copies for a few weeks. I'll call you then."

The sky to the west was colored red and orange. "Red at night, sailor's delight," Meg thought to herself. She was looking after the taxi and the next minute looking up at the heavens. "I wonder if such a night is ever followed by a 'red in the morning, AP's warning.'"

CHAPTER THIRTY

During an early morning swim Thursday, Meg remembered Althea's suggesting that she buy some hats from Sharon. After she returned to her room, Meg called Sharon Sheldon and put the question to her.

"What an idea! Look, I'm going over to the Quonset hut nearest the school today to work. We're going to have a silent auction to raise money for the school. It was Mrs. Fritz's idea. We're selling everything from the bomb shelter, plus an assortment of other items people are donating or want to get ride of--like my hats. You can get my hats then if you win out. All except the silk one I wore at Althea's wedding."

"I've never heard of a silent auction."

"People put their name and their bid on a slip of paper, and put the paper under the item. Highest bid wins. Haven't you ever raised money?"

"I sold Girl Scout cookies, somewhat reluctantly, and my sorority had rummage sales but myself, I didn't get any money from those. I worked for my money. My folks did auction cattle every couple of years."

"This is quieter than a cattle auction, thank goodness, and smells a lot better. Why don't you come over to the Quonset room and help me? I'll be there about 1000 hours. The other girls can't get there until after lunch."

"I'll be there. When will the auction be?"

"This Saturday. We're almost out of time. We have to have the auction room cleared for the kindergarten kids before school starts."

"Oh, dear, Sharon. I'm going to be out of town, going to Kyoto this weekend. May I put the hats on layaway?"

"I'll think about that. I'm currently busy pulling together some furniture polish and rags and vinegar to clean the items. Do you have any spare soap you could bring?"

"Lifebuoy and Ivory."

"Bring one of those and a bottle of water. There's such an assortment of material. Who knows what will work on what? Mr. Yamata said some of the items in the warehouse inventory were not his, and Mrs. Fritz said they weren't hers either. Everything is in addition to the ones she was purposely saving for a Monte Carlo auction. However, we don't have time to hold that type of auction before school starts."

"Yes, that sounded rather elaborate but a lot of fun."

"Moreover, we don't know where the items in the bomb shelter are originally from. No provenances that seem the most likely to indicate antiques. The American wares do not seem to be donations but some type of left-overs. Two GIs are moving the boxes over right now from the warehouse."

Meg replaced the phone and immediately looked for supplies that might help clean the items. Two empty Coke bottles went into her olive green purse. She'd fill them up with water in the little girls' lavatory. The slivers of soap she wrapped in a piece of newspaper.

She removed her camera and flash from her purse; the walk to school was already documented. But of course, whenever she left the camera behind, she could absolutely guarantee that she'd miss a great picture. True to form, she saw two snapshots she would've liked to have taken: first, two little *kimono*-clad, runny-nosed girls squatting by the curb holding chipped teacups to dolls' lips, and the second one was of another little girl with a baby strapped to her back.

The walk to the Village felt easy, carefree, and, somewhat gleefully she thought, was the first time she had walked alone for some time. No shadows trailing her that she could see, either, just the usual crowded sidewalks and familiar sounds, smells, and the slightly humid breeze in her face.

In the Quonset, all the kiddy furniture had been pushed against one wall. Three wood tables were leaning against another wall, and boxes made of cardboard, wood, or lacquer were around the door. Sharon and Meg snapped the tables' legs in place, and then the two teachers turned the tables over and lifted them upright. They placed a box on each to unpack.

Meg's first box had an assortment of items. "How do you want to organize all this stuff?" she asked Sharon.

"Let's put items for children––dolls, kites, lanterns, cloth toys, little statues that are unbreakable, for instance, on one end of your table. The lacquer chests we'll leave against a wall. Over here, let's place small items that are made of lacquer, next to them ones of cloisonné, and over on the last table, put anything of ivory or the big decorative items. If that doesn't work, we'll rearrange."

"Some things are certainly grimy. Probably were pulled from the rubble after a bombing raid."

"We'll try a dab of vinegar and water first, on the bottom, to see if that works, Meg. No, let's just rub them gently first, and maybe the dirt'll come off. Then we'll try vinegar, then your soap and water. If all else fails, we'll leave them as is."

"Got it." They started gently working with the rags on the ivory pieces.

"What happened to the stuff that looked like it came from the PX or commissary?"

"Taken back to the shelter for emergencies or discarded if trashy."

"Oh. Makes sense. Do you know when you're leaving for ZI?" Meg asked.

Sharon smiled. "In mid-September. It'll be a nice time of year to travel. Aren't many typhoons this late in the year. I won't get seasick on a Navy ship. The food is too good." She sang, "The Navy gets the gravy, and the Army gets the beans, beans, beans, beans."

"Indeed, I didn't eat much on the ship I came over on so I wouldn't know. I have heard the Navy does serve better food." Meg paused in her work and turned her questioning eyes to Sharon. "What's this box for? It doesn't have a lid," Meg asked with curiosity in her voice, handing the item to Sharon.

"I like these boxes, kind of a puzzle to open. Exquisite craftsmanship with the different colored wood pieces." Meg watched as Sharon pushed aside a panel on the end that let a panel on the side slide over, then one on other end slid out, and a lid opened.

Sharon exclaimed, "What a cute brooch inside. It may be gold. Have to have that appraised." She removed the pin, put it in her shirt pocket, and slid all the panels back into place on the small box.

Meg had begun unpacking a number of fierce looking dragons, dogs, and demons, when a knock sounded at the door.

Sharon answered it to find a Japanese girl on the doorstep who stuttered, "Ms. Sh-She'don. I din't know you here . . ."

Meg turned around as Sharon said, "Well, Fumiko Yamata, it's you. My husband––"

Fumiko noticed Meg, and her eyes squinted. Without warning, Fumiko pulled out of her *kimono* sleeve a red ball, about eight inches around with a face painted on it, aimed it at Meg, and then darted away down the street with it in her hand.

Meg first ducked, thinking it was being thrown at her, started to exclaim and go out the door after the girl when nothing was thrown--but suddenly a trembling started under her feet. She was thrown a bit sideways as an earthquake hit the building, grabbed the walls and shook them. Meg dived under a table, thankfully not the one that crashed down on one end, and Sharon braced herself in the entrance doorway. The tables holding the auction goods had items tumbling from them and on them, and one table collapsed.

Outside the American Village could be heard loud noises, probably buildings crumbling, roofs crashing, stone fences roiled. Then, the sirens on police, ambulance, and fire engines began wailing.

"What a fine mess this is! Do you think people are hurt?" Meg crawled out and stood, went to the door, and peered out but saw no damage to the houses in the Village.

"Japanese know how to handle themselves during a quake, Meg. The authorities are on top of responding quickly to any needing help."

"At least inside here it's the metal things that fell and not the vases," Meg said, surveying the floor around the collapsed table. She turned around as Sharon came over to help and asked, "Why did you stand in the doorway like that?"

The two ladies set the table back upright after snapping the legs more firmly in place.

"Standing in a doorway is an alternative to hiding under a piece of furniture. I couldn't have made it over here," Sharon replied.

"Is another quake coming? That one only lasted a few seconds."

"Don't think so but never can tell. Nagoya could be at the tail end of where the primary shake was."

"Wasn't that Fumiko Yamata at the door just before the earthquake?" Meg asked. The earthquake again left her with an odd feeling of unfinished business, the same uneasy feeling she had when she and Marty had been in the zoo earthquake.

"Yes. I don't know why she ran away but when the quake started she probably went to check on her poor father."

"What was that red ball she pulled from her sleeve to show me?" Meg glanced at Sharon.

"I'll eat my hat if you haven't been hexed," Sharon joked and smiled. "It was a *papier mache* figure with one eye colored in--colored in blue, notice--and she aimed it at you. When you *die*, she'll color in the other eye. She'll figure she brought on the earthquake to get you."

"Should I wear a garlic necklace?" Meg bent to pick up two more metal items to replace on the table.

"'Fraid that's for warding off vampires. I'll call Bill in a little while and tell him she's still around, pulling arcane tricks. I swear, I'm glad to be going home where the only thing to worry about is being soaped on Halloween. Or having air let out of the car tires. Did you notice how they use old tires here for the soles of those straw sandals, the *zoris*? Here it's like how it was back in the Depression era when people made sure that nothing remotely usable went to waste."

"I wondered why those straw sandals didn't fall apart on a rough alley way. I'll just keep my rabbit's foot in my pocket to protect me from the hex and hope she trips up or blows an inner tube under the soles of her *zoris* so that she has to stop to repair a flat if she's chasing me."

"I'll tell Bill we saw her here. Meanwhile, here, you kneel and hand things that crashed onto the floor back up to me. That'll be quicker than both of us stooping and standing with every item. We should have everything unpacked by noon. This afternoon we'll do the refurbishing."

"How'd Fumiko get in the American Village anyway? I thought she quit being a janitor at the school. Wasn't her Pass lifted?"

"Undoubtedly. Oh, the sentries could have recognized her from when she worked here. They're not supposed to be easy-going any more but I suspect they're lax. It's been a goodly number of weeks since servants were dismissed for thieving. Could be the guards were replaced, too, and the new ones don't know to screen native workers who appear to know what they're doing as they stride in the gates."

Meg finally stood and started unloading another box. "Oh, here's the dog with the broken ear that was in the Worth box I gave Colonel Jones. I bet I could use some clay and repair it."

"I doubt anyone'd bid on that. Take it with you as your pay for helping."

"When I receive my first paycheck, I'll donate a pence and ha'penny into the general fund," Meg rejoined. "Now, how do I insure that my silent bids win your two hats?"

"I'm not going to tell you. That'd be cheating. Just know that two bits ain't gonna win."

"Okay. I'll give you a sealed envelope with my bids for the two hats. For down payment on the layaway plan, I'd give you four bits. Total bid is a secret. Know that the envelope is to be opened after all the other bids, understand?" Meg was thinking rapidly that Sharon was trying to outguess her, and she was trying to outguess Sharon.

The two straw hats were on a chair. Meg tried them on, with her compact open, and eyed her reflection as she wore each one. "Oh, bother. I'll go ahead and pay you a buck each. Is that satisfactory?"

Sharon nodded, grinned, and said, "Cash on the barrel head."

"It'll be better than possibly buying some junky souvenir in Kyoto, I know. And, I'll have months to go back there if what I want isn't junk." She pulled out her wallet and passed the money over.

"You're not adding the four bits?"

"No, it's included because I didn't put them on hold," Meg retorted firmly.

"You're a hard bargainer. It's double what I expected, and I and the students of Nagoya American School, also the American Occupation, the Allied Command, and President Truman thank you for your donation on behalf of the future of America. The buck stops here––make that 'bucks.'" She waved the dollar scrip above her head.

"It's my pleasure, ma'am. Plus I have a free wounded dog to care for. However, as of this minute, I'm famished. Let's take a break. Is the commissary open?"

Sharon looked at her watch. "We better hurry. It closes at noon on Thursdays."

Sharon locked the door behind them. She said, "There's Annie Torleone over there with her new baby on their front porch. Let's say 'hello' and see if she liked the little earthquake."

A big sun hat shielded the red hair and fair face of the mother holding a tiny baby.

A large dog was watching them approach with interest. Its great jaws rested lazily on its large paws, and it sniffed the hair with a raised nose before returning to sleep.

"Hi, Sharon. Come on over. Yukiko almost has lunch set up. You have time for lunch and coffee?" Mrs. Torleone called.

"Yes, thanks, we were hurrying to grab a bite before the store closed. This is Miss Margaret Lowe, history teacher." Meg stood on the sidewalk and smiled a greeting.

"Ah, me lassie. You helped the Worth girl when she, Corey, and Stilwell found that body." Mrs. Torleone turned magnificent blue eyes toward Meg with thanks in her eyes.

"Yes. Unusual and terrifying for her. She upchucked several times in my wastebasket. Corey was great. Steady demeanor during the whole unpleasant discovery."

"So, this is Laurie Ann?" said Sharon, bending down over the baby.

"Best baby I've had. The boys were always screaming to be fed. She wakes up and gurgles."

"Did the earthquake do any damage to your place?" Meg moved up the steps onto the porch.

"No. This dog of ours, name of Stilwell, for General Vinegar Joe Stilwell," the dog raised its head when it heard its name and then slumbered again, "always warns us when a quake's coming. I swear he sounds like a cat, actually *mews* a few seconds before an earthquake. That's when I take to the out-of-doors. The boys are off playing ball somewhere, but they know to stay outside or crawl under something. Nothing breakable in this house, at all at all. Too many lumbering boys. They do keep their room as neat as if they're military recruits, though. Harry taught them that. When

I came home from the Base Hospital yesterday morning, they'd even prepared me a feast.

"What were you doing in the Quonset hut? You're not teaching elementary school this year, are you, Sharon?" Annie asked.

"No, Bill and I are leaving soon for the States. Meg and I were going through some items that the former principal had gathered for a rummage sale for a Monte Carlo night. I'm turning it into a silent auction this week, because most of the items are pretty but fragile, and it's hard to keep them nice when they are stored in the warehouse with all the heavy military supplies. The auction'll be Saturday 0900 hours to 1400. The notice will be in the paper tonight and tomorrow night."

"I'll stop by Saturday morning, squirrel away some souvenirs in case the boys get married some day. They don't think long range about their time here and, later, might enjoy having mementos from Japan."

"There are some nice things," Sharon acknowledged.

"Meg, Sharon: Corey is sure to ask what you know about who killed that guy on the lawn at the American School." She looked at her guests.

"I don't believe it's been solved. The victim was a local man, and it's really up to the Metropolitan Police, not us. We're only peripherally involved, Bill says, and that only because it was in the American Village where he was found," Sharon reported.

"Do stay for lunch. I'm not sure Yukiko heard us talking," Annie called over her shoulder, "Yukiko-san, please set two more places."

She patted the baby who was stirring. "I made a pot of ham and beans and some cornbread. Those boys eat everything in sight. After they stuff themselves at lunch, they'll probably have a peanut butter and jam sandwich for dessert."

Meg and Sharon sat in the other wicker porch chairs. The flowers near the porch were streaked red and white. "What are those?" Meg asked.

"I don't know. They look like camellias, I think. They were planted just after we moved in two years ago."

"Doubt we'll ever know. Oh, may I use your phone to call Bill?"

"Sure. Inside on the sideboard. I'm sorry I missed the Fujiyama slides."

"I can bring the slide projector over tomorrow afternoon and show you and the boys. It was a hard trip but one we'll talk about for years." She went inside to call Bill.

"What have you been doing this summer, except setting plans for the fall enrollment?" Annie's eyebrows rose knowingly at Meg as if to say, "I know you have met my sons, earlier at Gamagori and then during the crime scene we just discussed."

Meg nodded at the unspoken remark and replied, "Swimming, tennis, Kyoto for the weekend."

Sharon returned and sat back in a chair. "Told Bill about our visiting hexer," she said aside to Meg. Meg nodded.

"Here come the voracious appetites," Annie said, handing the baby to Sharon as Tory and Corey came charging across the road. "I'll go dish up the food. Not much in the way of a salad from the Army Corps' crops this time of year, I'm afraid. The boys don't care for salad anyway. They do eat fruit and that will be our salad and dessert. Harry will be here in a few minutes."

The boys greeted Mrs. Sheldon and Miss Lowe, ran into the house, and returned with splashes of water in their burr haircuts. "Where's Dad?"

"He'll be here, your mom said," Miss Lowe replied. "How much did you shake with the earthquake?"

"That was little more than a takedown tackle in football, right, Corey?"

"Good description. We just danced around a bit. How's our baby sister?" Corey asked, leaning over Sharon's side and peering at the little face. The baby opened her eyes and burped.

CHAPTER THIRTY-ONE

Meg hurried through the permission business once again, with Tamara at her side approving the transposition of their plans. The train trip cost a little over a dollar (in *yen*), each way, for coach fare. Meg briefly wondered aloud if she'd be riding on the "Dixie" because, she was saying to Tamara, they had completed a "fixie" on the ticket.

Three other ladies and four couples left early Friday with Meg from the Nagoya station for the tour of Kyoto. Other passengers in the car they boarded were from places all the way up north to Yokohama and Tokyo and were already tired.

Meg could not see that anyone on the platform––or later in the Occupation Forces coach––seemed particularly interested in her. She gave a sigh of relief.

The four ladies choose two seats facing each other. Meg was happy she had Sharon's straw hat on her head because the others wore summer hats, also.

The lieutenant introduced herself to Meg as Wanda Norton, said she was quartered at the Dai-ichi Hotel, and, knew Betty Carnahan. Unexpected by Meg, she moreover revealed that she had been the nurse on the cormorant trip and distinctly remembered Meg's fall over the side of the tour boat. She commented that Meg looked quite different in the daytime, clean, dry, and not heaving. Meg told her that Betty had mentioned her being there.

The other two ladies, sitting across from them, were military wives whose husbands were on TDY in Korea, by name Cornelia Postman and Patty Young. They passed the four-hour journey by sharing interesting personal histories and travel experiences. The latter discussion, though, found Meg silent. Coming to Japan was the first time she'd been outside of Missouri; and all of the others had been through the same type of travel as she had across the Pacific Ocean on a ship, followed by the whirl through the local registration offices in Nagoya. She had experienced nothing on that trip that they didn't already know. After this trip to Kyoto, she'd have more to share when similar conversations arose.

The outings they described could have filled a travel book: traveling by donkeys in South American; riding a barge on the Elbe; sailing in Hawaii; skiing in Colorado; kayaking in Alaska, all while accompanying their husbands' units, or in Wanda's case, transferring among bases with her own medical group. Meg's story about the black market swipes in Nagoya didn't quite fit the tenor of those adventures plus she was not sure if the information was hers to relate--she might be breaking some military law. The warnings from Bill, Robbie, and Marty had left her somewhat intimidated, an unusual feeling.

After the few hours on the train, having passed green hills and rice paddies, seen the always smoking wood-fueled vehicles and the oxen yoked carts, looked down upon small hamlets of one-story wood houses, some half-destroyed by bombs or earthquakes, the Kyoto Station appeared as the train slowed. They stood when the train stopped and exited down the steps to the platform. Their accommodations were at the Kyoto Hotel, not far from the train station and close to the Imperial Palace grounds in central Kyoto. They followed the Special Services non-com to the bus.

After they arrived and checked in, the four ladies met for lunch in the formal hotel dining room. Meg laughed out loud when she picked up the typed menu at her place, and she had to explain how frankfurters kept showing up to sate her appetite.

Kyoto Hotel
Lunch
Puree of Vegetable Soup
Steamed Frankfurters
Barbecue Sauce
Boiled Potatoes Hot Sauerkraut
Fruit Salad
Hot roll Butter
Dessert
Applesauce Cake
Coffee

After eating, they took a nice leisurely stroll of some six blocks around the Kyoto Hotel area. Along the way, they looked into the Imperial Palace grounds (actually there were three palaces including the Imperial) and continued back to the hotel.

Meg chatted to the other three as they walked. "I read that Kyoto has some 187 shrines, and all are supposed to be ON LIMITS, but some do have restricted hours when tourists may visit. The US declared Kyoto an Open City during the war, that is, not to be bombed, and that's why it is such an intact attraction and so mysterious like. It's a center of both Buddhism and Shintoism, their monuments as well as shrines. Some of what I'd call monuments are actually features of a landscape or garden. The main feature such as an enormous rock that attracts visitors." The excitement in her voice seemed to enchant the others.

At fourteen hundred hours, they took a brief bus tour around town to map out preferences for onsite visits for one look-see this afternoon and others on Saturday. Another tour might be squeezed in Sunday morning before they caught the train home. This evening they were all to attend a three-hour *Noh* play.

"The tour bus is scheduled to take us to that *Noh* play tonight. Our friend, Betty," she said to the lieutenant, "told me that it is really long. She found it incomprehensible but was glad she had seen it. I'll probably doze during it so poke me if I snore."

Because Meg was a historian somewhat knowledgeable about the temples, gardens, and palaces, the other three suggested that she choose their activities. Each tourist, upon registration in Nagoya, had been given a pamphlet with a description of a few of the most well known sites. Meg agreed to map out activities for Saturday and perhaps Sunday morning as well as this afternoon. She settled back in the seat, picked out a few of the best places sited close enough to each other so that they wouldn't have to rush and then offered up her suggestions. She enjoyed thinking about the history of each site.

She leaned across Wanda to include Cornelia and Patty, who were seated across the aisle. "Let's spend this afternoon at the Gold Pavilion *Kinkaku-ji* on the west side of Kyoto. We can go inside it, then go outside to take pictures of the temple from across its lake and also walk around studying the gardens."

"Sounds fine by me," Patty agreed.

"I want explore a few that we would remember clearly," Meg explained. The others nodded approval at the decision. Wanda yawned.

Meg proposed a plan for the next day barely stumbling across the Japanese names. She had found already found that the Japanese language was easy to pronounce, although she had to speak more crisply than she usually did in her soft Missouri drawl. It was intriguing trying to decipher the meaning of the shrines' names from her Japanese/English dictionary.

The Silver Pavilion *Ginkaku-ji* and the *Sanjusangendo* Temple were on the east side of Kyoto. She had studied the names last evening in Nagoya, deciding that *Gin* must mean silver and *Kin*, gold, after looking back and forth between the names of this afternoon's pavilion and the one for tomorrow. And, clearly the Temple's name referred to thirty-three something or the other, *san ju san*. Those two locations, the silver pavilion and the thirty-three unknown-somethings-temple, would take all of Saturday.

On Sunday morning, they could visit the *Nijo* Castle at 0900. The palace had nightingale floors and had already been on Meg's visiting list from remarks she had heard from her teaching colleagues who had been in Japan last year.

Meg looked around at her companions as the bus returned to the hotel and they walked into the dining room to have tea. She concluded her suggestions with a brief note of antique intrigue. "Those *Nijo* Castle floors were built to squeak a warning about intruders to the guards of the 1600s *shogun*, Tokugawa, at his summer place, *Nijo* Castle. *Nijo* is named for Second, *Ni*, Avenue from which one enters the grounds in the middle of Kyoto. Tokugawa had ruled a fourth of the Japanese lands, including the chief mines of coal, copper, gold, lead, nickel, and silver," Meg related. "He was a powerful, legendary man."

Lt. Norton commented quietly, "And American prisoners of war were forced to work in those very mines during our recent war wearing naught but a scrap of cloth and being fed only a scrap of food."

Meg looked at her with wonderment. "I'd not known that."

"Let's not talk about that here. We might be overheard and censored and sent home," Cornelia objected, then changed the subject to a disagreement of little importance, Meg observed. "This pamphlet says the *Nijo* Castle has replicas of the 16 petaled chrysanthemum crest of the Emperor. Our brochure here says nothing about any place having nightingale floors except for those in the *Hongonji* Temple, somewhere else in town."

"I noticed that, but other descriptions that I've read indicate that *Nijo* has them, too," Meg replied softly, realizing she'd better refrain from anything that resembled a lecture. "We'll find out for sure which is correct. I read a lot about Tokugawa in a history book, and that's where I found out about the floors and what they were designed to do. Anyway, we'll find out if it is so when we go there.

"If time permits later Sunday morning, we could also look in the East or West temples of *Hongonji* that Cornelia just mentioned. Or, maybe you'd rather check out the gift shop on Third Street before returning to the hotel for lunch?" Meg turned to look at the ladies seated across from her at the table to check their reactions as she sipped the fragrant, warm tea, surprisingly refreshing on a hot humid tiring day.

"No," Lt. Norton, sitting beside her, said decisively. "We have gift shops in Nagoya. I want to see both East and West temples before we leave, during Sunday morning."

"Roger that. We'll collect our luggage and belongings after lunch, then, for the return to Nagoya," Patty said. Cornelia agreed, also, with the lieutenant's statement.

Meg ran over the itinerary in her mind, anticipating her return to the tourist bus as soon as she refreshed her makeup upstairs. The Occupation Forces had imported nice, comfortable buses for scheduled daily routes as well as these tourist excursions. In contrast, the streetcars and trains for the Japanese were crammed full and looked dirty. Rusty. Pitted. Armaments for various Japanese military units had used all the steel available, including those tons of scrap shipped from the United States throughout the '30s. The civilian population had suffered in more ways than experiencing a lack of food.

#

At the Gold Pavilion Friday afternoon, a priest led them around the temple. He noted almost word for word what Meg had read in the pamphlet. The other ladies were starting to look bored as he intoned. "This temple was originally covered with gold foil, but it wore off a long time ago. A member of the Ashikaga Shogunate built it when he retired and entered the priesthood. Although it was not religious zeal that he wanted to display but the wealth and power of his clan. Many years later, this site became a temple for the Rinzai Sect of Buddhism. If Buddhists wish to put up a shrine in a Shinto district, the Shintoists would probably let them if they construct a Shinto shrine somewhere on the grounds––and vice versa. Shinto shrines feature the huge, red *torii* gates at the entrance."

He added, "There are many different sects in both religions. The Shinto priests are not allowed to marry. Now, perhaps you'd like to stroll in the garden. Just follow the paths." They took his dismissal and end of lecturing with sighs of relief.

On the walkway, another priest who could speak English told them many interesting things about Shintoism and ceremonies that they had not already read. He said that adherents have rules much like the Ten Commandments and have great regard for nature and its calming effect from all its beauty.

All three stories of the Gold Pavilion, mirrored in the lake, seemed to be in a meditative state. Meg became still as she was lost in appreciation of the small lake featuring an island in the shape of Honshu itself. The water was stocked with gold and black carp flashing briefly near the surface as they darted around. After first walking around the lake, she next wandered off taking pictures of the temple, the island, and flowers of the shrine. Finally, in back of the Pavilion, she photographed the God of Luck with its elderly benign face. Maybe with luck she herself would no longer have indigens tripping over her footsteps. So far, she hadn't noticed anyone trailing after her. Lucky that she had left town so quickly without much planning and that she had a rabbit's foot in her handbag.

"That's the first time I've seen a wooden building in Japan higher than a single story. Wonder why it doesn't fall down during an earthquake?" Cornelia murmured behind Meg's back.

"Maybe all these animistic gods keep it high and mighty," Patty offered.

"I think it's darling to appreciate nature. So many things to rejoice in. Did you hear about the practice of priests throwing beans out of the shrine porches to bring fortune in and cast demons out in February? I find that captivating," Wanda added.

"How about banging those huge bells to call the gods and sticking incense in a pot. Or, hanging messages to the gods on a tree by the shrine? Our churches have us pray in unison or silently. I guess we attract God by singing hymns," Meg suggested. "As off-key as I sing, my songs may hit heaven like a discord." *As this country sometimes hits me as being off-kilter.*

The afternoon in the garden was more humid and hot than Meg had experienced anytime back in Nagoya. Yet the unstressed amount of time she'd allowed herself had been a welcome distraction. It had resulted in a sense of contemplation and relaxation in spite of the perspiration damping her outfit and the other ladies' dresses and Norton's uniform. The dark, supernaturally strange temple had captured her imagination what with trying to imagine generations of Japs kneeling, bells knelling, priests needling the congregants. Or maybe people going to Shinto shrines and Buddhist temples didn't hear exhortations against sinning in these large, preternatural buildings.

The bus returned, and they wearily returned to the hotel.

After a dinner of hamburger and mashed potatoes, the ladies each retired to their rooms for a brief rest before they boarded a bus again, this time to the theater with the *Noh* play. Betty had described it perfectly as it turned out. Indeed, it was hard to follow with a few actors emoting and striding dramatically around. What an actor was emoting was unclear because a bland mask covered his face, but he did twirl his fan emphatically at frequent intervals. A trio of drummers seated alongside the west stage banged unfamiliar syncopation. Overall, Meg felt it cast a spell that was rather haunting . . . or daunting. Might result in nightmares.

During the play, Meg was poked twice by Lt. Norton. She shivered as she sat up, awake. Unlike the stories for the two operas that she had read about before attending their presentations back home, this *Noh* play made no sense, was senseless, but badgered her hearing and eyesight until she simply tried to shut down her feelings. She had read nothing about it to explain its plot.

Back at the hotel, she stumbled twice on the way to her room because she was worn "to a frazzle," as her mom would say. Cornelia murmured, "I tripped like that when I tried to wear some *geta*. The floor was too slippery to get a grip in the wooden shoes. Good thing I was next to our bed because I went down face first."

Meg grinned over at her. "I bet the *geta*'re now used for decorating your living room."

"You are correct. Rather pretty lacquered wood ones, as a matter of fact, on the bookshelf."

CHAPTER THIRTY-TWO

While going to the east side of town the next morning to visit the Silver Pavilion, Meg called their attention to the last page of their pamphlets. "No silver was ever used at this one because the *Shogun* died before it could be applied. Yet it still carries that name, just as the gold one did yesterday without any gold." They all grinned.

She added, "I read in another tour guide that it was built, not as a place of worship, but as a retreat for the *Shogun* to carry out his hobbies, such as enjoying flower arranging and the tea ceremony. He didn't take time to govern and therefore the power of the Ashikaga clan waned. Seems to be typical of former ruling families in every country, doesn't it?"

No one seemed to be paying attention to her so she shut up.

The two-story edifice featured a famous garden with a huge heap of sand shaped like Mt. Fuji or, as some brochures called it, the Silver Sand Sea. A priest informed them that rocks from all over Japan were sent as gifts to be added to the pile. A smaller sand pile was called "Facing Moon Platform," and the old *Shogun* sat there to watch the moon and meditate. Rocks and stone bridges dominated the brooding, bucolic garden, one that invited meditation.

Imagine sending a rock to a church! Meg commented that her twin brothers would have been vastly disappointed at Christmas if St. Nicholas had given them a piece of coal (which anyway was useful in winter), much less a rock. They would've thrown a rock far away in disgust while wishing to throw it at whoever sent it to them.

The ladies strolled around, looking up behind the temple at Mt. Higashi, its slopes covered with pines throwing dark shadows on the ground. The hill reminded Meg of the trip to the Nagara River and her dark, cryptic nightmare later that night. In contrast, the placid pond and green gardens were becoming a familiar sight, much like those they'd already viewed.

They moved back to the hotel to rest and partake of the same offering for lunch they'd had the previous day. At least the fruit plate differed. Upstairs afterward, Meg took off her shoes, hose, and garter belt, pulled on her huaraches, changed her dress, and splashed water on her face.

#

An hour later, they once again joined up in the long hotel lobby (with a wistful look at the comfortable cushioned chairs) and took off for the temple on the southeast side of Kyoto, *Sanjusangendo*. The afternoon at the "thirty-three somethings" was more interesting than their morning tour, although it featured strange, weird statues.

"The name came from the number of spaces between pillars, for some *odd* reason," Patty joked. She added, puzzled, gesturing at the long row of the goddess statues, "But why not name it for the thousand statues of the Goddess of Mercy? Now those are something for the sheer number if not for artistic value. If the Buddhists believed the Goddess would cure stricken people, then they sure had a lot of help here."

The chief image was the Thousand-handed Kwannon. In the back hall of *Sanjusangendo* Temple they found statues of 28 followers of the Goddess Kwannon, those gods of wind, thunder and so on who trailed her. The room through which the female foursome then exited held a marvelous statue of a praying woman and of a lean, bearded hermit.

"Why do so many warriors wear horrible masks? And ninjas wear concealing masks? They aren't holding up railroads or banks. And also why do those animals at the temple gates look so fierce?" asked Wanda. "Then in contrast, why do most of these statues have benign expressions?"

"Hum. Impalpable. For sure. And, in contrast, the *Noh* actors wore blank masks, and I thought those were just as scary, being expressionless. You know, I've never read any reason for any of those fierce or blank faces or masks. Maybe they were to become a nightmare that will scare little kids like 'the boogey man'll getcha if ya don't watch out,' and so they behave?" Meg replied.

The other ladies shook their heads. None could fathom the background reasoning.

These big dark temples contrasted sharply with the white clapboard churches back home, to say nothing of big airy granite churches with stained-glass windows that the sun peeked through sending rainbow arcs across the naves.

The guidebook revealed that for the past 350 years, an archery contest had been held here in January, using the long hall from archer to the target, 396 feet. A warrior from long ago still held the record. Meg briefly wondered if someone could hit a tennis ball that whole distance . . . baseball players certainly batted that far.

And a softball player, one Cally Paley, just six weeks ago, had described for her the eerie feeling he had during the dedication of the playing field, the consecration, appeasing some goddess or the other. She had listened in a detached fashion, merely hearing a ghost story, but now she knew what he meant. These dark weird temples created the same uneasy feeling in her. Meg remembered with gratitude that she still carried the rabbit's foot that Marty gave her. Strange how a little thingamajig does make one feel secure.

Nothing was scheduled for the evening, providing the tourists with an evening of small talk in the lobby over a tiny libation before early bedtime.

#

Unable to enter their Sunday morning destination until 0900, the ladies lingered over breakfast. Meg felt a pang of homesickness for some inexplicable reason. She glanced briefly at the other three ladies, slim, clean, confident, posture perfect, poster perfect. Her friends back home could replace them easily with the same demeanor, stance, and sense of well being, comfortable with themselves. They each had achieved something, whether it be marrying an officer or being an officer oneself or having college degrees.

They separately studied their maps indicating the layout of the Castle and its 70 acres. Notable for the ornate decorations inside the 33-room building, as well as 800 *tatami* mats, *Nijo* Castle was one of the Imperial retreats. The Emperor entered through a special gate with his crest on it, a huge 16-petaled chrysanthemum. The American quartet, and others who had also chosen this tour, entered through a more plebeian gate.

After crossing a bridge above a moat, they encountered a large sign featuring Disney characters at the corners. At the bottom corner, Mickey Mouse waved at a map in the center of the board while Pluto seemed sulky about something. At the top, Donald Duck with his three nephews on a corner opposite him blanketed the title.

NIJO CASTLE
Welcome
"The sKetch of the
Palace ground
Kindly advised
you to stroll by this route

Meg took pictures of her companions by the sign and had one of them take her picture. They wandered through some of the rooms. Hurrying along, the ladies decided not to explore the grounds but to continue on to the East and West temples of *Hongonji*.

As they had read in the brochure, the "*Hongonji* temples are the center of a sect of Buddhism, the Shin, most influential of all Buddhist sects, which was founded in 1224. St. Shinran, the founder, carved an image of himself and presented it to his daughter, and it is now in the altar. This altar is called the image of Flesh and Blood because it was varnished with lacquer containing the Saint's ashes."

"I wonder where they get all the red paint for the shrines and *toriis*, surely not from a saint's ashes! I never see anyone painting them, even at Miyajima, which is more colorful than here," said Cornelia. "The Fujiya Hotel located there, I must tell you, is also the most beautiful hotel that I've seen anywhere in the world. Pools to bath in, and one to swim in, curving balconies, and gorgeous adjunct buildings. You-all simply have to see Miyajima this fall. And stay at the Fujiya."

On the Buddhist shrine's porch in a glass case was a segment of thick rope made of human hair. When the shrine was built, devoted female Buddhists all over Japan cut off their hair to make a rope strong enough to raise the huge beams in the temple roof.

The glass case bore a message stating that, of the 53 ropes, "the longest one is 239 feet in length, 1.3 feet in circumference, and 2236 pounds in weight."

Meg turned over the words in her mind, speaking softly, "They had a long hair rope but no more *kin* or *gin*. We have gin to drink and kinship and heirs and longhair music. I know there's been some *kin*-shipping by a Nagoya Japanese-American family who are kin."

"Whatever are you muttering about?" the lieutenant asked.

"Just a play on words. Relatives have been shipping gold, I meant. I like congruent facts," Meg explained, as they exited the porch. "I guess the tour is over. Let's grab a bite to eat." Although she loved history and historical tours, this one was quite enough, already.

During lunch, she introduced a subject she wanted to have others speculate about to confirm her own conjectures. "If you wanted to deliver a message secretly here in Japan, how would you go about it?"

Wanda groaned. "If I myself wanted to send a secret message, I'd just pick up the phone and say something on the party line. If I wanted it to be garbled, I'd play 'telephone,' whisper in the first person's ear, and let it be whispered around the circle. That's always fun."

Cornelia said, "How about writing with lemon juice on paper and the recipient holds it over a candle? Or stuff a message in the knot hole of a tree?"

Patty chimed in, "Put a mark on a fence the way the hobos did during the Depression to signify a house where the lady'd give you a meal in exchange for doing a chore."

"Put a message in plain sight on a theater marquee. We can't read Japanese ideograms, so it'd only be for the natives," Cornelia joked again.

"Ideographs," Meg corrected under her breath.

Patty jumped in like a first grader, bouncing in her chair as she exclaimed, "I know! I know! Ask me! Ask me!" She paused dramatically, "Put a note under a rock with an 'X' marked on it!"

"Very good class. You've had your thinking caps on. No dunce caps in this class. And all messages and everything plucked from an area goes into the garbage and out to sea, like three men in a tub, rub-a-dub-dub," Meg said.

A nice thing about the American ladies was that they could contradict each other without either party feeling insulted. They deferred when someone else is speaking and looked directly at each other. No dropping of eyes or bowing here.

She was actually disappointed, and had a sense of ennui that no innovative ideas had occurred to her compatriots, none other than what she'd already thought of. Maybe those were the sum and total of transporting secrets about precious items that could be stolen. She'd already stirred and mixed their very ideas around in her mind. It was necessary for servants working in the American houses to have a way of communicating with the burglary plotters. Fake grocery lists seemed the most likely means, especially those tossed into the trash and picked up by the garbage trucks. Small, valuable, nonporous items could have taken the same route. Oh, right: the military police were taking care of the problem. No need for her to keep pondering it.

"We better wash our faces and get a hubba hubba move on ourselves. The train leaves in an hour," said Lt. Norton. "We'll be back home in good time for a nice, long evening to write letters about our trip. We'll be able to mail them before work tomorrow morning."

Suddenly, Meg felt tension drain from her body. That was surprising because she earlier had assumed that nothing had been bothering her but instead that the events had been amusing; her recommendations had been interesting; the possibilities had kept her engaged. But people other than she actually had the duty to solve crime and grime. Her mom used to admonish her frequently about the futility of wrestling with impossible tasks.

Once when Meg was eleven she was trying to tie the two ends of broken rubber band together and was whimpering. Mother said sharply, "Quit flaying a dead donkey. Leave what can't be fixed. Get up off your ass. Toss that band; get another one from the desk." That made Meg laugh with shock because Mom was usually so soft-spoken: she never swore. And so she herself would "go on" now as Robbie Jones would say and leave the band of cops to play on, rather than the strawberry blonde doing so. From now on, she would abandon attempts to solve the burglars' trail and the stabbings. She couldn't do it, anyway. Futility.

Same lunch at the hotel.

The return train trip Sunday afternoon would be hotter than that they had on Friday morning. Meg donned her chintz sundress. She pulled the huaraches from the suitcase and slipped them back on. Although she wasn't going to church, she donned the usual hat and gloves, ignoring the fact that they did not exactly go with huaraches. The hat and gloves she could remove in the train once it started north.

As the ladies disembarked from the bus at the Kyoto train station to await the boarding signal, Patty peered at Meg's huaraches. "What kind of leather are those made from?" she asked.

Meg giggled. "Spotted calf." She added nothing else by way of explaining the odd coloration of black dots that contrasted with the scrubbed white sides.

CHAPTER THIRTY-THREE

When Meg started across the Chiyoda lobby early that evening with her suitcase, Tamara appeared at her elbow, looking less frazzled than she had appeared after she first saw Kurt hurting in the hospital. Meg was also less frazzled because she knew no one could have been on her trail this weekend when she was suddenly out of town on Special Services buses in Kyoto.

Tamara pointed a long finger, bayonet-like, at her, straight from her shoulder. "You look bushed; let me help you with that case. Your purse is enough for one person to carry, after a three day trip to the south in this weather," offered Tamara. "Did you have a good time?"

"It was a good time if different is good. There were no casualties, no knifings. The shrines and temples were quite exotic, and we concentrated on seeing a few thoroughly rather than rushing all over town. Yes, I think it was a good trip. However, I am somewhat tired. I feel as flat as a punctured inner tube on my old bike."

"You sound unsure that the trip worth doing."

Meg struggled to turn her impressions into words––an unusual problem for her. With some hesitation she revealed some of her immersion into a religious cultural setting, strange culture, unfamiliar culture, unfamiliar and strange religions. It had been distracting with deadly quiet, but serene, gardens offset by dark hulking buildings and lots of effigies. "And Friday night, exhausted from the trip, we went to a weird ghostly show with atonal music. It went on and on and on."

She shook her body and handed over her suitcase. "Thanks for carrying that up for me. Yes, you need to see places in Kyoto in all their other worldliness. Enough said for tonight. Let me fetch my mail, Tamara."

She returned from across the lobby, shambling a bit as she looked at the envelopes. "Good, I have a letter from my intended, Walt Raleigh. He's in law school. Because he was immersed in classes and then studying for over 12 hours a day, we decided I could apply to teach here. He had been in the Pacific Theater during the war. How's Kurt, by the way?"

"He's really pale and in pain, but the docs saved the arm. He lost some nerves and muscle. No way to tell yet how much use of it he'll recover. We've been working over that poem I showed you. Let me have your keys, I'll open the door." She handed back the key and trotted off down the hall as she said over her shoulder, "I'll run and get the lyrics and music. Wait for me."

"What did you say you worked over?" Meg asked when Tamara came running in her door. Meg felt so tired that she knew comprehension would be difficult.

Tamara handed Meg a sheet. "We took out the fourth and last verses and used the lines from the last verse 'just climb on the Dixie, the train-clerk can fixie' repeated twice as the chorus. Here's the music."

"I can't read music." She yawned.

"Oh. I'll sing the two selections, one adapted from Robert Schumann's 'Hunting Song,' and one from a waltz by Frederick Chopin. We changed the notes to be continuous, without rests or notes and a half." Tamara blew on a pitch pipe, which made Meg wince, and sang the lyrics. "Which do you prefer?"

"Ask me tomorrow, and play it again, Sam." Meg yawned again. "I'm not in great shape to make such a decision tonight. Everything you played sounded as atonal as that music from Friday night. Sorry."

Tamara patted Meg's hand as she took back the sheet of lyrics. "All right. I'll sing it all the way through to you again tomorrow--no, make that Tuesday. I'm tied up tomorrow. We're excited about the possibilities. You had good ideas about the length of the lyrics and about classical music having a theme that could be adapted for them."

"Thanks." Meg roused herself enough to remember she had film left in her camera. If she used up the roll, she could put it in the mail tomorrow to be developed Stateside.

"Look, Tamara, I'm really tired. Let me take a picture of you and call it a night."

Tamara, posing with the pitch pipe against her mouth and holding a sheet of music she was ostensibly studying, looked professional as Meg took the last two snapshots left on her film.

"I'll give you that picture to put on your first album cover," teased Meg.

"Uncanny: that's exactly what I was thinking. I'm the muse behind the tone. Also, your mentioning homophones the other day clicked constantly in my brain, and I suddenly associated the word with xylophone--don't ask me how that happened. Because no one in Nashville is going to know how to play a *samisen* or any Japanese instrument, I think having in the background a tinkling xylophone would add the exotic touch. We'll discuss that later, too. Good night, Meg."

Meg made herself a cup of instant coffee with the hot water from the bathroom tap. She opened the letter she had from Walt. He was graduating at the end of the semester in January. He said he could catch a ship over if she could find them a tourist hotel to stay in while he studied for the Bar Exam. Some weekends, they could go exploring. He had already applied for a three-month visa. What a grand end to an unusual weekend, she decided, taking up her pen to write an enthusiastic reply. She was no longer tired.

But now wait, no way could she travel around to hotels and inns and shrines with a man––it wasn't seemly. An idea followed on that realization. Where had she read that a military man over here had married a girl back home by proxy? Via ham radio? With stand-ins? What had it been? Her old friend Patsy Berry had married Jerry Wrenslow, that's who it was, back home three years ago.

No problem working out the proxy wedding details with the Chaplain and his assistant Mitch Holland. She started sifting the problems into solutions. Bingo! She jotted off a long letter to Walt, outlining the positives. The main one was that they could apply for dependant housing, and she'd never let him forget that he was the dependant.

Picking up his letter and smoothing it out with her firm hands, she discovered a line written in his crabbed penmanship that she had missed; reading it, she laughed. *Let's get married when I arrive. I'll bring the rings.* He wrote without crossing his "t's" or dotting his "i's", probably from having to hastily take notes in his classes.

Meg tore up the letter she had written, tossed the litter in the air, kissed his letter, and wrote an acceptance. "*Te amo.* You may say *veni, vidi, vici.*" All she'd have to do was much less complicated than she had first thought, merely schedule the church and apply for civilian accommodations at the Maiko-Kan Hotel near the city. A few days ago, she'd heard a cleric say a license was $2: she could spring for that, for sure. That Maiko-Kan Hotel could be their residence as well as a place for their honeymoon because school was still going to be in session. Her letters to family and friends about the Kyoto trip were written with a dash of joy.

What a feeling of relief permeated her being. She had shaken her stalkers by mocking them with her "book list," by having Marty stare at them belligerently, or by leaving town and thus being out of sight.

As she settled into bed, lay there with the sheet pulled to her chin, her mind ran through contrasting scenes: Nagoya vs. Kyoto. Meg thought with warmth of her assignment to the American School in Nagoya, its being in the American Village, with the sunny Chapel, the Americans everywhere, the tennis courts, the ranch houses surrounding the soft-ball field. Comparing the locale with Oriental Kyoto brought up cold memories of dark, menacing temples, of Charon rowing across the Styx (poor Johnny Hill), of the vicious face on the card in her globe, of wafting superlunary spirits on Moon Viewing nights, of being hexed, and she shuddered once before falling asleep. Luckily, none of the dreams that she could recall next morning really haunted her. Dreamland must have exorcised the ghosts.

She did ponder the contrast between her impressions of Nagoya and Kyoto. No reading in books, no viewing of pictures, no listening to *Madama Butterfly*, no visiting of a local shrine had prepared her for the depressive feeling left by touring that temple-heavy Japanese city down south. It stayed hazy in her mind.

#

Seated at a nearby table as a distracted Meg ate a late breakfast, eventually Betty Carnahan leaned over and said she was taking a day of leave on this Monday morning. She wondered if Meg'd like to tag along to the housing office as she applied for dependant quarters and then go with her to an "On Limits" Japanese restaurant. She indicated a sheaf of long, tan sheets of official paper she had placed on a chair seat. Meg glanced at them and complained that she didn't understand why people in the military numbered each paragraph. Betty explained it was to expedite responses to questions regarding a particular paragraph. "And those are the papers I had to fill out to apply for housing."

Meg nodded at learning another tactic she would have to apply in a few months, finished eating, straightened her shoulders, stood up, and then smoothed down her blue polished cotton frock. They chatted while walking out of the hotel and down the street. "I'll just have to see how that numbering works because it might just be important for me to know. As to where we eat, I must say that I think soy sauce is too sharp tasting. I hope the café you chose has some other flavoring."

"Many things are on the menu such as noodles, *tempura, sushi, miso*––which is bean curd soup. I'd bet you haven't tried any of those yet."

"No, and as long as I can stay away from soy sauce, I'll sample new things. *Not* including the poisonous fish I've been warned about."

"Chefs like to flavor with lots of ginger; the problem with that is that you can taste it for days afterwards."

Inside the housing office, the two ladies stood against a wall while a young private talked with the seated clerk. "Sir, I'd like to move to a house." Hand on heart.

"What kind? Family, ill-repute, or nut?" replied the bored clerk looking up from a stack of papers.

"I met a nice Korean family, and I want to move them to a better place. They're working for a Japanese family now. I can afford it next week. I'm willing to move in with them." Hand went over the bristles of his crew cut.

"Are you out of your shrunken mind? We don't allow Occupation Forces to move in with the indigeens." The clerk slapped a meaty palm on his desk and glared at the soldier.

"Can I get some furniture?"

"Where's your requisition?"

"Where do I get it?"

The clerk rattled off his well-rehearsed spiel without pausing for breath. "You get it with your family's assignment of quarters from the Housing Priority List published the tenth of each month with preference due those who have spent the most time in temporary quarters and given blood regularly, and, naturally, according to rank. You're supposed to notify this Dependant Housing Section as soon as your dependants received port-call. You have to inventory and sign for furnishings for permanent quarters for your family within twenty-four hours after you accept quarters."

Betty whispered, "Good information."

"No, no, these are my family because Stateside, my folks was killed in a tornado."

"No, no, no––you're not still talking about the same indigeens," the clerk groaned.

"Yes, my girlfriend––" hand on heart and eyes lifted upward, sighing, "and her father and mother."

"I just bet. 'B' housing doesn't rate furniture."

"What's the difference?"

"$2." The clerk was slightly amused.

"$2?"

"Marriage license!" The clerk waved the private away and motioned to Betty Carnahan to step forward as Meg salted away the information about the price of a license and the procedure for being assigned dependant housing.

Betty completed the paperwork and handed it in with the papers she had brought. The orders transferring her husband from the Philippines were all in order, the clerk advised her, after she had also handed over copies of those. He told her they would be living at the Kanko Hotel until other dependant housing became available. She would be able to move in Wednesday, before she left Thursday for Yokohama to meet Dean.

Meg offered to help her move, which Betty gladly accepted, saying, "I also need some nice dishes. Let's go to the Noritake china factory tomorrow afternoon."

"I'm game. One of my brothers was joking around and broke Mom's good platter. Maybe I can find one to match the rest of her dinnerware."

Betty had been to two Japanese restaurants. The one she ushered Meg into was exotic: seating at dark wood, low tables; smelling of fried, steamed, and baked edibles; dim lighting from lanterns. The restaurant offered a complete luncheon menu, as opposed to most restaurants that featured a single entree.

They ordered one of each of the dishes Betty suggested, and both sampled them. Meg still found the rice tasteless, until Betty showed her how to add a little sauce that made it quite good. She didn't find out until later that it was soy sauce.

"I met Lieutenant Wanda Norton from your hospital on the trip to Kyoto. We had a leisurely tour of a few of Kyoto's attractions. It certainly was different from all the churches and courthouses back home. You should plan to take it this fall. Wanda said she was the nurse on the cormorant fishing trip when I fell overboard."

Betty nodded and took a sip of tea. "I told you that."

Meg continued, "How did you meet your Doctor Dean Carnahan?"

"After high school, I took a job in a drugstore. When the war started, I volunteered to wrap bandages for the Red Cross. So many men were called up that the pharmacist had me counting pills behind his counter when there was a rush, and he put his surly daughter in charge of the cash register."

"You're a pharmacist?"

"No, I thought I told you. I'm a pharmacist's assistant."

They both ordered more tea and another dish of *tempura*. "I'm not eating *sushi* because a friend said it had raw fish in it," Meg said.

"Yes, I think that's sometimes called *sashimi*. But, sometimes the rice is wrapped around vegetables. I don't know how to ask for it, though."

"That's the word for the raw fish she used, I remember now."

"To continue. I had taken every science class in high school. The gruff but kindly teacher--you know how a person can be both? --"

Meg nodded.

"--told me to go to the vo tech school and get trained. Afterwards, I took the Armed Services Battery of tests and could have enlisted. I decided to apply to Civil Service and was accepted. I met Dean when he was working at El Toro Army Air Base."

"Where's that?"

"In California, close to where I grew up. As the movies have it, we took one look at each other and were smitten."

"You said you applied here to Japan?"

"Yes. After he was transferred to the Pacific, we realized we'd be running into each other somewhere, somehow, if I asked for assignment here. I have more leeway to move than he does. I'm a G-2, that's Civil Service rank."

They split the bill and sauntered back to the hotel, gazing down narrow streets that had stiff bamboo poles tented overhead, each pole covered with variegated, plump colored lanterns.

They decided to visit the exchange bank before venturing to the Noritake factory the next afternoon. Meg said she was still weary and needed to rest the rest of the afternoon. Betty replied that she'd spend the time folding clothes.

Meg had two letters in her mailbox, one from her folks and the first one she had received from Sgt. Calhoun Paley since he'd gone to Z-1. She would be able to reply to these and mail the ones she had written last night at the same time.

The former sergeant was flying high, he reported. His daddy had sent the case of metal objects to a friend in Kansas City who sent them to a dealer in New York. The New York dealer phoned his daddy and offered $500 for the "Woo Shoo" coins, saying they were from China, from when the Silk Road trade was booming. His daddy bought a two-bedroom house near the college campus with the money.

Cally wrote that he was going to major in business, and his sister, Glory Anne, had decided on science. She would share her room with another girl from their town. And he thanked her for being his "Robin Hood."

Meg wrote a reply, referring but a little to their earlier adventure; she did mention that the Fritz couple were on the way back to the States. She added some comments about the softball team and the baseball team, the Nagoya Comets, and she tossed in a few hints for studying for tests in college. She sealed the envelope and then reached for the phone after one peal.

"Donna here. There's a ball game tomorrow night."

"Sure. I'd love to go. I'm going shopping with Betty in the afternoon, and then I'll have time to change clothes and meet you downstairs about seventeen hundred."

"I'll walk over straight from work and wait for you in the lobby."

CHAPTER THIRTY-FOUR

Meg settled into her room and prepared for bed, but sleep wouldn't come. She pushed the sheet and pillows to one side of the bed and slipped over to curl up on a chair, resting her head on the back of the cushioned chair, eyes closed.

Her soft nightgown had been a twentieth birthday gift from her mother, handmade from feed sacks, those cloth sacks decorated with pretty designs that held grist for the goats, chow for the chickens. She had left three nightgowns in a drawer when she went off to study for her bachelor's degree, to teach, and to study for her master's degree. She was delighted to find them seven years later when she went home to pack for this overseas trip. She now wore one every night for a week and aired it out in the daytime.

Stroking her cheek with the rabbit's foot, she thought lazily about the trip to the legendary Kyoto, full of history and mystery. She would have some photos enlarged on *matte*--rather than glossy--paper, and frame them. The one of the trees up the hill behind the shrine would look like a painting with all the shadows. Another one smaller, much smaller, of the up-close picture of the demon god's face would fit between her woodprints. Then those with vibrant colors might turn out to have captured a second of time in real life.

A wave of cool air that waved past her cheek startled Meg's dreamy visions away. Her heartbeat quickened to a gallop, though she didn't understand why. But then, just as suddenly she noticed the creak of a floorboard, impossibly close to her bed, and a sharp smell of soy sauce hit her nose. A dim figure had entered her door, slithering then quickly over to the bed.

With an arm raised high, it swiftly changed position: moonlight glittered on a dagger for an instant before it plunged downward, aiming straight where Meg's sleeping figure would have been.

Meg dropped the rabbit's foot down the nape of the *kimono*. The back of the collar traditionally gaped outwards a couple of inches––what was thought of locally as enticing.

The figure squirmed at the sensation trickling, tickling down its back. It shrieked "errrrrk," then whirled. A blank mask covered the face, under what appeared to be big, bulky hair. Meg grabbed a brass crane from the desk and hit the figure hard in the ribs, dropped the crane, gripped the upraised arm with her strong swimmers' hands, and pulled the body to the floor. A white mask slipped sideways on the face.

Her legs snarled in her nightgown, hampering Meg's attempts to subdue the figure, and she screamed, "HELP!! MURDER!! POLICE!!"

The figure slid on the floor, but then wrapped its legs around her and tried to toss her off, wrestled, tried to free the arm with the dagger, flipped about like a live electric wire, sparked out sentences and curses from behind a mask, "*Iteki!* Barbarians! *Gaijin! Iteki!* Traitors!"

Steps pounding snare, bongo, and bass drum beats, and also some swishing sounds, came down the hall. Ladies in various night garments piled into the room. Someone clicked on the overhead light. Tamara Talbot stepped on the arm holding the dagger, and Chloe plopped down on the stomach, both of them partially trapping Meg, too. With one eye obscured by the body and mess of silk, Meg noted her friends as she also looked at a geisha wig, elegant embroidered gown, and that blank facemask.

"Want me to knock the snot outta her?" Chloe offered, her fist pointed at the mask. The figure kept squirming under her weight. Meg just grunted and extricated herself from the pile, stood breathing hard, and glanced at her friends.

Matilda Patrick had the presence of mind to call an alarm to the front desk after stepping over the figures on the floor. "The desk clerk says he can't leave the desk, but he has called the APs to the ladies' hotel. He wants me to keep the line open so that they can hear what's going on."

Betty and Donna grabbed the figure's ankles to keep them from flaying about. The figure couldn't see anyone because the mask was to one side, but kept shrieking, "*Iteki*! Barbarian! *Gaijin*! *Iteki*! Traitors!"

The figure struggled mightily but was outnumbered, outweighed, and out of luck. Donna next tried to twist her robe belt around the figure's wrists but one hand firmly clutched a dagger under Tamara's foot on her arm and kept trying to free it. Betty was trying to help Donna by bringing up the other arm from her position on the other side of Chloe.

Arvada Norstad came in carrying the Durant book. "This was in the hall outside. Yours?" Her pale blue eyes, in a very pale face, were taking in the melee.

Meg was breathing hard and gritted out, after a brief glance, her words through her teeth, "Yes, it's mine." She tried to figure out how to grab the dagger without getting hurt.

Matilda still had the phone at her ear. She overrode the noise to inform them, "The desk clerk says a young girl in a *kimono* said Miss Lowe needed that book immediately and that she had to bring it to her hubba hubba. She left her *geta* at the entrance and hit her elbow on the railing when her *tabi* slipped on the stairs. He's talking to some APs who just arrived. They're listening at his phone now to what's happening in here."

Arvada muttered, turning over the heavy book, "It feels funny. I can't open it." She tugged on the shiny cover. "It's heavy as a door stop."

The figure almost wriggled the dagger free. "My fliends find funny book clues. I made book glues! Ha ha ha to you!"

Meg had heard that voice before. Fumiko?

"That's a *Noh* mask, Meg," Chloe said, keeping her seat on the figure, but looking over her shoulder at a blank, bland mask on the figure's face.

"I see that! Then it must be the male actor who takes women's parts," Meg replied.

Sgt. Laura Duncan strode into the room, on her belt a radio. "What's the ruckus? I was visiting upstairs when I heard brawling down here. Some turmoil had been called in, too. Oh, I might have known it was you, Meg. What's this about?"

Meg continued in a strained voice to Sgt. Duncan, "This he/she/it person tried to stab me, but I wasn't in bed, I was in that chair resting. I slugged her with a crane and screamed, and everyone piled in. It might be that male actor or maybe Fumiko Yamata."

"Stay there on the person, Chloe, Donna." Meg began to laugh giddily. She pounded the wrist on the floor; the intruder's arm resisted, twisting hard. Meg bent, grabbed the arm from under Tamara's foot and snapped the wrist sharply three times in rapid succession. The weapon fell. Hitting the wig with a huarache she grabbed off the floor, Meg knocked it off to reveal a shaved head.

Sgt. Laura Duncan ordered every one up, used Meg's blue headband to tie the intruder's arms behind the back, dropped the bathrobe belt, and peeled off the mask.

The unveiling revealed Fumiko Yamata's furious face, covered chalk white with rice powder; with the wig gone, her scalp gleamed, had been saved bare; still squirming, her body bent to the floor for the dagger. The movement revealed a jeweled sheath tucked into her *obi*.

Donna, Chloe, and Betty stepped closer to the wall. Meg sat heavily back into her chair.

"Well, if it isn't Miss Yamata, who's been hard to find," exclaimed Sgt. Duncan. "I guess you already know about your father, Miss." She turned to Meg and teased, "You almost got it right about who it is. But it's not the female impersonator, Kikuyo."

"I knew it was one or the other." Meg seemed puzzled.

Sgt. Laura Duncan remarked, eying the struggle, "What a day. First we try to interview Yamata-san and find him with his guts all over the *tatami* mats, head bowed on the floor in front of a shrine. Committed *hari-kari, seppuku*. Must have felt disgraced by something--or someone. Maybe the shutdown of his piggybacking thefts on the black market trade. Now you, Meg, almost had *your* innards all over a rag rug."

Arvada sounded puzzled as she asked loudly to be heard above the shrieking figure, "Why is Mata Hari involved?"

"Not Mata Hari, *hari-kari*, or *seppuku*. It's suicide by disemboweling," Meg explained in a loud voice, breathing hard while she frowned against the twists the figure kept doing toward her.

Sgt. Laura Duncan drew an upside down L across her abdomen. "Like that."

"Don't tell me any more. That's explicit enough." Arvada looked sick.

"All right. No more gut-wrenching descriptions."

Meg, studying the girl and shaking her head slowly at her, said, "Why? I found your Dolls' Day characters; and, your father was appreciative."

The figure was screaming, "You made me shame *Chichi*, my fatheh, you made me kill people to save his business! You dissipate his gold! You make him *seppuku*! I am *kami!* I hate United States and take it out of map! I hate his enemies! I hate you. I get you dead."

Laura Duncan calmly continued her own description of this day's events as she unwound the belt from the ankles and tried to turn the girl toward the door. "Down some stairs at Yamata's house, we found closets containing dozens upon dozens of rat chewed boxes of moldy rice, and trunks of stolen yen and scrip, jade whatevers, cigarette cartons, old jeweled swords and gold American style jewelry, from stealing and running the black market. He was, in addition, hoarding some weird stuff we could not identify. Preparing for Armageddon, I guess."

A stream of spittle hit Meg's nightgown before Fumiko Yamata took a deep breath and shouted in plain English, "I'm not a baby-san! I'm not a janitor! Not an actor! You made me wipe your shoes! I not a servant! Barbarian! I am a Lady! You Americans hanged my Lord dead!"

"Me? I didn't hang anyone," Meg protested. "I just got here."

Meg's brain was awhirl. This was a strange ending to the story about 'being hexed' that she'd been writing to her folks, Cally Paley, and Walt Raleigh. Now the Japanese maid had tried to kill her because she had *made* her clean the huaraches. Just have to laugh and shake the quaking. Fumiko being Kurt Salchow's *baby-san* when he was part of the investigation of her father; Yamata's suicide today; people going bonkers; the hoarding of inedible rice; kinship and gold temples: these things raced through her mind.

Meg took a shaky breath and spoke. "At first when my assailant turned, I thought it was the actor who takes girl's roles in the *Noh* Theater. That was because she was wearing a *Noh* mask. Days ago I had narrowed the murderer of those Japanese men and the captain down to either Fumiko or him or their associates." Meg looked around at her friends as she mused aloud.

Sgt. Duncan raised an eyebrow and said, "You care to explain what she just said? Why she was after you and so angry?"

"It's like this. Once upon a time, I asked her, when she was a Japanese janitor at the American School, to help me clean mildew from my huaraches, these sandals that I hit her with." Meg held up the mottled shoe. "I had no idea that she'd be insulted. I was working right along beside her. I've been told--as well as have observed--that the Japanese are 99 and 44/100 percent purely quiescent, either from being obedient to the Emperor or from having to be crowded into living on Honshu island's coasts because the mountains inland are too steep. Those are a couple of the explanations that I've heard, and I thought she wouldn't mind helping.

"I assumed she was working for the same reasons as every one of us do, i.e., to earn a paycheck. I told my friends here about her and her dad two weeks ago. Tonight when I saw a Japanese character sidle into my door in the dark, then raise an arm as if to stab me in bed, I put my rabbit's foot down her neckline in the back. That made her shudder, jerk, and screech. Pardon me if I giggle." Meg knew she sounded slightly hysterical, because she was.

"You hit her with this crane, too; its leg is broken," Betty said, moving forward and picking it up from the floor.

"Well, she reacted when the fur tickled her back, hesitated, gave me time to halt the knife thrust aimed for my heart, and hit her arm. The crane's leg was already broken. A friend found it at the Brass Pile. You and Dean can go look there, too, for something. I also found this incense burner." Meg knew she was rambling a bit as she indicated the brass souvenir and rubbed the knuckles of her right hand where she had hit them on the rug while snapping Fumiko's wrist.

Fumiko twisted violently against Sgt. Duncan's grasp on her tied hands, expostulating to Meg, "I'm not a traitor: *you* are. I protect my father from enemy, enemy, enemy. But he say I shame him when I protect. I am his *samurai*. You're guilty; you *baka, bad*. You ruin his business; you spy on shops; you must die! Youh fliends must die."

"I obviously ended up with a no-hitter, although I somewhere had inadvertently committed an error." Meg again laughed nervously after making what she realized was an inane comment and dropped her chin.

Seated next to the desk, Tamara opened a drawer and pulled out a pad of paper and a pencil from Meg's supply.

"What are you doing?" asked Meg. The collegiality of her older teaching companions and friends was easing the adrenaline flowing throughout her body. Her heart wasn't beating as fast, and her throat was not as tight as it had been.

"Composing a song for Kurt." Tamara looked at the ceiling. "Calling it 'Ambush at the Chiyoda Hotel. Circle your wagons, girls, don't bother to pin up your curls.'" She started writing. "I feel a bit giddy, riding my ditty."

Meg sighed, spoke loudly toward the phone, and gestured at the ladies. "What a scenario. Thank you all for your instantaneous response to my SOS." She wanted the cops downstairs to hear her, too, because she also wanted no trouble from––and to be no trouble to––the APs who had befriended her.

Fumiko never stopped struggling or ranting about honor, jade, gold, until she suddenly spoke clearly in high-pitched English. "I stabbed sneaky tattle tales!" Tears ran down the rice powder snow, making parallel tracks like skis had gone sliding on either side of her little nose. She went silent although she still squirmed.

Third grade teacher Chloe Volker looked startled as she exclaimed, "That Jap just sounded exactly like one of my students!"

Matilda hung up the phone. "Yes, I heard her, dear! She's dangerous. She's obviously insane. It's providential that we caught that girl red-handed, well, not red with blood on her hands, Meg, your blood. I'll help take her down, Sergeant. The APs said they are waiting on you to bring her down to the jeep."

Matilda's feet were wrapped in ankle high, beaded Indian moccasins made of deer-skin, a complement to her home-state of Arizona, accounting for the swishing sound that accompanied the harder footsteps pounding down the hall, running, answering Meg's holler for help.

"Won't you be embarrassed to be in your robe and slippers in front of the police*men*?" asked Chloe, taking in Matilda's outfit with a smarmy grin.

"Why should I be? I have on more clothes than you do at the swimming pool," Matilda retorted, gazing down at her tan chenille robe that covered her like brown sugar icing on a cake. She was helping restrain the smaller girl by firmly grasping a wriggling arm.

Meg groaned, "My wonderful reference book is destroyed, and I lost my rabbit's foot."

Sgt. Duncan gave her a noncommittal look. "Better than losing your life, I'd say."

Meg reached for the enameled stiletto on the floor, excited as she exclaimed, "But at least I have a souvenir, a real damascene sword, for my dad."

Sgt. Duncan preempted her with a gesture, picked the stiletto up with a handkerchief, and stowed it in her pocket. "Don't fool with that stiletto! It's evidence in three murders. Almost fourth or fifth ones."

"She must have been the one, Tamara, who cut Kurt's arm because he was betraying her and/or her father," Meg conjectured. Tamara looked up and nodded.

"You almost got that right, too," Sgt. Duncan looked back at Meg as she shoved the struggling Yamata girl out of the door and grinned, "but in the gut."

Meg gulped, caught Betty's eye, and concluded slowly, "This is surely *Noh* way to make a living."

EPILOGUE

The phone rang (too) early the next morning. "Miss Lowe, Corporal Aldrich calling for Captain. Torleone. He would like to see you this morning."

"Donna? Isn't that you?"

"Correct."

"How do you know Harry?"

"He's my superior officer here at the PIO office."

"I see. Would 1030 be convenient? Can you tell me what it concerns?" Meg's voice raised a bit as her mind raced: what had she done now?

"Yes as to the time. I have no idea as to what. See you then."

The phone rang again, and Sgt. Duncan asked how she was doing this fine morning. Meg excused herself to answer the door where Tamara and Chloe stood asking her the same thing. "I'm alive and kicking!" Meg told everyone, shut the door and said goodbye to Duncan.

After agreeing to the appointment, Meg rapped on the room next door and told Betty she had an appointment at the Public Relations office in midmorning. Betty just nodded and said solicitously that she hoped Meg had been able to sleep last night. Meg thanked her and with a shake of her head plus a small grin indicated that she was feeling just a bit weary because of the excitement but not from fear. Betty patted her hand and said she'd start packing. She accepted Meg's offer of her trunk, which they moved into Betty's room.

Meg stopped for a quick cup of coffee and a biscuit downstairs and then meandered out into the street to keep the appointment, now with a bit of fear about the looming meeting edging into her stomach.

Capt. Torleone had his door open when Meg, dressed in one of her new outfits, walked in. He greeted her while motioning her to a chair. "Come in. How have you been?"

"Fine. And you? And your wife and new baby?"

"Doing well, quite well."

"Do I call you 'Harry' or 'sir' in this office?"

"Neither or either. Most likely, a simple 'captain' would do. 'Miss Lowe, Margaret, Meg?'"

She smiled. "'Meg' will do, Captain."

"My son Corey said you treated the Worth girl gently and helpfully when the kids found the corpse."

"My job. I'm used to dealing with students who suddenly develop flu, chicken pox, measles, etc., in the classroom. Happens frequently."

"I understand. Everyone overseeing a number of younger people has to learn to move appropriately in a critical, unpredictable situation."

Meg settled back and looked around the room, her gaze fastening on a potted plant next to her chair. "That's a marvelous smelling plant. What is it?" She pointed to a vinous plant in a teal colored ceramic pot.

"Jasmine. Sometimes you can find a tasty jasmine tea in the restaurants."

"I'll look for it on the menus. Now that we've chatted a bit, I'm curious why I am sitting in the Public Information Office. Kindly enlighten me."

Capt. Torleone folded his hands behind his head and leaned back in his chair, studying the ceiling, giving her an occasional glance. "I asked Colonel Smithson for a copy of your application, transcripts, and letters of reference. I spoke with Mrs. Jones about her impression of you. Also, Colonel Jones and I had a long chat. The reason I was double-checking everything you've, er, done is easy to explain. The Mayor of Nagoya has requested you as an English teacher for his daughter and four of her friends."

Meg was bewildered. "Why me?"

Sitting forward at his desk, he said, "He was impressed with your manners at the funeral. And, I cannot have someone in the military serve that role . . . wouldn't look good."

"But I know a military wife is teaching English to little Japanese school kids. The new principal, Mr. Hines, an American, is teaching at Nanzan, The Catholic University. Or, why doesn't Mr. Yamata do it? He teaches Japanese to Americans." (No! Hari-karied!)

"Can't be a male: that would not be proper. Also, as to Yamata-san, in addition, he's not of the, let's say, upper crust. He simply wouldn't do," he mimicked a British voice in the last four words. "Those other people are teaching in formal educational establishments. This will be in the Mayor's home. Would you be willing to take it on?"

"But, I don't know more than a few phrases of Japanese. However would I communicate, translate, succeed?"

"The Armed Forces published a fine manual with anglicized expressions of Japanese sentences. The *kana* ideograms and certain expressions are in an appendix.

You'll have access to that to study beforehand. Last year, the Education Ministry selected 1,850 ideographs for daily use and stipulated that 881 should be learned in the nine years of compulsory education. There are 50 basic sounds in Japanese, although a couple are simplified pronunciation. Different districts have different dialects, just as in the U. S., but still understandable to native speakers."

"I see."

"The daughter is about fifteen and has had some training in the English language from a tutor. She was too old to start school when the educational system changed to include females after the war."

"Bless my stars. I'm stunned."

"Will you do it, or at least, consider it? The females are particularly interested in their rights under the new Constitution and need some help in interpreting them. I've obtained a copy of it." He handed her a long sheath of 14-inch long, flimsy paper.

"Well, that's right in my field. Of course, women in all the States weren't permitted to vote until the 19th Amendment passed in 1920, only 29 years ago. Wyoming, from the first, allowed female suffrage, and it was in that State's law books when it entered the union in 1890. Some other states, mostly Western, allowed female voting. Early on, of course, some colonies allowed widows to vote. I have noticed that the only time sex is mentioned in our Constitution is in the 19th Amendment. I'm curious to see what rights the Japanese Constitution mentions."

"It's Article 24."

She thumbed through the pages to the passage, glanced at it. "Impressive." She read it aloud.

> "Marriage shall be based only on the mutual consent of both sexes and it shall be maintained through mutual cooperation with the equal rights of husband and wife as a basis.
>
> "With regard to choice of spouse, property rights, inheritance, choice of domicile, divorce and other matters pertaining to marriage and the family, laws shall be enacted from the standpoint of individual dignity and the essential equality of the sexes."

Meg commented, "That Article may have been *promulgated*, but have any laws been passed to enforce it? If not, it'll be under the sclerotic management of the old guard. It also only addresses marriage. Anything else changing for females?"

"Look at Article 26, there." He nodded his head.

She read aloud again.

> "All people shall have the right to receive an equal education correspondent to their ability, as provided by law.
>
> "All people shall be obligated to have all boys and girls under their protection receive ordinary education as provided for by law. Such compulsory education shall be free."

Torleone replied, "And, well, that's all I know about the changes for females. The Constitution you have there was passed two years ago."

"I hope a copy of this goes to D. C. to the Library of Congress. It's time Japanese women had some rights."

He said, "It probably will because we helped with it. Good news for you: some women were elected to the first congress, that is, the Diet. The Mayor here was elected by both ladies and men."

"Hmmmm. This is exciting. My Stateside beau has been asking why I haven't met any Japanese. Here now is my chance. How do they know about me?"

"As I said, the Mayor and his wife were impressed with your manners at the Catholic funeral, although you didn't take a gift."

"Gift?" *For once, someone appreciates my manners—— with reservations, of course.*

"Back home, don't you take potato salad or baked beans to a bereaved family? My wife does."

"Yes. But I wouldn't take something like that to a church."

"No matter. You need to take a little gift every time you visit their home. They'll give you one each time. Just don't wrap it in white; that's for funerals."

"Oh, ho. Those things wrapped in white were on the table in the Cathedral refreshment room. Perhaps some guy at the Base craft shop would have an acceptable item. I can't spend much, maybe just a trinket."

"But, listen, you take the gift wrapped in some neutral color each time and remember to shed your shoes at the door. Shall I schedule the first lesson for a month from now? That enough time to prepare?"

"Yes," she responded slowly. "My high school classes will have their assignments by then. I think a weekday evening would be best, if that works out with the Japanese girls." How fine to be given a mission like this

374

"We will arrange that."

"What amuses them--by that I mean, what do they laugh out loud about? I've seen only little girls giggling behind their hands. I've noticed older ones merely smiling sometimes. Not laughing out loud."

Harry answered, "I've noticed some pictures of games played on certain holidays, cards, shuttlecock, and the like, where girls are smiling. That reminds me, I have something better to suggest. Three years ago, a new pack of the syllabary cartoon cards was published. Each card is based on a *kana* character but has a subtle message. Aphorisms, adages, axioms, maxims, often with a double meaning."

"I looked at the *kana* ideographs when I was trying to read the sole of a statue of Jesus."

Harry Torleone looked at her, startled.

"It was the sole of a foot, not an ephemeral soul, Captain. I think I found '*ri*,' as in *torii*."

"Let me think. The set I had also had '*ri*.' It is the beginning of a statement about Tojo behind jail bars. I have a pack of those cards somewhere. Mine're comments on the aftermath of the war in most part. Each syllable begins a word of a statement. I put them somewhere for my boys but forgot about them until now. I'll dig them out for you so that you can have them explained to you. That'll put you into the field of ironic statements they find amusing. It's a neat way of teaching their, well, let's say, it's their alphabet. Of course, that isn't anywhere near the 881 characters they have to learn. The daughter's tutor will work with you. She'll probably teach you the card game that's played by the whole family at New Year's time."

"I'd be happy to have those syllabary cards of yours. I'll take good care of them in case I can't find any myself. I'll study this copy of the Constitution in English. I wonder if any newspaper reports have been written about the new female suffrage; there was virtually nothing in the prior Constitution for common folk's rights."

"I'll ask around for you from the news organizations. Donna will give you the manual. Most of the headlines about the Constitution were about pledges of 'no more wars.' There was that one Article in the Constitution like you read out loud that concerned education rights, but somewhere one says all people are to be equal under the law, and no discrimination allowed."

"That's interesting. I'll see if it adds some sidelights I can discuss with the daughter and her friends. By the way, I have a small matter I'm curious about. Do I receive a stipend?"

"No. This is good will. And, soon, my office would like to have a photograph of you and the daughter and friends to publish with an article in the *Asahi Shimbun* and the *Nagoya Nugget*. Probably need the Mayor and his wife and your principal Mr. Hines in the layout, too."

"Oh. Really? So experience and publicity will be my compensation. Publicity would be the reason your office is overseeing this offer I gather. Public Information."

"Yes, I'll have the Mayor, his wife, and the tutor over to meet you first, before the picture taking."

"I'd be very happy to help those girls. Do I have to bow when I meet them?"

"Incline your head as you did when you met Loren and me at the Fritz blowout. Remember that the Mayor is head of the family and receives major deference. I note that what I'm describing as mannerly behavior is somewhat contradictory to what you'll be teaching to emancipated females. Go slowly."

"Whole project sounds interesting. Likewise, this gives me something to add to my World History class--the institution of a Constitution. I've studied quite a bit about Japan's history, and visited Kyoto shrines. I'll pick up the manual from Donna now. I know we're going to use Army manuals for the typing class. Students don't need constant supervision to learn from those because they're so well written. You told me this one about the Japanese language is excellent, too?"

"Yes, Meg."

Meg put on her gloves, lifted her handbag (its color matched the olive green leaves in her dress), and departed. She could flip through the manual tonight; having it is certainly better than trying to find a key Japanese word, with sentences illustrating its use, in the English-Japanese dictionary.

Donna handed her the manual and quietly said, "That was some shindig in your room last night. We'll talk about it when I see you tonight."

#

After collecting Betty, Meg entered the showroom at the Noritake china factory and immediately spotted a cabinet of platters. "I swear this is Mom's pattern. It's remarkably like hers. Her china was inherited from a European ancestor who entered the States in 1849. I wonder when that set was purchased. I'm not sure whether great grandma brought it with her or bought it after she arrived. My brother broke the large platter messing around with his twin when they were doing the dishes."

Betty's dimples deepened as she grinned. "That's a boy, for sure. I'd bet that a china factory manager always figures that if something is attractive enough to keep selling, like that particular pattern, why change it?"

Meg signaled a clerk, telling him that it had to be wrapped for shipping. He described the straw, paper, and wooden box that would cushion it adequately. The package would be delivered to her the next day.

Meanwhile Betty had been selecting an eight piece set with the design of tiny gazebos, flowers, and paths on the outer rim. She asked that it be packed like Meg's and delivered to the Kanko in two days.

#

Back at the hotel, the two ladies folded, stacked, and packed Betty's clothes and accouterments.

"I apologize that the trunk still has some moth ball odor. I did put in a bar of sandalwood soap. Your clothes may end up with an unusual perfume," Meg commented.

"It doesn't matter, Meg. I'll have a maid and a houseboy and a washing machine when we move into a house. Meanwhile, I'll have the hotel's servants. Somewhere I want to buy a lacquer coffee table before we go Stateside. They are sturdy but so light that it's incredible."

"I've read that the lacquer is tapped from trees the way maple syrup is, but, I don't know how it turns solid. Let's find out sometime. All these Japanese wares are made beautifully from a wide range of materials: bamboo, brass, clay, silkworms, lacquer."

"I have aluminum and leather packing supplies here," Betty laughed. Her aluminum suitcase and boxy make-up kit held a lot, but Meg's trunk had the bulk of the wardrobe. When she had left for overseas, Betty said, she had shipped her things to Nagoya in cardboard boxes that were long gone to the dump or that she had discarded into the ocean on the way over when she repacked her belongings.

She called down to the desk and asked to be scheduled for moving to the Kanko Hotel in tomorrow. The two had changed clothes before the storing of items, and they now congratulated themselves as a move that preserved their other outfits.

"Maybe we'll be able to move to a Japanese 'rehab' house some day. Dean is making a career of the Army, so we won't be going to a reppo deppo to get out on the points he's accumulated for length and type of service," said Betty. Her eyes filled with tears. "Sorry, I always cry when I'm happy."

"I know two houses that should be vacant, the one Captain Fritz had and the Sheldon's because they're leaving next month." Meg handed over a handkerchief. "Keep it, put it in your scrapbook with a note about 'tears of joy', or maybe 'Ode to Joy, Thanks Owed to Meg.' I hope you'll be crying often for happiness, my friend. Dean will love to see you so happy. Bye for now."

Meg excused herself with a pat on Betty's shoulder and went to the lobby to meet Donna Aldrich. Her pedal pushers and flats were a lot more appropriate than the outfit she had worn to the game after the wedding. No pearl strand would be broken tonight.

On the bus to the ballpark, Donna first recalled everything that had happened in the *Fuming Fumiko* episode last night. She had Meg laughing aloud by the time she had finished.

Meg closed that discussion by commenting, "So, finally, I found out why some people trailed me for a while. They were Fumiko's friends and reporting to her where I went. They stopped after I dropped the list of fictitious book titles: one title mentioned Fumiko, and that must have been too threatening." Meg punched Donna lightly in the shoulder as a way of thanking her for completely dissipating any remaining tension.

Donna next said she and Phil Tyler had been seeing each other when he could synchronize his schedule with hers. "He's been awfully busy lately. Too many boys going home, and the ones coming in replacing the old well-trained soldiers know little about what they're supposed to do. No, that's not correct. They do their duty, but it's after duty hours where they're into Big Band music and frolicking. He says they act as though this is summer vacation and that this will be the best vacation of their lives."

"What do you and Phil do on dates here?" Before Walt arrived, Meg told Donna that she needed to find some entertainment other than the Brass Pile, Nagoya Park, and the zoo.

Donna thought a minute. "We go to the Top Three Club to eat, dance. We play golf, come here to baseball games. Sometimes we go to the shooting range."

"I didn't know there was one you could go to out of hunting season."

"It's mandatory to keep up practice for us in military. I don't think you'd be allowed, you civilian, you. I'll check if you want. Might be able to go hunting."

"Never mind. I doubt that I'd get a license. If I did go hunting and shot some ducks, I wouldn't know what to do with the bounty. I'll concentrate on tennis."

"That's grand. You really learned fast. It's fun doing the doubles. We'll have to replace Sharon soon. There's entertainment too at the stages and movie theaters and even at the Chiyoda that you could attend."

As they waited for a bus, Meg wished she could capture even a sliver of the messages that often hit her senses--soft breeze, street smells, grinding or clanking traffic, slithery shoes sliding by or wooden ones providing reverberating clip-clops, monstrous collection of rainbow hues, the tastes of ginger and soy. Not a single photograph or slide could capture the sensory impressions she absorbed each instant. With Walt at her shoulder to experience the same sensations, they for sure would find a way to describe the ambience of the Orient.

AUTHOR'S NOTES

My appreciation to the following friends and relatives who read (and commented on) parts of the book: Glenda Schweitzer; Ann and Brad Van Horn; Lisa, Pete, and Adam Klaes; Doris and George Neil. Alaina Klaes provided technical help. Lisa even reviewed the whole shebang.

My deep gratitude goes to copy editor, Lacey L. Brummer, with her meticulous attention to usage.

QUOTED

Adams, Franklin Pierce. ((July 12 (or 10), 1910)). "Baseball's Sad Lexicon." *New York Evening Mail.* (First called "That double play again"). In Adams, F. P. *Innocent Merriment: An Anthology of Light Verse.* Garden City, NY: Garden City Publishing Company, 1945.

Dixon, Mort, and Warren, Harry. "Nagasaki." NY: NY. (c) Remick Music Corp, 1928.

Thayer, Ernest Lawrence ("Phin"). "Casey at the Bat: A Ballad of the Republic." (Sung in 1888). *The San Francisco Examiner,* June 3,1888.

The Constitution of Japan: Japanese Government Law Translation. Article 24 and Article 26. Washington, DC: Library of Congress, 1947. www.loc.gov

2010 World Book Multimedia Encyclopedia: Version 14.0.0 (r) World Book, Inc. (www.mackiev.com)

PARODIED

Coleridge, Samuel Taylor. (1798). "Rime of the Ancient Mariner." In *The Norton Anthology of English Literature*. (3rd. ed.). New York, NY: W. W. Norton & Co., 1975.

Gershwin, George, Gershwin, Ira and Heyward, Du Bose. "Summertime." *Porgy and Bess*. New York: Gershwin Publishing Corporation, distributed by Chappell & Co., 1935.

Jolson, Al. "Mammy." *The Jazz Singer*. Composed by Young, Joe, Lewis, Sam M., and Donaldson, Walter, 1927.

O'Hara, Geoffrey. "K-K-K-Katy." NY: Leo Feist. 1918. Distributed by the Choral Public Domain Library, 1999. http://www.cpdl.org

Service, Robert W. "The Shooting of Dan McGrew" in *The Spell of the Yukon*. New York, NY: Barse & Hopkins, 1907. (public domain)

Yellen, Jack, Bigelow, Robert Wilcox (Bob), and Bates, Charles. "Hard-hearted Hannah." New York, NY: Ager, Yellen & Bornstein, June, 1924.

REFERENCES

ASCAP: Composers, Authors, Publishers Copyright Clearance Center. ASCAP.com
(Used to check copyright for song by Dixon and Warren "Nagasaki")

Asian Americans. *The World Book Multimedia Encyclopedia.* Chicago: (c) 2010 World Book Inc.

(Reference for the emigration and laws in USA for Japanese)

Choral Public Domain Library. (1999). http://www.cpdl.org

(Used to check quotes and parodies)

Cline, Ray S. *United States Army in World War II. The War Department. Washington Command Post: The Operations Division.* Washington, D. C.: Office of the Chief of Military History, Department of the Army. Copyright: Orlando Ward, 1951.

(History of planning for invasion)

Dower, John W. *Ways of Forgetting, Ways of Remembering: Japan in the Modern World.* New York: The New Press, 2012.

(Checked for much background on Japan after August, 1945; *kana* cards)

Durant, Will. *The Story of Our Civilization: Part I: Our Oriental Heritage.* New York: Simon and Schuster, 1935, 1954, 1963.

(Meg's reference book: note that it uses 'Nofretiti' rather than 'Nefertiti' that we use nowadays)

Evans, Harold. *The American Century.* New York: Alfred Knopf, 1998.

(History of the 40s in the US and Japan and relations between)

Funk, Charles Earle. *Heavens to Betsy and Other Curious Sayings*. New York: Harper Collins Publishers, 1955, 1983.

(Used to check if certain colloquialisms were used back then)

Georges, Robert E. (Ed.) *Nagoya Air Base: Home of the Fighting Fifth_Air Force*. (pamphlet). Nagoya, Japan: (Base Personnel Services) (ca. 1950).

(Nagoya environs, services, hours of PX and commissary, hotels, rules, etc.)

Gordon, Beate Sirota. *The Only Woman in the Room*. Japan: Kodansha International, 1997, 2001.

(Reveals briefly how she helped write Japanese Constitution)

Hilgers, Lauren. "Factory of Wealth." *Archaeology*, pps. 30-35, Nov., Dec., 2012.

((Described Wu Zhu coins (misspelled by Calhoun Paley in his letter to Meg) used during Silk Road era))

ITI's LiteraryMarketplace.com

(Used to check copyrights on Adams' and Thayer's poems)

Lockridge, Barbara (Ed.). *The Torii 1948-1949: Yearbook of the Students_of Nagoya American School*. Nagoya, Japan: NAS, 1949.

(Overview of Nagoya American High School year)

Matsutaro, Shoriki. "Japan's Citizen Kane." *The Economist*, pps. 59-62, Dec. 22, 2012.

(Story of Babe Ruth in Japan)

Newman, Caitlin. "A Few Square Inches of Home." *World War_II*, pps. 69-73, Nov.-Dec., 2011.

(History of introduction of paperback books for GIs in WWII)

Shodo Taki. *Japan Today: A Pictorial Guide.* Tokyo, Japan: Society for Japanese Cultural Information, 1948.

(Major reference for everything related to Japanese 1940's culture)

2007 TIME Almanac with Information Please. Boston, MA: Pearson Education.

(Perpetual calendar; US Constitution)

questia.com/online library

(Used to check publishing house of R. W. Service)

MISCELLANEOUS

May 1948-July 1950: issues of the Nagoya American School newsletter; some issues of the *Nagoya Nugget* (the newspaper became *Comet and Stars* in March, 1950); *Pacific Stars and Stripes*; personal notes of adventures, scrapbooks with pictures, (ms. from 1980s), big black scrapbook of receipts, menus, etc., is the main reference

Printed in the United States
By Bookmasters